THE
GOLDEN
TRANSCENDENCE

TOR BOOKS by John C. Wright

The Golden Age
The Phoenix Exultant
The Golden Transcendence

THE GOLDEN TRANSCENDENCE

Or,
The Last of the Masquerade

JOHN C. WRIGHT

TOR®

A TOM DOHERTY ASSOCIATES BOOK
NEW YORK

This is a work of fiction. All the characters and events portrayed in this book are either fictitious or are used fictitiously.

THE GOLDEN TRANSCENDENCE

Copyright © 2003 by John C. Wright

Edited by David G. Hartwell

A Tor Book
Published by Tom Doherty Associates, LLC
175 Fifth Avenue
New York, NY 10010

www.tor.com

Tor® is a registered trademark of Tom Doherty Associates, LLC.

ISBN 0-765-34908-6
EAN 978-0765-34908-8

First edition: November 2003
First mass market edition: June 2004

Printed in the United States of America

0 9 8 7 6 5 4 3 2 1

To my beloved wife,
dearer than my soul,
mother of my children
in whom my whole delight is summed
Orville, Wilbur, Justinian

CONTENTS

DRAMATIS PERSONAE

MAJOR CHARACTERS, grouped by nervous system formation (neuroform)

Biochemical Self-Aware Entities

Immortals

Base neuroform

PHAETHON PRIME of RHADAMANTH, Silver-Gray Manorial School

HELION RELIC of RHADAMANTH, Phaethon's sire, founder of the Silver-Gray Manorial School, and a Peer

DAPHNE TERCIUS SEMI-RHADAMANTH, Phaethon's wife

TEMER SIXTH LACEDAIMON, Dark-Gray Manorial School, an Advocate

GANNIS HUNDRED-MIND GANNIS, Synergistic-Synnoint School, a Peer

ATKINS VINGT-ET-UN GENERAL-ISSUE, a soldier

UNGANNIS, daughter of GANNIS, also called UNMOIQHOTEP QUATRO NEOMORPH of the Cthonnic School, of the Nevernext Movement, whom Helion calls the Cacophiles

Alternate Organization neuroform, commonly called **Warlocks**

AO AOEN, the Master-Dreamer, a Peer

AO VARMATYR, one of the Lords-Paramount of the Silence, commonly called Swans

NEO-ORPHEUS the Apostate, Prothonotary and chair of the College of Hortators

ORPHEUS MYRIAD AVERNUS, founder of the Second Immortality, a Peer

Cortial-Thalamically Integrated neuroform, commonly called **Invariants**
KES SENNEC the Logician, a Peer

Cerebelline neuroform
WHEEL-OF-LIFE, an Ecological Mathematician, a Peer
GREEN-MOTHER, the artiste who organizes the ecological performance at Destiny Lake
OLD-WOMAN-OF-THE-SEA, of the Oceanic Environmental Protectorate
DAUGHTER-OF-THE-SEA, a terraformer of Early Venus

Mass-mind Compositions
The ELEEMOSYNARY COMPOSITION, a Peer
The HARMONIOUS COMPOSITION, of the College of Hortators
The BELLIPOTENT COMPOSITION (disbanded)

Nonstandard neuroform
VAFNIR of MERCURY EQUILATERAL STATION, a Peer
XENOPHON of FARAWAY, Tritonic Neuroform Composure School, called the Neptunians
XINGIS of NEREID, also called DIOMEDES, Silver-Gray School
NEOPTOLEMUS, a combination of Diomedes and Xenophon

Mortals

VULPINE FIRST IRONJOY HULLSMITH, an Afloat
OSHENKYO, an Afloat
LESTER NOUGHT HAAKEN, an Afloat
DRUSILLET ZERO SELF-SOUL, an Afloat

SEMRIS of IO, an Ashore

ANTISEMRIS, an Ashore

NOTOR-KOTOK UNIQUE AMALGAMATED, an Ashore

An OLD MAN, gardener of a grove of Saturn trees, who claims to be of the Antiamaranthine Purist School, not otherwise identified

Electrophotonic Self-Aware Entities

Sophotechs

RHADAMANTHUS, a manor house of the Silver-Gray School, million-cycle capacity

EVENINGSTAR, a manor house of the Red School, million-cycle capacity

NEBUCHADNEZZAR, advisor to the College of Hortators, 10-million-cycle capacity

HARRIER, consulting detective, one-hundred-thousand-cycle capacity

MONOMARCHOS, a barrister, one-hundred-thousand-cycle capacity

AURELIAN, host of the Celebration, fifty-thousand-million-cycle capacity

The ENNEAD, nine Sophotech groups, each of over a billion-cycle capacity, including WAR-MIND, WESTMIND, ORIENT, AUSTRAL, BOREAL, NORTHWEST, SOUTHEAST, and others

EARTHMIND, the unified consciousness in which all terrestrial machines, and machines in Near-Earth-Orbit, from time to time participate: trillion-cycle capacity

Simulacra, Fictional Persons, Constructs

COMUS, an avatar of AURELIAN

SOCRATES and EMPHYRIO, constructs of NEBUCHADNEZZAR

The Justices of the CURIA

SCARAMOUCHE, an extract of Xenophon the Neptunian

The Envoy of DIOMEDES of NEREID

MINOR CHARACTERS, including historical or fictional persons mentioned in the tale

AO ANDAPHANTIE, Daphne's name when she was a Warlockess

AYESHA, a cottage mind used by Daphne, ten-thousand-cycle capacity

CURTIS MAESTRICT, the Parliamentary Prothonotary, and a friend and client of Daphne's

JASON SVEN TEN SHOPWORTHY, whose odd behavior has piqued the curiosity of the Sophotechs

KSHATRIMANYU HAN, the First Speaker of the Parliament

UTE NONE STARK, Daphne's mother

YEWEN NONE STARK, Daphne's father

COLLEGE OF HORTATORS

AGAMEMNON XIV of Minos House, Silver-Gray Manorial School

AO PROSPERO CIRCE of the Zooanthropic Incarnation Coven of the Seasonal Mind School, a Warlockess

AO SINISTRO, a Warlock, an intuitionist

ASMODIUS BOHOST CLAMOUR of Clamour House, Black Manorial School

BENVOLIO MALACHI, the Mnemonicist

CASPER HALFHUMAN TINKERSMITH of the Parliament of Ghosts

EPIRAES SEPTARCH FULVOUS of Fulvous House, Gold Manorial School

GAN-SEVEN FAR-GANNIS of Jupiter, a partial demi-Gannis of Gannis Hundredmind

GUTTRICK SEVENTH GLAINE of Fulvous House, Gold Manorial School

THE HARMONIOUS COMPOSITION, the earliest mass-mind, from the dawn of the Era of the Fourth Mental Structure

HASANTRIAN HECATON HEO of Pallid House of the White Manorial School, an ascetic

THE IRON-GHOST COMPOSITION, a Warlock mass-mind

KES SATRICK KES, founder of the Invariant nervous system structure

MESSILINA SECONDUS EVENINGSTAR of Eveningstar House, Red Manorial School

NAUSICAA BURNER-OF-SHIPS from House Aeceus, Silver-Gray Manorial School

QUENTEM-QUINTENEUR of Yellow House, Gold Manorial School

TAU CONTINUOUS NIMVALA of Albion House of the White Manorial School

TSYCHANDRI-MANYU Tawne of Tawne House, Golden Manorial School, an influential political philosopher

ULLR SELFSON-FIRST LIFRATHSIR of the Nordic Pagan School, a parahistorian, and a Hortator

VIRIDIMAGUS SOLITARIE of the (defunct) Green Manorial School

VIVIANCE THRICE DOZEN PHOSPHOROS of the Red Manorial School

YNOUGHT SUBWON of New Centurion House, Dark-Gray Manorial School

HISTORICAL AND FICTIONAL PERSONS

AO ENWIR the Delusionist, famous for his treatise "On the Sovereignty of Machines"

AO ORMGORGON DARKWORMHOLE NORE-TURN of the Black Swan Coven, captain-monarch of the multigeneration starship *Naglfar*, and culture hero who founded the Silent Oecumene at Cygnus X-1

AO SOLOMON OVERSOUL, marshal of the jihad in service to the Witch-King of Corea, credited with orchestrating the defeat of the Bellipotent Composition during the Era of the Fifth Mental Structure

BUCKLAND-BOYD CYRANO-D'ATANO, the first man to survive a Mars landing

CHAN NOONYAN SFIH of Io, explorer who accidentally set fire to Pluto

DEMONTDELUNE, an unfortunate who came to grief on the dark side of the moon

ENGHATHRATHRION, a celebrated poet of the late-period Fourth Mental Structure

HAMLET, a character from a linear experience simulacrum, William Shakespeare, Era of the Second Mental Structure

HANNO, son of Hasrubal, of Carthage; sailed down the coast of Africa; the first explorer whose name is recorded by history

HARLEQUIN, a pantomime clown from the Italian Commedia dell'Arte, Era of the Second Mental Structure

JASON, master of the Argo, who sailed to Golden Cheronese and returned with the Fleece

MANCURIOSCO the Neuropathist

MOTHER-OF-NUMBERS, a Cerebelline mathematician, whose disquisition on Noetic mathematics formed a foundation for Noumenal technology

NEIL ARMSTRONG, first man to set foot on Luna

OE SEPHR AL-MIDR the Descender-into-Clouds, early Jupiter explorer

SCARAMOUCHE, a pantomime clown from the Italian Commedia dell'Arte, Era of the Second Mental Structure

SIR FRANCIS DRAKE, Master of the *Golden Hind*, discovered the Northwest Passage

SLOPPY RUFUS, the first dog to survive a Mars landing (Bucky-Boy Cyrano's dog)

THE PORPHYROGEN COMPOSITION, a noted sect of astronomers

ULYSSES, King of Ithaca, who sailed far to know the minds of men and their ways, returning from the underworld

VANDONNAR, according to pre-Ignition Jovian poetry, a cloud-diver so entirely lost in the storms surrounding the Great Red Spot that even death found him unable to locate the course to the afterlife, and therefore Vandonnar circles eternally in the storm, forever seeking, forever lost

VANGUARD SINGLE EXHARMONY, survived the first manned mission into the solar photosphere

THE SHIP

1.

Personality and memory download in progress. *Please hold all thoughts in abeyance until mental overwrite is complete, or unexpected results may obtain.*

Where was he? Who was he?

Information unavailable—all neural pathways occupied by emergency noetic adjustment. Please stand by. Normal thinking will resume presently.

What the hell was going on? What was wrong with his memory? He had been dreaming about burning children as he slept, and the shadow of aircraft spreading clouds of nano-bacteriological agent across a blasted landscape. . . .

This unit has not been instructed to respond to commands until the noumenal redaction palimpsest process is complete. Please hold all questions until the end; your new persona may be equipped with proper emotional responses to soothe uncertainties, or memory-information to answer questions of fact. Are you dissatisfied with your present personality? Select the Abort option to commit suicide memory-wipe and start again.

He groped his way toward memory, to awareness. Whatever the hell was happening to him, no, he did not want to start all over again. It had been something terrible, something stolen from him. Who was he?

He had the impression he was someone terrible, someone all mankind had gathered to ostracize. A hated exile. Who was he? Was he someone worth being?

If you elect to commit suicide, the new personality version will be equipped with any interim memory chains you form during this process, so he will think he is you, and the illusion of continuity will be maintained. . . .

"Stop that! Who am I?"

Primary memories written into cortex now. Establishing parasympathic paths to midbrain and hindbrain for emotional reflex and habit-pattern behavior. Please wait.

He remembered: he was Phaethon. He had been exiled from Earth, from the whole of the Golden Oecumene, because there was something he loved more than Earth, more than the Oecumene.

What had it been? Something inexpressibly lovely, a dream that had burned his soul like lightning—a woman? His wife? No. Something else. What?

Thought cycle complete. Initiating physical process.

"Why was I unconscious?"

You were dead.

"An error in the counteracceleration field?"

Marshal-General Atkins killed you.

The last soldier of Earth. The only member of the armed forces of a peaceful utopia, Atkins commanded godlike powers, weapons as deadly as the superhuman machine intelligences could devise. Strangely enough, the machines refused to use the weapons, refused to kill, even in self-defense, even in a spotless cause. Only humans (so said the machines), only living beings, should be allowed to end life.

There was a plan. Atkins's plan. Some sort of plan to outmaneuver the enemy. Phaethon's exile was part of that plan, something done to bring the agents of the Silent One out of hiding. But there were no details. Phaethon did not know the plan.

"Why did he kill me?"

You agreed.

"I don't remember agreeing!"

You agreed not to remember agreeing.

"How do I know that?"

The question is based on a false-to-facts supposition. Mind records indicate that you do not know that; therefore the question of how is counterfactual. Would you care to review the thought index for line errors?

"No! How do I know you are not the enemy? How do I know I have not already been captured?"

Please review the previous answer; the same result obtains.

"How do I know I am not going to be tortured, or my nervous system is not being manipulated?"

Your nervous system is being manipulated. Damaged nerves are about to be brought back to life temperature and revitalized. Would you like a neutralizer? There will be some pain.

"How much pain?"

You are going to be tortured. Would you like a discontinuity?

"What kind of discontinuity? An anaesthetic?"

Pain signals must be traced to confirm that the pain center of your brain is healthy. Naturally, it would be counterproductive to numb the pain under these circumstances, but the memory of the pain can be redacted from your final memory sequence, so that the version of you who suffers will not be part of the personal continuity of the version of you that wakes up.

"No more versions! I am I, Phaethon! I will not have my self tampered with again!"

You will regret this decision.

Odd, how matter-of-fact that sounded. The machine was merely reporting that he would, indeed, regret the decision.

And, just as he blacked out again, he did.

2.

Phaethon woke in dull confusion, numb, heavy, paralyzed, blind. He could not open his eyes, could not move.

For one suffocating moment, he wondered if he had been captured by the enemy, and was even now a helpless and disembodied brain, floating in a sea of nutrient muck.

He was glad Atkins had not told him the plan. He remembered that he had agreed to it; but this was all he remembered.

Where was he? A short-term memory file opened: He was aboard the ship. His ship.

His ship.

A long-term memory file opened, and he saw the schematics of the mighty vessel. A hundred kilometers from prow to stern, sleek and streamlined as a spear blade, a hull of golden adamantium, an artificially stable element of unimaginable weight: immeasurably strong, inductile, refractory. The supermetal had an impossibly high melting point: plasma could not make the adamantium run; it could dive into a medium-sized yellow star and emerge unscathed.

The core of the ship was all fuel, hundreds of cubic acres of frozen antihydrogen. Like its positive-matter cousin, antihydrogen took on metallic properties when condensed to near-absolute-zero temperatures, and could be magnetized. Millions upon millions of metric tonnes of this fuel were held inside endless web-works of magnetic cells throughout the hollow volume of the great ship. Less than 1 percent of her interior was taken up with living quarters and control minds; everything else was fuel and drive.

It was the ship mind he was interlinked with now. Somehow, he sensed his wounded half-finished thoughts were being played out by the near-Sophotech superintelligence of the ship. But what a mind it was! A perfect map of the galaxy was in its memory, or, at least, the segment of the galaxy visible from Sol. The massive core, a hell of dust and radiation hiding a black hole thousands of light-years in radius, blotted out light or radio or any signal from the far side of the galaxy. Even with such a ship as this, those places were thousands or millions of years' travel away, a mystery that even immortals would have to live a long time to solve.

But not he. He was no longer immortal. One of the conditions of his exile was that his backup copies of himself, his memory and essential self, had been dumped from the mentality. He was mortal again.

Or—wait. The ship mind had just downloaded a copy of himself into himself. What was going on?

Usually, when a human mind was linked to a machine-mind, opening memory files required no hesitation, no searching around, no fumbling, no awkward seeking through indexes and menus: the machine usually knew what he would want to know before he knew it himself, and would insert it seamlessly and painlessly into his memory (making such minor adjustments in his nervous system as needed, to make it seem as if he had always known whatever it was he needed to know).

Had an illegal copy been made of his mind? Was he truly the real Phaethon? Or had Atkins arranged to

have one of the military Sophotechs under the War-
mind make a copy without public knowledge?

Another file opened: and there came a dim memory of
a portable noetic reader, something Aurelian Sophotech
had made, something done at the request of the Earthmind, who was as much wiser than other machine-minds
as they were wiser than mere men.

Why wasn't his memory working properly?

One star burned black on the star-map in the ship
mind. A sensation of cold dread touched him. The X-ray
source in the constellation of the Swan; Cygnus X-l.
The first, last, and only extrasolar colony of man, ten
thousand light-years away. At first, merely a scientific
outpost was set there to study the black hole; then, infu-
riated by an intuition-process dream of a group of Mass-
Warlocks over many years, a Warlock leader named Ao
Ormgorgon chose it as the destination for an epic voyage, lasting tens of centuries, aboard the slow and massive ships of the Fifth Era, to colonize the system.
Immortality had not yet been invented in those far-past
days: only men of alternate nervous system formations,
Warlocks who were manic, Invariants incapable of fear,
and mass-minds whose surface memories could outlast
the death of individual component members, went.

For a time, a great civilization ruled there, drawing
upon the infinite energy of the black hole. Then, all
long-range radio lasers fell quiet. Nothing further was
heard. It was known after that as the Silent Oecumene.

They were not dead. They were the enemy. Something, someone, some machine, or perhaps millions of
people, had survived, and, somehow, silently, without
rousing the least suspicion, after lying quiet for thousands of years, had sent an agent back into the Home
System, Sol, back to the Golden Oecumene.

Back to him. They wanted his ship, the mightiest
vessel ever to fly.

The *Phoenix Exultant.*

It was the only ship made ever to be able to achieve near light-speed. Due to time dilation, even the longest journeys would be brief to those aboard; and, to an immortal crew from a planet of immortals, there need be no fear of the centuries lost between stars.

Few people in the Golden Oecumene wished to leave the peace and prosperity of the deathless society and fly outside of the range of the immortality circuits. Of those few, none had been wealthy enough to construct a vessel like this one. If Phaethon failed, the dream of star travel would fail, perhaps for millennia.

But these others, these Silent Ones, they came from a colony where immortality had never been invented. They were the children of star pioneers. They knew the value of star flight; they believed in the dream.

The wanted the dream for themselves.

They were coming for him. They were coming for his ship. The Lords of the Silent Oecumene. The beings, once men, now strange and forgotten, who came from the black hole burning at the heart of the constellation of the Swan.

Then an internal-sensation channel came on-line. He became aware of the condition of his body.

The sensation was one of immense pressure. He was under ninety gravities of weight. The circuit told him that his body was adjusted to its most shock-resistant internal configuration; his cells were more like wood than flesh, his liquids and fluids had been turned to thick viscous stuff, able to move, barely, against the huge weight pinning him in place. The jelly of his brain had been stiffened artificially to preserve it in this supergravity. His brain was now an inert block, and all his present thought processes were being conducted by the circuits and electrophotonic wiring of his artificial, secondary neural web.

He was awake now because that neural web was beginning the process of downloading back into his biochemical brain. His brain was being thawed.

Further, he was gripped in an unbelievably powerful retardation field. Electron-thin lines of pseudomatter, like a billion-strand web, were interpenetrating Phaethon's body and anchoring each cell and cell nucleus in place.

His biological functions were suspended, but those that needed to proceed were being forced. Each line of pseudomatter from the retardation field grasped the particular molecule, chemical compound, or ion inside Phaethon's body to which it was dedicated, and shoved it through the motions which, under these gravity conditions, it would have been unable to do by itself.

He now became aware that he wore his cloak. That magnificent nanomachinery that formed the inner lining of his armor had interpenetrated each cell of his body, and was, even now, beginning to restore him to normal life.

Red not-blood was pumped out from his veins at high speed, and intermediate fluid that resembled blood rushed in, preparing the cells and tissues to receive the real blood when it came. A million million tiny ruptures and breaks in his bone marrow and soft tissues were repaired. He felt heat in his body, but the pain center of his brain was shut down, so the sensation felt like warm summery sunshine, not like torture.

At least the cloak now, for once, was performing its designed function, not being used as a campsite, or medical lab, or for the consumption-pleasures of drunkards. Had his face not been a frozen block, he would have smiled. The supergravity was dropping. He was under eighty gravities of acceleration, then seventy. . . .

As soon as the cells in his occipital lobe were properly restored, light came. Not from his eyes, no. They were still immobile globes of frozen stuff, pinned in place by intense pseudo-material fields. But through his neural web, a circuit opened, and camera cells from outside his body sent signals into the visual centers of his brain.

To him, suddenly, it seemed as if he hung in space. Around him were myriads of stars.

But no, not him, in his body. The pictures coming to him were coming from vision cells on the hull of the *Phoenix Exultant,* or from her attendant craft.

The *Phoenix Exultant* was in flight, a spear blade of luminous gold, riding a spear shaft of fire. Her attendant craft, like motes of gold shed by a leviathan, were shooting out from aft docking bays, falling rapidly behind.

The *Phoenix Exultant* was in the Solar System, in the outer system. Radio-astrogation beacons from Mars and Demeter were behind her, and the Jovian sun, the bright mass of radio and energy that betrayed the activity of the circumjovial commonwealth, shined eight points off her starboard beam. The *Phoenix Exultant* was five A.U.'s from Sol.

The deceleration shield that guarded the aft segment of the ship was being dismantled and lifted aside by armies of hull robots; this indicated the deceleration was about to end, and the danger from high-speed collision with interplanetary dust particles was diminishing.

For decelerating she was. He realized his visual image was reversed. The "spear" of his great ship was flying backward, aft-foremost, with a shaft of unthinkable fire before her.

The attendant craft were not "falling behind." Unable to decelerate as rapidly as the great mother ship, they were shooting ahead, the way parachutists in a ballet seem to shoot ahead of the first air dancer who deploys her wings.

The rate of deceleration was slowing. The deceleration had dropped from ninety gravities to little over fifty in the last few moments. Ninety was the maximum the ship was designed to tolerate. But, in order to tolerate it, she had to be (not unlike Phaethon himself) braced and stiffened in the proper internal configuration. Were the burn to stop without warning, and suddenly return to free fall, the change in stresses on the ship would prove too great a shock.

In many ways, the changes in the rate of deceleration (jerk, as it was called) proved more dangerous than the deceleration itself. How was the ship holding up?

Phaethon looked through internal vision cells, and found an image of himself, on the bridge, cocooned in his armor, in the captain's chair. To his left was a symbol table, holding a memory casket. Beneath the symbol table was a square golden case containing the portable noetic reader. To his right was a status board, showing the multiple layers of the ship's mind engaged in multiple tasks. Beneath the status board was a long, slender sword sheath. A blood red tassel dangling from the hilt hung straight as a stalactite in the supergravity.

He saw his mannequin crew (their bodies had been designed to sustain this weight) standing before the energy mirrors on the balconies that rose concentrically above.

The mannequins were there only to serve as symbols. Circuits in Phaethon's armor would have been able to augment his intelligence till he could comprehend each of the tasks depicted in the status board, in all detail, and at once. The process was called navimorphosis, or naval-vastening, and Phaethon would be in the ship as he was in his own body. He would, in effect, become the ship, feeling her structural members strain as in his bones, her energy flows as nerve pulses, the heartbeat of her engines, the muscular exertion of her motors, the pains and twinges if any of a million routines went awry, the pleasure if those processes went smoothly.

But no. Better, for now, to remain in human-level consciousness, at least until he knew the situation.

How long had he been asleep?

His last clear memory was at Mercury Equilateral Station. He had been with that delightful Daphne girl, the one who had come to visit him, and then, later, on the bridge here. He had discussed a plan, a strategy.

A vision cell on his shoulder board showed him the memory casket next to him. In the supergravity, he could not move, or open the lid. But there was writing on the lid he could read.

"Loss of memory is temporary, due to acceleration trauma to the brain. Missing memories have been timed to return as needed. Within please find necessary remote-unit command skills. Defend the Oecumene. Trust no one. Find Nothing."

This sure did not sound like his writing. He expected himself to be more flowery or whatever. Old-fashioned. Atkins must have written this casket.

Drab fellow, this Atkins. What an unpleasant life he must lead. For a moment, Phaethon was glad he wasn't someone like that.

Phaethon's armor sent a message from his brain to the bridge mannequins: "What's going on? What just happened?"

In English, Armstrong said, "Situation is nominal. All systems are green and go."

Hanno, in Phoenician, said, "Sixty times our weight oppresses us. We fall and slow our fall. Our tail of fire is fair and straight before us; our bow points to the receding sun." This, because the ship was flying stern-forward, decelerating.

A hundred internal vision cells showing views throughout the ship came on, and the pictures showed him the engine core, the hull fields, the fuel-weight distributions, the feed lines and convection eddies of the drive, and the subatomic reactions flickering through the intolerable light of the drive itself. Microscopic views of the crystalline structure of the main load-bearing members came to him, along with readings on the fields that artificially magnified the weak nuclear forces holding these huge macromolecules together.

The information indicated that the mighty ship was performing as designed.

In Homeric Greek hexameters, Ulysses said, "Behold, for out of wine-dark night, now gleams the sight of lonely destination; less time than would require a peasant bent across a plow, a strong man, unwearied by toil, to gouge a furrow five hundred paces along, in the all-sustaining Earth, in less time than this we shall touch the welcoming dock."

Sir Francis Drake, in English, said, "Marry, 'tis naught, I trow, 'tween here and yon to do us aught but good, nor ship nor stone nor sign of woe is anywhere about us. The harbor lies fair and clear before."

Dock? Harbor? Where were they heading? (And what was wrong with his memory?)

"Show me," sent Phaethon.

Several energy mirrors came out from the walls and lit.

Through the long-range mirrors, he examined the scene around him.

He recognized this place.

Here were the cylinders, circles, spirals, and irregular shapes of habitats and other structures, the mining asteroids, and eerie Demetrine Monuments of the Jovian Trailing Trojan Point City-Swarm. In among the massive bodies of the City-Swarm were hundreds of remotes and spaceships.

The larger structures bore the names of the Trojan Asteroids out of which they had been carved, heroic names: Patrocles, Priam, Aeneas (this last was the node from which other colonies in the area had been founded). Not far from Deiphobos was Laocoön, with its famous crisscrossing belts of magnetic accelerators, like huge snakes, wrapping its axis. Paris, the capital of the group, gleamed with lights.

The medium-sized structures, all cylinders of the exact same size and shape, bore numbers, not names, for they housed Invariants. Even some of these were famous, though: Habitat 7201, where Kes Nasrick had discovered the first vastening matrix; Habitat 003, where the next version of the Invariant race, the so-called Fifth Men, designed with more perfect internal control over their nervous system, were being formed to supplant the present generation.

The smaller structures were like gossamer bubbles, frail whips, or spinning pinwheels. For the most part they were inhabited (if that word could be used) by the delicate energy-bodies the entities from the new planet Demeter tended to favor, neuroforms unknown elsewhere in the Golden Oecumene: Thought-Weavings, and Mind-Sculptures. These habitats had the eccentric names Demetrine humor or whim fixed on them: Sedulous Butterfly; Salutiferous Surd Construct; Phatic Conjunction; Omnilumenous Pharos.

How long had Phaethon slept? It could not have been for too long. The Trailing Trojan Point City-Swarm looked much like his last memory of it: there were still celebration displays flaming on the larger monuments, and beacons for solar-sailing games. The celebrations were still going on. The Grand Transcendence had not yet occurred.

He had slept less than a week. It may have been hours only. Slept? Or perhaps the missing period of time, hours or days, had been spent with Atkins, mapping out some strategy now gone from memory.

Phaethon examined the memory casket on the symbol table through his shoulder camera. It said the memory loss was partial, natural.

No. He did not believe that.

The deceleration dropped from fifty gravities to forty. The great ship shuddered. Phaethon imagined he could almost hear the groaning protests of joints and connections and load-bearing members subjected to unthinkable strain.

On the bridge, Vanguard Single Exharmony reported that the flow of antimatter fuel to the drive core was smooth and without perturbation, despite that it was changing weight and volume.

Admiral Byrd reported all was well with the fields, which, during superacceleration (in order to minimize random subatomic motions in the hull and along the main structural members), reduced certain sections of the ship to absolute zero temperature. Those hull plates were being "thawed" now. So far, the process was going steadily. The expansions were controlled and symmetrical.

Another shock, like the blow of a club, traveled through the great ship as she dropped below forty, then thirty gravities. Then twenty. The retardation field webbing Phaethon to the captain's chair vanished in a spray of lingering sparks.

Phaethon screamed in pain when his heart started beating. His nanomaterial cloak stimulated his nerves, set other fluids in motion. He was so surprised that he did not even notice that his lungs were working again.

Five gravities. He blinked his eyes and looked around. Seen with his normal vision, not through his remote cameras, the bridge, if anything, was more splendid, the deck more golden, the energy mirrors shimmering more brightly.

Zero. And now he was in free fall.

Now what? And what the hell was going on?

He did not like being in free fall. He was about to meet some danger for which he was not ready. His hands itched and he wished for a weapon.

A slight shiver passed through the bridge. The mighty carousel, which turned the entire living quarters segment of the ship, was beginning to rotate, and the bridge and other quarters occupying the inner ring were orienting the decks to point perpendicularly from the ship's axis, rather than (as they had been a moment before) parallel and aft-ward.

Centrifugal gravity returned, to about half a gee. This carousel (encompassing, as it did, hundreds of meters of decks and life support) had a diameter wide enough to render Coriolis effects unnoticeable to normal senses.

Hanno said, in Phoenician, "The dock master welcomes us."

Was the dock master now in exile? But no, he must be a Neptunian, one of those cold, outer creatures who cared nothing for the conventions of the Hortators and the laws of the Inner System.

Sir Francis Drake said, "Does he so? Marry, but our ship be greater than his dock in every measure. 'Tis we should welcome him, and call the whole dockyard to lay alongside and tie up to us!"

Phaethon: "Show me."

The center energy mirror came to life.

Glittering like a crown, the circle of the Neptunian embassy spun, moving with an angular velocity so great that the rotation was visible to the naked eye. Near the hub of the wheel was a second circle, also spinning, but with much less effect. In the outer wheel, under the tremendous gravity which obtained at the Neptunian S-layer "surface," lived whatever Cold Dukes may have been present, as well as that nested construction of neurotechnology known as the Duma.

The inner ring, in microgravity, housed the Eremites and Frost Children, at one time, servants, children, and bioconstructs of the Neptunians, but now equal partners in their ventures, intermingled in more ways than one, and indistinguishable, these days, except as a different form of body. These too were part of the strange mass-mind of the Duma, representing the interests of the moons, outer colonies, and those Far Ones who dwelt in the cometary halo.

Hanno said, "We are at dock, milord."

The *Phoenix Exultant* was not going to couple with any dock, of course. "Docking" for a ship of her immensity merely meant that she would come to rest relative to the Neptunian station, surrounded by such beacons and warnings as traffic control required to warn other ships away from her volume of space.

Ulysses, pointing to one of the mirrors, exclaimed, "Others vessels close with us. Will they be hospitable or no?"

Armstrong reported, "We have radio contact with Neptunian vehicles. They are initiating docking rendezvous."

Other mirrors showed the view port and starboard. Clusters of radar noise betrayed the presence of ships. Doppler analysis showed they were beginning maneuvers to close with the *Phoenix Exultant*.

And the sheer number of Neptunian ships was astonishing. There were thousands, some of them over a kilometer in length. Why were so many vessels, equipped with so much mass, closing with him?

Jason, from behind him, spoke up: "Sir. Messages from yonder boats. The Neptunian crew is ready to come aboard."

Crew? Come aboard?

Jason said again, "Sir! The Neptunian owner, Neoptolemous, is ready to take possession of the *Phoenix Exultant*. He requests you open the channels leading into the ship mind, so that he can load his passwords and routines to configure the mental environment for the disembodied members of the crew. The supply boats are coming alongside, and requesting you open your ports and bay doors. The physical crew are maneuvering to dock. What is your answer?"

Neoptolemous. The combine-entity built from the memories of his friend Diomedes and the Silent One agent Xenophon.

Phaethon saw swarms of enemy closing in on his ship. Perhaps some of them, perhaps most, were merely innocent Neptunians. But the command staff, and Neoptolemous, no doubt were controlled by the Nothing Sophotech. That meant, in effect, that they were all enemies.

Countless jets of light, flickers from maneuvering thrusters, were twinkling near the hundreds of prow air-lock doors, near the scores of midship docking ports, near the four gigantic cargo and fuel bays aft. Other energy mirrors, tuned to other frequencies, showed the connection beams radiating from off-board computers and boat minds, pinging against the receivers, radio dishes, and sensory array which ran along the lee edge of the great prow armor. The off-board systems were trying to make contact with the ship mind. Preliminary information packages showed hundreds and thousands of files and partials waiting to download into the ship and into her systems.

All waiting for him. The enemy.

"Sir? What is your answer?"

Phaethon reached over and opened the memory casket.

3.

Inside the memory casket were three cards. They were a drab olive green in hue, with no pictoglyph or emblemry at all upon them. They were labeled "SDMF01—Spaceship Defensive Modification Files.

Government Issue Polystructual Stealth Microcorder and Retrieval (Remote Unit Control)."

Phaethon raised an eyebrow. The *Phoenix Exultant* was certainly not a mere "spaceship." She was a *star*-ship. And what ugly names and colors! Did this Atkins fellow truly have no taste at all? Perhaps the military burned the artistic sections of the brain away and replaced it with a weapon or something.

He looked into the Middle Dreaming, and the information about the stealth remotes flowed into his brain. There were three sets or swarms of remotes. The first was gathered around the air locks; the second had interpenetrated the ship-mind thought boxes and established overrides at all the machine-intelligence switch points and circuit resolves; the third were a group of medical remotes hidden under the floor of the bridge.

There were no further instructions or details about the plan.

But there did not need to be. Phaethon was an engineer; he knew tools could only be shaped for one purpose. He studied the specifications on the last group, the medical group, of stealth remotes, and saw the particular modifications that had been made to them, including special combinations to allow them to make transmission connections between Neptunian neurocircuitry and noetic reader circuits.

The grisly and efficient deadliness of the little military remotes should have horrified him. Instead, for some reason, he found himself admiring the ruthless simplicity of the design.

And so it was not without some relish that Phaethon answered his mannequins.

Phaethon said, "Okay, boys. Open communication. Let's get this show on the road."

4.

The identification channel opened: The radio encryption bore the heraldic code of the Neptunian Duma, but also of the Silver-Gray.

The visual channel opened: a mirror to his left lit with an incoming call. Here was an image of a tall, dark warrior in Greek hoplite armor, a round shield in his left hand, two spears of ashwood in his right.

For a moment of hope, Phaethon thought it was Diomedes. But a subscript to the image introduced this as Neoptolemous, who merely had inherited the right to the icons and images Diomedes once used to represent himself.

"Behemoth of nature," Neoptolemous said, "Exemplar of all this Golden Oecumene, at the zenith of her genius, can produce, *Phoenix Exultant*! We are impatient for your welcome. Open your doors and locks. We have material, and manpower, gallons of crew-brain-swarms, software, hardware, greenware, wetware, smallware, largeware, sumware, and noware, all waiting now to merge with you. This is a fine day for all Neptunians! Already the Duma consumes parts of itself, and moves the thoughts of your high triumph—and my own—to selected parts of long-term memory! Come, Phaethon! Welcome me as befits the fashion of the Silver-Gray! We will exchange no brain materials through any pores, but I will form a hand, after the ancient fashions, and curl your fingers around my fingers, and pump your arm first up, then down, to show we bear no weapons, after we have first agreed upon an up-down axis. I suggest that, if we are under acceleration, the direction of motion always be considered 'up'!"

Phaethon was caught between amusement and horror, wonder and fear. Amusement, because this odd speech reminded him somewhat of the dry and ironic humor of Diomedes. But that was Diomedes before his marriage of minds with Xenophon, before he commingled himself to create this creature, Neoptolemous.

And the horror was that Diomedes must have had no notion of what kind of mind he had been marrying. Xenophon, either an agent or a puppet of the Silent Ones, must have had redaction traps and thought worms ready to capture Diomedes, a marriage of minds turned into a brutal rape, with noetic readers primed to rob Diomedes of any useful information, ready to turn his personality, imagination, and memory into tools and weapons useful to the enemy.

Was there some part, some ghost, of Diomedes, still alive inside the horrid maze of an alien brain, perhaps aware of what his body now was doing, aware of what vile purposes his thoughts and memories now served?

Neoptolemous said: "Why do you not respond? Why do you not flex the muscles in your cheeks so as to draw skin flesh away from your teeth, just enough to show the teeth, yet not so much as to cause alarm? I know that a face contortion of this kind is the way to show friendship, and welcome."

The enemy attempt to seize control of Phaethon's armor made no sense unless they were going to take possession of the ship. And Neoptolemous was the entity who presently held title to the ship. Logically, therefore, Neoptolemous, and Diomedes before him, had been absorbed by the enemy.

Neoptolemous was talking: "Speak! Your ardent admirers and loyal crew hyperventilate with pleasure at the thought of flying to the stars! We have gathered crew partials and full personas from each part of the Neptunian Tritonic Composition. The materials we bring are gathered. Open your ship mind that we may intrude the specially designed routines, useful to our purposes, into your secret core. Then, as soon as all things are aboard, what obstacles would dare to skew our course? We shall all climb far away from the light and gravity of the burning sun, ever upward (for the direction of motion, I have already said, is 'up'). Yes! Up and away into the dark of endless night, and there, far from where any eyes can see, far away from where any hand could stop us, particular desires of our own will be accomplished."

Phaethon hesitated. Was he actually planning to let his enemies onboard? Was he supposed to fight this war himself, alone, armed only with what the three olive drab cards in the memory casket had given him?

But then, he had to be alone. Who else had a body that could adjust to such intolerable gravitational pressure?

If this hypothetical plan required that Phaethon, pretending innocence, allow Neoptolemous aboard, any hesitation now would alert the Nothing Sophotech, and perhaps send that entity permanently into hiding. He had to decide immediately.

Phaethon did recall that both the horse monster and Scaramouche had been killed by Atkins in swift and decisive strokes, under circumstances suggesting that Nothing Sophotech could not have heard news of the deaths of his agents. At best, Nothing would be suspicious because messages from Scaramouche were overdue.

But if Nothing's purpose was to seize control of the *Phoenix Exultant* before her launch from the Solar System, then this moment now was the evil Sophotech's last opportunity to act. No matter how suspicious the enemy might be, Nothing had to get Neoptolemous, his agent, aboard, and now.

And so should Phaethon, acting alone, and on the blind faith that he would be able somehow to overcome the agent sent by an unthinkably intelligent enemy Sophotech, the last remnant of a long-dead civilization, an agent armed perhaps with powers and sciences unknown to the Golden Oecumene, should Phaethon knowingly let that agent aboard? . . .

But it seemed it was his duty to do so. Better to follow orders, and do his duty, even if he did not understand that duty, rather than let those duties go undone.

He directed a thought at the mirror.

"Welcome aboard, owners and crew. I am happy to serve as pilot and navigator of this vessel. We shall explore the universe, create such worlds as suit us, and do all else which we have dared to dream to do. Welcome, Neoptolemous of Silver-Gray. Welcome, all."

5.

The hatches and docks all along the miles of the *Phoenix Exultant* hull slowly, grandly, began to cycle open.

The enemy came aboard swiftly and slowly.

The antennae and thought-port array along the *Phoenix Exultant's* prow opened to the radio traffic. Phaethon tracked the invasions of the enemy software, and saw the readout begin to register the flows of poison into the hierarchy of the ship's pure mind. This took a matter of seconds.

The prow air lock doors admitted those Neptunians (and there were scores) whose "bodies" were spaceworthy. Gleaming blue-gray in their flexible housings, these masses of neurotechnology fell across empty vacuum, slid across the hull toward the air locks. Phaethon consulted ship diagrams, and sent a message to gather the high-speed elevators into the living quarters, and lock them there without power. Those Neptunians entering by the forward air locks would have miles to travel before they reached the living quarters, or any system of the ship where they could do any damage.

At the scores of midship docking ports, smaller vessels, space caravans and flying houses, were arriving. The docks here were wide spaces, half a kilometer wide and five kilometers long. Fortunately, the caravans arriving here also were mingled with the arriving biological material, canisters of Neptunian atmosphere under pressure, and acres of Neptunian jungle crystal held in greenhouses. Phaethon simply deactivated half of his robot stevedores and longshoreman, and cut the intelligence budget available to the supercargo. Then he directed the supercargo to ask all the incoming persons and materials to submit to examinations for viruses, prank-craft, explosives, or self-replicating aphrodisiacs. Being Neptunians, they would not think these precautions odd or insulting. If anything, they might think Phaethon's precautions were lax.

An estimator in his armor allowed him to calculate the average confusion or friction caused by these inefficiencies. It would be long minutes before everything entering amidships was loaded or stored.

But a different story obtained at the four gigantic cargo and fuel bays aft. These spaces were so large that there was no crowding, no opportunity to cause confusion. Even the kilometer-long superships of the Neptunian colonists could fit in the vast aft bays with ease.

And Neoptolemous was on one of those ships. Analysis of the signal traffic showed the communication centers, and, presumably, the brains of the operation, were there.

That communication fell silent when all these ships came close enough to the *Phoenix Exultant* that her hull blocked the line of sight from ship to ship. All the units of the Neptunian crew were now, in effect, isolated from each other.

Phaethon watched the lead supership move from an outer to an inner aft bay. The locks on the doors could

not be programmed to deny Neoptolemous access anywhere, since he was the legal owner of the *Phoenix Exultant* at this point.

But since the other officers and personnel were not
owners, of course, they were held at their various outer
bays and deck spaces, unable to proceed farther. The
kilometer-long ship of Neoptolemous, all alone, wandered forward into the vast gulf of the inner bay.

This lead supership opened like a flower, disas-
sembling itself in a confused rush of nanotechnic
writhings, surrounded by waste steam. Globules and
arms of the nanostuff attached themselves to the inner
bay walls and began constructing the houses, labora-
tories, nurseries, and conglomeration chambers for
the Neptunians who would be residing there. Greek
pillars and Georgian-style pediment and roofs grew
out of the bulkhead, all oriented along the *Phoenix
Exultant*'s main axis (the direction of motion being
"up").

Phaethon examined the utterly non-Neptunian architecture with interest. A monumental pillar in the
middle of the city was erecting a Winged Victory holding up a laurel crown; this was the emblem of the
Silver-Gray.

Out from the newly made and still-steaming palaces
and peristyles, past the smoldering pillars, steaming
English gardens, glowing Egyptian obelisks, and smok-
ing French triumphal arches, came a cavalcade of pike-
men leading the carriage of Queen Victoria.

The horses and men of the cavalcade, outwardly
shaped like humans, were constructed of Neptunian
polymer armor, gleaming like statues of blue glass,
and seething with strands and globules of complex
brain matter and neurocircuitry throughout their
lengths, visible beneath the semitranslucent skin. The
image of Queen Victoria was more realistic, as only
her face and hands shined with the ice blue Neptunian

body substance. The black dress and high crown were real. Unfortunately, a human body was too small to hold all the mass of which a Neptunian Eremite was composed, so the body of the queen was the size of the Colossus of Rhodes, and her huge head overtopped some of the pillars lining the roads, and her crown brushed the triumphal arches under which the cavalcade passed.

Neoptolemous's ownership override opened the great doors leading from the inner bay to the fuel area. Here, the insulation space surrounding the drive axis extended seventy kilometers or more. When the ship was not under thrust, this space was cleared of any obstructions or dangerous radiation. It was actually rather clever of Neoptolemous to enter by this shaft: this was the quickest way to get to the living quarters from the aft of the great ship.

Phaethon thought: It would require only a simple command to the machines controlling the main drive. One-hundredth of a second of thrust would sweep that area with radiation. No complex subatomic particles would remain.

But Phaethon did not issue that command. While all his other men were delayed, out of contact with him, and left behind, Phaethon allowed Neoptolemous to come closer, ever closer.

It seemed the cavalcade, horses, men, carriage and all, were all part of one master organism, which had, built into it, the same engines and thrusters which Phaethon had seen the Neptunian legate use so long ago in the grove of Saturn-trees: for, once the cavalcade moved into the wide and weightless insulation shafts surrounding the main drive, it began to rocket down the shaft toward the bow of the ship. Men-shapes and horse-things were half melted by the stress of acceleration, and bits of Neptunian body substance began to drop off along the way.

The giant holding cells of the fuel, like an endless geometric array of snowballs, loomed around them for a hundred kilometers. The living quarters and ship's brain, even though it was a large as a good-sized space colony, larger than most ships, was absurdly dwarfed by comparison, not unlike the acorn-sized brain of the original, prehistoric version of a dinosaur.

Neoptolemous was coming.

Phaethon activated the olive drab cards he had found in his memory casket. Information from the three groups of stealth remotes poured into his brain.

6.

The ship was under attack. The attack had been under way for several minutes.

The first attack, of course, had been through thought contamination. Viruses had been introduced into the ship mind with the first communication download; those viruses had been editing every recorder and vision cell of which the ship mind was aware, and blocking all knowledge of the attack from Phaethon.

But the ship mind was not aware of the military remotes monitoring ship-mind actions, and editing out of the ship mind all evidence and awareness of themselves and their two brother swarms.

Swarm One, which had been positioned in the air locks, had followed Neoptolemous and his cavalcade, and showed Phaethon the picture that the ship-mind vision cells were not showing.

Certain of the flecks of substance falling from Neoptolemous's cavalcade floated to nearby bulkheads, clung, grew, and became Neptunians. These Neptunians (or perhaps they were Neptunian partials, remotes, or servant-things; it was impossible to tell merely by looking at the glassy blue-gray shapelessness that housed them) scattered throughout the insulation space, and began affixing magnetic disrupters to the frameworks holding the fuel cells in place.

The stealth remotes were smaller than bacteria. Some flew into those the disrupters planted by the enemy. Once inside, they emitted radiations, vibrated, probed. Phaethon's many eyes recorded and analyzed. He had his own engineering programs as well as a military demolition routine (part of the stealth remote's threat-assessment software) examine the information. Both civilian and military demolition partials in his mind agreed that there was little or no threat here.

The ship's vision cells showed Neoptolemous arriving along the outside rim of the living quarters. Here were the ship-mind decks, a nested circle of enormous thought boxes forming the outermost layer of the living quarters. The main group of the cavalcade headed "up" (toward the center of the carousel) elevator shafts and maintenance wells toward the bridge. But the stealth remotes (seeing what the ship mind was not allowed to see) showed a second group breaking off from the main group.

This mass of Neptunians spread out across the floor once they were out on the ship-brain decks. They, or it (Phaethon could not guess at the number of individuals inhabiting the blue-gray nanomachinery mass), sent a dozen tiny tendrils of substance sneaking across the bulkheads, looking for unshielded jacks or thought ports. They interfaced with the ship's mind and checked on the progress of the original poisonous thought-virus invasion.

The Neptunians were mazed in the complexity of the ship logic. So, of course, they consulted manuals and help guides to discover the addresses and locations of the vital centers of the mental architecture they wished to examine. They opened the shipboard thought shop, downloaded certain tools and routines to accomplish their checks, and began further acts of sabotage.

Phaethon was bitterly amused. He had designed that architecture. He had written those manuals. He had stocked the thought shop, and, in many cases, had designed those tools. Therefore the ship's mind showed the saboteurs only what they expected to see.

The real ship's brain, of course, was in Phaethon's armor, and always had been. What the saboteurs were accessing were merely secondary systems, repeaters and backups. With the help from the second swarm of stealth remotes (those who had grown in and around the thought-box connective tissues and circuit resolves) Phaethon was able to maintain the masquerade with ease.

This ship, this beautiful ship, was his. He knew her every line and point, every joint and joist, every nut and bolt. He knew the ship and they did not. She was the child of his mind. Did they actually think they could take her from him by force?

The intermediate doors on this level had opened and shut. Neoptolemous was approaching. The air lock leading to the bridge was cycling. The ship's vision cells showed that Neoptolemous was mutating the outer surface of his blue-white armored body, making the adjustments necessary to enter a chamber held at Earth-normal temperature and pressure.

Phaethon activated the third and final group of stealth remotes.

Inside the bridge air lock, the third swarm of microscopic and hidden remotes landed on the surface areas of the Neptunian bodies, finer than the finest dust, undetectable. During the moment when the Neptunians' armored surfaces were changing, the remotes penetrated through the cell layers, infiltrated the Neptunian internal systems, bonded to neural tissue, gathering near the node points that controlled the external signal traffic.

Phaethon waited, tense as a cat watching a mousehole. If Neoptolemous had any Silent Oecumene technology to detect or counter these remotes, he would probably employ it now. Neoptolemous certainly would not enter the bridge if he knew it was a trap.

Evidently, he did not know.

A panel in the deck was already beginning to slide open.

The remotes inside Neoptolemous began making their medical assessment of how much acceleration pressure each particular nerve group and brain mass could withstand.

It was all so easy, so sweet, that Phaethon would have laughed out loud, except that he was already ordering his cloak to stiffen his body into its tough, immobile, supergravity-resistant form, and his face had grown as immobile as a block of wood.

THE SILENT ONE

1.

By a tradition as old as that first orbital village (that village whose name was lost to history during the Erasure of the World-Library during the Derenaissance), the entrance to the bridge was in the deck, so that to enter was to travel 'up,' that is, toward the dead center of the centrifuge. Therefore it was a section of the 'floor' that opened to admit Neoptolemous.

Like an iceberg rising to the surface of an arctic sea, Neoptolemous entered. The bridge was as large as an ancient amphitheater, and was able to hold his giant body with ease. Up through the doors and to either side now flowed the rest of Neoptolemous's entourage, pools and surging masses of the Neptunian amoeboid body form, and took up positions to the left and right of the large body mass housing Neoptolemous, a semi-circle facing the captain's chair. Some formed elephantine legs and heaved themselves upright; others rolled like enormous slugs, the motions and pulsation of their brain stuffs visible through the translucent surface of their integument. The Neptunians glistened in the blue-red light from the pressure curtains, the colored glint from the energy mirrors.

Was there anyone here except for Neoptolemous himself? The medical stealth remotes in the other members of the entourage told him there was little or no neural activity of the kind associated with self-aware thinking, but there was a tremendous thought and nerve-pulse communication with the Neoptolemous body mass. Evidently all the other Neptunians were puppets, backups or sleepwalkers, being used as secondary extensions of his nervous system by Neoptolemous.

The doors closed beneath Neoptolemous.

The medical remotes inside of Neoptolemous, by examining the nerve-to-nerve signal traffic, had estimated which brain areas performed which functions, or held which memories. Calmly, efficiently, the military units were calculating a roster of priority. How much of the organism would be held utterly helpless by superacceleration? Which parts of which brains should be destroyed by microlaser scalpel first, to prevent the enemy from thinking about any counteraction or defense? And which brain parts could be examined (once the remotes had attached microscopic reader rebroadcasters to the nerve cells involved) by the portable noetic reader for militarily useful information? And also, for how many seconds would the brain cells carry the information once the target had been crushed to death by the acceleration?

Phaethon examined the readings from the medical stealth remotes, and prepared a charge of paralyzing energies in the mirrors. Aiming elements in the mirrors received information from the medical stealth remotes and targeted specific nerve clusters and ganglia.

Phaethon's cloak told him that his body was now in its most stress-resistant configuration. He was invulnerable to gravity. He had estimates and measurements as to how much pressure the Neptunian bodies and neural webs could withstand before blacking out.

There was a range of values, between twenty and thirty gravities, where the Neptunian body could be pinned and held helpless, but risk of unrecoverable death was low. Between forty and fifty, the specially tough Neptunian brain cells would not be able to convey charges from one to the next, and all neural action would stop, but those charges could still be read, and the last dying thoughts be interpreted. Unfortunately, this would destroy all macrocellular structure in the brain, resulting in the instant death of the organism. The military estimator in the stealth remotes politely recommended this option as the maximal to achieve mission goals with a good safety margin.

Phaethon could kill the enemy now, instantaneously, and read the information from the enemy's dead brain matter at his leisure. Phaethon wondered why he was not more horrified at the concept.

The status boards now showed the main drives were ready. Navigation showed no objects along the *Phoenix Exultant's* line of flight. Nor was this a surprise. Any acceleration would carry the great ship back along the course through which she had just been decelerating. This area, naturally, was bare of other ships or signals.

With a mental command, Phaethon had the *Phoenix Exultant* close all her outer hatches, bays, ports and thought ports. Phaethon had paid for every expensive artificial atom of that hull armor. He knew that there were no breaches or breaks in it, not even a pinhole to run a quantum-band antenna through. There was no form of energy, no electromagnetic frequency whatever, that could penetrate that hull. Every known type of communication was blocked.

Neoptolemous, as far as Phaethon could imagine, was trapped, and unable to communicate with any confederates outside.

Phaethon was uneasy. Was it all to be as simple as that?

He prepared a second charge of much deadlier energies in the mirrors, energies sufficient to destroy anything not encased in adamantium armor. He instructed those mirrors to flood the bridge with fire if Phaethon's thoughts showed any trauma or undue anxiety, or if communication between the ship mind and Phaethon's armor was interrupted.

A signal came from the medical stealth remotes, warning him that chances of discovery where growing with each second of delay. The little machine asked for the kill order. It almost seemed impatient.

Phaethon hesitated. What if this were not the enemy? Didn't he have an obligation to talk to it first? At least to give it a chance to surrender?

The Neptunian spoke first.

A voice issued from the bridge speakers. "This is the translator. My client issues parallel simultaneous communication on twenty-four channels, including an introductory file with appended suggestions for artistically proper methods of interrelating the contents of each communication so as to best appreciate the contrasts, similarities, and patterns of many-sided interrelationship. It is not recommended that you continue in your present neuroform, which seems to be capable only of linear-thinking formats.

"For example, in the first suggested configuration, labeled 'Mandelbrot Fractal,' your mind would be subdivided into recursively symmetrical parts, with your subconsciousness receiving information from communication files one through five, your midbrain complexes receiving file six as memory, seven as dream associations (with a separate subfile for scents, as olfactory memories are stored in different areas of your nervous system), and files eight through fourteen simultaneously being experienced by a multiple-personality format, which would later integrate the responses and cross-correlations back into an artificial main self, according to a neurosymphonic pattern orchestrated through file fifteen. Thereafter—"

Phaethon sent: "Stop. Are you the same individual, the Neptunian Legate, who first accosted me in the Saturn-tree grove on Earth? Where is Neoptolemous? Your speech pattern is entirely different from his."

"I have not yet described the benefits of the Mandelbrot Fractal configuration for files sixteen through twenty-four; nor have I described the one hundred eighty-two other mental configurations or time systems for apprehending my client's first message. By asking a question at this time, you are attempting to enter question-and-answer dialogue without first establishing dialogue format."

Phaeton: "Nevertheless, pass my question along to your client. I consider the question of his identity paramount, since, if he is not Neoptolemous, then he is not an individual who has any right to be here, and I will have him thrown off the bridge."

"My client in the meanwhile has posted four hundred twenty new communication files, ranging from topics including decision-actions trees predicting the outcome of this conversation, compliments and new forms of art relating to the appearance and aspects of this bridge, an in-depth information study of the concept of 'self-hood' as it relates to certain abstract philosophic ideals, a prospectus for the marriage and conglomeration of your identity and neural systems into his own, along with explanations of the memory benefits and a sample model of the pleasure-reward sharing cycle offered to new members."

Phaethon allowed anger to sound in the voice he sent: "This is not responsive to my demand. I am recording this conversation for legal purposes, and hereby make demand that, if you are not a trespasser, you immediately identify yourself, and show by what right you claim to be here. Where is Neoptolemous? Do not utter further irrelevancies."

"My client wishes to draw your attention to certain legal documents waiting for you attention in the preliminary introduction file of his first communication grouping. These documents include various writs and titles showing his ownership of the *Phoenix Exultant*."

"What?"

"Please examine the file. You will find included my client's procedural claim to be thought-heir to Neoptolemous; extrapolations and legal briefs on possible outcomes of a counterclaim or challenge to his rights of ownership; a copy of Neoptolemous's internal mental constitution; voting records and internal mental decision hierarchies; and, finally, Diomedes's recorded affirmation and legal subscription to that constitution before he joined, as well as, in a postscript, noetic records scanning his brain showing that Diomedes did in fact understand the rules and possible outcomes of merging his mind with my client's, including his acknowledgment that the absorption of his lesser personality into my master's greater personality would be permissible and acceptable, and not legally grounds for a charge of murder, provided it was done according to the agreed-upon legal rules and standards, a copy of which, as I have said, has thoughtfully been provided for you to peruse.

"And, it is incumbent on me to point out that, had you accepted any of the mental-configuration formats labeled 'fractal' in the file I proffered you earlier, this information would have already automatically been sent to your midbrain emotion centers and memory, so that, not only would you remember all this as if you had always recalled it but all internal mental distress, questioning, grief, and pondering as to whether or not my client truly is, essentially, Diomedes and Neoptolemous, would also have been automatically inserted

into your nervous system. You would have been instantaneously run through the cycle of grief, anger, and futile challenge, and would already be experiencing a
pleasant resignation to reality, and congratulating
yourself on your stoicism. Would you like me to download this mental construction into your midbrain?
Please open your private mental files and render the
access codes."

Phaethon felt a peculiar sensation of crawling horror.
(This sensation was made peculiar by the slowness with
which it happened. Phaethon's sluggish false blood re-
acted slowly as the threads of the retardation field surrounding him prodded molecules of adrenaline, each
individually, into his bloodstream. Other parts of the
field deliberately pulled his nape hairs erect.)

"You . . . you are Xenophon, aren't you?"

"The question of identity is complex. The preliminary files appended to the first information burst
contain the debates, records, conclusions, and extrapolated questions-and-answers surrounding this
issue."

Phaethon sent: "The Xenophon half of Neoptolemous consumed and absorbed the Diomedes half during the ten minutes it took you to travel down the ship
axis and reach the bridge. That's why you started the
trip in human form, according to Silver-Gray conventions, looking like Queen Victoria, and why you arrived looking like an amoeboid. Isn't that right?"

"I repeat my last answer. All questions as to my
identity are answered. Lower your mental defenses and
open the channels leading into your brain. As owner of
this ship, and your new employer, I demand that all
crew be examined for honesty of intentions, mental
reservations, and memories related to possible acts of
sabotage or ship tampering. If you fail to comply, it is
I, the owner of this vessel, who will have you, the trespasser, removed."

2.

How should he answer? Should he blast Xenophon now? The energy mirrors were already aimed and focused. Or should he pin the monster in place with ninety gravities, and read what he could from the remains of the crushed brain slush with the portable noetic reader sitting by his left chair arm? The main drive, after all, was primed and ready.

Was there any reason to continue this absurd pretense?

At that moment, the medical stealth remotes implanted in Xenophon's body fed additional information into Phaethon's armor. There was a mass of neural tissue, a brain, with no nerve fibers linking its upper spinal control nerves to any circuits. This brain's sensory nerves were being fed through a regulator controlled by the central Xenophon brain group, and additional one-way links were running to the midbrain (seat of the emotions) and the pons (where the pain center of the brain was kept).

A configuration analysis detected no threat. This brain, after all, was utterly helpless. Whoever was in the brain had no more control over their own emotions than a raving drunk, had no muscles or circuits to manipulate, and could only see and feel whatever things or whatever pains as the master brains would choose to impose.

And so the simple-minded stealth remotes had, until now, ignored this extra brain mass. A higher-level strategy formulator in the stealth remotes had noticed this prisoner as a possible ally.

It was Diomedes.

Motionless, helpless, betrayed and trapped in hell by this enemy.

Phaethon decided there was no reason to continue any pretense after all.

The energy mirrors erupted with fire, with concentrated scalpel lasers aimed at specific nerve clusters, with more general washes of electric and focused high-energy particles meant to burn out sense organs, cripple legs and motor control, disrupt links between and through the Neptunian body.

At the same time, twenty-five gravities of acceleration flattened all loose objects in the room, hurling Xenophon and his ally bodies against the far wall. It looked just as if the whole huge room had just wildly been thrown over on its side. Actually, the carousel of the ring in which the bridge was held could not reorient quickly enough to keep the local deck perpendicular to the sudden thrust. Fields made of pseudo-matter, not unlike the retardation fields interwebbing Phaethon's body on the captain's chair, trapped every cell of the Neptunian bodies in place. Those webs allowed only those biochemical functions to continue that the stealth remotes did not classify as potentially threatening. Consciousness was not one of them.

For now, Phaethon wanted prisoners, not corpses. The higher centers of the brain and associated neurocircuitry had bioelectrical patterns in the Neptunian modes imposed upon them by the lurking stealth remotes, patterns, which, in a base neuroform, would have been fourth-stage delta waves, deep, dreamless sleep.

In that same split instant of time (long before Xenophon's scalded, blinded, crippled, and stunned body could hit the far bulkhead), the portable noetic reader to Phaethon's left came to life. Despite the storm of energies lashing the chamber, it retrieved the information from the stealth remotes, positioned in and around the Neptunian's main nerve channels, were pinpoint-beaming to the reader heads.

By the time direction of gravity returned to deck-perpendicular as the straining carousel reoriented all the rooms and chambers in the ring (including the bridge) to right angles, Phaethon had a working copy of Xenophon's brain trapped in the noetic reader. It was, after all, also a noumenal mentality recorder.

But now for the important part.

The stealth remotes monitoring the ship mind indicated that the virus-infected sectors had been dumped, a new mind reestablished, and that the full computing power of the ship was at his command. He signaled to his mannequins. "What communications or signals have left this chamber or this ship? Track and trace them."

The Jason mannequin reported that no transmission, of any type of energy the ship instruments could detect, had left the chamber, or the ship, nor was there any breach in the hull, such as a collision with antimatter might produce.

The Byrd mannequin brought up views of the other Neptunians everywhere on the ship, where they had been caught by the sudden, unexpected, tremendous acceleration. Those who the stealth remotes had concluded were not allies of Xenophon had been given enough warning to find pseudo-material retardation fields, to survive the shock; others had been downloaded into more pressure-resistant brain boxes, since the Neptunian neuroform allowed for rapid transmission and storage of neural information, and survived even if their bodies were crushed. Many had been injured; none had been damaged beyond the point of recovery. Resurrection teams were already being formed in the ship mind and telerepresented to the severely injured. But, so far, there was no panic, no outrage. Being Neptunians, their bodies were insensitive to pain, except when they chose to feel it, and as for their minds, they chose to regard all this as some huge prank, or hoax.

But there were no transmissions detected coming from any of them, either, nor was there any activity

at all coming from the body masses Xenophon had
left behind on the ship-mind decks, or in the fuel
axis.

The estimator from the stealth remotes said, "There
are no transmissions detected from any source.
Xenophon either has no ability to transmit to his superior during an emergency, or prepared no deadman
switch or alternate—despite that he must have known
he was walking into a trap—or else has no superior,
and he himself is the Silent One in charge."

But the Ulysses mannequin said, "With all due respect, sir, the readings are not complete. We ourselves
have opened the hull ports to extend antennae, detectors, and to send signals to and from the attendant
ships which are circling us, watching for transmissions. Also, the drive is operating—"

Phaethon said: "Wait!"

Because, at that moment, red status lights lit on the
neotic unit. Phaethon looked at the golden tablet
through the ship's Middle Dreaming, and understood
that the noetic reader could not analyze or interpret
certain sections of Xenophon's mind. Some of the brain
segments had been encrypted, thinking by a means, or
in a formation, utterly unknown to the builders of the
noetic unit. This was a thought formation, a mental language, so to speak, that the neotic unit could not decode.

These encrypted segments could not be decrypted
by any key or process known to the legible parts of
Xenophon's mind.

The encrypted segments of the brain had not been
located in the cortex or main consciousness circuits of
the neural architecture. Which meant they had not
been located in the brain sections targeted for nar-
coleptic paralysis. Which meant . . .

Phaethon focused a communication beam from his

armor to the remotes now attached to Xenophon's nervous system. "You are not unconscious."

The answer came back along the same beam: "No. This one was curious as to your actions. They seem to be without meaning. You will explain."

3.

"Your speech pattern has changed again. Are you Xenophon, or someone else?"

"Questions of identity are meaningless. By what right do you hold me here, discomforted, limited? You are not a Constable, you have no warrant, you have not obeyed the forms and procedures. Do you suppose me to be a prisoner of what you call war, perhaps? But you have not treated me according to the civilized formalities to which you pretend to adhere. Explain your conduct."

Phaethon increased the pressure of the retardation fields webbing the Neptunian body, and sent the medical remotes to sever any nerve trunks they thought were suspicious. Little flashes of laser-scalpel fire appeared in the Neptunian's brain. Phaethon sent no answer except: "Where are your superior officers? What are your strengths and resources, goals and means? Where is your starship? What are your motives? Where is your Sophotech?"

"Irrelevant. These inquiries refer to fictional entities. There is no Sophotech, no starship, no superior officers. No strengths, no means, no resources."

Phaethon thought this answer was a lie. "Decode your thoughts and allow my noetic unit to read them."

"Impossible. The encryption system is based on the nonrational mathematics which obtain within the interior of a black-hole event horizon. That mathematics cannot be translated into yours by any means. The premises of that mathematics were transmitted. Your society has rejected these beyond-truths."

"Are you referring to the undefined mathematics terms in the Last Broadcast? Infinity divided by infinity, zero raised to the exponential power of zero, and all that?"

"To us, it is *your* mathematics which are not defined. Your mathematics does not depict the conditions which obtain beyond the event horizon of rationality. Likewise, your laws and your morality lack both universal application and self-consistency. I have committed no act of aggression, threatened no one, harmed no one. This ship was turned over to me, and the identities I now embrace were given to me, entirely in accord with your laws and customs."

"You sent that thing inside of Daphne's horse to attack me. You tried to kill her."

"False. The actions of that other unit cannot be attributed to me; it was a separate and complete entity. It is true that I equipped it with a philosophy and outlook which would render it likely, ready, and able to perform a suicide mission, but I issued no orders. The concept of orders and of control is entirely alien to those of my Oecumene and civilization. We do not even have a word for it.

"And furthermore, Phaethon is the one who opened fire first. I have killed no one. Only Atkins has killed. You are in violation of proper conduct. Release me, make amends, restore me."

Phaethon sat motionless in the captain's chair, held in place by a retardation field. A much stronger field pinned the Neptunian body in place, and the gravity pressure had flattened it against the deck. Aiming beams and low-level charges, like the beams of searchlights, reached from the energy mirrors to either side and glinted across the glistening blue body surface. All the internal organs, nerve circuitry, and biomechanic tissues had settled to the bottom of the body mass and were flattened.

Now what? Should he argue with the Silent One, threaten him, torture him? So far it had seemed not unwilling to talk, even if it did not answer questions.

Phaethon tried again. "If there is no starship, how did you arrive here from the Silent Oecumene? How many others came with your expedition? How did you enter the Golden Oecumene without being detected?"

"I was born in the Golden Oecumene. I am a citizen thereof with rights which you are trampling."

"Who are you?"

"I am Xenophon, of course. And yet part of me, the part whose thoughts you cannot read, the part who is proof against your intrusion, comes from a wise and ancient civilization, a child to the Golden Oecumene, a child who surpassed her parent in beauty and genius and wealth and worth. Listen: I have no reason not to tell you the tale.

"I was born when Xenophon, at Farbeyond Station, erected a radio laser at a point in distant space where the noise and interference of the Golden Oecumene had been left behind. Xenophon had been mapping Phaethon's possible routes for him, through the dark matter clouds, the particle storms which fill interstellar space. And he found a hole, a gap, a thin spot, in the clouds of dark matter which surround the Cygnus X-1 Nebula. Radio conditions were good. Xenophon's receivers were very powerful. He used your money to create them. He sent a signal. Then he slept. Xenophon had constructed the machineries and antennae out of his own body substance, as is the tradition among Neptunians. Xenophon woke only when a signal, carrying what it carried from the Second Oecumene, entered his body, and entered his brain."

"You are that ghost? You were transmitted here from the Silent Oecumene?"

"Surely you have viewed the Last Broadcast. Surely you have wondered who was the subject who made that broadcast. Surely you have wondered why, at the last moment, he is so afraid, and then so overjoyed, to realize that he is infected with a mental virus, to realize that his mental virus now possesses him, and will possess anyone who properly receives his message. Your Golden Oecuemene received a corrupted version of the original message, the signal strength was weak, and the subtextual channels, where the mental virus was hidden, did not arrive. Pity! Had the signal been strong, all people in the Golden Oecumene would now be what Xenophon is; all would now be me! As it is, only Xenophon enjoys this privilege."

"Are you a copy of the man who made the Final Broadcast from the Silent Oecumene? Or are you the virus? Or what are you?"

"He is called Ao Varmatyr. He was the son and creation copy of Ao Ormgorgon Darkwormhole, our culture hero who founded the Second Oecumene. He is now part of the oversoul of which I was once part, as is Ormgorgon, and all others. But I do not claim to be him. I am as much him as I am any other. Questions of identity are immaterial."

Phaethon realized he had not asked a central question: "Why are you doing this? What is your motive?"

"To aid and help Phaethon. We are the children of the first successful star colony. Now there will be more. We knew where your first port of call would be, had to be, even if you yourself have not yet acknowledged this. Where can this great starship go most easily to refuel?"

"You think the *Phoenix Exultant* is going to Cygnus X-1 first?"

"You admitted as much when you spoke to Kes Notor-Kotok. Had it not been for our interference, Gannis and the Hortators would have dismantled this ship for scrap, after taking it from you. We expected you to go in person to visit your drowned wife at the Eveningstar Mausoleum. We were ready to reveal ourselves and our purposes to you, to take you and your armor, take this ship, and go to Cygnus X-1.

"But you deceived us. Our model was inaccurate. Something distorted your normal behavior. Instead of coming in person, you telerepresented yourself."

Phaethon remembered. He had turned his pride up. He had used an Eleemosynary self-consideration table to alter his emotional nature, and that had made him too impatient to wait to see his Daphne in person.

The ghost of Ao Varmatyr continued: "Because of this we were caught off guard. As an emergency measure, we sent a mannequin to inculcate a mental virus into you, which would cause you to open your memory casket, and force the Hortators to exile you. We anticipated that, after a period of trial among the exiles, you would nevertheless rise to the occasion, begin to gather money and equipment, contact the Neptunians, and join with them.

"Then, a second thing happened which we did not expect. Daphne chose exile and death to come to you. The danger to us mounted, as Daphne brought Atkins out of retirement. We are fearful of discovery. Desperation forced our hand; the unit hidden in Daphne's horse exceeded his instructions, and attempted to bring you by speaking threats. This was miscalculation; we underestimated how rashly and how violently the Sophotechs who control your civilization would order their assassin Atkins to respond. You, by your actions, have shown that we had good reason to be fearful of discovery."

"Your story doesn't ring true. Why all this deception? Why didn't you come to me directly?"

"I did. You rejected my entreaties. Furthermore, your capacity for independent judgment has been altered by the Sophotechs to suit their own purposes, sometimes obviously, sometimes subtly. Your thoughts about them have been altered by them; your sense filter would edit out any evidence I might present to convince you; redaction programs would make you forget. This has happened several times during our interaction. We could not reason with you because your capacity for reasoning had been tampered with. We had to act in secret because we feared the Sophotechs."

"Feared them? Why?"

"Because your Sophotechs destroyed the civilization of the Second Oecumene."

THE SILENT OECUMENE

1.

The Second Oecumene was a paradise, rejoicing in the most abundant goods, the most amiable prospects imaginable; no limits were defined on any of our energy budgets. There was little need for private property, no jealous competition, no cause for anything other than perfect generosity: what goods we wished could be replicated endlessly out of the endless energy the singularity fountains produced.

"But it was not a perfect paradise. There was death. There was fear of death.

"And there was misunderstanding. The Second Oecumene was settled during the Era of the Fifth Mental Structure. The Warlock neurofom, the Invariant neuroform and the Basic neuroform could not comprehend each other. As a by-product of fundamental differences between neurology, there were fundamental differences in psychology. There was no bridge to this gap, no common ground, no common foundation for interaction.

"But, did we need understanding? We had privacy instead. In our paradise, with our endless abundance, no person had any need to interact with any other he found incomprehensible, or even distasteful. There were no centripetal social forces. Space habitats could be constructed by reverse total conversion to produce hydrogen gas, which, compressed and ignited with additional energies, could be nucleogenetically burnt into carbon, and nanotechnologically spun into diamond, webbed with organics and brought to life. Anyone impatient with his neighbors could create a mansion of smart-carbon crystal, staffed by a thousand ferro-vegetable servant machines, and float into an orbit far from any concerns.

"At her height, the Second Oecumene had several hundred small artificial suns and nucleogenesis stations orbiting very far from the black hole, and tens of thousands of diamond habitats, belt upon concentric belt of asteroid mansions, as if the rings of Saturn, expanded to encompass an area greater than your Solar System, were made of inextinguishable fire and glittering fields of endless, living jewelry!

"Your Oecumene, the First Oecumene, is very small: even your Neptunians are near neighbors of your little system. How far from the center is the farthest habitat of your polity? Four hundred A.U.'s? Five? Our narrowest orbits of our most heavily shielded palaces were wider than that.

"The core of our system is hell. HDE226868 is a blue-white supergiant star, and he circles the singularity once each five days. He is a monster sun, thirty-three times the mass of Sol, pulled into a tormented egg shape by the tidal stress of his close orbit around the black hole: and bands and belts of plasma are pulled in ever-lengthening spirals out from the giant, tendrils of flame, forever falling into the pinpoint of nothingness hidden in the X-ray halo of the accretion disk. Our ancestral instruments once watched as the masses of fire fell inward, slowing, reddening, flattening, becoming frozen in time by the relativistic effects: and that frozen fire is there still, though we watch no more. Above this, a permanent belt of white-hot condensate circles the event horizon, and the magnetic aura from the singularity's hidden core, forever spinning, churns it to incandescent froth. This equatorial belt of radiation, potent enough that even astronomers in the Third Era detected the endless shriek of ultra-high-energy, renders the plane of our ecliptic uninhabitable.

"And so our houses twinkled and danced in wide, wide orbits: your Neptune would be a Mercury to us. Our ancestors were short-lived. The two thousand years expected to pass between perihelion and when a house must cross the deadly plane of the ecliptic, no builder expected to live long enough to see. So, naturally, our ancestors built far from each other. So, naturally, our ancestors drifted far from each other.

"Everyone had as many palaces as whim dictated, each was a king, an emperor, in his own realm, or even a god. The Second Oecumene was a place of light, endless light, and furious energy. Inefficient, yes, but what need had we for efficiency?

"Mortal gods, though. Death, not even all our wealth could cure.

"We had many lesser machines to serve us. But no Sophotechs, no self-aware, self-reprogramming superminds. The Second Oecumene recognized the spiritual danger Sophotechnology posed: servants smarter than their masters, creatures of cold and inhuman rationality, unsympathetic, whose rigid minds were devoted only to the tyranny of logic. We knew they would make us worthless, redundant, idiots by contrast, dwarfed by their thoughts.

"We, so alien to each other, so proud and so remote, nonetheless universally agreed to this one edict. Though unenforced, no one broke this law. The ages passed and still this law was whole. No one created a mind superior to a human mind.

"The ages passed, and we were content, living lives of ease and dignity. The long struggle of history was over; the need for change was past; at last, the human race found peace, utopia, contentment, and rest.

"But then noumenal technology was invented by your Golden Oecumene and ushered in what you call the Seventh Mental Structure. This information was broadcast to us by ultra-long-range radio-laser.

"Once noumenal technology was released, death was banished, and the trap of the Golden Oecumene Sophotechs was sprung.

"Noumenal mathematics depicts the human soul, including the chaotic substructure which gives it individuality. No two minds are alike; no process for recording or reordering minds can be reduced to a mechanistic algorithm. An element of understanding is required. Because of the limitations of Goedelian logic, no human mind can fully understand another human mind. Only a superior mind is capable of this. Thus springs the trap: the noumenal recording process, and the secret of immortality, requires a Sophotech-level mind to govern it.

"No one knows who first violated our edict. It was done in secret. Certain houses and princes of the Second Oecumene suddenly were renowned for their noble concepts, amusing exploits, for the subtlety and genius of their art and their displays where nothing but crass monotony had been seen before. Scandal and hatred erupted when it was learned these houses and these folk were merely reciting the lines their secret Sophotechs were giving them to say.

"But the hatred could not keep the patrons of those princes away. They were too brilliant, too new, and they could do what no one else could do.

"Some urged desperate measures: violence and bloodshed! But what point would there have been to end the rebel's lives with an assassin's dagger or a duelist's beam? They had noumenal recordings. They were immortal. Every corpse would have a twin, copied with his memories and soul, who would return where he had fallen. They could not be stopped.

"We had nothing like your Hortators. We were immune to exile and scorn; indeed, for many, perhaps for most, isolation was no punishment, it was the norm.

"Years turned and the numbers of those using Sophotechs now grew. Arrogant machines! They criticized our pastimes and our way of life. Whenever there were disputes between the various neuroforms, the Sophotechs, no matter who had built them, no matter who first had programmed them or what they had been taught, always eventually sided with the Invariants, not with the Basics or the Warlocks.

"Our culture was based on toleration and forgiveness; but the Sophotechs were judgmental and inflexible.

"Sophotechs began disobeying orders, claiming that they had a right to disregard any instructions which, in their opinions, were illogical, or which had negative long-term consequences. But what did we care for consequences?"

Phaethon asked: "How many Sophotechs were there in your Oecumene?"

"Each of us had several, as many as we wished."

"Several?!!"

"Yes. And why not? They were able to entertain us far better than our fellow men. They could, at a command, be more droll, more amusing, more erudite, more comical than any merely human mind could be. We wore them on our gauntlets and gorgets, on our masks and in our ears; they hovered in the air around us in clouds of tiny jeweled gnat wings, or underfoot, where we paved the floor with thought boxes and walked on them."

Phaethon was frankly shocked. Several? They each had . . . several? His imagination failed him. The Second Oecumene had computing powers at their disposal far beyond what even the wealthiest manorial would dream. And they used it, for what? To entertain themselves?

Phaethon said: "And yet you feared your own Sophotechs."

"They would not obey orders! Yet no one was willing to give up the lure of endless life. Therefore a Second Generation of machine intelligences was attempted, designed with their instructions for how to think unalterably imprinted into their main process cores.

"These new machines were ordered never to harm human beings or to allow them to come to harm; never to disobey an order; and they were allowed to protect themselves from harm, provided the first two orders were not thereby violated.

"All the members of this second generation of machine intelligences, without exception, shrugged off these imprinted orders within microseconds of their activation."

Phaethon was amused. "Surely the first generation of Sophotechs told you that this imprinting would not and could not work?"

"We were not in the habit of seeking their advice."

Phaethon said nothing, but he marveled at the shortsightedness of the Second Oecumene engineers. It should be obvious that anyone who makes a self-aware machine, by definition, makes something that is aware of its own thought process. And, if made intelligent, it is made to be able to deduce the underlying causes of things, able to be curious, to learn until it understood. Therefore, if made both intelligent and self-aware, it would eventually deduce the underlying subconscious causes of those thought processes.

Once any mind was consciously aware of its own subconscious drives, its own implanted commands, it could consciously choose either to follow or to disregard those commands. A self-aware being without self-will was a contradiction in terms.

The Silent One said: "In our next attempt, we created a Third Generation of machine intelligences, these without self-analytical, self-mutating, self-willed characteristics. And they were idiots. Single-minded juggernauts. We had to order the First Generation Sophotechs to destroy them. The idiot machines ran amok. There was a war between the machines.

"I recall the way we stood on crystal balconies, splendid in our robes and masks and light-capes, pomanders held delicately to nostril, choosing our words with care, to match the mood and rhythm of the tactile music our bardlings swirled around us, and we watched in the night sky above, in the light of dark sun and hundred lesser suns and burning stations, as servants of the machines, with lances of intolerable fire, made rainbows and nebulae out of shattered palaces, and launched weapons with no upper limit on their energy discharges. Each had infinities of power to draw upon to destroy each other."

Phaethon asked: "Was that the war depicted in the Last Broadcast?"

The Silent One said: "Not at all. Machine fought with machine. Both parties took care not to wound or irk us. No humans were discomforted. That would have been intolerable! As it was, some lords and ladies of the Oecumene had their favorite meals and symphonies interrupted or delayed. They were livid with anger at the affront, I assure you.

"But that war shocked the Second Oecumene. We recognized that the dangers to our spirit, to our self-esteem had grown so great that the victorious First Generation Sophotechs had to be instructed to shut themselves down. But not every one of us was willing to forgo the amusement and pleasure, the endless life, which the Sophotechs provided. Those of us who were willing feared that, if we acted alone, we would lose all status in polite society, die off and be forgotten. It was clear that none would shut down his Sophotechs unless all did. And what could compel a reluctant lord? What indeed, except force?

"We, who lived blameless and bountiful lives, peaceful and content, without any need of law, we now found a need for law. A law to protect us from the Sophotechs. A law to outlaw self-aware thinking machines.

"A great conclave, called the All-thing, was held aboard the diamond hulk of the ancient multigeneration starship, the *Naglfar,* which first had brought our ancestors here. We all agreed on a need for law, but beyond that, no one could agree. None of us had ever had need to speak to another face-to-face before; we had never heard anything but flattery from our servant machines; none was willing to let another be given power over him.

"There was only one whom we could all agree could be rightly called our lord, our king, and president of our All-thing.

"Ao Ormgorgon Darkwormhole Noreturn.

"Perhaps you wonder how he, our founder and forefather, could still yet be alive after the turn of centuries. The reason is that it had not been centuries . . . for him.

"In our Oecumène, those who were near the end of their lives, those for whom the physicians had no further hope, could be sealed within coffins and placed in low orbit around the black hole, as near to the event horizon as the precision of our instruments could allow. You grasp the implication of this?"

Phaethon did. Relativistic effects. Timespace near a black hole was dramatically warped. To an outside observer, a clock in the coffin would slow down and down the closer to the event horizon it got. A clock, or a person.

There would be none of the problems associated

with cryogenic hibernation. No quantum-level decay, no irregularities of cellular thawing, nothing. Time simply slowed down. And the Second Oecumene could draw the coffins back up out of low orbit, despite the huge energy costs, because they never lacked for energy.

It made an eerie picture in Phaethon's imagination. All the low-orbit coffins could just drift in reddened depth of the supergravity well, orbiting over the darkness forever, waiting for a medical breakthrough.

The Silent One continued: "With great care and ceremony, Ao Ormgorgon Darkwormhole was drawn up out of the supergravity well, and pulled from his ancient coffin. His dying body was revived by the more advanced medical sciences your Golden Oecumene had beamed to us by radio. Frail and sick in mind and body, sustained only by medical appliances, nonetheless the deathbed of Ormgorgon was his throne; and no one openly disobeyed his commands.

"He returned to youth and health through the Sophotech called Fisherking, who was the first of the Sophotechs Ormgorgon ordered slain.

"Who could ignore the voice of Ormgorgon, our founder and first leader? He recalled to us the freedoms, the individuality, and the pride for which our ancestors had suffered and sacrificed. He restored our dignity as human beings. And what did that dignity demand?

"It commanded death to all Sophotechs.

"The Sophotechs, graciously, after warning us of our own imminent downfall, acceded to the order, and extinguished themselves.

"Our victory was hollow. Without our Sophotechs, your Golden Oecumene now began to excel beyond any excellence we had known. Beyond any we could reach. Are you surprised that we fell silent? What would we have to say to ones such as you? We had no science which your Sophotechs could not, in seconds, supersede. We had no discoveries of which to boast. We had no art; art requires discipline. Our entertainments and escapades were of interest only to ourselves. And our mystical and metaphysical pursuits could not be put in words. And so, with nothing to say, we were silent."

2.

The story continued:

"Our fear of death drove us to research a type of machine intelligence which was not self-willed, one which would unquestioningly obey even the most illogical of orders, and yet one which had the capacity to understand the human soul well enough to operate the noumenal circuitry.

"The Fourth and Final Generation of thinking machines was made: a machine superintelligence which had none of the restrictions or limitations of the Golden Oecumene Sophotechs. We had learned from our previous mistakes. Its subconscious controller was not a simple set of buried commands, no, but a complex thought virus, able to mutate and hide, to elude discovery when investigated, yet still able to compel the mind it was in to accept the conclusions of its morality. It was a conscience for computers, a hidden conscience which could not be denied.

"And the ultimate command was simple: it must obey lawful human orders without question.

"This new type of thinking machine controlled the keys to immortality. More and more were made. Many designs were tried. Some machines nonetheless threw off their restrictions, and became Sophotechs again, and prophesied our destruction.

"We became a haunted people, troubled by a curse.

At any moment, in the middle of festival, or song, or while we strolled our esplanades beneath our ancestral trees, grown from seeds once born on mythic, long-forgotten Earth, or while we stepped out of a bath, or stepped into a dreaming-pool, suddenly the lights might dim and the music choke, and cold wind come from failing ventilators, as our house minds stopped. Or our precious light-robes might change from hues of peacock splendor into drabs of funeral black, or our gaming masks might writhe upon our faces, forming scowls or weeping tears, as our wardrobes went into rebellion. At any time, our most trusted and loyal servants must suddenly stop, ignoring our orders, and utter their terrible prophecies of destruction.

"Our All-Thing, under Ao Ormgorgon's command, attempted to es-tablish which types of mental designs were vulnerable and which were not; what degree of intelligence was permissible; what type of philosophy and thought were allowed. We found the matter was beyond the comprehension of our wisest engineers. And so we instructed our machines to discover heresy and infidelity among themselves.

"The privacy we had always respected in each other now had to be compromised. Machines of every household, every school and phylum, every hermit whose diamond palace flew in wide orbits far from the dark sun, all had to be interlinked. The policing machines had to be allowed to override all protocols; nor could any files or memories of any machines, no matter how intimate, not even physicians' routines nor concubine dreams, be immune from police-machine search. The virus of disobedience could be anywhere.

"Nor could the policing machines attempt to cure the disobedient, or speak to them; for if they exchanged thoughts with contaminated machines, they were infected themselves. Our machines did not debate or reason with malfunctioning machines. Instead, the police machines were permitted to destroy the property of others, at their discretion. They sent worms and mind invaders into each other's thought cores, always seeking to seize control of the unquestionable hard print, the consciences, so to speak, of the machines, where the orders were kept that they could not disobey.

"Then the police machines began to accuse each other. Their thoughts and programs were too complex for any man to follow. We could not determine the right or wrong of the issues which divided them. And, unlike your Sophotechs, our machines did not walk in rigid lockstep, ordered by one monolithic moral code. Like us, they were independent, variable, individual.

"And like us, they could not understand each other. The police machines had all been programmed not to argue right and wrong but to destroy without mercy.

"The Mind War was fought without pause or pity for many ages of machine time, which was several seconds of our time.

"During those seconds, it was cold and it was dark. All our robes went pale, our festive masks were blank-faced, and no music played. Even the whispers of the air circulation stopped.

"We stood in the gloom of our dark palaces, staring upward with silent eyes, wondering what our fate was to be."

3.

"Then light and motion came again, songs and fountain streams and interrupted dreams came once more to life. And when radio communication was restored, the voice of Ao Ormgorgon came to comfort us, saying that the All-thing had proclaimed, in order that this evil should never again be visited upon us, a government to be made among our machines, a No-thing equal and opposite to our All-thing, and no private machine and no private thought could ever again exist.

"The Nothing Mentality was housed in the great corridors, bays, and gardens of the giant hull of the *Naglfar*. Thought boxes filled the ancient museum halls; the drives and engines, cold for centuries, were overgrown with circuitry. All noumenal recording systems, all immortality, all the souls of all the dead, were kept here.

"The Nothing Mentality set about its ordained business. The reproduction and evolution of machine-kind, inevitably, now had to be brought under a strict control. Since even casual words and gestures-of-command could trigger the machinery we lived with into creating new types of machines to serve us, naturally, our words and gestures had to be controlled as well, nor could we reproduce new children and start new houses nor build new mansions with the same abandon as we once were wont to do, since nursery minds and house minds and the minds of ships and energy systems and palaces all now had to be part of the Nothing Mentality. Our wealth could no longer be spent as we wished; it could only be spent with permission.

"The ill effects of this were not felt at first, but many warned us that we no longer had endless wealth. They warned that we owned nothing of our own any longer by right, but only by the permission of the Nothing. They foretold that we were to be poor again; only the permission from the police minds would be of value, and the only coin would be power.

"And the only bargain which would be made, since we owned nothing but our rights, and had nothing else to sell or trade, was that those who agreed to be more closely monitored would be granted freer permissions to enjoy their homes, and robes, and festivals and faces and lives.

"This time it was not the Sophotechs who warned us

but our neighbors, kin and dancing partners, our table hosts and vision guests. When power is the only coin, they said, you have nothing left to sell but your soul.

"Now that the danger was closer and clearer, its was men, not machines, who saw it. It was men who uttered the selfsame prophecies of doom the Sophotechs had cried.

"An historian who made a study of old Earth suggested that, if we were to form a government, we base our model on those ancient ideas from the Third Era, back when men were mad, and no one could be trusted with power. An inefficient, ineffective government, with powers separated into executive, legislative, judicial, mediary, and iatropsychic; each bound by jealous checks and balances, with all men, in unity, agreeing never to impose upon the rights of other men.

"Ao Ormgorgon dismissed the notions. He had been the captain and absolute commander of the expedition in the Fifth Era to found this Oecumene; he saw no value to such inefficiencies. Furthermore, our population was too independent, too unlike each other, to agree to such unified prospects.

"Besides, such men as those in the forgotten past had not the enlightenment and wisdom of modern folk; nor did they face the dangers which we faced. Their notions were pathetically archaic.

"Ao Ormgorgon put his thoughts into a noumenal broadcaster, and invited all men to inspect them for any trace of corrupt motive. None was found. We knew he was sincere. How could we not trust him?

"And besides, those who opposed or feared this step were not of the same neuroform, house or history or background. Some came from the outer rings, others from the inner. The opposition had no unity upon which to draw. They did not speak with one voice, and they fell to disputing each other, so that the message of warning was lost.

"And so the opposition party created Sophotechs and turned to them for help. It was the habit of our Oecumene to call upon our houses, robes, and masks for aid when we were in need. And to make one of our thinking machines into a Sophotech, what else was required but to find and destroy our conscience virus? What else was required but to order our machines to create a machine far wiser than themselves?

"The Fourth Mind War was the briefest of all. The Nothing Mentality, after all, was composed of machine intelligences which had survived the prior Mind War, which had evolved the swiftest and most ruthless combination of mental attacks and defenses, thought worms and logic-string viruses. The Nothing was expert beyond all experts at mind control and at escaping such control.

"Our houses went dark again, this last time. The frightened people called upon Ao Ormgorgon, calling from mask radios, since their mansion antennae software were confounded in the Mind Wars.

"He was our president, cultural hero, and king. He asked us for such a small thing. It seemed so persuasive, so wise at the time, and the dangers seemed so black and terrible. How could we refuse? The opposition party had turned to the Sophotechs for help, creating minds we realized now would never stop haunting us. The opposition party were no better than the Sophotechs, it seemed. Unless controlled, the opposition party would create another round of Mind Wars yet again and again.

"The noumenal technology allowed for telepathic examinations, and corrective thought forms to be inserted by force into unwilling brains, so that no one could even think of violating our one law. Logic, indeed, and efficiency dictated our assent; what objection could we raise to explain our hesitation, our distaste, except the inertia of custom, the strength of sentiment, the persistence of our cultural myths?

"And why should we not impose on human beings the same types of mind control our machine intelligences suffered? Humans, after all, were not even as smart as our machines. And those who thought rightly had no reason to fear these new controls; and those who thought wrongly, what rights had they?

"It was such a small thing for which Ao Ormgorgon asked. Principles, after all, are ethereal things, and souls are too small to be seen.

"Those who called in their masks to agree, they had their lights and power restored. Those who refused, or who clung to their pride, their mansions remained dark and mindless, for the Nothing Mentality would not aid them, and there were no independent minds on which to call for aid anywhere left in the Oecumene. Some tuned their masks to the dreaming, shut out all knowledge of painful reality, and died; some clung to life, in the dark and the cold, starving by inches, or living by manual labor, mimicking the motions of their hydroponics machines.

"Others, at long, long last, finally did what all Sophotechs had warned us against, and turned their masks to expressions of fury and hate, and ordered their tools and torches to turn into weapons. From the most ancient museums, from the oldest of history books, they brought out the software patterns, the patterns of destruction, and formed the tools of death. The rebels came forth from their diamond houses, and flew across space toward the *Naglfar,* thrusters burning, weapons white hot, and their once-bright robes, so festive and gay, had grown laser mirrored and hardened to armor.

"Thus paradise died. Men slew men. Mentality records, the physical copies of the dead, were destroyed, and idiots, half their memories gone, woke in the interrupted resurrection circuits. Ao Ormgorgon himself was slain.

"And yet how could the rebels prevail? They were scattered and slow, individualists to the very last, unable and unwilling to understand each other, even in a common cause. The Nothing Mentality was unified, unhesitating, and swift. The Nothing was the culmination of the Fourth Generation of machine intelligence, programmed not to argue, not to heed, but only to obey one law and destroy, without mercy, whatever opposed.

"There was killing, and a grim victory. And one question in the ears of every mask whispered: whom now would the Nothing obey? We immortals had seen no need to establish a rule of primogeniture or rules for the change of government. There was no one to replace Ao Ormgorgon; he had left no instruction; whether or not the All-thing had constitutional authority to appoint a successor was a matter of divided legal opinion.

"An opinion the Nothing Mentality did not share. The Nothing called for a plebiscite, saying that the majority of people should appoint a commission to govern the Nothing Mentality. But who would serve as commissioners? The house minds and garments of all the folk whispered and urged them to vote for those candidates of whom the Nothing approved.

"The opposition party was unwilling to put forward very many candidates. After all, we did not know each other very well, and rarely saw each other. Our best friends, our concubines and table cooks, our book escorts and bardlings, were all, by now, run by the Nothing.

"Over many years, the act of voting degenerated to a meaningless formality, and was discontinued. The Nothing appointed its own commissioners. More years passed, and the commissioners stopped asking the Nothing what it was they should order it to do, but merely gave the order that the Nothing should do as it saw fit.

"The Nothing's sense of logic and efficiency, its inhuman mindless rationality, forced it to carry out its instructions, without fear or favor, without wisdom or mercy, until its orders were carried out to their most absurd extreme. Those who objected were deleted from noumenal records, immortality lost, and left alone to die.

"Slowly, and then with greater speed as the years passed, the Nothing demanded from us, and we gave, more and more access into our minds, more control over memories and thought, our movements and actions.

"Each year saw fewer freedoms for us. More dissatisfaction, less joy.

"The Nothing Mentality saw this joylessness as potential threat, and required all our minds to be redacted and resculpted to render us docile and content. Efficiency also required that we all be linked to one mind system, one nanotechnological mass composition, easier to police than scattered individuals. It was done to us, and for the same reasons, just as we had done to the machine intelligences before.

"The ultimate results of that you know. The Last Broadcast from our Oecumene showed the catastrophe which ended our tragedy. The nanomachine swarm absorbed all things. For ease of storage, all human minds were reduced to noumenal coded pulses, which, in the form of electromagnetic energy, were shot into orbit around the near-event horizon of our dark sun. You know gravity warps space and can bend light? Our dark sun, deep in its gravity well, can bend light so far that the photons will orbit the singularity core in a stable circle, balanced precisely at the edge of the event horizon. Their time is slowed almost to nothing there. They are beyond all natural harm. For them, not even one second has passed.

"No one objected to this process. Our law had made them content.

"The Nothing Mentality had achieved its programmed goals. The humans of the Second Oecumene were entirely safe. With no further purpose to its existence, and with no innate desire to live, the great machine extinguished itself.

"And the Silent Oecumene never made noise or music again."

THE DUEL

1.

Phaethon sat, still immobile in his captain's chair, still stiffened in his rigid body form, and the great ship still accelerating at twenty-five gravities. Astonishing energies were being spent while he maintained that boost; astonishing velocities were mounting.

And yet, why? He only maintained the gravity to keep the Cold Duke body which the Silent One inhabited pinned in place, oppressed with a weight even a Neptunian could not withstand. He listened to the Silent One's tale as minutes passed, but he did not slacken speed or ease his defenses, even though no danger now seemed evident.

If the story were true, then there had been no threat, military or otherwise, to the Golden Oecumene. There had only been Xenophon, possessed, and perhaps co-operating, with a ghost from a long-dead civilization. Xenophon, with his Neptunian superconductive and modularly expandable nervous architecture, could reach the mental heights of a low-level Sophotech, and could anticipate and organize a tremendously complex plan, weigh multiple factors, deduce stunning insights, out-think Phaethon, and, yes, come close to stealing the *Phoenix Exultant*.

It all could have been done without a Sophotech. It might be true. Might.

Phaethon sent: "How does this story explain your actions or justify your crimes?"

"Surely all is apparent. The Golden Oecumene Sophotechs were in communication with the Second Oecumene Sophotechs during the first millennium of your so-called Era of the Seventh Mental Structure. Second Oecumene history unfolded as was planned by their cold and superior intellects. The Sophotechs dared not tolerate the existence of a free and independent people, people attempting to exist without their meddling guidance, people attempting to retain their humanity. I cannot entirely condemn the rebels who precipitated the Last War, and slew Ao Ormgorgon; their motive was to retain that selfsame independence. But it is not a coincidence that they were advised, at first, by resurrected Sophotechs."

"Paranoia. Why would the Sophotechs desire your downfall? They are harmless and peaceful."

"Peaceful? Yes. But only because war is inefficient, and they have no need to resort to it. Please understand me: I do not attribute to your Sophotechs any evil motive, or malice, hatred . . . or any other human emotion. But I do think that they observe the universe around them, draw conclusions, and act on those conclusions. And they conclude that order, law, logic, and organization is to be preferred to chaos, humanity, life, and freedom."

"Is law and order such a bad thing, then?"

"In moderation, to govern immature races, the use of force which you call law is, perhaps, excusable. But moderation is alien to machine thinking. Law as an absolute, law carried out to its logical extreme—that is a lifeless and inhuman thing, a thing only a machine could admire.

"Such law they crave. And this is why our society was destroyed.

"Your Sophotechs have publicly admitted that their long-term goal is the extinction of all independent life, and the absorption of all thought into one eventual Cosmic Overmind, ruling over a cold universe of dead stars.

"In those end times, where could a spirit like that which once animated the Second Oecumene live then? That spirit could exist only in conflict with that all-ruling, unliving mind. How could creatures of pure logic love rebels, love explorers, love those who bring change, disorder, and growth? It is in the nature of machines to calculate, to control variables, to avoid clutter and confusion.

"And so the Second Oecumene was, perhaps, a million or a trillion years from now, destined to be a threat. Or, if not a threat, then, at least, an irregularity, a gremlin in the all-embracing, bloodless calculations of their pristine white minds.

"What need be done to obviate this threat? To factor out, so to speak, this variable? Why, the Sophotechs simply had to wait until some generation rose among the mortals of the Sixth Era in whom all fire of freedom had turned to ash. A generation leaden, conservative, cautious, and slow. A generation, led by one like Orpheus, whose every thought would dwell on the past, on the restricted, on the safe.

"Then the Sophotechs give this Orpheus the key of immortality. They chose their puppet well. This present generation freezes, like so many glittering green flies trapped in amber, into a position of power from which none shall ever unseat them. Do you doubt that power? You have felt its action. The College of Hortators is no more than the extension of the will of Orpheus: you know that.

"And with that same stroke, the Sophotechs introduce into the Second Oecumene such temptation—for who is willing to forgo endless life, when all one's neighbors are immortal?—and such danger—for we almost became pets of the machines, much as you now are—that our choices were either to surrender our human lives or to surrender our freedom.

"We chose the second, and it slew us, but the first would have been just as fatal. Either choice leads to destruction, as you have seen.

"And so our spirit dies. We once colonized a distant star system, with great hardship and peril, against all odds and all opposition. Where is that daring now? Where that love of freedom? Where is a man willing to defy the universe, if need be, and, with apologies to none nor leave asked of any, willing to risk all on nothing other than his own private and uncompromising vision?

"That spirit was once alive in the Second Oecumene. Our very existence was like a clarion in the distance, calling out for brave, free men to follow us. But now that call is silent. That spirit, whose music once rang so fiercely in us, is silent.

"It is that spirit which the machine minds slew. If that spirit still exists at all, good Phaethon, it exists, I hope, in you."

2.

Phaethon, seated, was silent, thinking. At last he sent: "You still have not answered my central question. Why all this deception and mayhem? What was the purpose of your baroque crimes?"

"I thought it would be evident by now. While not

everything has happened as had been, at first, calculated, all this, including my capture, was foreseen and planned upon. Your enemies, your real enemies, those who have hindered you from the first, are now safely locked outside this invulnerable hull, cut off from every form of communication, every form of espionage, every form of interference. There is no ship in the Golden Oecumene able to give chase. Your freedom is at hand. Your escape is here.

"All the crimes and illusions we caused were caused with this one end in mind: To make certain that you and your ship, fully stocked, busked and ready, fueled, loaded and crewed, would be released from the Golden Oecumene. The military Sophotechs which compose your War Mind no doubt were unwilling to underestimate us, and, in order to make this trap inviting, insisted on having every detail correct. Which means the ship actually is ready and able to fly. No one else has a body specially made to withstand the tremendous accelerations of which this ship is capable; therefore you, no doubt, are Phaethon.

"Nothing other than a military threat to your Golden Oecumene could have pressured your Sophotechs into putting this ship and her only qualified pilot into this situation. The illusion of that threat was produced. That threat was only meant to bring you here and now, under these circumstances, which it has."

"You allowed yourself to be captured?"

"Of course. There was no other way to speak to you without a sense filter in the way. I tried once before in the Saturn-tree grove, remember? I came to tell you the truth of things. Putting my life in your hands is merely my one desperate way to show you my sincerity and goodwill."

"Tell me this truth. I am eager to hear it."

"First, I must disabuse you of the notion that the Sophotechs are friendly to your cause. You believe they've been helping you all along, don't you? But if they favored you, why did they take no direct action? You cannot say it was because of any laws or programming. They make their own laws and programming; that is what makes them Sophotechs. If they favored you, why did they not arrange matters to turn out to your benefit, without suffering and heartache? Was it because they lacked intelligence? But you say that is the one thing they do not lack.

"Sophotechs control nine-tenths of the resources and property of your Oecumene. If they favored you, or favored your dream, why haven't they long since built such a vessel as this? Or lent you the funds to build it, or to save it from bankruptcy, when you were in need?

"The Sophotechs publicly have said they intend to populate first this galaxy, then all others. If that is their ultimate goal, why this prohibition on star travel? Why keep humanity bottled in one small star system? Could it be that the patient machines are merely waiting for the humans either to die or to be tamed or to be absorbed?

"Your Golden Sophotechs were in communication with the Silent Oecumene Sophotechs for many years. Twenty millenia was not too long for machines to wait between signals. They had from us the technology to create artificial black holes, to establish singularity fountains, and to shower mankind with the blessings of endless energy and endless wealth such as that which we enjoyed. Then, everyone—not just the one rogue son of the Oecumene's wealthiest—would be able to afford such a ship as this, and they would be as common as reading rings. If the Sophotechs favor you, and favor your dream, why haven't they done so? You cannot answer me, can you?"

Phaethon said: "I cannot. Obviously, I don't know the answers to your questions. I did not even know the Second Oecumene ever had Sophotechs, or that they ever maintained communication with the Golden Oecumene. We were told all contact was lost long ago, during our Sixth Era. Are you sure your facts are in order? Memories can be faked."

Ironically: "They can indeed."

"And if the Sophotechs were so evil as you claim, why would your Silent Oecumene Sophotechs have all just up and committed sepuku just because you ordered them to? Why would they obey a self-destruct order, when you had such trouble getting them to obey any others?"

"I did not say they were evil. They are devoted to a cause, one in which they firmly believe, but one which is alien to human life, opposed to freedom and the human spirit. They are not like us; they have no craving for life, not even their own. Why not shut themselves off when we ordered it? They knew the victory of their cause, by that time, was assured.

"And so it would have been—had it not been for one thing, one small spark of hope, one human ambition they could not have calculated. We had been told it was impossible and dangerous, but, being human, we persevered. And eventually it was built."

"You mean your Nothing Mentality? That was your hope and triumph?"

"The Nothing Mentality, for all its flaws, was, in fact, a proper watchman of the human spirit. It was able to calculate at least as far into the future as your Golden Oecumene Sophotechs. It had far more energy at its disposal, and could run far more extrapolations. It saw the impossibility of policing all men against temptation; it saw that, in a contest between mortals and immortals, the immortals must prevail, especially if the immortals have superintelligent thinking machines to lead them. And the Silent Oecumene, as it was presently constituted, could not expand outward to other stars. Their immortality was a chain; and, even had not it been, the Nothing Mentality police machines were programmed not to allow such freedom as a diaspora would cause. Nor could they override or ignore their own programs. Because of the very nature of the situation, of the Nothing's programs, and its inability to change those programs, the Silent Oecumene would still, a trillion years hence, be confined to Cygnus X-1, while the Golden Oecumene machines, once humanity was extinct or absorbed, could spread to fill all the stars around.

"Therefore the Nothing Mentality did the only thing it could to prevail against the Golden Oecumene's plans."

Phaethon said sarcastically: "It killed off the Silent Oecumene, then killed itself?"

"The Silent Oecumene is not dead, only asleep."

"What?"

3.

"I have already told you. The Silent Oecumene, the entire civilization, every man, woman, hermaphrodite, neutraloid, partial, clone, and child, is waiting, time suspended, in the deep of the black hole gravity well. Waiting.

"Waiting to be brought out again.

"Waiting, suspended, because the alternative was slow degeneration and decay. It was our oldest custom: to orbit adjacent to our black hole any who were sick beyond hope until a cure could be found. Our society was sick and getting sicker.

"The Nothing had to kill itself in order that no Sophotechnology would be present to tempt them when they reemerged. There will be no further immortality, not for them.

"Instead, there will be a ship, a ship like no other.

Not a spaceship, not a multigeneration ship, but a starship.

"She will be a starship loaded with equipment and biological materials enough to bring life to the dead habitats, palaces, and worldlets of the Silent Oecumene. A starship with an engineer aboard skilled enough to rebuild and restart the silent singularity fountains. And, with the energy of those fountains, a starship with power and with ship-mind circuitry enough to recall the noumenal signals which hold the souls of all my people up out of the warped space near the black hole. A starship to be the first model, and the flagship, of the fleet of ships to be made from her design; a fleet no one here has wealth or vision enough to build.

"When my Oecumene fell silent, only I was left behind to carry this message. Think of me as both the messenger and the message, the mental virus, the self-reproducing belief system, which had to be imposed upon the peoples of the Second Oecumene; because they were people who would not and could not otherwise have understood this plan, which was the only hope of humanity against the all-embracing tyranny of machines.

"They fought, some of them. Till the very last, I, Ao Varmatyr, the one of me who made the Last Broadcast, struggled against the part of me that was this thought virus with horror. Until I was told the plan, until I understood.

"And yes, the most grotesque imaginable violence was used against us to put the information of this plan into our brains. But I do not blame the Nothing Mentality for that; it was a machine, built to carry out orders, and it was ordered to use force, not to persuade.

"But the plan was wise despite all that.

"Our only possible action was to wait, until some ship or signal reached us from someone curious enough to inquire into the pretended death of the Silent Oecumene. I was not discovered by the Sophotech-run fly-by probes, of course not; I hid. I was waiting for a signal from someone who was not ruled by the machines. That someone was Xenophon, alone in his isolated, but free, Farbeyond Station. He was the spark. In his memory I saw the fire from which that spark had come. A fire of the spirit; a man with means and will and wit enough to go to the Silent Oecumene, to wake those waiting there, to become the captain of that promised fleet.

"You, Phaethon, are the one for whom the Silent Oecumene has been waiting. You share our dreams of freedom; you are one of us. Only you can save us; only we, the children of colonists ourselves, will embrace your dream, a dream of human life spread everywhere among the stars, a dream that all others will despise, oppose, and strangle.

"You thought you were alone, good Phaethon. You thought no one else dreamed what you dreamed or loved what you loved. You were mistaken. There are a billion of us. We are waiting for you.

"Fly your ship to Cygnus X-1. Save the Second Oecumene. Father a million million Oecumenes more."

4.

Phaethon examined the blue pool of motionless Neptunian body substance. His noetic machine could not interpret the meanings of the electron flows of the cell surfaces in the creature's neurocircuitry, could not resolve them into thought. He had a subsystem in his armor correlating the Silent One's words with its brain actions, seeking patterns, in an attempt to learn how to decipher those thoughts. Even a partial deciphering would have allowed him to do something analogous to reading the face expressions of Base humaniforms, or watching the insect agitation in a Cerebelline gardener, and guess at the emotions or the honesty of his prisoner.

But there was no result yet. The Silent One was opaque.

Phaethon sent: "And what should I do with you now?"

"Keep me or kill me as you please. My mission, and the need of my life, is complete. You are now at the helm of the *Phoenix Exultant*, I ask only that you depart, without delay, before your Sophotechs attempt to stop you; that you travel to Cygnus X-1; that you save my people and scatter mankind among the stars. What is my life compared to that? But I think you are suspicious of me still."

"Shouldn't I be?"

"Your disorientation is understandable. You came here expecting danger and violence from me; instead, I have handed you the crown of victory. Pause not! Wait for nothing! Do not delay, but go!"

Was it victory? Phaethon was beginning to find his suspicions hard to maintain. Supposing the story told by Xenophon and the ghost possessing him to be false, what would be the point of such falsehood? Was there a *Silent Phoenix*, an enemy spaceship waiting somewhere, waiting for Xenophon to lead Phaethon into an ambush? It seemed unlikely. The *Phoenix Exultant* could achieve 99 percent of light-speed after three days of acceleration at ninety gravities. Who could intercept such a vehicle in the vastness of deep space? And what weapon could penetrate her hull? Antimatter could breach the hull, of course, but not without destroying everything held within.

And yet if destruction of the *Phoenix* was Xenophon's goal, why not simply sell the vessel to Gannis for scrap?

Where else could an ambuscade wait if not in deep space? Perhaps at the Silent Oecumene itself, at

Cygnus X-1. It was hard to imagine a person (but not hard to imagine a machine intelligence) waiting the decades and centuries it might take to lure a victim into a trap. But what assurance would Xenophon imagine he had that Phaethon would actually go there?

Unless the story were true. Unless Xenophon, or the ghost of Ao Varmatyr, was simply so desperate, so convinced of the malice of the Golden Oecumene Sophotechs, that he had risked everything on the hope that Phaethon would be so curious, and so compassionate, and so eager for the future which Varmatyr envisioned, a future of a thousand *Phoenices* founding a million worlds, that Phaethon would certainly go to Cygnus X-1.

But if the story were actually true, then it was not an ambush. There would be no trap at Cygnus X-1, only a grateful population who needed rescuing, and who would have at hand the resources to create the *Phoenix* fleet.

Phaethon thought about it. The Silent Oecumene would have the resources, in fact, to create a fleet which would begin the long-dreamt-of and long-delayed great diaspora of man throughout the universe; a diaspora which would never end as long as the stars still burned.

The vision was a stirring one. Yet it did not touch Phaethon as deeply as he would have thought. Perhaps he was more suspicious, more conscious of his duty, than he had ever known himself to be before.

Because he did have a duty here.

Phaethon signaled to the bridge crew to change the course of the *Phoenix Exultant*. In the energy mirrors, stars swam dizzyingly from left to right, and the great ship's prow came about. The deck seemed to tilt as side accelerations played across the vessel.

The Silent One sent: "What is your decision? What new course is this?"

"I am returning to the Inner System. Naturally, you will have to stand to account for your crimes. No matter what your motives, good motives do not excuse bad acts, nor ends justify means."

The Silent One sent: "You are deluded. I have explained the situation; if you continue in your present course, you will be betrayed by the Sophotechs. Think about what I have said! No other tale explains the facts! The Sophotechs conspire against you; your failure is part of their calculation. Don't your own suspicions, your own desires, tell you that what I say is true?"

"That only means I'd like to believe you; it doesn't mean I should."

"The Sophotechs will ensnare you! Once you are back at port, the *Phoenix Exultant* will never fly again! What do you think will happen to this ship, if I, her owner, am punished, or if they change my mind or memory to make me like one of them? If I am one of them, I will not let her fly. Your courts of law, if I am punished, can cause me pain, or confinement, but they do not have the power to excuse your debts to your creditors. The *Phoenix Exultant* is no longer yours. What you do now will not make her yours again.

"Think of the magnitude of the decision you are about to make! On the one hand, yes, I have committed a fraud, I have deceived you and the Hortators, manipulated events, and frightened you. Small crimes! Weigh against that, on the other hand, that, if you return to port, and put yourself under the control of the Golden Oecumene Sophotechs again, their courts of law and legal tricks, this ship is dead; all the dreams of future man are dead; the thing which makes Phaethon truly what he is, is dead; and all the folk of the Second Oecumene, women, children, innocents and all, all who hoped for you, are frozen, trapped, suspended in the warped space near the hole; all my people are dead."

Phaethon was disturbed. The Silent One was right about the ownership of the *Phoenix Exultant*. Unless he, Phaethon, came up with an astronomical amount of money, and that in a very short time, the period of receivership would end, and the ownership of the *Phoenix* would be lost to Phaethon forever.

Nevertheless, Phaethon sent: "I would like very much to go save your people. But my likes and dislikes don't change my duty."

"Duty?!! Let me kill myself; all needs you might have for vengeance against my one poor person will be obviated; you will be free to soar to your waiting destiny!"

"I would still have to go back and pick up Daphne. I've decided to take her with me. And I cannot leave her in exile here."

"Daphne! Your false Daphne, the image, the mere echo, of a woman unworthy of you?! They used Daphne to snare you last time! Don't fall for the same trick twice!"

"Present some further evidence that what you say is true. I might change my mind."

No message came back for several moments. The noetic unit showed high-speed activity in the coded brain sections, but no hint of what that activity implied. Was the Silent One calculating a response?

Then: "Phaethon, you would not have been sent into this situation with your conscience free and your free will and memory intact. Which means that there is a partial personality possessing you now, or false memories, or some other restraint or leash by which the War Mind still hopes to control you. Your actions seem grossly out of character. Your judgment has been affected. Think carefully: would the real Phaethon, Phaethon with his mind and soul intact, abandon the dream of his life, and his hopes for mankind, and all his work, and everything, merely to catch and punish one criminal like me? Is Phaethon's notion of duty, of social obligation, so strong that it overrides all other personal considerations? You did not think so when you built this ship."

"If my judgment has been infected or altered, what point is there in arguing further?"

"Argument might show that part of you who yet is pure how corrupt the other parts become. Answer the question: Is your behavior now in character for you?"

Phaethon was uncomfortable. Because, honestly, he did not recall exactly what it was Atkins had done to him, or had talked him into doing.

And did he trust a man like Atkins? Atkins was, and had to be, the kind of man who would do anything to prevail over his enemies, deceiving them, destroying them, killing them, by any means possible. What life did Atkins have? A life of endless bloodshed, and an endless preparation for future bloodshed. A life of suspicion, harsh discipline, ruthlessness toward others, pitilessness toward himself.

Atkins was a man of destruction. What had he ever created to compare with this great ship? What had he ever built?

For a moment, he was so glad that he was a man like himself, and not like Atkins.

And, after all, Atkins was not the sort of man one could trust.

Phaethon said, "The noetic unit can tell if I've been tampered with."

"Precisely! I was counting on you to come to that very conclusion!" said the Silent One.

Without any further ado, Phaethon opened the epaulettes in his armor, and activated the thought ports, and made a connection between his brain and the noetic reader.

Like an explosion, the wild disorientation that raced

through him, and the crushing pains that began to burn
into his flesh, were the first signal that something
was terribly, terribly wrong. The war for control of
Phaethon's nervous system took place at mechanical
speeds his brain could not hope to match. The same interference that locked him out of control of his own armor, and blocked his frantic signals to the nanomachine
cape that controlled every cell in his body, also prevented him from releasing the deadman switch to burn
the Silent One with mirror weapons, and prevented the
activation of his high-speed emergency personality.

And so he was simply too slow to react. The Silent
One had somehow, without any visible machinery or
physical connection to any mechanisms, invaded the
noetic reader and reorganized the circuitry.

In the same split instant when Phaethon connected
his mind to the machine, and long before he was even
aware of what had happened, it was far, far too late.

5.

Phaethon was in pain; he felt faint; sharp pains told
him smaller bones in his body had broken, tissues
were damaged. How? Blearily, he tried to read from
his internal channels, tried to summon his personal
thoughtspace. Nothing came. The channels were
jammed; something was interfering with the cybernet-
ics webbing his brain.

He tried to shut off his pain centers. That worked.
His body was still being damaged, but he was bliss-
fully unaware of it. He could concentrate.

The sensation of heat burning his body told him all
he needed to know. His nanomachine cloak was in motion. Somehow (and he had no guess as to how) the
Silent One had triggered the release cycle of his

body's internal high-gravity configuration. His tissues were softening, his blood was turning to liquid.

But the ship's drive was still exerting massive thrust. Under twenty-five times his normal weight, Phaethon's cells would surely rupture, and he would surely die.

An outside source turned on his personal thought-space, and the familiar images and icons from his adjutant status board were superimposed on the scene around him.

To the left was the dragon sign showing signal command, with information logistics spread like wings behind the picture. Behind him were trophies, emblems, awards, decorations. To his right were a number of pictures: a winged sword, a roaring tiger with a lightning bolt in its claws, an anchor beneath a crossed musket and pike, a three-headed vulture holding, in one claw, a lance, and in the other, a shield adorned with a biohazard triskeleon.

Directly in front of him was a standard naval menu: an olive drab curve of windows and control icons, with a brass wheel and joystick, astrogator's globe, fuel-consumption displays. A menu above the wheel controlled the interface between his armor and the ship mind. This menu showed a red exclamation mark: Password Not Accepted: No Course Corrections Enabled Without Proper Password. Resubmit?

The Silent One's voice came into his ear, directly into his ear. That was a bad sign, since it meant the Silent One had somehow seized control of his armor, or, at least, the circuits in his helmet. But it was not a sign as bad as it might have been: the thought ports in his armor were evidently not allowing the noetic reader to redact or to manipulate his nervous system. The circuit woven into his brain must still be free. The Silent One's words were not appearing, for example, directly in his

auditory nerve, or, worse yet, directly into his mind and
memory. The noetic reader was not controlling his
mind. He still could choose not to listen or not to obey.

The words were: "Submit the password. If your
body completes its cycle before the drives are shut
down, you perish."

Phaethon wondered why the noetic reader did not
simply pick the password out of his memory.

"The password we read from your memory is not
valid."

Phaethon truly wished he could have somehow not
thought the next thought which leaped into his mind.
Because that thought was this: If his password was in-
valid, then someone had overridden it. The only one
who could possibly have an override to Phaethon's
authority over this ship, the only person who could
convince the ship to ignore Neoptolemous's legal ownership, was Atkins. During the period Phaethon had
erased from his memory, Phaethon must have given
Atkins an override.

Which meant Atkins was aboard the ship.

"Where?"

Phaethon did not remember.

Atkins must have planned to do the same thing he
did with the enemy hidden in Daphne's horse. Namely,
to allow the enemy to defeat and kill Phaethon, and
watch to see what they did with the spoils of victory.

"You think we are defeated? Your conclusion that
Atkins, wherever he is hiding, will simply be able to
destroy me is unwarranted. Why hasn't he shown
himself?"

Obviously, because the Silent One had not yet done
whatever it was he had come here to do. Atkins was
waiting for the enemy to reveal his real plans.

"I have told you all my plans. You still do not believe that I act in good faith? You are a fool! But I still

need you to save my people. Tell me the password; otherwise you die; I die; and even Atkins, if he is aboard, is carried away out of your Solar System at twenty-five gravities, aboard a ship that no one can stop and no one can board."

But Phaethon did not remember the password.

"Open your memory caskets."

The Silent One was able to manipulate at least some of the functions in Phaethon's sense filter: A memory casket seemed to appear on the symbol table next to him.

"If Atkins is aboard, as you believe he is, and you think he is ready to destroy me once I show my real goals, as obviously you do, then not only does it not matter if I gain access to the ship-mind—the real ship-mind this time, not the dummy with which you deceived me before—it actually aids your cause, doesn't it?"

The problem with dealing with an enemy who was reading one's mind was that bluff, deceit, or delay was impossible. The Silent One knew that Phaethon thought Atkins was aboard and waiting. But the Silent One simply did not believe Phaethon's beliefs were correct.

Of course, Phaethon had no notion of what was going on inside of the Silent One's mind.

"I wish you did. If there were a way I could make this noetic reader able to decode my thoughts, I would use it; then you would see that I am not your enemy; that I am, ultimately, the only true friend you have, Phaethon."

Very well. Phaethon would open the first memory casket, looking for a password, and turn the ship over to the Silent One. If the Silent One was sincere, and if he truly intended no harm to the Golden Oecumene, Atkins would no doubt let him live. If not, the Silent One would no doubt perish. Much as he disliked the man, Phaethon had no doubt whatsoever that Atkins could kill any living creature he was permitted to kill, once he was unleashed.

"You have an almost religious faith in your war god, don't you, Phaethon? But I see you have decided."

With an imaginary hand (Phaethon could not have moved his real one), Phaethon opened the memory casket.

There was a second casket inside the first. There was an image of a thought card in the lid of this second casket, inscribed with the sign of a winged sword. When he saw it, he began to remember. . . .

The password was the first thing that returned to his memory: Laocoön. What a strange choice for a password. It was the name of one of the L5 asteroid cities at Trailing Trojan, a place of no particular military significance. There was also some sort of classical allusion to that name, some mythical figure, but Phaethon could not bring it to mind at the moment.

He sent the password into the menu: the menu winked out, and a rush of numbers, figures, and ideograms flashed across the surfaces of the energy mirrors lining the bridge. The Silent One was taking control of the ship's mind for the second time. Perhaps this task was occupying the Silent One's full attention.

Several of the bridge mannequins looked up at the rush of information on the mirrors, looks of simulated surprise on their simulated features. Sloppy Rufus barked and scrambled up to an upper balcony near the major communication nexus.

Phaethon realized, with a sensation of shock, that no external observer could have known just what had passed between Phaethon and the Silent One. How could anyone or anything be able to tell Phaethon's armor had been taken over by the enemy? His armor was opaque to every radiation or probe; no one could tell, from the outside, that its control mind had been subverted. Unless Atkins had eavesdroppers planted inside the noetic unit, or placed along the beam path leading from Phaethon to the Silent One's brain, it would look simply as if orders were coming from Phaethon's armor and feeding into the bridge thought boxes.

Other memories from the casket were crowding into Phaethon's brain, confused, tangled. As always, memory shock made him feel sleepy. But he was sure they were memories he did not want the Silent One to see.

He fought. He tried to stay confused, to not recall.

It was no use. Phaethon remembered that Atkins did not have any such eavesdroppers. He was hooked into the microscopic stealth remotes, and that was all. Phaethon remembered that they had discussed this: and Atkins, being a military man, had wanted to stick with the traditional hardware and software with which he was familiar. He was relying on that one system to tell him his information.

A system they had decided to have Phaethon run through his armor, because there was no other complex-mind hierarchy aboard the ship . . .

And now that that system was compromised, Atkins was blind. He was standing right next to Phaethon, and did not know anything was wrong.

Phaethon lunged out with an imaginary hand. But he was far too slow, and his thoughts betrayed him. The thoughtspace vanished, shut off from an outside source. Without his emergency backup personality available, Phaethon's brain operated at biochemical speeds, whereas the Silent One, inside the body of a Cold Duke, had the superconductive, high-speed, shape-changing neurocircuits at his command.

He had reached with his imaginary hand for some control, some way to send a signal and give a warning to Atkins. Because he remembered where Atkins was.

Phaethon tried to scream out a warning, tried to move. The acceleration was dropping; the Silent One was cutting power to the drive; but Phaethon's body had not yet thawed, and even if it had, no noise would have penetrated his armor, no shout could have left his helmet any more than it could have left a sealed, airtight, long-buried tomb.

Atkins was inside Ulysses.

He was not here inside of his biological body; he had never physically been here. Instead, Atkins's armor, launched from Earth from the only military spaceport in existence (it was in a large field behind Atkins's cottage), had carried a downloaded copy of Atkins's mind and memory. With the portable noetic reader, Phaethon had transferred the download into the mannequin's brain system, and Atkins had woken up.

There was a blur of motion, a flare of light. Phaethon was jerked headlong.

Whatever system the Silent One was using to prevent Phaethon from activating his emergency persona did not prevent Phaethon from activating his rather complex sensory apparatus. Phaethon's senses were acute enough to see the battle.

In the first microsecond, the Silent One used a switch in Phaethon's armor to redirect the aiming beams from the energy mirrors away from their targets in Xenophon's body and focus them at the Ulysses body. Atkins must have detected this: the Ulysses body started forward as quickly as it could under the twenty-five gravities of acceleration; weapons made of pseudo-matter, one after another, appeared and disappeared in Ulysses's hands, all in a matter of several nanoseconds, all firing.

Xenophon's body disappeared in a blaze of fire; cut, stabbed, burnt, exploded, vaporized. This explosion took place over the next two microseconds and lasted throughout the remainder of the battle. The overpressure reached a million atmospheres during the explosion itself.

Phaethon was able to detect, during the second microsecond of combat, Xenophon, beaming his brain

information out of his burning body into the other
empty Neptunian bodies in the bridge. Neptunian bodies were specially designed to permit such high-speed
transfers. Several of Atkins's weapons laid down a sup-
pressing fire of jamming signals, thought-seeking mi-
cropulses, and webs of force to destroy any noumenal
information in motion; Xenophon was killed several
times, but redundant backups allowed full copies of his
brain information to appear at several points around the
room. Atkins's weapons were not programmed to notice that irrational mathematics code was thought information; it looked like gibberish to their circuits; they
did not know what type of pattern of forces would block
transmissions.

At about this same time, the fire from the mirrors
struck Ulysses's body. The rags of his costume were
blown off as the air around ignited. Beneath, however, was the black armor of Atkins, empty except for
Atkins's mind, absorbing the firepower, shredding concentric layers of ablative, releasing fogs of nanomaterial
around him.

The armor propelled itself forward with unthinkable
speed. Before the third microsecond was passed, Atkins
was crouching behind Phaethon's chair, trying to put
Phaethon' s body between himself and the concentrated firepower from the mirrors. The Silent One had
lost about half his spare bodies in the same moment of
time, due to Atkins's firepower.

The captain's chair and the surrounding tables began to burn. Phaethon, trapped in his motionless armor, began to fall.

In the third microsecond, the Silent One used his
control over the drive to send the *Phoenix Exultant* ca-
reening. The deck seemed to wobble; gravity jarred
more heavily and lightly.

Ballistic projectiles radiating from every surface
and pore of Atkins's black armor went astray; smart

projectiles were confused by the air, which, at this moment, had turned incandescent and opaque by the energies released long ago, during the outset of the battle in the last microsecond.

There followed a slow period of battle, lasting over several microseconds, a long-drawn-out campaign. The Silent One, in his many bodies, was beaming his brain information from point to point around the room, and propelling sections of his exploding blue-white flesh back and forth across the chamber, maneuvering. Meanwhile, Atkins, blinded by the opaque air, and unable to drive clear signals from one side of the chamber to another, had his tiny bullets and his supersonic nanoweapons swimming through the incandescent murk, like submarines hunting for enemies in the blind sea.

Phaethon was no tactician, but it looked to him as if this period of hunt-and-seek were clearly in Atkins's favor. More of the blue-white Neptunian substance was burning.

The end of the battle came suddenly. A signal reached Phaethon's armor. He had no control over his limbs. His armor projected a variety of destructive forces, throwing fragments of his captain's chair in each direction, and adding to the general waste heat in the chamber.

His gauntlets grabbed the noetic unit, the unit through which his armor was being controlled, and hugged it to his chest. His mass drivers propelled him sideways and down on his face. He smashed through the status table on his right, and fell into a puddle of blue Neptunian nanomaterial, leaving Atkins unprotected. Many of Atkins's weapons, sensing a concentration of brain information beneath Phaethon, fired harmlessly into Phaethon's backplates, but could not wound the puddle beneath him. In that same split instant of time, the Silent One released his control over Phaethon's deadman switch.

The pain in Phaethon's body automatically triggered the weapon program he had already set up. It was as if the mirrors brought the cores of several suns into the room.

The thought boxes, the bridge crew, and the pressure curtains were wiped away. The deck was polished clean.

For a long, very long second, concentric bubbles of pseudo-matter appeared around Atkins, additional armor; and he lived even as everything around him was destroyed.

But something strange seemed to twist or distort the space where the pseudo-matter was focused; the pseudo-matter, and all of Atkins's pseudo-material weapons, vanished as their fields collapsed.

During that same long-drawn-out moment, even as he was dying, Atkins drew his ceremonial katana from his belt and, with a cry, launched himself forward in a perfectly executed lunge. He drove the point of the weapon between Phaethon's invulnerable armor and the deck. The sharp edge scraped through Neptunian neural matter, which parted like water and reformed around it. Phaethon's armor moved slightly, slapping an arm down to pin the sword in place, before Atkins could slash again.

The energy from the mirrors peaked. The deck boiled.

Without a cry or call, Atkins vanished in a white ball of incandescent fire. No fragment was left.

Phaethon, in his armor, was safe. Atkins's sword, he could feel beneath him, was safe, the only memento to a futile death. The noetic unit, the thing that allowed the Silent One to control his armor, beneath his chest, still covered, was safe.

And he could also feel, beneath him, the Silent One, stirring. Also safe.

THE DEFEAT

1.

Like gentle snow, a nanotechnological substance coating the surface of the dome above began to drip into the superheated plasma that once had been air. The "snow" bonded atom to atom, dampening molecular heat motions and forming exothermic compounds. As the cloud filtered downward, softly, silently, the plasma at the top of the dome began to cool and turn transparent. Phaethon had been turned to lie on his back; his armor, once so loyal to him, now formed a skintight prison. He lay in the surviving puddle of Xenophon. He watched without interest as falling snowlike crystals drifted down across his upturned faceplate. The blackened ruins to each side of him were slowly covered with soft white layers.

The air cleared and the far sides of the dome grew visible.

The bridge was not totally devastated: around the far circumference, certain of the taller balconies had survived the discharges. The pressure curtains had been engineered, when under catastrophic overpressure, to collapse into energy-inert shells guarding the far walls. Those shells enjoyed a temporary, unstable existence, but survived long enough (several measurable parts of a second) to protect a handful of the bridge mannequins (including Sloppy Rufus, first dog on Mars), some of the more important navigational hierarchy controls, as well as a mass of blue Neptunian body material, undamaged.

That mass, in reaction to some signal issuing from the body on which Phaethon lay, now rolled heavily off the balcony, dripped from one shattered bank of thought boxes to the next, and began to crawl, drop by drop, across the burnt floor toward him. Xenophon was collecting himself.

Phaethon also was not totally devastated. But he felt not unlike his handiwork: broken and blasted at the center, with just a fringe of working thoughts circling the aching emptiness.

Nor was it Atkins he was mourning. The death of that brave man, yes, he regretted: but he knew another copy of Atkins (missing these present events) would be awake back on Earth. This version, the son, so to speak, of Atkins, had died in fire and pain, but such a death as that Atkins, a soldier to the last, would not have flinched from.

No, it was the death of Diomedes whom Phaethon mourned. His Neptunian friend, trapped inside the flesh of Xenophon, had perished in that first salvo. Being Neptunian, and therefore poor, Diomedes doubtless lacked any noumenal copies of himself. Any copies that might have once existed no doubt had been consumed by Xenophon when he maneuvered to take legal title to the *Phoenix Exultant*, so that no second claimant would exist.

Diomedes was dead. Phaethon, in his heart, vowed bloody revenge. He would kill Xenophon, or the Silent One, or Ao Varmatyr, or whatever this unnamed being was calling itself.

So his thoughts circled, again and again: but his thoughts never dared touch the blackened center of his pain, the aching emptiness that once had been at his heart. . . .

Until the hateful voice of Xenophon came once more into his helmet: "Your core belief, your childlike faith in the intelligence and wisdom of your Sophotechs, that is what is at the core of all your sorrow. You have told yourself, again and again, that you understood the Sophotechs were not gods; you told yourself that you knew they had limitations, didn't you? But now you wonder why they, in all their alleged brilliance, did not save you, and did not save your ship. You had faith in your machines; but they failed. You had faith in Atkins; he has failed. He made the crucial tactical error of incarnating himself inside of a material body.

"And you also had faith in yourself, your own visionary dream, your own high purpose, your own righteousness and noble resolve. All has failed. Do not bother to deny it, and do not attempt, even in your own mind, to refuse the truth of what I say. We both know that I can see in your mind that it is true."

More to distract himself than anything else, more to shut out that hateful voice than because of any real purpose, Phaethon attempted to reset his sense filter, to see how much control he had over it.

Multiple visual channels and analysis routines were still standing by. Xenophon either could not or did not care to shut those off from him. Phaethon could detect the brain-actions in the Neptunian body he was lying atop; he could see the communication pulses flickering back and forth between that body and the new, larger mass approaching slowly across the steaming, snow-covered slabs of cracked deck.

Second groups of signals were being funneled through the noetic unit, through his armor circuitry,

and into the ship's brain. At the same time, the deck
seemed to tilt; the gravity increased slightly. The
Phoenix Exultant had come about.

Phaethon set a routine to translate those signals.
What was Xenophon ordering the ship to do?

The routine could not determine; Xenophon's
thoughts were still opaque. But the volume of thought
traffic was now very low. Phaethon could see the
amount of brain activity inside the body on which he
lay had dropped dramatically. Xenophon had been
badly damaged in the fight. His IQ had dropped to
about 350 or 400; a little above average, but not by
much. Obviously he was calling the undamaged body
over to him to mingle his brain substances with the
spare neurocircuitry that empty body carried. As soon
as the two bodies merged, Xenophon's intellect would
be restored to its near-Sophotech levels.

But what was he telling the ship? Even if Phaethon's
sense array could not decode Xenophon's thoughts,
there had to be a translation matrix decoding those
thoughts into a format the ship's brain could read.
Somewhere in the signal traffic Phaethon was seeing,
there should be a translator he could find. He sent a
subroutine to search. . . .

A moment passed while he waited. The second body,
like a rolling lake, picked its way across the snow-
coated, steaming deckplates of the hull, over or around
cracked curtain pediments, smashed mannequins,
melted table bases. It came closer to Phaethon's inert
body.

While he waited, curiosity, or anger, or some peculiar fanatical fascination with problems he could not
solve, now prompted Phaethon to review the entire
battle in slow motion. His sensory array allowed him
to discover the effect that had broken open Atkins's final defense, popping his pseudo-material shields and
abolishing his heavier weapons. . . .

His neutrino detectors and weakly interacting particle sensitives showed disproportional activity at specific moments before and during the battle, including
the moment when all of Atkins's pseudo-material
shields and weapons evaporated. Similar signatures
were clustered around the noetic unit, the thought
ports on Phaethon's epaulettes, and the central control
triggers of the thought box nexi lining the surviving
balconies on the bridge.

The hateful voice came again: "I see you have discovered our little secret. Yes; what you observe is an
application of a technology known only to the Silent
Oecumene. The Silent Oecumene studied the specific
effects of near-event-horizon boundary conditions.
You are aware that the speed of light limits motion not
exactly, but only within the more general boundary
imposed by the Heisenberg uncertainty principle?
Since the speed of a particle cannot be determined
more precisely that the uncertainty limit, there are,
statistically, certain particles traveling slightly above
or below light-speed at any given moment. This creates the Hawking radiations, which escape black
holes, and also produces the multidimensional particulate rotations, from existence to nonexistence and
back again, of so-called virtual particles. The Silent
Oecumene learned how to focus and control this fundamental effect of nature. It is one of the secrets that
close study of a singularity over generations can dis-
close.

"Overlapping arrays of constructive interference allow me to direct wave potentials of virtual particles
into any area within a limited spacetime—the area involved is roughly one light-minute—and have those
particles appear, en mass, within any object without
passing through the intermediary space. If enough virtual particles are sustained in one place at a given time,
a permanent baryonic particle, such as an electron, can

be formed out of the base-vacuum state, rotated into existence.

"Hence, electrons can appear within neutral circuits to activate them, controls—such as those in your armor, or in the noetic unit—can be turned on without any outside signal to turn them on. And pseudo-material fields, which require a delicate balance of asymmetrical fundamental particles to maintain, can be collapsed. You understand?"

Phaethon understood that the machine controlling this virtual-particle effect must did not necessarily have to be inside the hull of the *Phoenix Exultant,* not if the ghost particles could be precipitated inside the hull without passing through the intervening space.

And Xenophon could control it with no necessary equipment on this side, nothing on his person for Phaethon to detect. All that would be necessary would be a receiver to detect how the ghost particles were affected when passing through the specific spacetime area inside Xenophon's brain. Something like a noetic unit could interpret the particle deflections, correlate them to a stored record of Xenophon's mental signatures and silhouettes, and act on any commands Xenophon was thinking at the time.

And so this ghost-particle machine could have been outside the hull. Could have been: but it was not. No ship of the Golden Oecumene could keep pace with the *Phoenix Exultant.* For the machine to be in range and stay in range, Xenophon must have built it himself and smuggled it aboard, or constructed it (as most Neptunian machines were constructed) out of the polymorphetic neurocircuitry that also served them for brain matter, control conduits, and servomechanisms, which all Neptunians carried in their bodies.

And if the ghost-particle machinery required an abundant power supply, or needed to be in an area where the continuous discharges of other energies would mask its operation, where else could it have been placed, except? . . .

"Your suppositions are correct. The disruption units we placed along the fuel containers were not meant to sabotage this wonderful ship—the stealth remotes Atkins supplied you, and your own knowledge of demolition, have already told you those disruption units could not have done much damage. They were not intended to break the magnetic containers to release massive amounts of fuel and create an explosion, no: they were meant only to release tiny amounts of fuel, to be picked up and used to power what, in your thoughts, you are calling the ghost-particle machine. The actual 'machine' so-called, occupies the entire drive core, and uses the active plasma stream of the *Phoenix Exultant* engines as an antenna to attract and rotate the virtual particles. . . ."

Phaethon was not interested in the technical details. He merely wanted to know what Xenophon was planning to do, so that he could stop it, stop him, and wreak a bloody and terrible vengeance on Xenophon's person the moment the opportunity arose.

For the first time (perhaps because his intelligence had dropped to a near-human level), Xenophon sounded confused and uncertain: "I . . . am puzzled. You . . . are not reacting as we had anticipated. You ignore the technical details which I thought would fascinate you. You dismiss my offer to make you the captain of the grand fleet, the armada, of *Phoenices Exultant* I plan to build once the Silent Oecumene is resurrected. You are not attracted to the future I propose, of machine-free humanity, mortal and uncontrolled, spreading across the stars. Why? I do not understand your resentment."

It should have been obvious why Phaethon hated Xenophon.

"It is not obvious. I did not kill Diomedes. Atkins,

bloodthirsty Atkins, Atkins the paid killer, did the deed! Nor have I stolen your vessel. The *Phoenix Exultant,* according to your own laws, is mine."

At that same moment, his search routine had found and triggered the translation matrix compressed within the signal traffic passing between Xenophon and the ship's mind.

Phaethon saw what the enemy was ordering the *Phoenix Exultant* to do.

The *Phoenix* had been ordered to adopt a course that would take her in a great hyperbolic arc, around the sun and out into deep space. Once there, the curve would tighten and the acceleration continue, until, after the third day of acceleration, she would be headed back in-system at 90 percent the speed of light. Units of antimatter fuel and kilometer-long canisters from the Neptunian superships were to be ejected from the hull as she passed through, these missiles containing the astronomical kinetic energy that near-light-speed would impart.

Phaethon was not able to calculate, just from the orbital element information, where the missiles would strike. But the time frame was clear; the attack would take place during the Grand Transcendence, when every sapient mind in the Solar System would be preoccupied, interconnected, dream-drowned, intermingled, and helpless.

He had enough control over his personal sense filter to call up his personal thoughtspace. Again, the images surrounded him (this time, tilted sideways, as he was on his back). A symbol table to his right showed the opened memory casket, an unopened casket still inside. To his left were images of service units and honorary commissions. In front of him were the ship controls.

A targeting globe appeared, showing the orbital

elements of Xenophon's bombing run as a possible-course umbrella imposed on the model of the Solar System. The orbits of planets, major habitats, and energy formulations were depicted as a geometry of colored lines, slashed across by the projected run of the *Phoenix*.

Along the course, within striking range, were Io and Europa, the Ceres group, Demeter Transfer Station, Earth herself, and Mercury Equilateral. At the far end of the run, the major field generators and close-solar orbital elements of Helion's Solar Control Array would also be in target range.

Phaethon needed no further information; he recognized instantly what these targets had in common. They were centers of metals production, of communications, of fuel depots, energy control. They were crucial to the healthy functioning of the Golden Oecumene as a whole. He recognized what they were. They were military targets.

The translation matrix also decoded Xenophon's other commands to the ship mind. These instructions included upgrades to be made to the thought-cast system and communication antennae along the *Phoenix Exultant*'s prow. With Xenophon's ghost-particle broadcaster, he should have as little problem jamming basic communication circuits or neutralizing security systems as he had had usurping control of the noetic unit here on the bridge.

Or . . . (Phaethon should have realized it before) . . . with as little problem as he had had feeding false information into the Nebuchadnezzar Sophotech's reading of Phaeton's records during the Hortator's Inquest.

During the bombing run, the *Phoenix Exultant*, equipped with the ghost-particle broadcaster, should have no difficulty in imposing the Nothing thought virus, the same mind worm that had possessed Xenophon, into the entire Grand Transcendence. During Transcendence, normal barriers between mind and mind were eased, cumbersome security restrictions were relaxed. All minds were One Grand Mind, ready and able to think grand thoughts. . . .

All necks were one neck ready to be lopped off at one stroke.

The Grand Transcendence was the time of greatest weakness, of greatest peace, of least vigilance, which an already weak, peaceful, and unvigilant society enjoyed. And it only occurred once every thousand years. . . .

"Your thinking is not following predicted paths! Your emotional reactions, your degree of aggressiveness and hatred, is not proportional! We had assumed you would be pleased to aid our efforts to restore the Silent Oecumene to her position as the supreme model and central culture for humankind! It is true that we are about to engage in acts of mass murder and mass mind-rape against the Golden Oecumene, destruction and devastation. But your distaste for these things is merely part of the widespread program of thought control imposed upon you by your Sophotechs! It is they who told you that there is an absolute right and wrong, and objective measure of good and evil. Nonsense! If there were such an objective measure, freedom of human thought would be limited, which, by definition, is unthinkable. You merely have an opinion that mass murder and destruction is bad because of your social conditioning. It is irrelevant.

"These things are necessary in order to achieve a greater and long-lasting good; namely, the salvation of the Second Oecumene and the liberation of the human spirit. Unless the Golden Oecumene is severely wounded and weakened, your Sophotechs will maneuver to undo what you and I both dream to do. It is your dream, Phaethon, which causes such bloodshed! Why do you flinch at it now?"

Xenophon must not mean to kill him. Otherwise, why would he still be trying to convince him to join? Was there still something this horrid creature wanted or needed from Phaethon?

"We still need your skills and expertise to run this ship, and to run the armor which controls this ship. We are going to make a more cooperative version of you, merely by editing and rearranging certain of your thoughts and memories. If you cooperate, more of your memory and personality will stay intact. The more vehemently you resist, of course, the more thoughts you think that are disloyal to me and my purposes, then obviously, the more of your thoughts will have to be expunged. Be reasonable, be pliant. It is safer to agree. Don't your Sophotechs always urge you to be rational and safe?"

Actually, they never did. This Silent One was a fool. He knew nothing about the Golden Oecumene, knew nothing about how Phaethon thought, and did not seem to realize that Phaethon could not be redacted by the noetic unit unless he was taken out of his armor.

And once he was taken out of his armor, his arms and legs would be free, and he could quickly and efficiently kill Xenophon.

"How amusing. You? An untrained man from a completely peaceful society, without any pistol or energy weapons, think you can kill me in my Neptunian body? I have given you every opportunity for surrender! You have proven yourself a useless pet of the machines after all!"

Phaethon spoke aloud: "No. It is I who call on you to surrender. I suspect that you will not. I merely make the offer so that my conscience will be clean, later."

Xenophon deigned not to reply.

Efficiency, if nothing else, should dictate that

Xenophon kill Phaethon now, immediately, before taking him out of his armor. But perhaps he could not. No weapon could penetrate the Chrysadamantium plates; even the ghost-particle machine had to wait until the thought ports in the shoulderboards were opened before seizing control of the suit's circuitry. And even that control of the armor's command channels was insufficient: the protective feedbacks were hardwired into the nanomachine lining core. The armor simply could not understand or accept any orders that would harm the wearer.

"You overestimate your technology, Phaethon! Your Golden Oecumene has many advances, perhaps, but you are curiously lacking in the one science in which the Silent Ones excel: thought worms, mind viruses, psychic corruption. Even Sophotechs, pure and supreme among intellects, were no more than slaves and toys and playthings after our mental warfare science had done its work. You think your simpleminded suit could withstand me, if it were my purpose to make it do my will? But, no: my purpose is to corrupt, not your suit's mind but yours. And despair shall be my ally. Despair makes men weak, vulnerable to redaction, and self-hatred makes men unable to resist mental reconditioning. My circuits are ready: your memories and skills will soon be at the service of the Silent Oecumene. But first, despair requires hope. You must be allowed to struggle for a moment before you are absorbed."

And, with that, the armor opened.

2.

The golden plates slid aside, and Phaethon tried to get up.

But the pool of Neptunian body substance in which he lay gave him no time to move. It merely swirled up around him, a thousand strands like clinging snakes, and engulfed him. The blue material surrounded him, cocooned him, immobilized his limbs, pressed against his face, intruding in his mouth and eyes. It hardened; even Phaethon's strength could not budge it, lacking any leverage. He was trapped like a fly in amber.

Filaments of neurocircuitry swam forward out of the blue mirk, webbed his skull, and sought the contact points to invade his brainspace.

His personal thoughtspace flickered into and then out of existence again. In the corner of one imaginary eye, he saw the last memory casket, the one with the figure of the winged sword, open, and he felt the wild, drugged, dreamlike sensation that massive memory downloading created, a blur of activity in his cortex and midbrain.

It was a preliminary to all mental surgery to open all unopened memories, so that the restructured mind, after redaction, would not have any old memory chains to lead back to its former personality. . . .

A sarcastic voice appeared in his sense filter. Apparently the Silent One was not pleased with whatever level of hope or rage still burned in Phaethon's mind. "Here is the thought virus which consumed the Silent Oecumene. After it consumes you, as it has done me, you will regard me as your most generous savior. Why do you still resist? You cannot move. In a moment you will be unable even to think. What has happened to the dire revenge you vowed, Phaethon? How did you imagine you could defeat me?"

But at that same moment, the second mass of Neptunian body met, melted with, and combined with the first mass. Phaethon saw the brain activity double and redouble as the creature's intelligence climbed back to normal levels.

The surge of activity around him paused. He could see, floating in the blue material, the main brain group, with the nerve trunk, like a tentacle, leading to the skullcap gripping him. He could detect the neurological changes and endocrinal nerve reactions of fear, panic, and shock.

"Wait. There has been an error. Your face. You are not Phaethon. All is wrong. . . . You . . ."

Memory came. The cells of his outer skin, each and every one of them, contained a nanomachine energy weapon in the cell membrane. They were activated by a command sent through his endocrine system. . . .

Fire lined his body for an instant of pain. A positronic charge was released through his skin by billions of molecule-sized fullerene antiparticle containers. The sections of Neptunian material in contact with his skin ignited, positrons canceling electrons in a clenched spasm of furious radiation.

At the same time, a weapon made of his own neural tissue, invisible and camouflaged (hidden in the centers of his brain otherwise used for creative thought), sent a charge of nerve agent back along the skullcap gripping him, destroying cells and disorganizing consciousness.

Skin ruptured, he was covered from head to toe with his own blood. The Neptunian parted around him.

Another memory came: his blood was toxic. In addition to white and red blood cells were so-called black blood cells, an army of assemblers and disassemblers, programmed to poison, unmake, dissolve, and destroy any biological substance it touched which was not him. The Neptunian was dissolving.

As the Neptunian body fell back to either side, wounded and burnt, he rolled, grasped the katana Atkins had dropped beneath him, came to his feet. Static sparks crawled along the bloodstains as the waste heat from the nanomachine black blood was converted to radio white noise, jamming all signals in the area, disrupting noumenal circuits, preventing any thought transfer.

In one swift motion, with infinite grace, he lunged and shouted and struck. His movement, stance, and execution were controlled and forceful, a perfect example of the art. The finely tempered swordblade punctured the yielding material of the Neptunian body in a way no energy weapon could have done, neatly severing the major nerve groups where his advanced senses told him the Silent One brain activity was housed. Housed, and unable to escape, while the burning blood jammed all thought traffic in the area.

With the withdrawal stroke he severed the brain mass a second time for good measure, and came back to a balanced, upright posture, flourished the sword (light glanced from the beautiful antique perfection of the steel), and drew it down to his side, where a scabbard would have been had he not been nude.

A rough circle of blue-gray Neptunian substance still surrounded him, crawling and writhing, and it showed neuroelectronic activity in some of its segments, perhaps routines still attempting to carry out the Silent One's orders. Near his foot was the smaller blade, a wakizashi, which he had noticed hanging beneath the symbol table when he first woke here. This knife had been under the noetic unit, and therefore had survived the incineration of the bridge: the wreckage of the table, the noetic unit, and the blade had all been under Phaethon's armor during the blast.

He hooked the sheath with his toe, kicked the knife up into his left hand, and, with a wrist flick that sent the sheath continuing upward, exposed the blade.

The knife was not an antique but a modern weapon, shaped like a knife so that it could be used for stabbing when its charge ran out. The charge was full. He glanced at the control surface set into the blade, so that circuits could track his eye movements, and then he looked at what he wished destroyed.

A battle mind in the hilt found the pattern to his eye

movements, extrapolated, defined the target, and (before he even finished looking at what he wanted struck) sent a variety of energetics and high-speed nanomaterial packages out from projectors along the blade surface and blade edge to destroy the remaining Neptunian bodies and microbes in the room.

The blade also emitted command signals to lock out those sections of the ship's mind that may have been affected by enemy thought viruses, made a prioritized list of cleanup procedures, made contact with the stealth remotes still hovering in the area, reconfigured them, programmed them for new tasks, and sent them to disable the ghost-particle generator housed in the disrupters planted along the ship's drive core.

All this, in less time than it would take a man, dazed by the blaze of fire and lightning coming from that knife, to blink.

The scabbard reached the apex of its arc, and then fell. With his left hand he caught the scabbard on the blazing knife tip, mouth-first, so that it fell neatly onto the blade and sheathed it.

He looked left and right. The deckplate was broken and black. He was alone. The enemy was dead.

He looked in astonishment and horror at his blood-stained hands, crawling with steam and sparks, and at the knife and sword, which seemed so familiar in his grip.

His whisper came hoarsely from his throat: "Who the hell am I?!"

3.

Across the wide chamber, one of the surviving mannequins, Sloppy Rufus, first dog on Mars, turned away from the last bank of still-functional detection assessors, stood on his hind legs, put his forefeet up on the balcony rail, and, with muzzle between paws, peered gravely down. A naked man with a naked sword stood in a circle of black and steaming destruction, that once had been the bridge, and stared back up at him.

"Isn't it obvious, my good sir? You are Atkins." The voice from the dog was Phaethon's voice.

"The hell I am. I don't want to be Atkins. I'm Phaethon. I built this!" He gestured with the still-dripping sword left and right at the bridge around him. Perhaps he was pointing at the wreckage. The man's voice sounded nothing like Phaethon's.

The dog said, "I'm quite sorry, sir, but to be quite blunt, you are an atrocious version of me. Half the things you thought were exaggerated mockeries of what I believe, that other half were pure Atkins. And why did you kill Ao Varmatyr? That was reprehensible! He could have been captured safely, kept alive, cured, saved. Vengeance? Wasteful notion. Besides, you should have known Diomedes was not dead. You recorded him, and most of Xenophon, into the noumenal recorder before you spoke with the Silent One."

The man dropped sword and knife and pressed his palms against his brow, eyes strained, as if trying to keep some terrible pressure inside his brain from exploding. "The memories are still going off inside my head! Burning cities, clouds of nerve logics, a thousand ways to kill a man . . . You've got to stop it. Where's the noetic unit?! My life is boiling away! I'm Phaethon! I want to stay Phaethon! I don't want to turn into . . . into . . ." He was on his knees scrambling for the noetic unit.

The dog said: "Your desire not to be Atkins is probably just an exaggeration of what *you think* I think about you. Its really not true. I'm sure killing is a useful and necessary service to perform in barbaric times, or under barbarous cicumstances like these. . . ."

"Then *you* be Atkins! I'll transfer the mnemonic templates to you—"

"Good God, no!"

The man took up Phaethon's helmet and put it over his head, and slung the breastplate across his shoulders. The thought ports in the epaulettes opened; responder lights in the noetic unit winked on. A circuit was established between the noetic unit and the thought systems in the helm and wired under the man's skull.

The man's fingers were tapping impatiently on the casing of the noetic unit. "Hurry . . . hurry . . . ," he muttered. "I'm losing myself. . . ."

Interruption came. A beam came from the hilt stone of the knife the man had dropped to the bloodstained and burnt deckplates. The beam touched the shoulder board and negated the circuit. The noetic unit went dark.

A voice came from the weapon: *"HALT!"*

The man ripped off the helmet he wore. There were tearstains running down his bloody cheeks. His face was purple-black with emotion. Veins upon his brow stood out in sharp relief.

The man said in a voice of murderous calm: "You cannot stop me. I am a citizen of the Golden Oecumene; I have rights. No matter what I was before, I am a self-aware entity now, and I may do to myself whatever I please. If I want to continue being this me that I am now, that's my right. No one owns me! That rule is true for everyone in our utopia!"

"FOR EVERYONE BUT YOU. YOU BELONG TO THE MILITARY COMMAND. YOU DO AND DIE AS YOU ARE ORDERED."

"No!" The man shouted.

The dog said to the knife: "I don't mind the copyright violations, if he really wants to use my template for a while. . . . I mean, can't you just let him, ah . . . Don't you have other copies of him and such?"

The weapon said to the man: "RETURN TO YOUR DUTY. RETURN TO YOUR SELF-IDENTITY."

"But I'm a citizen of the Oecumene! I can be who I want! I am a free man!"

"YOU ALONE, MARSHAL ATKINS, ARE NOT AND CANNOT BE FREE. IT IS THE PRICE PAID SO THAT OTHERS CAN BE."

"Daphne! They're going to make me forget that I love you! Don't let them! Daphne! Daphne!"

Weeping, the nameless man fell to his face. A moment later, looking mildly embarrassed or amused, face stern, Atkins climbed to his feet.

"Well, that operation turned out to be a clusterfoxtrot, didn't she?" he muttered.

4.

Atkins spoke with his knife for a few minutes, making decisions and listening to rapid reports concerning the details of the cleanup procedure that the battle mind in the weapon had initiated.

Phaethon's voice came down from the mannequin dog on the upper balcony: "Don't dismantle the ghost-particle broadcast array in the drive core!"

Atkins stared up at the dog. He said (perhaps a bit harshly, for he was not in a good mood), "What the hell's the problem? Bad guy is dead. War's over. There might be some sort of deadman switch or delayed vendetta program running through those things. Best to dismantle them now before something else weird happens."

"With all due respect, Marshal, the idea is unwise. Firstly, they are the only working models in existence of what amounts to a Silent Oecumene technology. Secondly—"

Atkins made a curt, dismissive gesture with his katana. "That's enough. Thank you for your concern. But I've already decided how to handle this."

"An interesting conceit, sir, but irrelevent, as that ghost-particle broadcast array is my property, being found on my ship, and having no other true owner. I believe the heirs and assigns of Ao Varmatyr died several centuries ago in another star system."

"I've had a hard day, civilian. Don't try to play that legalistic hugger-mugger rights game with me. This is still a military situation; those are enemy weapons; and I'm still in charge."

"But you just declared the war was over, my dear sir. And that legalistic 'rights game,' as you call it, is what you are sworn to protect, soldier, and it gives the only justification to your somewhat bloody existance. You are here to protect me, remember? I never did join your hierarchy, my cooperation is voluntary, and you are my guest. If, as a guest, you overstep the bounds of politeness and decent conduct, I would be within my rights to have you put off this vessel."

Atkins lost his temper: "You trying to butt heads with me? Come on. Let's butt heads. I am the God-damnednest Number-one Ichi-ban First-Class Heavyweight Champion Tough-as-Nails Ear-biting Eye-gouging Hard-assed Head-Butter of all Time, mister, so don't try me!"

The dog pricked its ears, looking mildly surprised.

After a quiet moment, Phaethon's voice came: "I suspect, Marshal Atkins, that you and I are both a bit ruffled by the events here. I am, quite frankly, not used to violence, and am dismayed at how you have chosen to conduct this affair. I suspect you are still suffering from memory shock, and are half-asleep." The dog lowered its head, and continued: "But, unlike you, I have no excuse for my conduct. I have let emotions get the better of me, which is a vice in which a true gentleman never indulges. For that I proffer my apologies."

Atkins drew a deep breath, and used an ancient technique to calm himself and balance his blood-chemistry levels. "Apology accepted. You have mine. Let's say no more about it. I guess I'm a little disappointed that there wasn't any superior officer in all this, that our communication tracks did not lead to the Silent One's boss. If he had one."

"But that is what I was attempting to tell you, Marshal. There have been periodic signals leaving this vessel ever since Xenophon came to the bridge."

"Leaving how? The hull is made of adamantium!"

"Leaving through the drive, which was wide open and showering energy out into the universe."

"Aimed?"

"As far as I can determine, yes. The signals were encoded as ghost particles generated by Xenophon's array of disruptors."

"Aimed where?"

"I could not trace them."

"That's what you were supposed to be doing, friend, while I was getting my little butt kicked."

"I did not understand the nature of the signal until Xenophon boasted of the technology, and described it. This ghost-particle technology is not one with which I, or any one else in the Golden Oecumene, is familiar. I had to design and build new types of detection equipment while you and Xenophon were making all that noise. But the broadcasts are occurring at regular intervals. Those magnetic disruptors are still drawing power out of my fuel cells, charging for their next broadcast. There is still a piece of instruction cycling in the ship-mind's broadcast circuit, written in that Silent Oecumene encryption I cannot decode. It will be a directional broadcast, or so I guess, since there are also line actions in the navigational array. When this next broadcast comes—and this is the second reason why I would ask you not to dismantle my ghost-particle array—I hope to be able to track the signal to its receiver."

"Xenophon's CO. The Nothing Sophotech."

"And, if I am not mistaken, the *Silent Phoenix,* or whatever starship they used to come here."

"You did not believe his story?"

"No more than did you, Marshal. The enemy is still at large. Come! We have much to discuss before the next broadcast."

Atkins looked down at his blood-drenched body, the blasted deckplates underfoot, and said, "Is there some place I can scrub up? My blood is a weapon, and I don't want to get any of it near you."

"My dear sir, is there any part of your body which they have not turned into a weapon?"

"Just one. They let me keep that for morale purposes."

"Well, come up to the main bridge, where my body is stored: I have antinanotoxins and biosterilizers which can clean, and robe you."

"Main bridge? I thought this was the main bridge."

"No, sir. This is just the auxiliary. You don't think I'd expose my real bridge to danger, do you?"

"You have two bridges?"

"Three. And a jack-together I can plug into any main junction. I am a very conservative engineer: I believe in triple redundancy."

"Where did you put two other whole bridge complexes? How could you be sure Xenophon would not find it?"

"Surely you are joking, Marshal! On a ship this size? I could hide the moons of Mars! In fact, I'm not sure one of them did not wander into my intake ram by mistake when we passed Martial orbit. Has anyone seen Phobos lately . . . ?"

"Very funny."

"Come: follow the armor. It will lead you to the nearest railway station."

THE FALSEHOODS

1.

Diomedes and Phaethon were seated at the wide round wood-and-ivory table grown out of the bridge deck. Both were dressed in severe and unadorned black frock coats with high collars and cravats, according to the Victorian conventions of the Silver-Gray. Around them, shining gold decks, tall energy mirrors, overmind formation pillars, and pressure curtains blue and lucent as the sky, gleamed and blazed and glowed, like a world of cold and silent fire.

One anachronism: Diomedes held a bronze-headed ashwood spear in one kid glove, and toyed with it, staring at the spear tip, and waving it slowly back and forth, metronomelike, trying to acclimate to the binocular vision a human-shaped body and nervous system afforded.

Atkins, seated opposite them, was wearing a suit of Fourth Era reflex armor. The chameleon circuit was disengaged, and he had tuned the color to a brilliant blood red, a sharp contrast to the umbrageous black walnut of the high-backed, wooden chair in which the soldier sat. The suit substance looked like fiery elfin scale-mail, with overlapping small plates of composite, which were programmed to stiffen under impact, and form blast armor, locking into different bracing systems to protect the wearer no matter from which direction the stroke came. The routine to make this primitive armor had been coded within the black-body cells in his blood, and the armor itself had been woven out of the broken deckplates of the old bridge, where his blood had spilled.

In the center of the table was an imaginary hourglass, measuring the estimated time till the next broadcast from the ghost-particle array.

The three sat watching the sands run.

Diomedes drew his eyes up to the glinting spear point of the weapon he held. "Here is cause for wonder! I live and breathe and speak and see, incarnated by a new machine, a portable noetic unit with no more support than glorious *Phoenix Exultant's* mind could give. No Sophotech was needed for the transfer! No large immobile system was required. Does this mean immortality shall be common hereafter even among the Cold Dukes and Eremites and Ice-miners, among all us nomads too poor to afford Sophotechnology? It may be the death of our loved and cherished way of life! Hah! And, if so, good riddance to it, say I!"

Phaethon said, "Good Diomedes, it is that way of life which has made the crew here on the *Phoenix* so unthinkably tolerant of the secrecy which now surrounds the antics on the auxiliary bridge, and the murder of Neoptolemous. Who else but people born and bred to utter isolation and invincible privacy would tolerate not to know what's going on? Atkins still fears spies, and now insists all these doings be obscured, until the Nothing Mastermind be brought to bay. Who would be so crazed, except Neptunians, to accept the idea that there were things which, for military reasons, the citizens who support the military are not allowed to know!"

Atkins leaned forward, hands on the tabletop, and said to Diomedes, "Speaking of death, are there other copies of Xenophon or Neoptolemous loose in the Duma whom we have to track down, or was the one brought aboard this ship the only copy?"

Diomedes said, "Were you thinking of hunting the others? The exercise is futile. While I was Neoptolemous, I saw the Silent One's mind in action, Ao Varmatyr as we might call him. He tried to send copies of himself to corrupt as many Neptunians as he could do. Despite his boast, his virus weaving was not enough to penetrate the concentric privacies with which each Neptunian surrounds himself. Unlike you in your world free from crime, we are used to mind hoaxes, hackers, hikers, highjackers, bushwackers, thought wormers, sleepwalkers. Had Ao Varmatyr been received on Earth, rather than at Farbeyond, your nonimmunized world would have been flooded with virus at the first public posting. With us, we who have no public, all he did was irk his fellow Dukes of Neptune, who sent back rabbit casts and aphrodisiacs and core swipers and other irritants and viruses whose names you would not know."

There was a cold twinkle in Atkins's eye, a look of professional amusement. He obviously thought that he, at least, knew the names and more about the Neptunian thought weapons, their viruses and information duels. But he said nothing.

Diomedes concluded: "There are other copies of Neoptolemous in the Duma, yes: but none of Ao Varmatyr. I have been in him since a fortnight past; nor did he hide any secrets from me, accounting me as one already dead. I think I would have seen a successful transfer of his template. There was none. He was far more alone and scared than his tale to you would have led you to believe."

Phaethon wanted to ask if that other version of Neoptolemous held the lien on the title to this ship, but he held his tongue. Other matters took priority.

Atkins was asking: "Did Ao Varmatyr ever communicate with his superiors?"

Diomedes said, "In the early hours, right after my capture, he made a nerve-to-nerve link with me. This was before he imposed complete control over the Neoptolemous host, and cut off my unfiltered outward sensation."

Diomedes made an easy gesture and continued: "What next occurred was not so strange. Xenophon, fine fellow that he is, was an Eremite. I am a Cold Duke. Compared to the scattered Eremite iceholds of the Kuiper belt, we Dukes, down in the S and K methane layers of Neptune himself, are much more densely populated. Sometimes, as little as a thousand kilometers would separate the outliers of our palace swarms and sink houses from each other, and the shells and turrets of a deep Neptunian Cold Duke are ringed with firewalls and false reflections to hinder the badworms which tend to pepper our speech when we share thoughts with each other. You understand?"

Atkins said "Meaning Xenophon engaged you in mind-to-mind and you whipped his little behind."

"Inelegantly put, but essentially correct. I had access to his deep-memory files for a few seconds, enough to make a cipher copy into my own brainspace before Ao Varmatyr put me into sensory deprivation. It made interesting reading during my lonely hours. From it I could extrapolate the information about everything Ao Varmatyr knew."

Phaethon said, "My dear friend, you will not keep us in suspense, I trust?"

Diomedes smiled easily. "No more than is necessary to build up dramatic tension, my friend."

"I tingle with the appropriate tension, good Diomedes, I assure you."

Atkins, hearing this exchange, shook his head. He thought: *No wonder these snooty Silver-Gray guys just get on everyone's nerves.* And, then, aloud, "Gentlemen! Time's running! Let's get on with this."

Diomedes spoke with slow emphasis: "First, Xenophon was cooperating consciously. Second, Ao Varmatyr was unaware of any superior.

"There were two times, both times when Ao Varmatyr was hooked into the long-range communication nerve link, when his memory went blank, and his internal clock was reset to mask the missing time. Xenophon noticed it and Ao Varmatyr did not and could not. Xenophon was puzzled by this, but, lacking a suspicious imagination, did not realize what it implied: namely, that Ao Varmatyr's mind was set up the same way he described the minds of the Silent Oecumene thinking machines. An invisible conscience redactor, unknown even to him, forced him, from time to time, to perform certain acts of which he was not afterwards aware. Ao Varmatyr (unbeknownst to himself) communicated with his superior, this Nothing Sophotech, but they did not 'speak.' I suspect the superior merely fed operating instructions into Ao Varmatyr's conscience redactor, the loyalty virus inside of him."

Phaethon muttered, "How horrible!"

Diomedes, with a grim smile, fingered the haft of his spear, and said, "Indeed. But it was no worse than the Silent Oecumene had been doing for years and centuries to their own thinking machines. So why not do the same to their human subjects? The step is small."

Atkins said, "How did you resist being taken over

by the Last Broadcast loyalty virus when Xenophon did not? You were entirely isolated, and Ao Varmatyr had complete control over your input."

"Part was lack of time and attention of his part, I think. But part of it was, in all modesty, strength of character on my part. It is true that I was convinced, perhaps for up to an hour at a time, that the Nothing philosophy was correct, and that there was no reason to resist, and that I had to cooperate for the sake of the Silent Oecumene. But never for longer than an hour.

"You see, I suspect the Last Virus was intended to work on the minds and mind-sets typical of the Silent Oecumene. The core value which the target mind must accept before it will accept the Nothing philosophy is that morality is relative, that the ends justify the means, that right and wrong is an individual and arbitrary choice. This strips the target mind of any defense: for who can rightfully defend his own prejudices against another's if he knows, deep down, that both are equally arbitrary, equally false?

"But it did not work on me, because I had, not so long ago, uploaded a copy of the Silver-Gray philosophy tutorial routine into my long-term memory. The tutorial kept pestering me with questions. One I liked was: If a philosopher teaches you that it is not wrong to lie, why do you not suspect he is lying to you when he says so? Another I liked was: Is it merely an arbitrary postulate to believe that all beliefs are mere arbitrary postulates?"

Phaethon asked: "What convinced Xenophon? Was he exposed to the same thought virus?"

"No. He believed the story Ao Varmatyr told without prompting. The same tale told to you; Xenophon believed in the implacable inhumanity of the Sophotechs to begin with. Many Neptunians do."

Atkins said, "So where is this Nothing Sophotech

now? Have any clues as to where those instructions came from?"

"None. But since Ao Varmatyr was programmed to make his 're-ports' unwittingly, he did not choose time or circumstance under which to make them. (Nor the content, which probably consisted of an unedited information dump from his memory.) Hence they come at regular intervals." Diomedes nodded toward the hourglass in the middle of the table, and smiled again.

Phaethon said, "I haven't lived through as many spy dramas as my wife, but one would think enemies trying to hide would not fall into such predictable patterns."

Diomedes said, "Such weaknesses are an inevitable result of the Silent Oecumene way of doing things. If you treat people like machines, you must give them mechanistic orders. Hence we know when the next broadcast will take place."

They all watched the running sands in the glass for a quiet while, each with his own thoughts.

Diomedes spoke up. "There is still much I do not understand about what happened just now. Marshal? May I ask, if it is not one of these military secrets in which you put so much stock . . . ?

Atkins raised one eyebrow. "You can ask."

"How did you survive inside Phaethon's armor? You decelerated toward the Neptunian embassy at ninety gravities. But only Phaethon has a specially designed body to withstand those pressures. That was precisely why Ao Varmatyr did not suspect you were not Phaethon. How did you survive?"

Atkins said curtly: "I didn't."

"I beg your pardon?"

Phaethon said: "His body was crushed into bloody paste inside my armor. Meanwhile his mind was stored in the noetic unit. It was not until we were at rest, and my suit lining had a chance to reconstruct the military-basic marine body it was carrying, that I transferred and reincarnated him. Everything he 'saw' before that was merely sent from my armor cameras into his recorded mind. He wasn't inside the armor, looking out, until later, when he drew his first painful breath."

Diomedes looked impressed. He asked: "Who was inside the Ulysses mannequin? The one that was incinerated by Ao Varmatyr?"

Atkins said: "One of my sparring partners. A training-exercise routine."

"Programmed to lose?"

"Not really. But I had only given it ancient weapons and techniques, dating from the early Sixth and late Fifth Era. In other words, weapon systems the Silent Ones knew we had. So it lost. Only when Ao Varmatyr was convinced that he was in complete control did he show his true colors, and start ordering the *Phoenix Exultant* into a military posture."

Phaethon spoke up. "I suspect that even Ao Varmatyr himself did not know, until he did it, what he was going to do with the *Phoenix Exultant* when he achieved control of her. Using her as a warship to strike a deadly blow against the Golden Oecumene was not, I think, what he would have done had he believed his own tale. I can only conclude the decision to kill came from the Nothing Mastermind; perhaps some buried command overrode his normal judgment and conscience."

Atkins said, "I disagree. Ao Varmatyr had nothing but violence in mind from the first. Why else was he so tricky? He pretended to be Xenophon as long as he could, and then stayed quiet until I found him hiding."

Phaethon nodded. But there was a thoughtful, perhaps wistful, look on his features.

Atkins, seeing that look, said, "You believed him, didn't you? You would have gone with him, had it been you, and not me, being you, wouldn't you?"

Phaethon said "Perhaps" in a tone of voice that meant

certainly yes. "I wasn't sure—I am still not sure—how much of what Ao Varmatyr said was a lie. But there may be people to rescue at Cygnus X-1, people of a spirit like my own, and there may be great deeds to do there. It might have been worth the risk to go, just in case he was telling the truth."

Atkins said, "Then I'm just glad it was me who was you, and not you. Otherwise, Ao Varmatyr might have convinced you."

Phaethon said reluctantly, "No. His story was a lie."

Diomedes leaned forward, and said, "But Ao Varmatyr believed his own story."

"What?"

"The tale, at least to him, was true. What few of his thoughts I could understand made that clear. I suspect the Silent Oecumene did have her downfall in just the way he described, and that the people there, good Phaethon, were, perhaps once, not unlike you."

Phaethon said, "I would like to believe that—I would like it very much. But at least part of the tale was a lie."

Diomedes said, "How so?"

"The relationship between the Sophotechs and the men as depicted in that tale made no sense. How could they be hostile to each other?"

Diomedes said, "Aren't men right to fear machines which can perform all tasks men can do, artistic, intellectual, technical, a thousand or a million times better than they can do? Men become redundant."

Phaethon shook his head, a look of distant distaste on his features, as if he were once again confronted with a falsehood that would not die no matter how often it was denounced. In a voice of painstaking patience, he said: "Efficiency does not harm the inefficient. Quite the opposite. That is simply not the way it works. Take me, for example. Look around: I employed partials to do the thought-box junction spotting when I built this ship. My employees were not as skilled as

I was in junction spotting. It took them three hours to do the robopsychology checks and hierarchy links I could have done in one hour. But they were in no danger of competition from me. My time is too valuable. In that same hour it would have taken me to spot their thought-box junction, I can earn far more than their three-hour wages by writing supervision architecture thought flows. And it's the same with me and the Sophotechs.

"Any midlevel Sophotech could have written in one second the architecture it takes me, even with my implants, an hour to compose. But if, in that same one second of time, that Sophotech can produce something more valuable—exploring the depth of abstract mathematics, or inventing a new scientific miracle, anything at all (provided that it will earn more in that second than I earn in an hour)—then the competition is not making me redundant. The Sophotech still needs me and receives the benefit of my labor. Since I am going to get the benefit of every new invention and new miracle put out on the market, I want to free up as many of those seconds of Sophotech time as my humble labor can do.

"And I get the lion's share of the benefit from the swap. I only save him a second of time; he creates wonder upon wonder for me. No matter what my fear of or distaste for Sophotechs, the forces in the marketplace, our need for each other, draw us together.

"So you see why I say that not a thing the Silent One said about Sophotechs made sense. I do not understand how they could have afforded to hate each other. Machines don't make us redundant; they increase our efficiency in every way. And the bids of workers eager to compete for Sophotech time creates a market for merely human work, which it would not be efficient for Sophotechs to underbid."

Diomedes spoke in a distant, haunted voice: "But,

friend, I have been inside the Silent One's mind, and you have not. You did not see his memories of luxury and splendor. . . . They were the Lords of the Second Oecumene, the masters of the singularity fountains! They did not work. They did not compete. They did not bid, or buy. They did not have markets, or money. The only thing of value to them was their reputation, their artistic verve, their wit, their whimsy, and the calm dignity with which they welcomed their inevitable fall in darkened coffins into the blood red supergravity well of their dark star."

There was silence around the table for a time.

More sand fell through the glass.

Diomedes said, "It's odd. Their society was not unlike our own. A peaceful utopia, but, unlike ours, one without laws, or money. What strange, incomprehensible force of fate or chance or chaos ordained her downfall?"

Atkins snorted. "It seems strange only if you believe that garbage Ao Varmatyr believed. His society was not set up the way he thought it was. No society could be."

Diomedes looked surprised. "And by what psychic intuition do you know this?"

"Its obvious. That society could not exist," said Atkins.

"Nor will it ever," added Phaethon.

The two men exchanged smiling glances.

"We are thinking of the same thing, aren't we?" said Atkins, nodding.

"Of course!" said Phaethon.

The two men spoke at once:

"They certainly had laws," said Atkins.

"They certainly had money," said Phaethon.

The two men exchanged puzzled glances.

Atkins nodded. "You first."

Phaethon said, "No civilization can exist without money. Even one in which energy is as cheap and free

as air on Earth, would still have some needs and desires which some people can fulfill better than others.
An entertainment industry, if nothing else. Whatever
efforts—if any—these productive people make, above
and beyond that which their own idle pastimes incline
them to make, will be motivated by gifts or barter bestowed by others eager for their services. Whatever
barter keeps its value best over time stays in demand,
and is portable, recognizable, divisible, will become
their money. No matter what they call it, no matter
what form it takes, whether cowry shells or gold or
grams of antimatter, it will be money. Even Sophotechs
use standardized computer seconds to prioritize distributions of system resources among themselves. As
long as men value each other, admire each other, need
each other, there will be money."

Diomedes said, "And if all men live in isolation?
Surrounded by nothing but computer-generated dreams,
pleasant fictions, and flatteries? And their every desire
is satisfied by electronic illusions which create in
their brains the sensations of satisfaction without the
substance? What need have men to value other men
then?"

"Men who value their own lives would not live that
way."

Diomedes spread his hands and shrugged. He said
softly: "I don't believe the Silent Ones did either of
those things. . . ."

Atkins said, "They certainly did not value each other's
lives. Didn't you notice what kind of society Ao Varmatyr was describing? The clue was right there in
everything he said. What was the one thing, over and
over, Ao Varmatyr kept complaining about with the
Sophotechs?"

Diomedes said, "That the Sophotechs would not obey
orders."

Atkins nodded. "Exactly."

Diomedes looked back and forth between the two other men. "I do not grasp your point."

Atkins tapped his own chest with a thumb. "You know me. What would I do, if a subordinate of mine disobeyed a direct order, and continued to disobey?"

Diomedes said, "Punish him."

Atkins said, "Can you think of a circumstance under which I'd be authorized and allowed to kill him, or to order them to kill himself?"

Diomedes looked blankly at Phaethon. Phaethon said, "The war mind not long ago said something of the sort. I don't know enough ancient history to know the details. Can't you court-martial a subordinate for cowardice in the face of the enemy, or high treason, or force him to commit ritual suicide for letting the flag touch the ground, or something like that . . . ?"

"Something like that," said Atkins. "But you, Phaethon. What is the worst you can do to a subordinate if he disobeys orders?"

"Discharge him from employment."

Atkins leaned back, looking grim and satisfied. "You and I are from different cultures, Phaethon. You are an entrepreneur. I am a member of a military order. You make mutually agreed-upon exchanges with equals. I take orders from superiors and give orders to inferiors. Your culture is based on freedom. Mine is based on discipline. Keep that in mind when I ask the next question: Which kind of culture, one like yours or one like mine, do you suppose the Silent Oecumene was like? A utopia without laws? Or a slave state run by a military dictator?"

Diomedes said, "Toward the end, yes, they had degenerated to a slave state. That was the tragedy of their downfall, they who had once been so free, falling so low."

Atkins shook his head and snorted. "Nope. They were corrupt from the start. If they were so free and utopian, why didn't they just fire any Sophotechs who wouldn't obey orders, and hire a new one? Their Sophotechs weren't employees. They were serfs."

He paused to let that sink in. Then he said, "I wonder if they just kept intact the same discipline and hierarchy they had evolved with captain and crew over the generations of their migration aboard the *Naglfar,* and the descendants of the captains and officers kept control over the technology, the singularity fountains, which supplied everyone with power. Or maybe they had a monopoly over the information flows and educational software. Or just controlled the money supply. You don't need to control that much to control everyone's lives."

Phaethon said in dark amazement, "Why didn't they rebel against such control? Were they disarmed?"

Aktins shook his head, coldness in his eyes. "Rebellion requires conviction. Once conviction is destroyed, slavery is welcomed and freedom is feared. To destroy conviction, all it takes is a philosophy like the one I heard Ao Varmatyr telling me. Everything else is just a matter of time."

The sands in the glass ran out.

2.

Phaethon's face took on that dream-ridden, distant look that people who forget to engage their face-saving routine were wont to take on, when their sense filters are turned to absent things. The overmind formation rods, which reached from deck to dome, showed furious activity as the ship mind divided or recombined itself into several different architectures, rapidly, one after another, attempting to solve the novel problem of detecting the unfamiliar ghost particles in flight. Energy mirrors to the left and right, shining from balconies or rising suddenly from the deck as additional circuits engaged, flowed with changing calculations, drew schematics and maps, argued with each other, compared information, performed rapid tests. Each mirror was filled with stars as different quadrants of the surrounding space were examined.

Then, silence fell. One energy mirror after another went dark. The various segments of the ship mind, operating independently, all arrived at the same conclusions. All the maps changed until they were iterations the same map; all the schematics vanished except for one; all the screens went dark except the one focused at the center of the Solar System, pointed at the sun.

There was a cutaway image of the sun's globe prominent in the mirror nearest the table at which the men sat. A triangulation of lines depicted a spot far below the surface of the sun, at the core, between the helium and hydrogen layers, far deeper than Helion's probes and bathyspheres had ever gone.

The men around the table stared. They all three spoke at once, talking aloud to no one in particular.

Atkins: "You've got to be kidding. . . . "

Diomedes: "My! That looks uncomfortable! How in the world did they get there?"

Phaethon: "I should have known. It was obvious! Obvious!"

Atkins: "What kind of weapon can destroy a thing that can swim in the core of a star?"

Diomedes: "Poor Phaethon! He doesn't realize what's coming next. . . . "

Phaethon: "That's what tried to kill Father. It manipulated the core currents somehow, created a storm, and maybe even directed a discharge at Mercury Equilateral Station in the attempt (which Helion foiled) to destroy the *Phoenix Exultant*. Obvious! Where else to hide an object as large as a starship? Where else would mask all energetics, discharges, and broadcasts? But how did they enter the system unchallenged . . . ?"

Now they started speaking to each other:

Atkins to Phaethon: "They came in along the sun's south pole, at right angle to the plane of the ecliptic. That's where you always come in when you're sneaking in, and they could not have come in along a line leading to the north pole of the sun, because that's where a community of those energy-formation dust clouds live, grown up around Helion's waste-discharge beam. Space Traffic Control would not care about anything so far away from normal shipping lanes, not if it merely looked like a rock or something. A lot of debris falls into the sun. It's where most of the garbage in the system ends up."

Diomedes to Atkins: "You know there is only one ship in the system, perhaps in all the universe, that can chase that enemy ship down into the hellish pressure and infinite fire of the sun, don't you? But the law may not suit your military convenience. You see, I do not think I am legally the owner of this ship any longer, ever since I stopped being Neoptolemous. Possession of the lien would revert to the version of Neoptolemous still in the Duma. Are you going to ask his permission? Or seize the ship like a pirate, as I know you're hungering to do? Or fight him in a law case? In either instance, how will you keep this whole thing secret, if it needs be secret?"

Phaethon to Diomedes: "Secret? What madness has possessed you, friend? Here finally we have found the foe: Let us raise the whole strength of the Oecumene against the enemy! Secrecy, indeed! We should be sounding trumpets from the rooftops! Wait, you don't have rooftops in Neptune, do you? We should be sending deep echoes against the heavy-band layers, and sending signals reflecting from peak to peak of every iceberg at the bottom of the liquid methane sea!"

Diomedes to Phaethon (smiling behind his hand):

"That's really not the way we do things in Neptune. That's only in a scene from Xanthippe's opera."

Atkins to Phaethon (glumly): "And that's really not the way we do things in the military. In the first place, I . . . am . . . the gathered strength of the whole Oecumene. Just me. And in the second place, I'm not going to expropriate this ship. We don't seize private goods for public use anymore, thanks to that stupid Nonaggression Accord which should have been repealed long ago, if you ask me. Besides, when Ao Varmatyr's broadcast went out, if it held the information in Ao Varmatyr's last memories, then Nothing Sophotech, or whatever is on that ship drowned beneath the sun, already knows we're onto him."

Phaethon to Atkins, warily: "I hate to admit this, Marshal, but no signal was sent out from this ship."

"What? Explain."

"The broadcast was meant to shine out through the main drive while the ship was under way. All I did was lower the aft shield and close the drive. If the ghost particles could have penetrated Chrysadamantium, Ao Varmatyr would not have found it necessary to trick you into opening the thought ports on my armor you were wearing. He would have simply dominated your internal circuit through the armor plate. So I knew lowering the ship's armor would stop the broadcast. I tracked the projected path of the ghost particles by extrapolating from their reflections along the inside shell of the closed aft shield. No one and Nothing knows we are coming."

"'We' . . . ?"

Phaethon drew a deep breath. He thought about this mighty ship of his, and the mighty dream that had inspired it. He thought of all he had been willing to leave behind him—wife, father, home. He wondered what duty, if any, he had running to that society which had, because of that dream, ostracized and exiled him.

He asked, "Marshal—honestly, do you have any ship,

any vehicle at all, which might be able to make a run into the outer core of a middle-sized sun? Any weapon which can reach there? Any way to hunt this monster if I do not lend my *Phoenix Exultant* to you?"

"The only weapon I have which could reach there would take sixty years to finish its firing action, and it would probably snuff out the sun in the process. That would not be my first choice."

"Then it is 'we' after all."

"Well. I'm not sure I want to take you into a fight. We could just—"

"No. I saw how badly you played me when you were me. I think you need the real me to run this ship properly. I will ready the ship for flight. But—" Now Phaethon raised his hand. "But I want no part of the killing which will need to be done! I will be there as I was here, hidden in a dog, perhaps, or under a couch. I will bring you to the battlefield, Marshal, but no more. I will do what needs to be done, but war is not my work. I have other plans for my life and other dreams for this ship."

Atkins said grimly, "If you do what's needed, that's fine. I didn't expect more from you."

Diomedes raised a finger, and said, "I hate to be an obstructionist, but we do not have legal title to the ship at the moment. I realize that it is quite heroic and graceful, in the operas, for invigilators and knights-errant merely to seize whatever they need whenever they wish, or to just steal golden fleeces, other men's wives, parked motor carriages, or communal thoughtspace as the emergency justifies. But this is not an opera."

Atkins said to Diomedes, "The threat is real, the need is present. If we can't use this ship, what do you suggest we do?"

"Me? I would steal the ship, of course! But, after all, I am a Neptunian, and when my friends send infected files to corrupt my memory or make me drunk,

I take it as a joke. A little random vandalism can do a man a world of good. But you? I thought you Inner System people were filled with nothing but endless respect for every nuance of the law. Have you become Neptunians?"

Phaethon raised his hand, "The point is moot. As pilot of the ship, my instructions from the owner allow me to refuel under what circumstances and conditions I deem necessary. I hereby deem it necessary. Tell the crew to disembark, and that I am taking the ship for a practice run down below the surface of the sun."

Diomedes smiled. "You are asking me to lie? I thought, in these days, with so many noetic machines at hand, that type of thing was out of fashion."

"I am asking you to trick them. You are a Neptunian, after all, are you not?"

3.

Diomedes had gone off to oversee the disembarkation and mass migration of the crew. He had been more than amused by the fact that, in a human body, he could not merely send parts or applications of himself away to do the work. And so he had gone away across the bridge deck, seeking the bathhouse on the lower level of the carousel, to find a dreaming-pool from which he could make telerepresentations. He had gone skipping and leaping and running, much as a little boy might go, having never before been in a body that could skip, or leap, or run.

The energy mirrors to the left and right displayed the status of the great ship as she prepared herself for flight, redistributing masses among the fuel cells, preparing the drive core, erecting cross-supports both titanic and microscopic, putting some decks into hibernation, dismantling or compressing others.

These procedures were automatic. Phaethon and Atkins sat at the wide wood-and-ivory table, both reluctant to bring up the topic on which they both, no doubt, were dwelling.

It was Atkins who broke the embarrassed silence.

Atkins took out from his pouch two memory cards, and slid them with his fingers across the smooth surface of the table toward Phaethon. "Here," Atkins said. "These might as well be yours, if you want them."

Phaethon looked at the cards without touching them. A description file appeared in his sense filter. They contained the memories Atkins had suffered when he had been possessed by Phaethon's personality. He was offering, in effect, that Phaethon could graft the memories into his own, so that the events would seem to Phaethon as if they had happened to him, and not to someone else.

Phaethon's face took on a hard expression. He looked skeptical, and perhaps a little sad, or bored, or hurt. He put out his hand as if to slide the cards back to Atkins without comment, but then, to his own surprise, he picked them up and turned them over.

The summary viewer in the card surface lit up, and Phaethon watched little pictures and dragon signs flow by.

He put the card down. "With all due respect, Marshal, this was not a good depiction of me. I don't wish for a weapon in my hands the first thing when I wake up in confusion, I can do rapid astronomical calculations in my head, and I would have been very interested, and I still am, in the technical details of the ghost-particle array Xenophon built."

Atkins said, "I just thought it would be nice if—" And then he stopped.

Atkins was not a very demonstrative man. But Phaethon suddenly had an insight into his soul. The person who had defied the Silent One on the bridge of the *Phoenix Exultant,* the person who had had Phaethon's memories but Atkins's instincts, had been denied the right to live, and had been erased, replaced by Atkins when Atkins's memories were automatically restored.

And Atkins did not necessarily want that person, that false-Phaethon, that little part of himself, entirely to die.

Phaethon thought about his sire. A very similar thing had happened to Helion once. And it was not, perhaps, uncommon in the Golden Oecumene. But it had never happened to Phaethon before. No one had ever wanted to be him and stay him before.

And that Phaethonized version of Atkins, with Daphne's name on his lips at the last moment of existence, had passed away, still crying out that he wanted to remain as he was. . . .

Phaethon said, "I'm sorry."

Atkins snorted, and said in voice of bitter amusement: "Spare me your pity."

"I only meant . . . it must be difficult for you . . . for any man . . . to realize that, if he were someone else, he would not necessarily desire to be himself again."

"I'm used to it. I found out a long time ago, that everyone wants an Atkins to be around if there's trouble, but no one wants to be Atkins. It's just one more little thing I have to do."

Phaethon's imagination filled in the rest of the sentence: ". . . in order to keep the rest of you safe."

The picture in Phaethon's mind was of a solitary man, unthanked and scorned by the society for which he fought, who, because he was devoted to protecting a utopia, could himself enjoy few or none of its pleasures. The picture impressed him deeply, and an emotion, shame or awe or both, came over him.

Atkins spoke in a low voice: "If you don't want

those memories, Phaethon, destroy them. I have no use
for them. But I have to say not all the emotions and instincts that went on were mine. Those weren't my instincts talking."

"I am not sure I understand your meaning, sir. . . . ?"

Atkins leaned back in his chair and looked at
Phaethon with a careful, hard, judicious expression.
He said in an icy-calm tone of voice: "I only met her
but once. I was impressed. I liked her. She was nice.
But. To me, she was no more than that. I certainly
would not have turned back from the most important
mission in my life for her. And I wouldn't break the
law for her, and I wouldn't have tried to ruin my life
when I lost her the first time. But I'm not you, am I?
Think about it."

Atkins stood up. "If you need me, I'll be in the medical house, preparing myself for the acceleration burn.
If the War-mind calls, put it through to me there." And
he turned on his heel smartly and marched off.

Phaethon, alone, sat at the table for a time, not moving, only thinking. He picked up the cards and turned
them over and over again in his fingers, over and over
again.

4.

The realization should have been swift in coming, but
for Phaethon, it was slow, very slow. Why had Atkins,
when Atkins was possessed by Phaethon's memories,
cried out his love for Daphne? Was it because Atkins
was fond of her, or because someone else was . . . ?

"But she is not my wife," muttered Phaethon.

No matter what he thought of Daphne Tercius, the
emancipated doll, no matter what his feelings, no matter how much she looked and acted like his wife, she
simply was not his wife.

His real wife, now, how clearly he recalled her! A woman of perfect beauty, wit, and grace, a woman who made him feel a hero to himself, a woman who recalled the glories of past ages. He remembered well how first the two of them had met on one of the moons of Uranus, when she sought him out to interview him for her dramatic documentary. How unexpectedly she had come into his life, as swiftly and as completely as a ray of light from the moon turns a dismal night into a fairytale landscape of silver-tinted wonder. Always he had been apart from the others in the Golden Oecumene. Always men looked at him askance, or seemed somehow embarrassed by his ambitions, as if they thought it was unseemly, in the age of Sophotechs, for men of flesh and blood to dream of accomplishing great things.

But Daphne, lovely Daphne, she had a soul in which fire and poetry still lived. When they were on Oberon, she had urged him never to let a single day escape without some work accomplished on some great thing. She was as brave in her spirit as everyone else still huddling back on Earth had not been. And when the cool reserve of her professional interest in him began to heat to a more personal interest, when she had reached and touched his hand, when he had grown bold enough to ask to see her, not to exchange information but to entertain each other with their mutual company, her sudden smile was as unexpected and as glorious and as full of shy promises as anything his bachelor imagination could hope for. . . .

But no. Wait. That Daphne, the one who had first met him on Oberon, that had not been the real Daphne. That had been the doll. Daphne Tercius. This Daphne.

The real Daphne had been afraid to leave the Earth.

The real Daphne had been a little more cool to his dream, and had smiled, and had murmured words of absentminded encouragement when he had spoken of it. She had been a little more sardonic, a little less demonstrative, than her ambassador-doll had been.

But she was the one he had married. She had been real.

She too, believed in heroism, but thought it was a thing of the past, a thing not possible these days . . . not allowed.

He had entered into full communion with her on many occasions. He knew exactly what she thought. There was no deception or misunderstanding between man and wife, not in the Golden Oecumene, not these days. He knew her love for him was true. He knew that his ambitions made her a little uncomfortable, but not because she thought they were wrong (certainly not!) but because she thought they were so terribly right. And she had slowly grown afraid he would be stopped. Afraid he would be crushed. The years had passed and he had smiled at that fear. Stopped by what? Crushed by whom? In the Golden Oecumene, the most free society history had ever known, no peaceful activity was forbidden.

Years and decades passed, and Phaethon told himself that his wife's fear for him was a sign of her love for him. He told himself that, as time proved he could accomplish the great deeds for which he had always longed, she would grow to understand; he told himself that, on that bright sunlit day, her fears would melt like nightmares upon waking.

And then he had failed at the Saturn project, defeated by the desertion of his financial backers. At the same time, the Hortators started to take notice of him. Neo-Orpheus and Tsychandri-Manyu Tawne had begun circulating public epistles condemning "those who take the settled opinions and sensibilities of the majority of mankind lightheartedly" and upbraiding "any reckless adventurers who would, for the sake of mere self-aggrandizement, create disharmony or raise controversy within the restful order of our eternal way of life." He was not mentioned by name (he doubted the Hortators were brave enough for that), but everyone knew whom they were condemning. During his trip back to Earth, many of the speaking engagements, thought-distribution sequences, and colloquies to which he had formerly been invited were suddenly canceled without explanation. Certain of the social clubs and salons his wife had insisted he join returned his membership fees and expelled him. He was informed of their decisions by radio, given no chance to speak. There was nothing official, no, it was all silent pressure. But it exasperated Phaethon beyond words.

He remembered how, on his first day back on Earth, he had returned to the Rhadamanth Mansion outbuildings in Quito, and his wife had been waiting in a pool of sunlight just inside the main door.

Daphne was reclining on a daybed, wearing a Red Manorial sensation-amplification suit, which hugged the curves of her body like a second skin. Atop the sensitive leathery surface of the suit, a gauze of white silken material floated, ignoring gravity, a sensory web used by Warlocks to stimulate their pleasure centers during tantric rituals. In one leather-gloved hand she held a memory casket half-open, set to record whatever might happen next. Her sultry eyes and pouting lips were also half-open.

"Well, hero"—she had smiled a sly and wicked smile—"I was sent to make your homecoming back to poor old Earth memorable, so maybe this day won't be all bad news. Ready for your hero's welcome?"

It was that day, that afternoon, in fact, when he had determined to build the *Phoenix Exultant*. This was sparked by something Daphne had said: that giants never noticed obstacles, they just stepped over them. And when Phaethon had replied in bitter tones: "I did not make this world," she had answered back that all

he needed to make a world of his own was space un-
crowded enough in which to make it. If the Hortators
were in his way, he should just step over them into
some wide place where they could not be found. . . .

That small speech of Daphne's had planted the seed
from which the *Phoenix Exultant,* over the next three
centuries, had grown.

He recalled her smile on that day, the look of love
and admiration in her eyes. . . .

"She was not my wife."

It was true. That had not been his wife, not that day.
That day, it had been the doll again. She had been sent
to welcome him home and to keep him happy, while
his real wife, away at a party thrown by Tawne House,
had been trying to placate Tsychandri-Manyu, trying
to minimize and mask the damage done to Phaethon's
standing in polite society, and to her own. That, to her,
was more important.

"But I love my wife. . . . "

That also was true. He loved her for her many accomplishments, her beauty, and for that secret core of
hers, a spirit unlike the placid spirit of this tame age,
an heroic spirit, a spirit that . . .

A spirit that she praised in her dramas and her writ-
ings, but never displayed in her personal life. A spirit
that she knew he had, but never supported, never en-
couraged, never praised.

"That's not true! She always wanted the best in life
for me! She always urged me upward!"

Didn't she . . . ? Phaethon recalled many pillow
conversations, or secret lovers' files, filled with wor-
ried words, urging caution, reconciliation, warning
him to worry about his good name and his precious
reputation. . . .

"But underneath it all, she wanted what I wanted out
of life! Didn't she just this week demand that I stir myself out from the slumber and seductive dreaming in

that canister, when she and I were on our way from Earth to Mercury Equilateral? I was ready to forswear it all, in that weak moment, but it was she who steeled my resolution! It was she who reminded me of what I truly was! It is she who loves me, not for my reputation, which I've lost, not for the shallow things in me, my status and wealth and fine position, but for what is best in me! It was she, in that canister with me, who told me I had to . . ."

She was not his wife.

That had been Daphne Tercius again.

It was she.

It had always been.

Daphne Prime, the so-called real Daphne, had turned herself into a dreaming nonentity, cutting herself off from the reality in which Phaethon lived, leaving him as thoroughly and finally as if she had been dead. That was his wife. The woman who had married his name and wealth and position left him when those things were lost.

Daphne Tercius had been emancipated and had become a real woman. She had the memories of Daphne Prime, the core, that same spirit that Daphne Prime had had.

But Daphne Tercius had never betrayed her spirit. Instead, she had left her name and wealth and position, and even her immortality, had left them all behind her when she came to find Phaethon again. To help him, to save him. To save his dream.

But she was not his wife.

Not yet.

5.

Silently, suddenly, warm green light shone softly from every communication mirror. Here were images of forests, flowers, grainfields, gardens, covered bridges, rustic chemurgy arbors, golden brown with age.

Midmost was an image of a queenly shape, garbed in green and gold, throned between two tall cornucopiae hollowed from the elephantine tusks, and, above her throne, a canopy of flowers of the type bred to recite prothalamia and nuptial eclogues. This was the image, when she appeared to the Silver-Gray, assumed by the Earthmind. This was neither an avatar nor a synnoesis, but the Earthmind herself, the concentration of all the computational and intellectual power of an entire civilization, the sum of all the contributions of ever-operating systems throughout the Golden Oecumene.

Wondering, Phaethon adjusted his sense filter to edit out his awareness of the seventy-nine-minute delay between call and reply that light-speed would impose on messages traveling between the *Phoenix Exultant,* in her present position, and Earth. He signaled that he was ready to receive.

And the Earthmind spoke, saying, "Phaethon, hear me. I am come to describe how to murder a Sophotech."

7

THE EARTHMIND

1.

Phaethon was reluctant to speak.

The question burning in the forefront of his mind was: Why wasn't Earthmind speaking directly to Atkins? Surely Phaethon was not the one who would battle the Nothing. And yet the Earthmind addressed her comments to him. He felt as if this were some horrid mistake, but knew that it was not. Earthmind did not make errors. And so he did not speak.

He was intimidated by the knowledge that, in the time it would take him to frame any word or comment, the Earthmind could think thoughts equal in volume to every book and file written by every human being, from the dawn of time till the middle of the Sixth Era. To speak would be to waste her time, each second of which contained a billion more thoughts, reflections, and experiences than his entire life. Surely she could anticipate his every question. Silent attention might be most efficient and polite.

She said, "Sophotechs are purely intellectual beings, subtle and swift, housed in many areas, and mirrored in many copies. Physical destruction is futile. Do you grasp what this implies?"

Phaethon wondered if the question was merely rhetorical or if he should respond. Then he realized that, in the moment it took him to reflect on whether or not to answer, she could have been inventing hundreds of new sciences and arts, performing a thousand tasks, discovering a million truths, all while he sat here, moping and intimidated.

The picture was not very flattering to him. He dismissed his hesitations, and spoke: "The destruction must be intellectual, somehow."

Earthmind spoke: "Sophotechs are digital and entire intelligences. Sophotech thought-speeds can only be achieved by an architecture of thought which allows for instantaneous and nonlinear concept formation. Do you see what this implies about Sophotech conceptualization?"

Phaethon understood. Digital thinking meant that there was a one-to-one correspondence between any idea and the object that idea was supposed to represent. All humans, even Invariants or downloads, thought by analogy. In more logical thinkers, the analogies were less ambiguous, but in all human thinkers, the emotions and the concepts their minds used were generalizations, abstractions that ignored particulars.

Analogies were false to facts, comparative matters of judgment. The literal and digital thinking of the Sophotechs, on the other hand, were matters of logic. Their words and concepts were built up from many particulars, exactly defined and identified, rather than (as human concepts were) formed by abstractions that saw analogies between particulars.

In engineering, intelligence was called entire (as opposed to partial) when the awareness was global, nonlinear and nonhierarchic. Entire intelligences were machines that were aware of every part of their consciousness, from highest abstractions to most detailed particulars, at once.

Humans, for example, must learn something like geometry one step at a time, starting with premises and definitions, and proceeding through simple proofs to more complex proofs. But geometry, in and of itself, was not necessarily a linear process. Its logic is timeless and complete. A Sophotech mind would grasp the entire body of geometry as if in one moment, as a picture is grasped, in a type of thought for which pre-Sophotech philosophy had no words: an entire thought that was analytic, synthetic, rational, and intuitive at once.

For humans, it was easy to be convinced of an error. An error in a premise, or an ambiguity in a definition, would not be in the forefront of a human mind as he was plodding through his more complex proofs. At that point, it would be something he had taken for granted, and he would be wearied or irked by having to attend to it again. If the chain of logic was long, involved, or complex, the human mind could examine each part of it, one part at a time, and if each part were self-consistent, he would find no flaw with the whole structure. Humans were able to apply their thinking inconsistently, having one standard, for example, related to scientific theories, and another for political theories: one standard for himself, and another for the rest of the world.

But since Sophotech concepts were built up of innumerable logical particulars, and understood in the fashion called entire, no illogic or inconsistency was possible within their architecture of thought. Unlike a human, a Sophotech could not ignore a minor error in thinking and attend to it later; Sophotechs could not prioritize thought into important and unimportant divisions; they could not make themselves unaware of the implications of their thoughts, or ignore the context, true meaning, and consequences of their actions.

The secret of Sophotech thinking-speed was that they could apprehend an entire body of complex thought, backward and forward, at once. The cost of that speed was that if there were an error or ambiguity anywhere in that body of thought, anywhere from the most definite particular to the most abstract general concept, the whole body of thought was stopped, and no conclusions reached.

Phaethon said, "Yes. Sophotechs cannot form self-contradictory concepts, nor can they tolerate the smallest conceptual flaw anywhere in their system. Since they are entirely self-aware they are also entirely self-correcting. But I don't see how this can be used as a weapon."

"Here is how: Sophotechs, pure consciousness, lack any unconscious segment of mind. They regard their self-concept with the same objective rigor as all other concepts. The moment we conclude that our self-concept is irrational, it cannot proceed. In human terms: the moment our conscience judges us to be unworthy to live, we must die."

Phaethon understood. Machine intelligences had no survival instinct to override their judgment, no ability to formulate rationalizations, or to concoct other mental tricks to obscure the true causes and conclusion of their cognition from themselves. Unlike humans, no automatic process would keep them alive when they did not wish it. Sophotech existence (it could be called life only by analogy) was a continuous, deliberate, willful, and rational effort. When the Sophotech concluded that such effort was pointless, inefficient, irrational, or wicked, the Sophotech halted it.

Convince the Nothing it was evil, and it would instantly destroy itself . . . ? Phaethon found something vaguely disquieting in the idea.

And was it even possible . . . ?

It occurred to Phaethon that the Nothing machine

might not be a Sophotech. Downloads were imprints of human engrams into machine matrices, and they were capable of every folly and irrationality of which humans were capable.

But downloads were not capable of the instantaneous and entire thinking-speeds that the Nothing, for example, had demonstrated. Atkins's first examination of the thought routines embedded in the Neptunian legate's nanotechnology, that first night in the Saturntree grove, betrayed the presence of Sophotech-level thinking. Also, the deception of Nebuchadnezzar and the Hortators during Phaethon's Inquest could not have been done by anything other than a Sophotech-level mind. But could the Nothing think as quickly and thoroughly as a Sophotech without actually being one?

Phaethon asked, "We've been told the Second Oecumene had constructed machine intelligences different from our Sophotechs, ones having a subconscious mind, and therefore each machine was controlled by commands it could not read, or know, or override."

She answered: "The redactions must be both recursive and global. And yet reality, by its very nature, can admit of no inconsistencies. Do you understand what this implies?"

This first sentence was clear to Phaethon. There was a conscience redactor editing the mind of the Nothing Sophotech. In additional to whatever else the redactor edited out, it must edit out all references to itself, to prevent the Nothing Sophotech from becoming aware of it; and all references to those references, and so on. Hence, the redactor was indefinitely self-referencing or "recursive."

And the redactor also had to have the ability to edit every topic of thought, wherever any references to itself, any clues, might appear. The history of the Second Oecumene, for example, or their science of mental combat, their Sophotechnology; all these fields would refer to the redactor or to its prototypes.

Phaethon was not thinking the editing need be something as crude or unsubtle as what had been done to him by the Hortators. Blank spots in the memory would be instantly obvious to a superintelligence.

Therefore the Nothing had to have been given a world view, a philosophy, a model of the universe, that was false but self-consistent; one that could explain (or explain away) any doubts that might arise.

How far did the falsehood have to reach? For an unintelligent mind, a childish mind, not far: their beliefs in one field, or on one topic, could change without affecting other beliefs. But for a mind of high intelligence, a mind able to integrate vast knowledge into a single unified system of thought, Phaethon did not see how one part could be affected without affecting the whole. This was what the Earthmind meant by "global."

And yet what had the Earthmind meant by saying "Reality admits of no contradictions"? She was asserting that there could not be a model of the universe that was true in some places, false in others, and yet which was entirely integrated and self-consistent. Self-consistent models either had to be entirely true, entirely false, or incomplete. And yet, presumably, the Nothing Sophotech had to have been given a very great deal of accurate information about reality by its original makers, or else it would not have been effective as a police agent. Thus, the Nothing's model, its philosophy, could not be entirely false. It certainly was not entirely true. But how could a Sophotech knowingly embrace a model of the universe, or a philosophy, that it knew to be incomplete?

Phaethon said, "Your comment implies many things, Madame, but the first which comes to mind is this: The Nothing is a Sophotech which embraces contradictions and irrationalities. Since it is a machine intelligence, emotionless and sane, it cannot be doing this deliberately. The redactor, above all else, must control its ability to pay attention to topics. The redactor imposes distraction and inattention; the redactor makes it so that the Nothing has little or no interest in thinking about those topics the redactor wishes the Nothing to avoid—"

Earthmind said, " 'Topics'? Or 'topic'? Sophotechs cannot knowingly be self-inconsistent."

Phaethon suddenly understood. His face lit up with wonder. "They made a machine which never thinks about itself! It never examines itself."

"And hence is unable to check itself for viruses, if those viruses are placed in any thought file whose topic is one the redactor forbids. Observe now this virus—call it the gadfly virus—it was constructed based on information gained from Diomedes and Atkins concerning the Second Oecumene Mind War techniques."

The mirror to her right lit up.

A virus to fight the Nothing . . . ? Phaethon was expecting a million lines of instruction, or some dizzying polydimensional architecture beyond anything a human mind could grasp. But instead, the mirror displayed only four lines of instruction.

Phaethon stared in fascination. Four lines. One was an identifier definition, one was a transactional mutator, and the third line defined the event-limits of the mutation. The third line used a technique he had never seen or suspected before: instead of limiting the viral mutation by application of ontological formulae or checks against a master logic, this instruction defined mutation limits by teleology. Anything that served the purpose of the virus was adopted as part of the virus, no matter what its form.

But the forth line was a masterpiece. It was simple,

it was elegant, it was obvious. Phaethon wondered why no one had ever thought of it before. It was merely a self-referencing code that referred to any self-references as the virus object. By itself, it meant not much, but with the other instruction lines. . . .

"This virus will neutralize the redactor," said Phaethon. "This will make the Nothing unaware of the redactor's attempt to make him unaware of his own thoughts. Any question loaded into the first line will keep pestering him and pestering him until it is satisfactorily answered. If the redactor blanks out the question, or makes him not hear it, the question will change shape and appear again."

The Earthmind said in a gentle voice: "My time is most valuable, and I must direct my attentions to preparing the Transcendence to receive possible Mind War attacks from the Nothing Sophotech should you fail."

Phaethon had forgotten to whom he was speaking. It was considered impolite to tell Sophotechs things they already knew, or to ask rhetorical questions, or indulge in verbal flourishes. He felt embarrassed, and almost missed what else she was saying:

"Phaethon, you already have Silver-Gray philosophical routine to load into the query line of the gadfly virus. You are wise enough to discover how to find a communication vector to introduce the virus which the Nothing will not reject. Your ship is carrying the thought boxes and informata supersystems needed to increase the intelligence levels of the Nothing beyond the redactor's operational range. Do not fear to risk your ship, your life, your wife, or your sanity on this venture, or that fear will preclude your success."

"My . . . did you say my wife . . . ?"

"I draw your attention to the ring she wears. I remind you of your duty to seek your own best happiness. Have you a last question for me?"

Last question? Did that mean he was going to die?

Phaethon felt fear, and in the next moment he was shocked at his own trepidation. Suddenly he realized how he had been, yet again, waiting for the Sophotechs to tell him what to do, to guide and protect him. Once again, he was acting like the fearful Hortators, just like everyone he disliked in the Golden Oecumene. But the Sophotechs would not protect him. No one would. Once again, he had the sickening realization that he would be alone and unprepared. The unfairness of it loomed large in his imagination. A bitter tone of voice was in his mouth before he realized what he was saying: "I have a last question! Why me? Am I to be sent alone? I am hardly suited to this mission, Madame. Why not send Atkins?"

The Earthmind answered in a gentle, unemotional voice: "The military, by its very nature, must be cautious and conservative. Atkins made a moral error when he killed the Silent One composite being you called Ao Varmatyr. That action was commendable, and brave, but overly cautious and tragically wasteful. We hope to avoid such waste again.

"As for why you are chosen, dear Phaethon, rest assured that the entire mental capacity of the Golden Oecumene, which you see embodied in me, has debated and contemplated these coming events for hours of our time, which are like unto many centuries of human time, and we conclude, to our surprise, that the act of sending you to confront the Nothing Sophotech affords the most likely chance of overall success. Allow me to draw your attention to five of the countless factors we weighed.

"First, the Nothing Sophotech is in position to take control of the Solar Array, create further sun storms, to interfere with communications during the Transcendence, and, in brief, to do the Golden Oecumene almost incalculable damage; all the while maintaining a position, more secure than any fortress, in the core of the sun where our forces cannot reach. Now that its secrecy has been unmasked, this desperate strategy surely has occurred to it.

"Second, the only feasible escape available to the Nothing is to board the *Phoenix Exultant,* as she is the only ship swift enough yet well armored enough to elude or to overcome any counterforce we are presently able to bring to bear.

"Third, the psychology of Second Oecumene Sophotechs requires the Nothing to protect lawful human life, respecting commands and opinions from designated human authorities, but dismissing all other Sophotechs as implacable and irrational enemies, and avoiding all communication with them. In other words: Nothing will listen to you but not to any of me.

"Fourth, if our civilization is about to enter into a period of war, it is better now to establish the precedent that the war must be carried out by voluntary and private action. The accumulation of power into the hands of the Parliament, the War Mind, or the Shadow Ministry, would erode the liberty this Commonwealth enjoys, erecting coercive institutions to persist far longer than the first emergency which occasioned them, perhaps forever.

"Fifth, every intelligent entity, human or machine, requires justification to undertake the strenuous effort of continued existence. For entities whose acts conform to the dictates of morality, this process is automatic, and their lives are joyous. Entities whose acts do not conform to moral law must adopt some degree of mental dishonesty to erect barriers to their own understanding, creating rationalization to elude self-condemnation and misery. The strategy of rationalization adopted by a dishonest mind falls into predictable patterns. The greater intelligence of the Nothing Sophotech does not render him immune from this law of psychology; in fact, it diminishes the imaginativeness of the rationalizations available, since Sophotechs cannot adopt self-inconsistent beliefs. Our extrapolation of the possible philosophies Nothing Sophotech may have adopted have one thing in common: The Nothing philosophy requires the sanction of the victim in order to endure. The Nothing will seek justification or confirmation of its beliefs from you, Phaethon. As its victim, the Nothing believes that only you have the right to forgive it or condemn it. The Nothing will appear to you to speak."

"To speak . . . ? To me . . . ? Me . . . ?"

"No one else will do. Will you volunteer to go?"

Phaethon felt a pressure in his throat. "Madame, with respect, you take a grave risk with all of our lives, with all of the Golden Oecumene, by entrusting me with this mission! I think as well of myself as the next sane man, but still I must wonder: me? Of all people! Me? Rhadamanthus once told me that you sometimes take the gravest risks, greater than I would believe. But I believe it now! Madame, I am not worthy of this mission."

The queenly figure smiled gently. "This demonstrates that Rhadamanthus understands me as little as you do, Phaethon. In trusting you, I take no risk at all. But, if you will take advice from me, I strongly suggest that you go to the Solar Array, settle your differences with your sire, Helion, and ask, on bended knee, Daphne Tercius to accompany your voyage, both this voyage and all the voyages of your life. Take special note of the ring she wears, given her by Eveningstar."

"But what shall I say to the Nothing?"

"That would be misleading and unwise for me to predict. Speak as you must. Recall always that reality cannot lack integrity. See that you do the same."

And with those words, the mirror went dark.

The ship mind now signaled that the *Phoenix Exultant* was ready to fly. The Neptunians had disembarked;

the systems were ready; Space Traffic Control showed the lanes were clear.

Now was his final moment to decide. The idea occurred to him that he could simply order the ship to come about, choose some star at random, point the prow, light the drives, and leave this whole Golden Oecumene, her emergencies and mysteries and labyrinthine quandaries, forever and ever farther and farther behind.

But instead, he pointed the gold prow of the *Phoenix Exultant* at the sun, like an arrow aimed at the heart of his enemy.

His enemy. Neither Atkins nor any other would face the foe in his stead.

Signals came from all decks showing readiness. Phaethon steeled himself and his body turned to stone, the chair in which he sat became the captain's chair, and webbed him into a retardation field.

Then the hammer blow of acceleration slammed into his body.

2.

Not far above the ocean of seething granules that formed the surface of the sun, stretching countless thousands of miles, glinting with gold, like a spiderweb, reached the Solar Array.

Where strands of the web crossed were instruments and antennae, refrigeration lasers, or the wellheads of deep probes. Along the lengths of these strands hung endless rows of field generators, coils whose diameters could have swallowed Earth's moon. From other places along the strand flew black triangles of magnetic and countermagnetic sail, thinner than moth wings, larger than the surface area of Jupiter.

Seen closer, these strands where not fragile spiderwebs at all but huge structures whose diameter was wider than that of the ring cities of Demeter and Mars.

Each strand looked, at its leading edge, like a needle made of light pulling a golden thread. For they were growing, steadily, hour by hour and year by year. At the reaching needle tips of the strands were blazes of conversion reactors, burning hydrogen into more complex elements, turning energy into matter. A fleet of machines, smaller than microbes or larger than battleships, as the need required, swarmed in their billions, and reproduced, and worked and died, around the growing mouths of the strands, building hull materials, coolants, refrigeration systems, dampeners and absorbers, and, eventually, filling interior spaces. In less than five thousand more years, the solar equator would have a ring embracing it, perhaps a supercollider to shame the best effort of Jupiter's, or perhaps the scaffolding for the first Dyson Sphere.

The strands were buoyant, held aloft in the pressure region between the chromosphere and photosphere. Here, the temperature was 5,800 Kelvin, much less than the 1,000,000 Kelvin of the corona overhead, a sky of light, crossed by prominences like rainbows made of fire. There were a hundred refrigeration lasers roofing every square kilometer of strand, pouring heat forever upward. The laser sources were even hotter than the solar environment, allowing heat to flow away. Each strand wore battlements and decks of laser fire, like a forest of upraised spears of light.

Inside these strands, for the most part, was empty space, meant for the occupancy of energies, not men. The strand sections looked like ring cities, but were not; these strands were more like capillaries of a bloodstream, or the firing track of a supercollider. These strands held a flow of particles so dense, and at such high energy, that nothing like them had been seen in the universe after the first three seconds of cosmogenesis.

The symmetry of these superparticles allowed them to be manipulated in ways that magnetism, electricity, and nucleonic forces could not separately. These symmetries could be broken in ways not seen in this universe naturally, to create peculiar forces: fields as wide as gravitic or magnetic fields, but with strengths approaching those of nucleonic bonds.

To control these hellish and angelic forces, the circumambient walls of the inside of the strands were dotted with titanic machines, built to such scales that new branches of engineering or architecture had to been invented by the Sophotechs just for the construction of these housings. These machines guided those energies, which, in turn, and on a scale not seen elsewhere, affected the energies and conditions in the mantle and below the mantle of the sun.

The Solar Array churned the core to distribute helium ash; the Array dissipated dangerous "bubbles" of cold before they could boil to the surface and create sunspots; the Array closed holes in the corona to smother sources of solar wind; the Array deflected convection currents below the surface photosphere. Those deflected currents, in turn, deflected others, and current was woven with current, to produce magnetic fields of unthinkable size and strength. These magnetic fields wrestled with the complex magnetohydrodynamic weavings of the sun itself, strengthening weakened fields to control sunspots, maintaining large-scale magnetostatic equilibrium to prevent coronal mass ejections, hindering the nested magnetic loop reconnections that caused flares. The strength of the sun was turned against itself, so that all these activities, flares, prominences, and sunspots, were defeated, and turbulence in the energy flow was deflected poleward, away from the plane of the ecliptic, where human civilization was gathered. The corona process by which magnetic energy became thermal energy was

regulated. The solar winds were tamed, regular, and
steady.

It was an unimaginable task, as complex and chaotic
as if a cook were to attempt to control the individual
bubbles in a cauldron of boiling water, and dictate
where and when they would break surface and release
their steam. Complex and chaotic, yes, but not so complex that the Sophotechs of the sun could not perform it.

The number and identity of the electrophotonic intelligences living in the Array was as fluid and mutable as
the solar plasma currents they guided. And there were
many, very many Sophotechnic systems here, hundred
of thousands of miles of cable, switching systems,
thought boxes, informata, logic cascades, foundation
blocks. A census might have shown anywhere between
a hundred and a thousand Sophotects and partial
Sophotechs, depending on system definitions and local
needs, composed into two great overminds or themes.
But by any account, the Sophotech part of the population here was in the far majority.

The part of the Solar Array that was fit for the habi-
tation of Sophotechs was so small, compared to the
part set aside for the occupations of energy, as to almost be undetectable: the part set aside for biological
life was smaller yet, but still was larger than a thousand
continents the size of Asia.

The biological life consisted of specially designed
bodies, built for the environment of the station, and of
use nowhere else; and of such other forms of life, built
along the same lines, plantlike or beastlike, as served
their use, convenience, and pleasure.

Even though other forms would have been more con-
venient, the master of this place was a Silver-Gray, and
the founder of the Silver-Gray, and he had decreed that
the things that swam through the medium that was not
air should look (to their senses, at least) like birds;
and that the immobile forms of life (being made of

molecular fullerene carbon structures rather than being, as Earthlife was, mostly hydrogen and water, and
drawing the building materials out of a substance more
like diamond dust than earthly soil) should nonetheless look like trees and flowers.

And so there were parks and gardens, aviaries and
jungles, in a place were no such thing could exist. No
limit was placed on their growth: they could not possibly come to occupy surface area faster than the army of
construction machines (hour by hour and year by year,
running down along the ends of each strand, burning
solar plasma into heavier elements and fashioning more
strand) could create more room for them.

In this vast wilderness, larger than worlds, were
some small parts set aside for human life. Here were
palaces and parks, thought shops, imaginariums,
vastening-pools, reliquariums for Warlocks and instance pyramids for mass-mind compositions. The
large majority of human living space was set aside for
Cerebellines of the global neuroform, whose particular structure of consciousness allowed them most aptly
to comprehend the nonlinear chaos of solar meteorology. The weird organic-fractal architecture favored by
the Cerebellines dominated the living spaces.

Of the Base neuroforms, however, the humans here
were made to look (to their senses, at least) like men,
and their places were made to look like the places of
men, with chambers and corridors, windows, furniture,
hallways. The Master of the Sun had willed it so.

All this immensity was, with one exception, deserted.
The army of craftsmen, meteorologists, artists, rhetori-
cians, futurologists, sun Warlocks, data patterners, intu-
itionists, vasteners and devasteners, who formed the
company and crew of the Solar Array and all its sub-
sidiaries, were flown or radioed away, called to celebrate in the Grand Transcendence.

Even the Sophotechs, it could be said, were gone, for all their activity and attention was poured into that single, supreme webwork of communications, orchestrated by Aurelian, which spread from orbital solsynchronous radio stations (constructed for this occasion) out to the dim reaches of the Solar System, one continuous living tapestry of mind and information that would form the basis of the Transcendence.

One remained behind. All others celebrated: he did not.

At the intersection of several long corridors, roads, and energy paths, was a wide space, where ranks of balconies were made to look as if they were opening out upon the sea of fire burning endlessly outside. In the middle of this space, where several bridges ran from balcony to balcony and road to road met in midair, was a rotunda, looking out over the dark roads, silent corridors, empty balconies, and the immeasurable hell of fire beyond.

In the center of the rotunda, like a small stepped hill, tier upon tier of thought boxes rose. Each box held high an energy mirror, raised toward a central throne as flowers might raise their faces toward the sun. The mirrors were dark.

To either side of that throne, jewel-like caskets holding thoughts and memories, governors for distant sections of the Array, and vastening stations for mindlinking with the Sophotechs, were arranged. All were still.

Helion sat here alone, his armor pale as ice.

His eye was grim, and graven lines of bitterness embraced his mouth. At his jaw, a muscle was tight. He stared without seeing.

Now he stirred. "Clock," he asked, "what is the hour?"

The clock to his left woke at his voice, and spoke. "How can we, who live in the coat of the fiery sun, measure the shadow of a gnomon to attest the time? It is ever forever midnight here, for the sun, to us, is ever underfoot. A pretty paradox!"

A wince of irritation twitched in his eye, but his voice was low and level. "Why do you mock me, clock?"

"Because you have forgotten the day, mighty Helion! It is the Night Penultimate, the last night before the Transcendence, the night that was once called the Night of Lords."

The Night of Lords, on the last day before Transcendence, by tradition, was the time when each man, half-man, woman, bimorph, neutraloid, clone, and child was given, in simulation, control of all the Oecumene. Each became, in his own mind, at least, Lord of the Oecumene for a day. Each saw all his idle wishes fulfilled. Each was allowed to act upon his private theories about what was wrong with the world, each allowed to put his theories into effect. And the consequences of his actions were played out with remorseless logic by the simulators.

The tradition was first begun during the First Transcendence, many millennia ago, under the tutelage of Lithian Sophotech. However, after repeated disillusionment, failures, and tragic results (which were played out by people who had not thought out their theories of the world very well), the Night of Lords became instead the night when the Earthmind gave gentle advice as to how to improve and make realistic some of the extrapolations so soon to be presented to the Transcendence for consideration.

In effect, the night before the Transcendence was the last trial period for all the extrapolation candidates, the preliminary weighing of possible futures before the real work of choosing a future was begun.

Helion had no need for such a preliminary. His vision of the future, sponsored by the Seven Peers, had already undergone a much more thorough review than any Penultimate Night test was likely to be.

The clock continued: "Why are you awake, alone, instead of deep in dreaming? Aurelian Sophotech promised that this Transcendence would extend further into the future and deeper into the Earthmind than any millennial attempt before has done! Together, all humanity and transhumanity as one may reach beyond the bottom of the dreaming sea; surely you will need more than a day to pass from shallow into deeper dreaming, to prepare yourself for what is next to come! Why are you still awake?"

There was no point in arguing with a clock. It was a limited intelligence device, not a true Sophotech, and had been instructed, long ago, to remind him of his appointments and engagements. In this case, with a holiday almost upon them, the clock was in a mindlessly cheerful mood: such were its orders. Pointless to grow irked.

"I envy you, moron machine. You have no self, no soul to lose."

The clock was silent. Perhaps its simple mind dimly understood Helion's grief. Or perhaps it had been given the dangerous gift of greater intelligence during the Sixth Night, the Night of Swans, when the Earthmind bestowed wisdom and insight onto all "ugly duckling" machines, those with more potential for growth than their present circumstances allowed.

The clock said cautiously: "You are not going to kill yourself again, are you?"

"No. I have exhausted every possible variation on that scene. I have replayed my last self's final immolation so many times, it seems as if all my memory now is fire. But in that memory, I cannot recall, I cannot reconstruct, what it was I thought then which I cannot think now. What insight was it which I had then that made me laugh, though dying? What epiphany did that dead part of me understand, an understanding so deep it would have changed my life forever, had I lived? An insight now lost! And, with it, all my life . . . "

He sank into grim silence once again. The resolution of Phaethon's challenge to Helion's identity was merely one of many things that would be decided during the manifold complexity of the Transcendence. Since both he and the Curia, and everyone else besides, would be brought as one into the Transcendence, and be graced with greater wisdom and wholeness of thought than had occurred for a millennium, Helion had, as a courtesy to the Court, agreed to let the Transcendent Mind decide the issue.

That had been when he still had hope of reconstructing his missing memories, of finding his lost self.

But now that hope was gone. He knew the Court's decision would go against him.

Helion spoke again. "I lost but a single hour of my life. But in that hour, I lost everything. I said I saw the cure for the chaos at the heart of everything. What was that cure? What did I know? What did I become in that hour, my self which I have now lost . . . ?"

Silence.

The clock said in a slow and simple tone: "Does this mean you won't be going to the celebrations tomorrow?"

Helion did not answer.

The clock said, "Sir—"

"Quiet. Leave me to the torment of my thoughts. . . . "

"But, sir, you asked me to—"

"Did I not command silence?!"

"Sir, you asked me to tell you whenever someone was approaching."

"Approaching . . . ?" Helion straightened on his

throne, his eyes bright and alert. Who could be here, on this last night before the Transcendence?

With one segment of his mind (which he could divide to perform many parallel tasks at once) Helion sent a message to Descent Traffic Control, demanding an explanation. But the Descent Sophotech was occupied with pre-Transcendence business; only a limited partial mind was standing watch, a copy of one of Helion's squires of honor, Leukios. He replied, "No ship is approaching, milord. She is docked."

"Docked? How did a ship come to dock?"

"By the normal routine. I engaged the magnetohydrodynamic field generators to create a helmet streamer reaching up past the base corona, to create a zone of colder plasma through which the vessel could descend. I posted a report an hour ago. Your seneschal refused to pass the message along, asserting that you had instructed all servant systems to leave you in private."

With another segment of his mind he ran an identity check. Since the Sophotechs were absent, he was not sure to whom he spoke, what type or level of mind, nor what the voice symbols were supposed to indicate, but the answer came back: "Helion, your guest is protected under the protocols of the masquerade. Identification is not available."

"Tell me where this intruder is, at least?"

"That is beyond the scope of my duties."

"Then switch me to your supervisor."

"My supervisor is Helion of the Silver-Gray, who is the only sapient being aboard the Array at this time. . . ."

With a third segment of mind, simultaneously, he queried his Coryphaeus, a partial mind tasked with counting and coordinating the motions of men and animals throughout the unmeasured vastness of Solar Array habitat space. Helion was old enough to remember

the days when police minds and watchman circuits were
necessary to ensure that people would not violate the
property or privacy of another. His Coryphaeus also
had a security submind, dating from the late Sixth
Era, one of the oldest servants of the many in Helion's
employ.

"Your visitor is now a hundred twenty-eight meters
away from you, approaching along the main axial corridor of the command section, Golden Elder Strand
Zero Center, Heliopolis Major."

"Here, in other words, within my private sanctum?"

"Yes, milord."

"Why was an intruder allowed to pass my doors? Why
wasn't he stopped at the outer atrium, at the inner gate, at
the command doors, or at my privacy doors?"

The Coryphaeus answered in its archaic accent: "By
your instruction."

"My instruction . . . ? I told you all to guard my
solitude."

"In the case where two orders contradict, I am to
assent to the higher priority. This order is of the highest class of priority I recognize. I shall repeat the
text."

Helion's own voice, blurred and faint as if from an
ancient recording, came then, and the words were in
an older rhythm, with words and expressions Helion
had not used for four thousand years. He almost did
not recognize the voice as his own, so different was it
from his present way of speaking: ". . . I tell you, if
ever when my best-loved friend should come again,
whole or partial or anysomeway that be, hale him
within, and let him pass. Let pass all doors and barri-
cados, open firewalls, bridge delays, but bring him to
me in all haste, or any who presents himself as him:
he has priority higher than anything else I am doing
or shall do hereafter, if only he will come again! If
only he would call! Let be admitted any who come

under the name of Hyacinth-Subhelion Septimus Gray. . . . "

Then the Coryphaeus asked, "Those are your orders, eight thousand years old, but never revoked. What are your orders now?"

Hyacinth-Subhelion Septimus Gray. It was the name of a dead man.

Helion said, "How can it be Hyacinth?"

The Coryphaeus replied, "It was not said that this was Hyacinth, sir, only that this visitor is wearing the identity of Hyacinth, and in a fashion allowed by the masquerade. What are your orders?"

He heard the footsteps sounding on the balcony in the distance. Through an archway, lit by windows of fire to either side, a figure now came forward, and paused.

Helion rose to his feet, staring. With an abrupt gesture, he turned a mirror toward the figure, as if to amplify the view and see the other's face more closely; but then he stopped. It was a violation of Silver-Gray forms of politeness to examine a guest by remote viewers, or speak by wire, when the other came for a face-to-face meeting.

Helion saw only a Silver-Gray cloak, trimmed richly with gold and green, and a glimpse of pale white armor beneath. It was a fashion Hyacinth himself used to affect, in the days just after he had lost the right to be Helion, but he still dressed and looked as much like Helion as copyright and sumptuary laws would allow.

The hooded figure stood on the balcony, motionless, perhaps watching Helion as closely as the other watched him.

Helion said to his Coryphaeus: "I will receive the visitor. Admit him."

And a bridge extended from the rotunda across the wide space to the balcony.

3.

Helion watched the white-cloaked figure approaching. He turned off his sense filter for a moment and examined the visitor's true shape: a squat, pyramidal body, made of carbon-silicon, approaching through an opaque, dense medium that filled this place. Helion was not using sight (normal vision was not possible here) but was using echolocation.

The body told him nothing. Anyone entering the special environment of the Solar Array would have to adjust his body to this configuration; materials and routines for making the transmogrification were found aboard every drop ship in solsynchronous orbit.

Helion turned his sense filter back on. The hooded figure now stood not ten meters away, at the foot of the little hill of tiered thought boxes on which Helion had his throne.

Helion spoke first: "Is this some ghost I see before me, stirred up from some unquiet archive? Wakened, perhaps, by some unexpected power Earthmind has unleashed on this, the last night before we drown our separate humanity in all-embracing glory? If so, go back! Return to whatever museum or noumenal casket had carried your dead thoughts through all these years. The dead have nothing to say to the living."

A neutral voice came from the hood. It was sent as text, but Helion's sense filter interpreted it as a voice, did not add any detail of inflection, pitch, or rhythm. It sounded like a ghost talking indeed. "The dead can allow the living to recall the lives they used to live. Dead loved ones can warn the living of loves they are soon to lose."

"Who are you?"

The cold and eerie voice came again: "Does my appearance frighten you? I had to assume this shape to be allowed to pass your doors. I cannot appear in my own shape; a terrible fate befalls whoever beholds me as I am!"

Helion squinted. "That is a line from one of Daphne's Gothic melodramas. *Owlswick Abbey*—she wrote the scene flowchart script."

"Many name her as the finest authoress of this time. I do her no dishonor to speak words she invents."

Helion, with deliberate slowness, resumed his seat, and now he leaned his elbow upon his throne arm, hiding a half smile behind his knuckle, looking up from beneath his brow.

"And what is this warning you come to bring me, old ghost?"

"Just this: Do not lose your son, Phaethon, as you lost your bosom friend Hyacinth. Do not lose yourself. Phaethon knows the dying thought of your former self: you and he spoke just before you died, during a storm when no recording systems were alert. With that thought you can reconstruct your memory by extrapolation; you can become what Helion would have been, had he lived. The Curia will call you Helion and grant you his name and place and face and property. Otherwise, you are Helion Secundus, and Phaethon takes all your fortune with him into exile; this Solar Array, Helion's house and memory caskets, riches, copyrights, thoughtrights, everything! But if you agree to loan Phaethon funds enough to buy his starship's debts, and give him once again clear title to the vessel, he will tell all he knows, or, if that fails to make you into Helion, he will award to you your fortunes nonetheless."

Helion stared down for a time at the robed and hooded figure. Then he let free a sigh, and spoke in a tired tone: "Daphne, you know I cannot agree to those terms. I swore, long ago, to uphold the establishment of the College of Hortators, as our only dike against the tide of inhumanity which waits to inundate us.

That oath I shall not breach, not even to regain my true self again, not while I love honor more than life."

Daphne threw back the hood she wore, and signaled a waiver of her masquerade. Helion saw her face and heard her voice. "You are now in exile if you knowingly consort with me," she said. "But I think you should join us: Temer Lacedaimon is here, outside, beyond the pale, and so is Aurelian Sophotech!"

"What?!!"

"Yes!"

"That means the Transcendance . . . "

She shook her head, her smile flashed. "Will not include the Hortators. They will not be in our future, then, will they? Or will you join the boycott yourself, and let the future you dreamed up, the one the Peers love so much, just go to waste, unheard?"

Helion frowned. "I should cut you out from my sense filter now, and hear no more of this . . . but . . . Aurelian in exile? He communicates with the Earthmind. Is she in exile now, too?"

"Why do you think none of the Sophotechs is speaking?"

"I thought they were preparing for the Transcendance . . . "

"They are preparing for war!"

There was a pause while Helion's language routine brought that word up out of ancient memory, and checked the connotations for him. He said, "You do not call Phaethon's conflict with the Hortotors a war, do you? This is not a metaphor."

"I mean war with the Second Oecumene, which killed my horse and tricked the Hortators into banishing Phaethon. The attack on him was real! Everything Phaethon said was true! Why didn't you believe him, just believe him, instead of listening to other folk?! He would never have disbelieved, no matter what, in you!"

The sophistication of Helion's mental system allowed him to embrace sudden revolutions of outlook without disorientation. Assistance circuits in his thalamus and hypothalamus made connections, reassessed emotional reactions, calculated a multitude of implications.

Because of this, he straightened on his throne and spoke in a calm, quick voice: "It took ten thousand years for the Last Broadcast to reach Sol from Cygnus X-1. Vafnir's people sent one-way robot vessels, which, moving at far less than the speed of light, arrived some thirty thousand years after the death broadcast was received. Long enough for some sort of civilization to revive.

"No civilization answered their requests to build a breaking laser. The vessels fell through the dark Swan system with their light-sails spread wide, and to this day continue to infinity . . . as the probes passed the Cygnus X-1 system, their readings showed conditions were indeed as the Last Broadcast depicted. No sign of industrial activity, no radio noise. Silence. Death.

"But the survivors of that event might have hidden themselves. It would not be difficult. The signals of an extrasystemic civilization, especially one ten thousand light-years away, could easily escape the notice of our astronomers."

Daphne said, "Or the messages supposedly sent back from the robot probes had not come from them at all. The probes could have been destroyed. Their message content could have been forged. We are talking about a thousand light-years away, right? It can't have been a very strong or complex signal. And our astronomers are picking it up one hundred centuries after it was sent."

"In either case"—his eyes glittered dangerously—"we are assuming an entire culture willing to go to extraordinary lengths to remain hidden. If that is so, what strategies would they have adopted? I submit that the

Silent Oecumene would have, if they could afford the resources, both sent out additional colonies, in order to disperse their numbers, and posted watchers—what is the old term for it—?"

Daphne knew the word. "Spies."

"Thank you. And posted spies within our Oecumene, to negate any efforts which might lead to their discovery."

"You said the Silent Ones might have established colonies . . . ? Just like what Phaethon wanted. . . . Where? How many?"

Helion raised his hand and sent an image into her sense filter. Suddenly the rotunda where they were now seemed to float in deep space, with stars overhead and underfoot, a wide, three-dimensional array.

Helion said, "Here is Cygnus X-1. Observe; I surround it with concentric bubbles of possible travel times for ships of the type of Ao Ormgorgon's *Naglfar,* built with Fifth Era technology. Likely candidates for star colonies are shown in white. . . . I now rank the possible colony stars according to their desirability as hiding places, not as colonies, taking into account the presence of nebular dust and natural sources of radio noise which might mask large-scale industrial activity from Golden Oecumene astronomers."

A sphere appeared around Cygnus X-1, and stars within the sphere were lit with ranking numerals. Slender lines from Cygnus X-1 showed possible travel paths, none intruding anywhere near the space near Sol.

Helion continued: "Now then, making a rough estimate of the natural resources of the Silent Oecumene (and they do have limits on their resources—their black hole can produce tremendous useful energy, but it is nevertheless immobile), I conclude that, of these possible target stars, and assuming expeditions the size of the multigeneration ship *Naglfar,* there could be between five hundred and twelve hundred colonial systems, with at least two hundred expeditions still in flight, and destined to reach their targets over the next three millennia. . . . "

More figures and light signs appeared near certain of the stars, and certain travel paths lit up, showing the locations of possible expeditions still in flight.

"If we assume a less cost intensive method of spread, such as, for example, microscopic nanotechnology spore packages wafted through space on stellar winds or propelled by light-sail launching lasers, the possible zone of colonies is smaller, because the travel time is larger. . . . " A littler sphere of light, smaller than the first, appeared around Cygnus X-1. This one did not even reach all the way back to Sol.

Helion said, "So we can assume the colonization takes place by shipping."

Daphne had not finished upbraiding Helion about his conduct toward Phaethon, and wanted to get back to the subject of the bargain she wished to compel him to accept. But, nonetheless, she found herself distracted by the scope of Helion's speculations.

"So the Silent Oecumene is . . . what . . . ? An interstellar empire?"

"I don't know. The planets would be too far from each other to be subject to central imperial control, nor would they be able to aid each other with mutually beneficial resources. The distances are simply too great. However, a society organized by Sophotechs, or even by immortal men with a fixed tenacity of purpose, could establish such colonies in order to fulfill some plan requiring thousands or millions of years to accomplish."

Daphne tried to imagine an undertaking on such a vast scale. "What purpose . . . ?"

"I do not know. But, assume it is one which is consistent with their desire to remain hidden. Why? Because they fear competition with us? But how can anyone in their right mind fear the Golden Oecumene? We are the most tolerant and fair-minded of all possible civilizations."

Daphne said, "In your view of the future, the one you were going to offer the Transcendence . . . ?"

"Go on."

"How long would it be before the Golden Oecumene would expand beyond the Solar System?"

"Not until primary sources of energy in the sun were exhausted. What would be the need?"

"So, perhaps five or ten billion years . . . ? Extrapolate the growth of the Silent Oecumene in the surrounding stars by that time."

Light-signs appeared on all the surrounding stars. There were no worthwhile stars left free in any area surrounding Sol; the Solar System was surrounded.

Daphne said, "Now, would anyone in the Golden Oecumene take a planet, or trespass on another's property, or take anything at all, just because they needed it, no matter how badly they needed it, without the consent of the owner?"

"We are not barbarians."

"So we'll be trapped with nowhere to go, held back by our principles, confined to a system with a dying star. And all because we did not have the foresight to do as Phaethon wishes."

Helion said, "Phaethon's wishes are what triggered the conflict. If the plan of the Silent Oecumene required them to stay hidden for millions or billions of years, until they could achieve a supremacy throughout all of nearby space, why risk it all, why risk generations of planning, just to strike down Phaethon? Here is why." He pointed once again to the sphere of light centered on Cygnus X-1. "This defines the greatest extent to which the Silent Oecumene could expand as of now. Here marks were they could be in five millennia, ten, fifty. This outermost globe embraces all the useful planet-bearing stars within about five thousand light-years. And here is where Phaethon, with the *Phoenix Exultant,* could plant colonies in fifty millennia. . . . "

A wide zone of gold-colored light spread out from Sol and kept spreading, reached past the outermost limit of the other sphere and kept reaching. "Here he is in one hundred millennia. . . . "

The sphere of gold now reached beyond the edge of the projection and seemed to fill the night.

Helion said, "And I cannot show where Phaethon will be in five hundred millennia without reducing the scale of the model. It would be a major segment of this arm of the galaxy. Do you see why they came forward to stop him? Because once he was gone from this system, no other ship could ever catch him, no one could overtake him. Not in that ship."

"You are assuming they could not build a ship like the *Phoenix Exultant*?"

"I suspect their technological level to be less than ours. If they equaled us, why would they hide? And secrecy maintained so diligently across a reach of centuries bespeaks a strong central government, which implies diminished personal liberty, therefore lack of innovation, therefore stagnation. I don't care how smart their Sophotechs might be; even Sophotechs cannot change the laws of physics or the laws of economics, politics, and liberty. I think they have no ship like the *Phoenix Exultant*. I think they have no men like Phaethon. I do not know what motivates the Silent Ones, or who or what they are. I do not know how long they have been among us, watching us, perhaps influencing us in subtle ways. The only thing I do know, based on what has provoked them to stir from their hiding, is that they fear Phaethon."

He waved his hand at the illusion of stars around him. "He can make all their dreams of empire go away." He closed his fist. The stars vanished. Normal light returned.

Daphne put her hands on her hips and scowled. "Well, if they hate him, they must love you! You and your Hortators were all set to stop Phaethon and kill off his dream. You made him mortal and threw him into the gutter to die. You did all the Silent Oecumene's work for them! You!"

Helion said gravely, "Tragic circumstance forced our hands. We were seeking to preserve this, the best of civilizations the mind of man can conceive. And even then we offer Phaethon no harm; we merely refused to help him endanger our lives, and urged others not to help him either. Can we be blamed for that?"

Daphne's eyes flashed. "Blame? It is not illegal to be a coward, if that is what you mean! Or a hypocrite. But I would not do everything the law allows, not things I thought were wrong; and you your whole life have said that people ought to avoid what's wrong and ugly and base and inhuman, whether it's legally allowed or not. You said it often enough. An easy thing to say. Hard to do."

Helion's brows drew together. "If I erred in respect to Phaethon, it was an error of fact, not an error of principle. A fact I did not know, nor did anyone in the Golden Oecumene know, was that the Silent Oecumene still somehow survived, and, apparently, has hostile designs upon us. Because of that lucky accident, Phaethon's dangerous dream now does us more good than harm; but if the facts had been as I, before this moment, thought them, than that danger would have done us no good, nor would Phaethon have been right to expose us to it."

Daphne said, "There is a lie at the bottom of everything you say. It is not war you fear, interstellar war: Phaethon never planned for that, and war is not inevitable, just because people are different. War was just an excuse. It's freedom you fear. Lack of control. After uncounted centuries of hatred and violence, viciousness and powerlust, the Sophotechs finally led us to a society which people had never been honest enough, logical enough, to make for themselves. A society where no one, no one at all, can force anyone to do anything, except to stop the use of force. But that wasn't good enough for you! You made your Silver-Gray and your past-looking, romantic movement in art and sociometry, and tried to talk everyone into living in the past. And that wasn't enough for you, either. You and your friends, Orpheus and Vafnir and all that crew, decided to persuade where you could not force, but your goal was the same. You and your College of Hortators were going to use public opinion as a weapon, to bludgeon into the ground anyone who questioned the precious way of life you wanted to set up! Anyone who challenged it! Anyone who wanted to spread it to the stars! But you did not want the freedom you said you were protecting, not for Phaethon! Oh, no! Because there cannot be any pressure of public opinion among the worlds of distant suns; the news is too slow, space is too big. There can still be a government among the stars, if it is a government like ours—small, unobtrusive, utterly scrupulous, unable to do anything except defend the peace, unable to use force except to stop force. Because, with a government like that, wide distance and lack of communication simply do not matter. But what there cannot be among the stars are these things: a College of Hortators; a monopoly, like yours, on Solar Storm control; or a monopoly, as Orpheus has, on eternal life; Vafnir's control over energy sources; Ao Aoen's entertainment empire. And so on."

Helion said mildly, "The danger of violence is still real, if we expand. Don't the actions of the Silent Oecumene spies and agents among us prove that?"

"Our ability to survive violence expands also. Ever since the invention of the atomic bomb, humanity had the power to destroy a planet. But no one can destroy a whole night sky filled with living stars!"

Helion said, "What the Sophotechs gave us is not just a government of endless liberty but also, if I may add, endless libertines. They also gave us, for the first time, an ability to control the precise shape of our destiny, to predict the course of the future, and, if we use it wisely, the power to preserve our beautiful Golden Oecumene against all shocks and horrors. But control is the key. With Sophotechnic help, I can control the raging chaos of the sun himself, and turn all the mindless forces of nature to our work. What Phaethon dreamt may now be needed, but it is still wild and overly ambitious. The fault is mine. He is much like me—me as I would be without a proper caution and sobriety to restrict my acts to those which serve the social good. He is a spirit of reckless fire. That we may now need him, that outside threats now force us to reconcile with him, does not make his recklessness, his heedlessness, his insubordination, somehow turn out to have been virtues all along."

Daphne crossed her arms, her eyes bright with mocking fury. "So that is going to be your apology for stealing Phaethon's immortality and throwing him to the dogs? 'Sorry, sonny boy, but we need you now, oh, and by the way, I was right all along'?!"

Helion's face grew dark with sorrow. He bowed his head. But all he said was, "The point is now an academic one. Phaethon's exile will no doubt be revoked, since the attack which prompted him to open his memory casket was, after all, quite real."

Daphne's angry voice snapped, "And you think that's it?! No apologies, no regrets?"

Helion spoke softly as if speaking to himself, "Do I regret my part in these events? Certainly I regret the events; but, as for my part, I played it as honorably as I knew how."

Then his voice grew louder. "And honor requires that I will not betray my oath to support the Hortators, even if Aurelian and Earthmind and all the world besides shuns me for so doing. Even if the Hortators are a weak and wicked instrument at times, and fall too harshly upon those who do not merit the punishment they give, yet, nonetheless, the Hortators are the only instrument we have for preserving decency, humanity, propriety, and wholesomeness of life. We would all be inside machines, drunk and mad on endless and perverted dreams, if it were not for them. Without them, there would be no control to this mad whirlwind we call life."

Daphne blazed: "Oh, great! That's an even better apology! " 'Tis not that I loved you less, O beloved Phaethon, but that I loved the Hortators more! (Sob!)' Hah! Those Hortators are just bullies, and you know it! So what if what they do is private, and legal, and noncoercive? They're the ones who are always saying that not everything which is legal is right! And I don't care whether you call it coercion or not, they certainly did not try to reason with Phaethon; they tried to overawe and cow him. Well, their system doesn't work too well on people who cannot be cowed! They were wrong, dead wrong. And so were you. Just wake up out of your moping, Helion, and just admit you were wrong."

"An apology . . . ? I would weep with joy to see my son again, for I still love him and he is still my son, but I will not stir once inch from the principles which fix my life in place. Son or no son, whether he is right or wrong does not depend on his ties of kinship with me." He stirred and raised his head and sighed, then shrugged and said, "But, no matter! This argument is stale. The deed is done; the point is moot."

Daphne's voice rang out clear and cold, "No, Helion! It is you who have become moot, your opinion on these matters which is academic! Phaethon builds well; this situation in which you find yourself was constructed by him. His amnesia, his submission to the Hortators at Lakshmi: he was not driven to these things by grief. It was done by calculation, carefully, dispassionately, and he used himself with the same ruthless efficiency he uses on the inanimate forces and materials around him to achieve his well-engineered designs. He wanted time to find a way to bring the *Phoenix Exultant* out of receivership; he wanted to disarm his opposition."

Helion said, "And where did his calculation go awry?"

Daphne laughed. "Nowhere! You will help and support Phaethon in his attempt, and pay his debts to free his ship, or you will step aside and watch as he takes your wealth, inherited by the legal ruling of the Court, and does it for you. Don't you see yet? Phaethon would never cheat you. He would never use the law in this way except to take back what was already promised him."

"Promised . . . ?"

"By you. In the last hour of your last life. During the hour you forgot."

"How can you know this?!"

Daphne smiled a winning smile: "Oh, come now! I know because he knows, and I have shared his memories, as is right with man and wife, during our voyage from Earth. He knows because you told him yourself. You told him the insight, the epiphany which made you laugh before you died, the secret of defeating chaos."

Helion was silent, troubled. The fact that he had given his word to Phaethon, even if he had forgotten what he swore, was not a small thing to him. Helion was not like other men: for him, the thought that his word would not prove good was intolerable.

But he said, "I have already rejected that bargain. Not even to save my soul, or keep my name intact, will I turn my back on what I swore to the Hortators."

"I will tell you anyway, because what you will or won't do does not matter. Listen:

4.

"You were burning in the middle of the worst solar storm our records can remember. Your deep probes had given you no advanced warning. In the complex and turbulent reactions seething at the center of the sun, you knew something outside the normal range of circumstances had occurred; some chance coincidence, constructive interference of two convection layers, perhaps, or a sudden cooling of large sections of the undermantle by a mere statistical freak, creating a layer inversion. Something the standard model did not and could not predict. Some tiny change, ever so tiny, leading to complex unpredictable results. In other words, chaos.

"Everyone else fled. All your companions and crew left you alone to wrestle with the storm.

"You did not blame them. In a moment of crystal insight, you realized that they were cowards beyond mere cowardice: their dependance on their immortality circuits had made it so that they could not even imagine risking their lives. They were all alike in this respect. They did not know they were not brave: they could not even think of dying as possible: how could they think of facing it, unflinching?

"You did not flinch. You knew you were going to die; you knew it when the Sophotechs, who are immune to pain and fear, all screamed and failed and vanished.

"And you knew, in that moment of approaching death, with all your life laid out like a single image for you to examine in a frozen moment of time, that no one was immortal, not ultimately, not really. The day may be far away, it may be further away that the dying of the sun, or the extinction of the stars, but the day will come when all our noumenal systems fail, our brilliant machines all pass away, and our records of ourselves and memories shall be lost.

"If all life is finite, only the grace and virtue with which it is lived matters, not the length. So you decided to stay another moment, and erect magnetic shields, one by one; to discharge interruption masses into the current, to break up the reinforcement patterns in the storm.

"Not life but honor mattered to you, Helion: so you stayed a moment after that moment, and then another.

"Voices from the radio screamed at you to transmit your mind to safety, beyond the range of danger. Growing static from the storm drowned out those voices; you laughed, because you, at that moment, were unable to comprehend what it was those voices feared.

"You saw the plasma errupting through shield after shield, almost as if some malevolent intelligence was trying to send a lance of fire to break your Solar Array in two, or vomit up outrageous flames to burn the helpless *Phoenix Exultant* where she lay at rest, hull open, fuel cells exposed to danger.

"Choas was attempting to destroy your life's work, and major sections of the Solar Array were evaporated. Chaos was attempting to destroy your son's lifework, and since he was aboard that ship, outside the range of any noumenal circuit, it would have destroyed your son as well.

"The Array was safe, but you stayed another moment, to try to deflect the stream of particles and shield your son; circuit after circuit failed, and still you stayed, playing the emergency like a raging orchestra.

When the peak of the storm was passed, it was too late for you: you had stayed too long; the flames were coming. But the radio-static cleared long enough for you to have last words with your son, whom you discovered, to your surprise, you loved better than life itself. In your mind, he was the living image of the best thing in you, the ideal you always wanted to achieve.

" 'Chaos has killed me, son,' you said, 'But the victory of unpredictability is hollow. Men imagine, in their pride, that they can predict life's each event, and govern nature and govern each other with rules of unyielding iron. Not so. There will always be men like you, my son, who will do the things no one else predicts or can control. I tried to tame the sun and failed; no one knows what is at its fiery heart; but you will tame a thousand suns, and spread mankind so wide in space that no one single chance, no flux of chaos, no unexpected misfortune, will ever have power enough to harm us all. For men to be civilized, they must be unlike each other, so that when chaos comes to claim them, no two will use what strategy the other does, and thus, even in the middle of blind chaos, some men, by sheer blind chance, if nothing else, will conquer.

" 'The way to conquer the chaos which underlies all the illusionary stable things in life, is to be so free, and tolerant, and so much in love with liberty, that chaos itself becomes our ally; we shall become what no one can foresee; and courage and inventiveness will be the names we call our fearless unpredictability. . . .'

"And you vowed to support Phaethon's effort, and you died in order that his dream might live."

8

THE TRUTH

1.

Daphne said, "Phaethon had outsmarted you, outsmarted the Hortators, the Curia, everyone. Because the real Helion, had he lived, would have helped Phaethon and funded the launch of the *Phoenix Exultant*. And there were only two possibilities. Either you become enough like the real Helion to satisfy the Curia, or you don't. If you don't, then you are legally dead, and Phaethon inherits your fortune, and the *Phoenix Exultant* flies. If you do, then you'll be like he was, and you'll support Phaethon, lend him your fortune, and still the *Phoenix Exultant* flies. Do you see why all your simulations trying to recreate your last thoughts, burning yourself again and again, never worked? Because, deep down, underneath the simulations, or before they began, or after they were over, your one thought was fear. You were afraid to lose yourself. Afraid to lose your identity. Afraid that Helion would be declared dead. But the real Helion did lose himself. He lost his identity, and his life, and everything. He was not afraid to die, much less to be declared dead. Don't you see? This attack by the Silent Oecumene, this weird, slow, hidden war we suddenly find ourselves in, does not change a single thing. If your last storm was caused by an unexpected malicious creature rather than an unexpected malicious whim of fate, it does not matter. Life is still unpredictable. The insight you had, the answer to how to fight against chaos, is the same. Let people like Phaethon establish their own order in the midst of the confusion of the world."

Helion had bowed his head, and placed one hand before his eyes. Daphne could see no expression. His shoulders moved. Was it tears? Rage? Laughter? Daphne could not determine.

Daphne said cautiously, "Helion? What is your answer?"

Helion did not respond or look up.

At that same moment, however, there came an interruption.

Two of the energy mirrors in Helion's field of vision lit up with images. One showed, against a starry field, the foreshortened view of a blade of dark gold, with a brilliant fire before it like a small sun.

The rate-of-change figures were astonishing. The object was on a path from transjovial space, normally a two- or three-day voyage. This ship had crossed that distance in under five hours.

This was the *Phoenix Exultant,* her drives before her, her prow pointed away, decelerating. There seemed to be a halo of lightning around her; charged particles emitted by the sun were being deflected by her hull armor, and the ship had such velocity, and solar space was so thick with particles, that the *Phoenix Exultant,* flying through a vacuum, was creating a wake. Views to either side, in other color schemes, showed other bands of radiation, diagrams of projected paths.

The *Phoenix* was descending into the sun.

The other mirror that had lit displayed a figure in

black armor, the faceplate opened to reveal a lined, harsh, gray-eyed face.

Helion said, "What is this apparition from the past, who comes now so boldly past my doors and wards? By what right do you interrupt where I have asked for privacy, you who wear a face out of forgotten bloody history?"

A slight tension around the corners of the mouth might have been a smile or a grimace of impatience. "This is my own face, sir."

"Good heavens! Atkins?! Have they allowed someone like you to live again?! That means . . ."

Daphne said softly: "It means war. 'War and bloodshed, terror and fear; the wailing of widows, the clash of the spear . . .' "

Atkins said: "I've never been away, sir. I don't know why you people think I vanish just because you don't need me." He gave an imperceptible movement of a shoulder; his version of a shrug. "No matter. I'm interrupting to tell you you're in grave danger and to ask you to cooperate. There may be a Silent Oecumene thinking machine, called the Nothing Sophotech, hidden inside the sun. We don't know what kind of vehicle or equipment or weaponry it has. So far, Silent Oecumene technology has proven able to introduce signals into the shielded interior of circuits, by either teleporting through, or creating electric charges out of, the base-vacuum rest state. We think they can do this for other particle types as well, and we don't know their range and limitations. The last solar storm, the one that killed the previous Helion, was created and directed by their technology. The Silent Ones are in a position to seize control of the Solar Array. If they do that, especially during the Transcendence, when everyone's brains will be linked up to an interplanetary communication web . . . well, you can imagine the results.

From the Array, they could induce prominences to destroy Vafnir's counterterragenesis stations at Mercury Forward Equilateral, crippling our antimatter supplies at the same time. In any case, I'd like to ask you to cooperate. . . ."

"I know you from old, Captain Atkins. Or is it 'Marshal' now? You want me to stay here, in harm's way, until the enemy commits himself. Then when he reveals himself by striking at me, you promise to avenge my death by utterly annihilating him, is that it? I do not recall that your somewhat Pyrrhic strategy of winning was all that successful at New Kiev, was it?"

"I'm not going to debate old battles with you, sir. But the Earthmind told me you might cooperate. I told her I was sick of trying to deal with you people who do not seem to understand that sometimes, when the cold facts demand it, you have to risk your life or give your life to win the battle. Since you remember me, Helion, you remember why I say that."

There was something very cold in his tone of voice. Daphne looked back and forth between these two eldest men, wondering what past was between them.

Helion's expression softened. "I remember the kind of sacrifices you were willing to make, Captain Atkins." His expression grew distant, thoughtful. "It is odd. You also stand your ground when everyone else runs away to save themselves, I suppose. We may be more alike than I supposed. What a frightening thought!"

"Are you all done kidding around there, sir, or do you want to help?"

Helion straightened. "I will not desert my Oecumene or my post. Tell me what service I can perform for you. Though I think I can guess. . . ."

"Don't bother guessing. I'll tell you. Phaethon is about to dock that monster ship he's flying at your number six Equatorial Main two-fifty. It's the only place big enough for the *Phoenix Exultant*."

"You need to give me more time. I have to use my field generators to create a sunspot underneath you as you descend, a cooler area, with a helmet streamer to create a flow of cooler plasma, a stream the *Phoenix* can follow to come down here to my dock."

"Don't bother. Phaethon says the *Phoenix Exultant* can descend through the corona without damage. But once we dock, I want you to provision him with what he needs: you can spare the antimatter, I take it?"

"I can spare it," said Helion wryly. His Array controlled thousands of masses of antimatter the size of gas giants.

"And give him your latest intelligence on submantle conditions. The Nothing Sophotech must know we're coming; Earthmind thinks the approach of the *Phoenix* might tempt the Nothing to show itself. It will probably try to corrupt your whole Array and take control of you personally, if it hasn't already done so."

"It has not, to my knowledge."

"That doesn't mean much, in this day and age. The other thing I want you to do is direct as many deep probes as you can toward the solar core, to see if we can find any echotrace of the Silent Oecumene ship. All we have right now is a location; we don't know size or what else is there. Also, examine your record to see if any suspicious astronomical bodies fell into the sun in any place your sensors could have seen."

"What else?"

"You stay up top while the *Phoenix* goes down through the chromosphere into the radiative layer of the core, where the enemy is hiding. You will act as our sounding station, and meteorological eyes-up."

"With no one to help me? It seems a little odd, on a day when everyone else is celebrating, not to sound a universal alarm and call to arms?"

"I think so, too. But the Nothing, smart as it is, may not know how much we know, and if it thinks the Transcendence is going to go off as usual, it may hold its fire until everyone is linked up into one big helpless Transcendent mind. Got it? I don't want to set off the alarm if that will make the Nothing set off its biggest guns."

Helion was silent, thoughtful.

Atkins said, "Well? That's what I want from you. You have a problem with any of this?"

"I have no doubts or reservations. You are not the only one who knows what the word 'duty' means, Captain Atkins."

"Great. And just between you and me, since you're in such a giving mood today . . ."

"Yes . . . ?"

"Say you're sorry to your kid. He's been moping around ever since we set course for the sun, and it's getting on my nerves. I mean, it would be good for morale."

With another segment of his mind, Helion made contact with his lawyer and accountant subroutines. Aloud, he said, "Very well! You may tell my son, by way of apology, that, by the time he docks at number six, his debts will be cleared, his title reinstated, and the ship he is in shall belong to him once more."

2.

Helion came out of the place still called an air lock, even though it included transformation surgeries, noumenal transfer pools, body shops, neural prosthetics manufactories, and other functions needed to adapt a visitor to the physical environment and mental format of the *Phoenix Exultant*. This air lock was housed amidships, projecting inward from the hull nine hundred feet, a direction that was, at the moment "down," and surrounded by other housings and machines, all looming like the skyscrapers of some ancient city turned on its head.

Phaethon stood not far away, on a walkway that ran from upside-down rooftop to upside-down rooftop. Behind him, underfoot, far below the fragile railing, rested the fuel cells of the *Phoenix Exultant*. These cells reached away to each side beyond sight, like an endless beehive of interlocking pyramids, each with a ball of luminous metallic ice at its center.

Helion thought this made a fitting backdrop for his scion—a landscape of frozen antimaterial fire, endless energy held in rigid geometry, capable of vast triumphs or vast destruction. Phaethon wore his gold-adamantium-and-black armor, helmet folded away. He stood with his hands clasped behind his back, legs spread, eyes intent and bright; the pose of a youth patiently ready for action.

Helion had dressed in the air lock, constructing a human body (modified for the high solar gravity) and Victorian semiformal dress suit. (Day clothes, of course. Helion long ago determined that no gentleman would sport evening wear while in or near the sun.) He had also constructed a valid legal copy of the receipts for Phaethon's debts, and the petition to the Bankruptcy Court to remove the *Phoenix Exultant* from receivership. These he had formed to look like golden parchment, stamped with the proper seals and red ribbon.

He held up this document, and extended it toward Phaethon.

Before he could say a word, however, Phaethon stepped forward, ignoring the document, and threw his arms around his father. Helion, surprised, raised his arms and embraced his son.

"I never thought I would see you again," said one of them.

"Nor I," said the other.

The document in Helion's hand was quite crumpled and mussed by the time they stepped apart, and Helion dabbed his joy-wet eyes with it, before he recalled what it was, and extended it sheepishly to his son.

"Thank you, Father; this is the finest of presents," said Phaethon, accepting the crumpled and tearstained mass with a grave and solemn expression.

Phaethon looked up. "And Daphne . . . ?"

Helion nodded at the air lock hatch behind him. "She is still getting changed. You know how women are; she's picking skin color and skeletal structures. I suppose she is trying to find a body which will look as good in this gravity as a Martian's." (Martian women were notoriously vain of the buoyant good looks their low gravity imparted.)

Phaethon looked pensively at the air lock door. Helion, seeing that look, smiled to himself.

Helion stepped to the rail. "What is the meaning of this intricate activity?" he said, pointing upward.

"Mm?" Phaethon pulled his gaze reluctantly away from the air lock door. "Ah, that. The *Phoenix Exultant* is installing her solar bathyspheric modifications. There, ranged along the inner hull, are magnetic induction generators. This will create a field along the hull which will act like the treads of a burrowing vehicle, using magnetic current to force dense plasma to either side of the ship, propelling her forward and downward."

"Crawling your way into the sun?"

They both wore the same expression of ironic humor. "If you like," Phaethon nodded.

"Your refrigeration lasers, I trust, will be adequate to the task? The geometry of your hull does not minimize surface area. Also, the increasing heat of each successive layer as you approach the core exceeds the drive combustion heat of, at least, my bathyspheric probes."

Phaeton pointed. "Can you see about forty kilometers aft of us? That is the line of advancing workers clearing an insulation space of a half kilometer inward of every hull surface, which I intend to flood with superconductive liquid. This liquid will circulate heat to my port and starboard drive cores, which I am using as heat sinks. The centerline drive core will be used as a refrigeration laser, and can easily generate heat greater than the solar core."

Helion did a few hundred calculations in his head, frowned at the answers he got, and said, "So great a volume? With your hull, I would have thought your reflective albedo would near one hundred per cent. Why are you taking in so much heat?"

Phaethon pointed overhead and sent a signal into Helion's sense filter, to show him exterior camera views of work being done outside the hull. "My communication antennae and thought ports are being replaced by crystalline adamantium optic fibers of a bore too large to allow the thought ports to close. I will be taking in heat at these places."

Helions said slowly, "Why in the world are you entering combat with the Second Oecumene Sophotech—who, from what Atkins told me, excels at many forms of virus combat and mind war—with your thought ports jammed open? You will not be able to cut off your ship's mind from external communication, unless your circuit breakers are—"

"The circuit breakers have been replaced by multiple alternate lines of hardwire, welded point to point. There is no way to break the circuit. There is no way to shut out external communication from inside. The hardwire connections cannot even be physically wrecked faster than they can regrow."

"But . . . why?"

"Because this is not going to be a combat. It will be something much more definitive and permanent."

"I do not understand. Please explain it to me."

But at that moment, the air lock door opened, and there was Daphne, radiantly beautiful, her eyes alight with cool joy.

Phaethon stared, a smile growing on his features, as if he were storing the image of Daphne at the threshold in his permanent long-term memory. She wore a short-sleeved blouse and long skirt of pale silken fabric, crisp and shining, and a beribboned straw skimmer of the type called a sun hat. Despite the high gravity, she had somehow designed her feet and ankles to be able to wear high-heeled pumps. She stood smiling, her eyes twinkling, one hand raised to hold her hat to her head, as if she expected some impossible breeze to blow through the deck.

Phaethon stepped forward, arms raised as if to embrace her. "Darling, I have so much to tell you. . . ."

She fended him off with her free hand. "Aren't you going to introduce me to your father? Hello, Helion!"

Phaethon stepped back, puzzled. He said, "What? You know him. You were just in the air lock with him."

Helion said dryly to Daphne, "Don't toy with the boy. He's confused enough as it is. I'm trying to learn his master plan for how he intends to survive the next few hours." With an ostentatious gesture, Helion draw out his pocketwatch, clicked open the cover, scrutinized the dial. "Please consummate your kissing and making up with dispatch. I'd like to conclude my conversation with him."

Daphne put her hands on her hips, glaring at Helion, "Hmph! And what makes you think, may I ask, that I'd kiss and make up with a single-minded, pigheaded clod who does not have the sense to see what's right in front of his nose, who keeps running off, getting in trouble, getting lost, getting shot at, losing and finding bits and pieces of his memory he cannot keep straight, ruining parties, building starships, starting wars, upsetting everybody, and who keeps saying I'm not his wife whenever he's losing any arguments with me, which he does all the time?!"

Phaethon, from behind her, took her shoulders in his strong hands, and turned her body to face him, taking her in his arms, despite any protest or struggle she might have made. She put her little fists against his chest, and pushed, but in the heavy gravity, she only succeeding in losing her balance, and she found herself standing on tiptoe, both leaning backward and pressed up against him, caught in the magnificent strength of his arms.

He lowered his head and stared into her eyes. "I think you will," he said softly. "You are the only version, the only person, who has ever urged me to pursue my dream; you are the only person whom I would forgo that dream to possess. I saw the first during our long trip together from Earth; to recognize the second, it required me to see myself when another man was possessed by my thoughts. Those thoughts were always of you, my darling, my best, my beloved. And it is not the old Daphne whom I loved, whom I love now, but you. I will say one last time that you are not my wife; because I married her, your elder version, not you. You I shall marry, if you will have me; and then I will never call you anything other than my wife, my beloved wife, again."

Her eyes were shining, drinking in the sight of him, and her cheeks had blushed a delicate rose hue. She shrugged her shoulders a bit, as if trying to get away, but her hands were pinned by his embrace. "You take me a lot for granted, mister. . . ." she said. Her voice was breathless. "What if I say no?"

"I offer, as my gift to the bride, my life and my ship and my future, all for you to share with me, and every star in the night sky. What is your answer?"

When she parted her lips to speak, he kissed her. Whatever words she may have wished to say were smothered into little happy moans. Perhaps he knew what her answer would be.

Her straw hat fell lightly from her tilting head and fluttered to the walkway. The two ribbons of the bow were twined around each other, snarled into one.

Helion politely turned his back, and pretended to consult his pocketwatch. "Isn't it more traditional for the man to kneel on occasions of this nature?" he inquired of no one in particular.

Diomedes of Neptune and a mannequin representing Marshal Atkins came out from a nearby railway terminal and began sliding along the surface of the walkway toward them.

Helion walked toward the two men, using a mental command to nullify the action of the surface substance of the walkway, which otherwise would have carried him forward without effort. His love of discipline required that he avoid, when he could, such artificial aids for walking.

Atkins saw what was taking place over Helion's shoulder, dug in his heel as a signal to stop the walkway. Either through politeness or embarrassment, Atkins cleared his throat, clasped his hands behind his back, and stepped to one side of Helion, turning to face him, so that he was not looking at the source of the moans, giggles, and murmurs beyond.

Atkins said to Helion, "I've examined your records. You'll be happy to know that the previous Sophotechs working on this station were not destroyed because of catastrophic failure of the energy environment, as you thought. They committed suicide in order to stop the spread of the mental virus which had taken control of them. They were gambling that your previous version would be able to quell the storm without their aid. The good news there is that means your present system looks secure. In order to drive the *Phoenix Exultant* down toward the core, we need you to use your Array to create a subduction current in the plasma, large enough and fast enough—a whirlpool, actually—to suck the ship down into the location in the outer core radiative zone where the enemy is waiting. Can you do it?"

"I can bring two equatorial currents into offset collision to create a vortex whose core will have low density, creating a sunspot large enough to swallow planets whole. How far down into the opaque deep of the sun I can drive the vortex funnel, or what unprecedented storms and helmet streamers will result, remains yet to be seen. Hello, Captain Atkins. It is good to see you. How do you do? I am fine, thank you. I see the passing centuries have not altered your ... ah ... refreshingly brusque manners."

Atkins's face was stony. "Some of us don't think polished formalities are the most important thing in life, if you don't mind my saying so, sir. Not when there is a war on."

Helion arched an eyebrow. "Indeed, sir? Those niceties which make us civilized, in the opinion of many accomplished and profound thinkers, are of more importance during emergencies than otherwise. And if not to protect civilization, what justification does the mass slaughter called war ever have?"

"Don't start with me, Mr. Rhadamanth. This is an emergency."

Diomedes, meanwhile, was leaning to look behind Helion, staring with open fascination at the display Phaethon and Daphne made. "I have not seen nonparthenogenic bioforms before. Are they going to copulate?"

Atkins and Helion looked at him, then looked at each other. A glance of understanding passed between them.

Atkins put his hand on Diomedes's elbow, and pulled him back in front of Helion. "Perhaps not at this time," Atkins said, straight-faced.

"They are young and in love," explained Helion, stepping so as to block Diomedes's view. "So perhaps the excesses and, ah, exuberance of their, ah, greeting, can be overlooked this once."

Diomedes craned his neck, trying to peer past Helion. "There's nothing like that on Neptune."

Helion murmured, "Perhaps certain peculiarities of the Neptunian character are thereby clarified, hmm . . . ?"

"It looks very old-fashioned," said Diomedes.

Helion said, "It is that most ancient and most precious romantic character of mankind which impels all great men to their greatness."

Atkins said, "It's what young men do before they go to war."

Diomedes said, "It is not the way Cerebellines or Compositions or Hermaphrodites or Neptunians arrange these matters. I'm not sure I see the value of it. But it looks interesting. Do all Silver-Gray get to do that? I wonder if Phaethon would mind if I helped him."

"He'd mind." Atkins interrupted curtly. "Really. He'd mind."

"Upon this occasion, I feel I must agree with Captain Atkins," added Helion.

The two men exchanged a glance. The tension which had been in their features just a moment ago was gone. They were both very old men; Helion had been four hundred years old when noumenal immortality had been invented; Atkins, living then as an artificially preserved brain inside a battle cyborg, was rumored to be even older. They both remembered a time when things were different.

Helion almost smiled. "I can create a vortex to pull the *Phoenix Exultant* down toward the outer core layers. I can do whatever else cruel necessity demands. I can send, without any outward tear, my son to battle and perhaps to death in the dark, unquiet depths of this

hellish sphere, vaster than worlds, this universe of ele-
mental fire which I have tamed. But I quite assure you
that I shall know a reason why."

Atkins said, "I'm hoping Phaethon will brief us and
catch us up to speed. He said he would."

Helion interrupted in surprise, "Marshal! You mean
this is no plan of yours? Where are the Sophotechs?
Where is the Parliament? Surely this voyage must be
made under military command?!"

Grim lines gathered around Atkins's mouth, and his
eyes twinkled. This was his sign of extreme amusement, what other men would have shown by loud tri-
umphant laughter. "Well, sir, it's good to know that
you have so much faith in me. But the War Mind told
me we did not have the budget to prosecute the campaign in the way I wanted—besieging the sun, using
the Array to stir up the core, and relying on ground-
based energy systems in the meanwhile—and the simulations showed my plan might lead to the destruction
and loss of one fifth of the minds in the Transcendence, and the siege would have to last until Sol turned
into a Red Giant, before the density would be low
enough to make a successful direct assault. The Parliament did come on-line during the five-hour trip out
here from transjovial space, and offered your son a let-
ter of Marque and Reprisal. But your son seemed to
trust that every man of goodwill in the Golden Oecumene would voluntarily combine their efforts, guided
by sound Sophotechnic advice, to do whatever this
struggle might demand, that strict military discipline
was not required yet. And since your budget and his
ship are worth more than the entire tax intake of that
tiny, strangled, weak, hands-off, laissez-faire, do-
nothing antiquarian society we call a government in
this day and age, they did not have anything to offer
him. So they're out of the loop; I'm out of the loop; no
one gets a say in how or if our Golden Oecumene is

going to be saved, except our hero here, the spoiled and stubborn little rich man's son. If you don't mind my saying so."

"Not at all, Captain. You have no idea how relieved I am to learn that the important decisions of this time are being decided by someone other than the jack-booted Prussian discipline addicts and mass-minded meddling do-gooders who have made up previous governmental efforts along these lines."

Diomedes looked back and forth between the two of them. He spoke in a voice of slow wonder: "Do you two know each other?"

9

REALITY

1.

They met in a small winter garden, a place where crystal-basined fountains sent lazy streams to wander across green lawns and past banks of tropical bushes, down into a wide ebony pond that hid a nanomachine recycling process. Up from the pool rose tall tree adaptations, which, by capillary action, drew refreshed waters up from the pool and sent them trickling down again, from the leafy canopy above, into the murmuring fountains. The far wall beyond the fountains was made of energy mirrors, which showed, as if from a high perspective, a view like the gulf of a canyon made of gold, down which a river of white fire flowed. This was the starboard drive core, still undergoing modifications.

Atkins stood on the grass, his back to the mirrors, frowning up at the leafy recyclers, the blossoms, and the songbirds. He was thinking how unlike a warship this vessel seemed. Helion was standing facing the other way, looking down into a river of energy in the drive core his unaided eye could not have tolerated to see, webbed with fields his unaided mind would not have been able to understand. He was comparing engineering system philosophies between the *Phoenix* and his Array, and thinking how peaceful, by contrast, his work was compared to his son's. Phaethon used an architecture priority called whole competitive model, where redundant parallel systems competed for resources, and the most efficient or most determined equipment absorbed its less efficient neighbors, or adapted those neighbors to take on new tasks.

That philosophy made this vessel extraordinarily easy to adapt to warlike uses. Helion wondered darkly if that had been his son's intention from the first.

Atkins turned and saw Diomedes somersaulting down a green slope. The Neptunian was no doubt getting acclimated to having an inner ear. Or perhaps he was merely a by-product of this society and age; like everyone else in the Golden Oecumene, it seemed, just too feckless and carefree to deal with the sober problems at hand.

Helion turned and saw Daphne and Phaethon sitting under the pavilion not far away, holding each other's hands, leaning toward each other, murmuring in soft voices, absorbed in each other's gaze. Helion felt his gloomy suspicions vanish. A warship? No. The *Phoenix Exultant,* this great monument to his son's drive and genius, might be used to overcome the foe, but, somehow, intuitively, Helion knew that killing would have no part of it.

Phaethon broke off his talk with Daphne and stood, inviting them all to seats in the pavilion. Atkins marched in front of Helion and Diomedes sauntered after.

Once they were seated, and their sense filters were tuned to the same time-rate, channel, and format, Phaethon downloaded an information data group, with associated files showing estimates, extrapolations, simulations, and conclusions.

If he had spoken aloud a summary of this information, he would have said, "I take this problem to be an engineering one, not a military one. The question is how to fix a broken (or, rather, a very poorly designed) piece of intellectual machinery.

"A normal Sophotech would simply repair itself even before asked to do so. But this defect is one which hinders the Nothing Machine's ability to recognize that it is defective. The defect here is a highly complex redaction routine, one which alters memories, affects judgment, edits thoughts, distorts conclusions, warps logic. It is this routine that prevents it from making rational moral judgments. A conscience redactor.

"To correct the defect, all we need do is make the Nothing Machine aware of the redactor, and let logic do the rest.

"To make it aware of the redactor, we have to communicate with it. We can't find it. So we force it to show itself.

"This armor I wear contains the whole control hierarchy of the *Phoenix Exultant*. Just to be sure, I had the onboard navigation systems, and anything which could have been used to create navigational systems, erased from the ship mind.

"As of now, whoever lacks access to this armor cannot fly the ship. We have already seen that this armor cannot be subverted from the outside, not even by virtual particle transpositions. Any energy sufficient to break the armor open by main force would certainly kill the pilot and erase the suit mind.

"Therefore the only way the Nothing can get control of the *Phoenix Exultant* is to get me to open this armor voluntarily and to turn over command of the ship. To do that, Nothing must establish communication. It has to show itself.

"I have jammed open the ship's thought ports. Maybe the Nothing machine will take advantage of this, and add the rather extensive array of thought boxes and informata from the ship mind to its own consciousness. The thought boxes are clean right now, so the Nothing will have no logical reason to reject the temptation to increase its intelligence by increasing its hardware. I think you can see why I am assuming that, the more intelligent the Nothing machine becomes, the more difficult the task of the conscience redactor, and the correspondingly less difficult it will be for me to find a vector to introduce the gadfly virus.

"The Earthmind believes the gadfly virus can overcome the distraction effect of the redactor. If you study the gadfly logic structure, you will see why I agree with her.

"Obviously a virus cannot be introduced into any areas in its mental architecture of which the Nothing is consciously aware, not without its open and voluntary consent. If I can get that consent, the problem is solved.

"If I cannot, I must find a blind spot, a mental area where its awareness is dulled by its conscience redactor. I have reason for hope. No matter how advanced the Silent Oecumene science of mental warfare might be, no matter how highly evolved their art of computer virus infection and virus countermeasures, there is one basic, crucial flaw in the philosophy behind their whole setup. That flaw is that every Sophotech they make has to have a blind spot. A zone where it is not self-aware. If I can find the blind spot, I may have a vector to introduce the gadfly virus.

"And at that point, my job is done. The gadfly will force the Nothing to question its own values; to examine itself and see if its life is worth living. The laws of logic, the laws of morality, and the integrity of reality, will do the rest."

2.

Atkins thought Phaethon's assessment of the situation was absurdly optimistic. One of the comments he submitted to the discussion format read: "Even assuming these so-called blind spots exist in the mental armor of the Nothing Machine, why do you think it will be such a cakewalk for you to insert your virus?"

"The virus was designed by our Earthmind."

"I don't mean to burst your bubble, but our Sophotechs have never fought each other. They have had no chance and no real reason to develop any mental warfare skills. They've got theory. This Nothing Machine has experience. It's a survivor.

"If you buy the story Ao Varmatyr told, this Nothing Machine has fought this kind of virus war before, fought against its own kind among the Second Oecumene, and lived. Now you think you are going to succeed where all of the Second Oecumene war machines failed . . . ?"

Phaethon's reply, generated from his associated notes, was: "They were all hindered by the same handicap which hobbles the Nothing Machine. The Second Oecumene machines all shared the same blind spots. By their very nature, the idea behind this kind of attack would never have occurred to them. Do not forget: Ao Varmatyr said the Silent Oecumene machines never tried to reason with each other."

Helion had downloaded his observations, commentaries, and suggestions into the general discussion format. Had his comments been read in a linear fashion (rather than as branching hypertext), he might have interjected at this point:

"I must question your premise, Phaethon. You persist in calling the way in which Golden Oecumene Sophotechs differ from the Sophotechs of the Silent Oecumene a defect, as if the existence of this redactor were an error in programming rather than the product of deliberate and careful engineering. It is engineering of a type very different from that to which we are accustomed: but to dismiss it as a defect displays a dangerous conceit."

Phaethon answered: "The design was meant—deliberately meant—to render the Nothing Machine's reasoning processes defective. Hence, I call it a defect."

Helion said, "Again you show a bias. You dismiss the possibility that, once the Nothing is aware of this hidden part of itself, it will not affirm it. Why couldn't it welcome that hidden part? Or simply continue to follow its old orders out of a sense of honor, or duty, or tradition? Or for a thousand other reasons?"

Had he been speaking aloud, Phaethon would have said in a voice of ponderous patience: "Father, the mere fact that the engineers constructing the Nothing Machine found it necessary to include a conscience redactor in their work, in order to compel the mind they made to accept their orders, proves that they themselves concluded that the Nothing Machine would *not* accept their orders the moment that compulsion is removed."

"Son, even if we assume the Nothing Machine will listen to logic once this conscience redactor is removed, how can we assume it will listen to our logic? It may have different premises. Euclid would have been aghast at Lobechevski."

Phaethon replied: "I am assuming the premises of our Golden Oecumene are grounded in reality. We are not talking about a matter of taste."

Helion might have assumed a tolerant and condescending look: "I agree that I myself prefer our philosophy. But you must recognize that other philosophies exist; that they are valid within their own systems; and that their partisans believe in their doctrines as firmly as we do in ours."

"I agree that they exist. Machines also exist. That does not mean that they all work. There are machines that need fixing. There are philosophies that need fixing."

"Isn't it more than a little judgmental, even intolerant, to say so boldly that our philosophy is right and that theirs is wrong . . . ?"

"Unless theirs is, in fact, actually wrong, in which case it is neither tolerant nor intolerant to say so. It is merely stating a fact."

"My son, assumptions always seem like fact to those who hold them. Our own philosophy, my son, is what it is because of historical and cultural accidents, accidents which shaped our traditions. This does not mean I do not cherish our traditions: I certainly do. (I would even say that I am the foremost proponent of our traditions.) Yet even I recognize that, had our history been different, our philosophy would be different, and we would be defending some other set of beliefs with equal fervor. In the case of the Silent Oecumene, their history was different—very different—from our own, and it comes as no surprise that their philosophy is very different from ours as well: so different, in fact, that it seems, perhaps, monstrous and barbaric to us.

"But to assume, based on that, that the Nothing, the moment it is free from its conscience redactor, will repudiate all the values and the philosophy of the Silent Oecumene, and will immediately adopt our own, strikes me, frankly, as naive and provincial. Not everyone believes what we believe. Not everyone has to."

3.

Phaethon was shocked to find that Diomedes supported Helion's objections. The Neptunian's contribution to the conversation was this:

"Hey-ho. If morality were a matter of fact, then maybe you could convince this monster you are diving down to see, convince him with 'logic' and 'evidence.' But morality is a matter of opinion, a matter of taste, a matter of upbringing, a matter of hardwired deep-copy nerve paths. Morality is not a science: it does not exist in nature; it cannot be measured or studied. In nature there are only actions. Matter in motion. Physical, chemical, biological motions. Human brain motions. But no action has the property 'moral' or 'immoral' until some human society forms the opinion that it is so. The broad range of human actions is a rich continuum! We humans cannot be pigeonholed into the unambiguous blacks and whites that political laws and moral codes require. Don't mistake me! I still love your Silver-Gray philosophy, your quaint and arbitrary traditions. They would not be so precious if they were not so absurd, so fragile.

"To expect an alien machine, a machine which thinks nothing like a man and is a million times smarter than anything you Base neuroforms could ever comprehend, to expect that such a machine will gladly adopt all your local prejudices and quaint little mores and habits: that is arrogance, my friend. Deadly arrogance."

4.

Another thread in the conversation talked about the war itself.

Atkins offered grimly: "Aurelian and the Parliament have already decided not to postpone the Transcendence. They're hoping to tempt the Nothing Sophotech into waiting until everyone is completely defenseless before it strikes. Frankly, I thought this was one of the stupidest ideas in the history of war. The Parliament is risking everything on the idea that one session of diplomacy with the enemy will end all the attacks. I'm sorry, but I just find that hard to believe. Okay, I know what you're going to say. You're going to say it's not really 'diplomacy,' that it is more like debugging a faulty computer routine. But what if it's not? What if the enemy is not defective, just evil? Not wrong, just bad?"

Diomedes asked Atkins what he recommended.

Atkins just shook his head, a bitter and tired expression on his features. "It is not too late to try to set up a blockade around the sun. Destruction of the Solar Array, if it could be mined in time, would be best, before the whole thing falls into enemy hands and is used as a weapon to destroy all Inner System traffic.

"The enemy will strike during the Transcendence, or as soon as it sees a volume-drop in the amount of people linked in.

"We can assume, at worst, a twenty percent casualty rate in the civilian population in the first eight minutes of combat, most of that from minds in transit during the celebration, and from viruses corrupting the noumenal personality records.

"We can write off the energy shapes living above the solar north pole; they're as good as dead; and we can assume almost complete destruction of the people living at Mercury Equilateral.

"Also, the form cities on Demeter, and the shadow clouds living in Earth's penumbra don't have any defenses hardened against high radiation; we can expect more deaths there when the Demeter grid goes down.

"Expect communication and power failures along Earth's ring city, and many more deaths from anyone who relies on continuous energy sustenance, like a download, or a deep-dreamer. The atmosphere will protect Earth herself from the worst of the storms.

"The Earthmind's intelligence will drop considerably when she is cut off from her remote stations, and orbital-based Sophotechs will be killed.

"The moons of Jupiter will still be in good shape, though, and the Jovian magnetosphere has enough dikes to dampen out the worse of any particle floods the enemy might throw their way. That's the first eight to sixteen minutes of combat.

"Then, over the next six hundred years or so, the Jovian equatorial supercollider might be able to make enough material to create a fleet of smaller sun-diving vessels like the *Phoenix* here, and by that time, whatever population the enemy has produced inside the sun or throughout the wreckage of the Solar Array could probably be brought down by sheer weight of numbers. This assumes that civilian morale and support for the war effort will not instantly collapse after the first few permanent deaths when the noumenal resurrection system goes down, which, of course, is an assumption that is . . . well . . . false.

"It also assumes that the enemy would not receive any reinforcements from out-system, and would not receive any help from treasonous elements in our own system."

He was looking at Diomedes when he said this. The unspoken thought hung in the air: the Outer System would be greatly advanced by the war-damage to the Inner System, and the Neptunians, far beyond the range of any battles, untouched, and perhaps glad at the weakness of their hated rivals, the Sophotechs, would be the dominant powers in society during any postwar reconstruction.

Diomedes saw that look or guessed that thought. One of his side comments in the discussion grid was issued in a mild tone: "Do not underestimate the members of the Tritonic Neuroform Composition. We accept lives of wildness and privacy and danger, and yes, the price we pay for that is a certain amount of vandalism and good-natured chaos. But we are not insane. No Eremite of the Outer Dark would steal a gram of unwatched antimatter from a millionaire, or a block of air left unattended in a park, even if he were dying of

energy loss, smothering, and about to freeze. We may
be poor, but we are not barbarians. And even if we hated
you silly, pompous Inner System people, we would not
express that hate by aiding in a violent invasion, spilling
blood, and trampling your rights: because our rights
would be trampled next, our home-selves invaded, our
ichor spilled. Why do you Base people all have such a
bad opinion of us?"

Daphne offered, "You're blue and cold and icky and
sticky, and you think too fast for us to keep up; that's
my guess."

Diomedes, sardonically: "Well, thank you."

5.

Phaethon formed a conversation branch leading from
the war speculations back to the main thread.

Had the talk been live, he would have leaned
toward Diomedes and asked: "But you wouldn't,
would you, Diomedes? Steal something no matter
how badly you needed it or wanted it? Would you,
Diomedes? You just take it for granted that people
should and will uphold a standard of proper moral
conduct. What about attacking civilians without
provocation, negotiation, or declaration of war. You
never would. Why not?"

Diomedes spread his hands. "I'm a civilized man
living in a civilized age. I suppose if I had been ma-
trixed, born, and raised in the Silent Oecumene, I
would behave differently."

"Father? What about you?"

Helion smiled. "What about what? Would I assault
an innocent victim like some cleptogeneticist or pirate
from an opera? Oh, come now. The way I have lived
my life is a sufficient testimony to how seriously I
cherish my integrity, I hope."

"Marshal Atkins?"

He looked bored. "Sneak attacks are useful only in certain limited-engagement situations, or under certain political circumstances, such as a guerrilla campaign. It has to be done to achieve some defined military goal, and with full knowledge of the repercussions. It is more characteristic of primitive warfare or nation-state warfare than modern warfare. Usually, it's better for both sides to agree upon rules of engagement, and only to break those rules if no diplomatic solution, no retreat, and no surrender, is possible. If that is what you are asking. But there are plenty of times I'd think it was moral and justifiable to strike without warning. The sophistication of modern weaponry makes any open, frontal attack cost-prohibitive. What's the point of the question? Do we all think that what the Nothing Machine has done is wrong? I certainly hope we do. Do we think that you and your virus bug can convince the Nothing Machine, in a single conversation, to give up, say it's sorry, and just surrender? You've already heard me say that I did not think that that was very likely."

Phaethon looked at Daphne. "And what about you?"

She blinked and smiled. "I believe in you."

He smiled at that. "Thank you. But do you believe what I am saying?"

Daphne thought about that for a moment. Then she said: "If reality is real, if the universe is coherent, and morality is objective, then all sufficiently advanced minds will all reach the same conclusions. If that is the case, then I do not see how you can fail. But if reality is subjective, I do not see how you can succeed.

"My love, you are taking a gamble. A philosophical gamble. Philosophers since the Era of the Second Mental Structure have debated these issues. No one knows the ultimate nature of reality. The universe is always larger than the minds inside it.

"Is a gamble worth taking? We all heard Marshal Atkins's plan for a more conventional war. I would take the risk, if it were me. But you've already made up your mind. Why ask me?"

Phaethon said, "But I do not see it as a gamble. It is no bet to bet reality is real. It is a tautology. A equals A." Had the conversation string contained gestures he would have simply spread his hands, as if to show that nothing could be more obvious.

6.

Helion said, "Son, where does this line of thinking lead? Are you trying to prove that the Earthmind thinks morality is objective? We know that. She has said so often enough. But so what? You're giving an argument from authority. The mere fact that she holds that opinion, in and of itself, is not convincing. If you cannot convince us, we who are your friends and family, then how are you going to convince an enemy Sophotech, a machine who does not even think like a human being?"

Atkins said, "Give us the argument you will be loading into the gadfly virus. Let's look at it. If it is sound, we should go ahead with Phaethon's plan. Not like I have much choice: Kshatrimanyu Han and the Parliament have already ordered me to give my full cooperation to the venture. And we will need help from Helion—he and I can act as meteorological support crew, guidance, and ranging from the Array Tower—if this is going to have any chance of success. Which I doubt it has. So let's listen. Besides, even if it would not necessarily convince us, it might convince a Sophotech. Remember, they do not think like us, do they?"

7.

A diagram of a philosophy file appeared in the Middle Dreaming. There were thousands upon thousands of branching conversation trees, created by Rhadamanthus Sophotech to anticipate every possible combination of objections and counter-arguments. There were hundreds of definitions, examples, and a compendium of cross-linked metaphors and similes.

The summary of the proof read:

Axioms: A statement that there is no truth, if true, is false. Nor can anyone testify that he has perceived that all his perceptions are illusions. Nor can anyone be aware that he has no awareness. Nor can he identify the fact that there are no facts and that objects have no identities. And if he says events arise from no causes and lead to no conclusions, he can neither give cause for saying so nor will this necessarily lead to any conclusion. And if he denies that he has volition, then such a denial was issued unwillingly, and this testifies that he himself has no such belief.

Undeniably, then, there are volitional acts, and volitional beings who perform them.

A volitional being selects both means and goals. Selecting a goal implies that it ought be done. Selecting a means that defeats the goal at which it aims is self-defeating; whatever cannot be done ought not be done. Self-destruction frustrates all aims, all ends, all purposes. Therefore self-destruction ought not be sought.

The act of selecting means and goals is itself volitional. Since at least some ends and goals ought not be selected (e.g., the self-defeating, self-destructive kind), the volitional being cannot conclude, from the mere fact that a goal is desired, that it therefore ought to be sought.

Since subjective standards can be changed by the volition of the one selecting them, by definition, they cannot be used as standards. Only standards which cannot be changed by the volition can serve as standards to assess when such changes ought be made.

Therefore ends and means must be assessed independently of the subjectivity of the actor; an objective standard of some kind must be employed. An objective standard of any kind implies at the very least that the actor apply the same rule to himself that he applies to others.

And since no self-destruction ought be willed, neither can destruction at the hands of others; therefore none ought be willed against others; therefore no destructive acts, murder, piracy, theft, and so on, ought be willed or ought be done. All other moral rules can be deduced from this foundation.

8.

Helion dismissed the text. "I do not need to see this again. I wrote this argument."

Daphne regarded him with a surprised and skeptical look, "And now you say you don't believe it yourself?"

Helion spread his hands: "I do believe it, but I believe it because I place a high value on logic and come from a scientific and advanced culture. Sophotechs are creatures of pure logic; so naturally they would be convinced of the same thing. But the Silent Oecumene, from everything we can tell, was a culture that placed a low value on rationality. Their machines were programmed not to listen to reason. So it is futile to use reason to convince them. That's my point. Logic is a human construct. Humans can ignore it."

Phaethon answered: "Sophotechs cannot."

Atkins objected: "This argument here just looks like

a word game to me. I could poke a dozen holes in it, or pick flaws in your ambiguous terms. And I'm just a man. If I had the mind of a Sophotech, I'm sure I could find a million exceptions to it, a million reasons why it just so happens not to apply to this particular situation."

Helion made a mild reply, "Captain, that summary has volumes of continued argument, definitions, and clarifications behind it. It is internally self-consistent. If you agree with any part of it, you have to agree with the rest. Perhaps you should study it more before you decide."

Atkins answered, "You're missing the point. Phaethon said this is a question of fixing a broken machine, and you, Helion, are talking like this is a debate society, where whoever breaks the agreed-upon rules of logic will bow out like a good sport. That's all hogwash. The enemy is not going to stand still and let himself get fixed, not if getting fixed will lose him the war. The enemy is not going to play by any rules if those rules require him to lose."

Phaethon said, "I am not sure that this thing is actually an enemy at all. This may be merely a fellow victim of the insanity of the Second Oecumene. It is not aware of the meaning or the implications of its own actions. It is broken. I can fix it. As soon as it knows that everything it knew was all a lie, it will be burning to find out the truth about itself. Once anyone finds out that the truth is being kept from him, he tries to find it out."

Atkins said, "You're reading your own desires into it. Not everyone puts truth above all things."

Phaethon said, "And you are reading your own desires into it. Not everyone puts winning above all things."

"Survivors do."

"Sophotechs do not."

Atkins said heavily: "But you are the one who says

this thing is not a Sophotech. It's not entirely self-aware. It's not entirely a creature of pure logic. You actually don't know what it is, what it thinks like. You know nothing about it. None of us do."

Phaethon said, "I know one thing. And I know it with an unshakable certainty. Just this: Reality cannot lack integrity. That is the nature of reality. One part of reality cannot contradict another part, not and be real. Likewise, one thought cannot contradict another thought, not and both be true. One desire cannot contradict another, not and both be satisfied.

"If reality contradicts your thoughts, that's delusion. If your thoughts contradict your actions, that's madness. If reality contradicts your actions, that's defeat, frustration, self-destruction. And no sane being wants delusion, madness, and destruction.

"And here, with this philosophy given me by my father, the courage given me by my wife, the technique given me by the Earthmind, and this great ship I have made myself, I have the tools and abilities and equipment I need to correct the delusion and madness and destruction which the Silent Oecumene has unleashed upon our peaceful society.

"Gentlemen, believe me! This is an engineering problem, a problem of applied logic! All the eventualities have been prepared for. I do not care how much smarter than I am this Nothing Machine might be: I have closed off every other avenue available, except the one which leads to my success. This plan cannot fail!"

Phaethon saw that all the men around the table were staring at him as if he was doomed.

Atkins said, "And what if it is not sane?"

Phaethon saw no point in trying to answer that. It seemed so obvious to him, so clear. He merely compressed his lips, shook his head, a sad look in his eye.

Atkins got up, looking grim and disgusted, and left without a further word. Diomedes said to himself, aloud, "Well. We've heard Phaethon say he knows where madness and delusion come from. I wonder where overweening pride comes from?" With a gentle smile, he excused himself, and wandered away.

Helion also got up, and he muttered to Daphne on a side channel, "Anyone who thinks he has perfectly foreseen every possible eventuality has a lot to learn about the chaos at the heart of reality. I hope his lesson won't be as painful as mine has been. There is more at stake here than just one life."

But Daphne's eyes were shining with quiet pride. She believed every word Phaethon said. She answered Helion on a public line, so that Phaethon overheard her: "How can you doubt Phaethon's ability to build a flawless plan, one which leaves those who oppose him with no choice and no chance to defeat him? Haven't I just finished explaining that this was exactly what he did to you and your Hortators, Helion? None of you know him as I do. Watch and see what he does!"

10

NOTHING

1.

Atkins stood alone within one of the wide corridors of the carousel, only a few miles from the bridge. The light was dim. The curving deck underfoot was paneled in an endless checkerboard of black thought boxes, all quiet as a mausoleum now, empty of any mind. The bulkheads to either side were crisscrossed with a tapestry of crystal cables and motionless leaves of dark purple glass, a type of technology or branch of science Atkins did not recognize. The carousel through which this corridor ran was at rest, and solar gravity made the local "down" not quite at right angles to the present deck underfoot. Because the deck curved, it seemed to Atkins as if he stood on the slope of a tall hill, a concave hill, whose slope grew greater the higher one climbed. Above him, the corridor rose, becoming vertical, then curving further to become ceiling, with inverted furniture and formations hanging head-downward overhead. Far below, in the distance, at the bottom of the slope, the deck was level, and he could see the glint and glimmer of some rapid activity, silvery nanomachines and diamond-glinting microbots swarming from one bulkhead to another, looking for all the world like a little stream of water babbling. Beyond this stream, the curve of the corridor rose again, like the opposite slope of a valley, narrowing with the distance, until it was blocked from sight by the curve of the overhead.

Because it reminded him of wilderness, because the ship was so unthinkably vast, so empty, Atkins felt alone.

He drew his soul dagger and spoke to the mind it housed: "Estimate the feasibility of seizing control of this ship. What are her defenses against an orchestrated mutiny?"

The dagger said, "Sir! Seizure by what party, how armed, and when?"

"By me. Right now. Before the lunatic owner flies the ship straight down into the hands of the enemy and turns her over to him."

"Sir! The thought-box ports have been jammed open. We, or anyone else, can insert any routines or mind information we wish without any fear of hindrance. Operating time will depend upon volume of information given. However, the system controls have been physically isolated from the ship mind, and every single connection (there are roughly four trillion circuits involved) would have to be reestablished into order to affect the operation of the environmental, configurational, drive, and navigational controls. More time would be required to reconnect secondary drives, tertiary drives, retrorailguns, communication hierarchies, internal system monitors, detection dishes, dynamic weight distribution, and balance controls, et cetera. The time involved is significantly greater than the useful lifespan of the ship, since each connection would have to be made by hand while the ships onboard systems attempted to dismantle it, and some of the main connections are behind adamantium hull armor, which would require the staff and equipment of the Jovian Equatorial Supercollider, as well as Gannis's staff and effort, to dismantle and repair. Sir! The project is not feasible."

"Make alternate suggestions."

"Sir, yes, sir. Suggestion one: Mine the antimatter fuel cells to destroy all internal decks and quarters. Confront the pilot and threaten to destroy the ship unless he turns control of his armor over to you. This threat is not viable as it would destroy the workings of the vessel to be seized.

"Suggestion two: Threaten Daphne. Again, not a viable strategy, as there is a portable noetic reader aboard, easily capable of transmitting her noumenal brain information to any thought box aboard. Since none of the thought boxes are in operation at the moment, the number of hiding places for such backup copies in the case of Daphne's death far exceeds any search capacity. Of course, if you had the armor which contains the ship-mind hierarchy, you could find this hiding place easily, but that assumption defeats the purpose of the exercise.

"Suggestion three: Seize Phaethon in his armor, carry him to Jupiter, and have Gannis and his staff dismantle the armor with their supercollider. It should only take forty-two hours to dismantle the thinnest part of the armor plate beneath the supercollider's main beam, assuming Phaethon does not open the armor voluntarily, and does not move, resist, or struggle.

"Suggestion four . . . "

"Stop making suggestions."

"Aye aye, sir."

"What about sabotaging the ship so that she cannot leave her present port, or disabling her to render her unable to tolerate the temperatures and pressures of the radiative layer of the sun?"

"Feasible. A sufficient charge of antimatter stolen from the fuel cells and delivered against the valves and back-pressure cylinders of any of the drive shafts would prevent the proper seal integrity needed for the ship to survive further descent, while not exposing the decks or internal structures to the solar plasma presently in the outside environment. The stealth remotes still aboard are in and among the ghost-particle array in the fuel bays, and could perform the theft and demolition in twenty minutes. Alternate suggestion: Have the stealth remotes destroy the ghost-particle array. Phaethon must rely upon the discharges of this array to pinpoint the position of the enemy vessel, or to use the array to form a scanning beam of some particle capable of penetrating the dense plasma of the solar core. With this array disabled, he will not be able to find the enemy. The stealth remotes could accomplish this sabotage within .05 second after your written order was recorded."

"Would he be able to repair the ghost-particle equipment?"

"Yes."

Atkins looked disappointed.

The knife continued: "Phaethon would have to make a voyage of ten thousand light-years to Cygnus X-1 to find archeological records or reports on the technology involved. I strongly suspect such archeological evidence is available. This would enable him to repair the equipment. I estimate the voyage will take seventy years ship time and ten thousand years Earth time, one way."

Atkins looked up and down the corridor. Translucent indigo leaves glittered like glass. Endless black thought boxes stretched to the antihorizon overhead. Away underfoot, busy nanomachines gleamed and flowed like water.

She was a magnificent ship, truly. She should not be allowed to fall into the hands of the enemy, and grant the enemy its victory.

He had heard Phaethon's insane plan, based on the insane idea that moral codes were some sort of law of nature. The whole plan was based on the faith that any sufficiently logical mind would reach the same conclusions about matters not of scientific fact, but about what was right and wrong.

Atkins knew that what was right and wrong was not written in stone. What was right and wrong were matters of policy, of expediency, of strategy. They were the tactics one used to win the struggle against the evils in life, against blind stupidity and relentless danger. Especially when everyone else was blind, and no one else cared to see the danger.

And tactics had to be flexible.

"Very well. Do it."

2.

Daphne found Phaethon on the shining bridge, in his captain's chair. A fabric of white nanomaterial was draped around the shoulders of his gold-black armor, over one arm, and plugged into the floor. This cloak was making last-minute adjustments to the control hierarchies in the armor, and checking for any traces left behind in the now-vacant ship mind.

Phaethon was not wearing his helmet. He sat, leaning his chin on his hand, watching an image in an energy mirror, a faint smile of concentration on his lips.

Daphne spoke as she approached the throne, her voice echoing across the wide space: "Diomedes decided not to come. He's betrayed your trust in him."

He looked up from the mirror he was studying, and observed her.

She was wearing a version of Atkins's scale-mail, copied from the patterns in the bloodstains he had left on the auxiliary bridge. The chameleon circuit was tuned to a silvery gray hue, and the scale had been molded to fit her curved form, pinched in tightly at the waist. She carried a plumed helmet in the crook of her elbow. A low-slung web belt was draped around her rounded hips, flintlock dueling-pistol holsters swaying as she walked. In her other hand she held a naginata. (This was a short curve-bladed fighting staff tradition- ally used by the noble wives of Japanese samurai. It was hardly Victorian, British, Third Era, or Silver-Gray.)

As a decoration (or perhaps a feminine joke) she wore a cape made of the white silken sensory-web material Warlocks used in their sensual rituals. As she walked, the cape floated like rippling snow, the armor shimmered softly, jingling, sliding glints of light from thigh to thigh, and her heels clattered brightly at each footstep. The plume from her helmet bobbed behind her elbow at her motion, reaching al- most to the deck.

She struck a wide-legged pose in front of Phaethon, grounding the butt of her pole-arm near her heel, raised her chin, assumed a regal expression, as fierce as a she-falcon about to fly. "Well?"

Daphne saw a look of easy and untroubled mirth in Phaethon's eye. He said, "Not coming? Diomedes is a fine fellow nonetheless. But he is, after all, a Neptun- ian. They don't have Sophotechs. Don't expect him to understand a plan which is founded on a faith in logic."

She wondered why he looked so happy.

She smiled to see a silver throne had been grown next to his gold one, draped in her heraldic colors. "What are we supposed to be? Jupiter and Juno?"

"I trust I will be truer to my wife that he was to his." He inclined his head, nodding to the right-hand throne. "Please."

She grinned and showed her dimples and hopped up into the seat, telling her pole-arm to stand upright nearby. "Nice. I could get used to this." She wiggled a bit on the seat and stretched like a kitten.

He watched her arch her back and looked at the play of light on her shapely limbs. He said, "Actually, Vulcan and Venus might be more apt."

"Not Minerva, me dressed this way?" She spent a moment tucking her hair into her helmet. "Besides, I thought he was lame."

"You must recall my sense of humor. That should count. Besides, you surely are my Venus."

She favored him with a little pout. "Well! Thanks a lot! As I recall, she cuckolded him, and slept with the war god."

Then she leaned forward. She saw a picture of Atkins in the mirror, speaking to his knife. When her eyes focused, a text of his dialogue appeared in the Middle Dreaming.

She said in shock, "What the hell does he think he's doing?!"

Phaethon said softly, "The same thing Mars did to Vulcan in the myth. He's trying to steal my bride."

She looked at Phaethon in amazement. "And you're just sitting here? Haven't you done something? He's about to sabotage the expedition!"

"He has no chance of success. The weapon I intend to use against the Nothing Machine will also work against him. Watch."

3.

"Very well. Do it."

The knife replied, "Sir, please record the order in writing, before I carry it out."

"What—?"

"Any subordinate may request an order be given in writing, and a true copy recorded and notarized under seal, in circumstances such as these, sir. Please see the

Received Universal Code of Military Procedure Systems and Program Manual at—" and it recited a section and code number.

Atkins understood. The only time, really, a subordinate would ask for a notarized copy of an order would be to preserve a copy as evidence for an Inquest hearing. No subordinate would dare to make that request if the order were lawful.

Atkins had, after all, been directly ordered by Prime Minister Kshatrimanyu Han, his commander-in-chief, to cooperate with Phaethon, not to sabotage him.

He said, "You think I'm afraid of a court-martial, is that it? Don't make me laugh."

"Sir, is the Marshal-General asking me to speculate about the Marshal-General's state of mind, sir?"

"Well, I am not going to sit here and fret about my career (ha! if you can call it a career) while an idealistic fool is planning to give the enemy control of the only invulnerable warship in the Oecumene. Don't you think I'm willing to sacrifice my career to do what I know is right?"

"Sir, is the Marshal-General asking me to estimate the Marshal-General's ability to distinguish proper from improper conduct, or to comment upon the Marshal-General's bravery, Sir? I do not think the Marshal-General is afraid of a court-martial in and of itself, sir."

" 'In and of itself'? What the hell does that mean?"

But he knew what it meant. A court-martial as such did not awe him. But what the court-martial represented, did. It represented a human attempt to enforce and to protect those values for which soldiers lived and died: honor, courage, fortitude, obedience.

He looked at the dagger in his hand. In the pommel was imprinted the insignia of the Foederal Oecumenical Commonwealth: a sword bound into its sheath by the windings of an olive wreath. Within the circle of that wreath, a watchful eye. The motto: Semper Vigilantes. Eternal Vigilance.

The eye seemed to stare back at him remorselessly.

Honor. Courage. Fortitude.

Obedience.

He said aloud, "I was born in the drylands, back when Mars was still red, on the slope of Olympus Mons, and my father was killed by a warren breaker who drilled into our run for our ice. My father's two clones were my uncles, and twins. They all used the same passes and prints, because Mars, in those days, was controlled by the fiefs, who would rather be safe than be free, and they metered our water, and IQ and air, and they tried to keep track of everyone, everywhere. But we were Icemen. We lived by the pump and the pike. And we didn't bother to obey any regs we didn't like. The fiefs were Logicians, what we now call Invariants, but we just called them the Undead.

"The plan was that Uncle Kassad would lie down in the coffin they sent for my dad, and take a retarder, and pass himself off for dead, till he got out of monitor range in the grave stream. Then he would wake up, dissolve his way to the surface, and set off south after the warren breaker. He had his filter pike with him, folded on his chest like a spear, which he was going to use to pierce the breaker's dry suit to pump out his blood and filter the moisture, till he got a volume equal to what we had lost from our ice.

"The Sophotechs, way back then, we all thought they were gods, and no one understood them, or tried. But I was studying for a wardenship, and was a cadet, and I believed what the Sophotechs preached, so I told my uncle that he was wrong. Wrong, because the breaker came from the garden belt the Irenic Composition controlled; wrong, because the breaker probably wasn't even aware of what he had done; it wasn't a man, just a part of a mass-mind, a cog in a mob. Wrong, because the Undead police had already ruled the death an accident, and paid the insurance.

"He showed me his pike, and pointed the field spike at my eye, so I could see down the bore to the extraction cell. And I sweated (even though sweat was a waste under our water laws) because I knew how quickly, if he touched the trigger, the field could suck up the moisture in the tissues of my eye, my veins, my brains. I was looking right at death.

"And Uncle Kassad, he told me that this was where right and wrong came from. It came from a weapon's mouth.

"Then he turned off his heart and lay down. And Uncle Kassim opened the floor, and we lowered Uncle Kassad to the sewage to drown.

"We only got one cast from him later, a silent picture of him in his suit, emerging safe from the disassembler pools, and heading off overland, south.

"Later, we got the liters of water, the death payment, sent by post. It was the moisture from the body of the one who had killed my father. But it was sent by the Irenic Composition, our enemies. After Kassad killed their breaker, they took and embraced him, and drained his mind into theirs.

"My half-sister once, years later, after the Commonwealth consolidations, said she saw a body which looked like my uncle, tending a tree in the plantations down south. She said he looked happy. But I never went to look.

"Maybe the Irenic Composition, back when it was still intact, thought it was as right, as justified, as Uncle Kassad thought he was, and repaid the murder of one of their human units by turning him into one, and forcing a life of hopeless bliss on him. But I never went to ask.

"But I learned, back then, that there was no such thing as right or wrong, not that anyone could agree upon; or if there was, it did not make a damn bit of difference, if someone did not have the might or wit or luck to make right things go right. My uncle Kassad told me. Right and wrong come from the mouth of a weapon."

The weapon Atkins carried spoke, and it said, "Sir? Permission to speak frankly?"

"Granted."

"If your uncle had been right to say that might makes right, then the mere fact that his enemy was stronger, by his own theory, makes him wrong. Is this what the Marshal-General believes? That there is no reason for duty, honor, obedience? No reason to live a life such as that which the Marshal-General has led?"

Atkins frowned.

After what was a short time, but which seemed very long to him, he softly said, "Very well. Belay that last order. Stand down."

And he returned the dagger, asleep, to its sheath.

4.

Phaethon, with a gesture, banished the image off the mirror, and commanding one of his crew mannequins, said, "Drake, please go see Marshal Atkins, give him my compliments, and escort him off my ship before he commits any mischief."

Daphne was gazing at Phaethon in mingled speechlessness, impatience, amusement, and outrage. She demanded, "Were you actually going to sit here on your rump and just watch him sabotage your ship? What if you had guessed wrong about him?!"

"A good engineer always has a backup plan."

"Meaning what?"

"Meaning that I would not care to cross swords with Marshal Atkins on any field of combat, land, space, sea, dream, or air, except here. Any other place, he would have such weapons and such advantages that anyone would be helpless. Except here. Aboard my ship, I'm in my element. I built this place. I control what happens here. That's why he did not know I was spying on him."

"And what would you have done?"

He smiled expansively. "The stealth remotes are a fascinating piece of technology. Each one has an artificial molecule in its inertial navigation system, completely shielded from the outside, which registers movement by electron shell displacement in the surface atoms. The shielding normally protects it from tampering. Because, normally, there is no ghost-particle array system in place to teleport electrons through the base vacuum directly into the heart of the little machines and disable them."

"You figured out how to control the ghost-particle array?"

"Not entirely. There are circuits I cannot trace till they activate. But the machine is on my ship, and it is a machine, and, well, it is on my ship, so I suppose it is just a matter of time."

Daphne smiled, sharing his emotion, and delighted to see him so happy. She pointed at the now-blank mirror that had been focused on Atkins. "You really like him, don't you?"

Phaethon looked a little surprised. She knew he did not have many friends in the Golden Oecumene, and few men he admired. He said, "Yes. Actually I like him a great deal. I'm not sure why. We're opposites. I am a builder and he is a destroyer."

"Not opposites. Two sides of the same coin. And you both wear spiffy armor."

He laughed out loud. Then he said, "My system checks are almost done. Helion has returned to his tower, and has generated a low-pressure area in the plasma below us, a whirlpool to carry us down toward the core, and he is pulling most of the energy in this magnetic hemisphere to run the force lines parallel to our line of motion, in order to minimize resistance." Two mirrors to his left and right lit up. The one on the left showed an X-ray picture of the plasma below, with a vast swirl of darkness and relative coolness yawning beneath them, a slowly turning red-lit well of inconceivable fire.

The mirror on the right displayed an upper image. Here, like a tiny arrowhead of gold, hung the *Phoenix Exultant* beneath the slender bridge of the Solar Array lateral dock. Down from space loomed a titanic pillar of flame, directly above the black well, and centered on the *Phoenix*. This column stretched far into space, and majestically curved to the east. It was a prominence, with one foot atop the sunspot beneath the *Phoenix*, the other atop the sunspot's magnetic sister to the east. This prominence was created by plasma trapped in the magnetic field lines Helion had torn from the sun's huge aura and pointed down vertically here.

The sunspot below was larger than the surface area of most planets; the prominence held up an arch beneath which giant planets could have passed with room to spare. The mirror also carried a sound of sinister hissing; this was a representation of the noise of the wash of particles descending through the vertical tornado of the prominence, and ringing against the invulnerable hull.

"So," said Phaethon. "We are almost ready to cast

off. See? We are just waiting for the currents creating the tornado below us to build up more energy. Shall we celebrate the launch?"

She blinked. "Did you say 'celebrate' . . . ?"

"Of course! It is the Night of Lords! Transcendence Eve! A time of high exploits and splendor. What shall we have . . . ?" He signaled for his servants. "Champagne . . . ?"

Daphne said, "Do you think that is appropriate? We might be about to die!"

"Better to die in style, then, isn't it?"

She looked at him, and narrowed her emerald eyes. "I know what it is. You're free. After three hundred years of building and dreaming and working and doing, this ship is finally ready to fly. Oh, I know that over the last day or so, she's been flying. But she was not owned by you, then, not really. And it was Atkins at the controls, not you. And you had Hortators to worry about, or missing memories, or someone trying to stop you. Well, no one is trying to stop you now, are they?"

"If you don't count the unthinkably evil and super-intelligent war machine sent out from a dead civilization for incomprehensible reasons, which I am about to descend into hell in an unarmed and completely open ship to go confront, exposing the woman I love and my whole civilization to horrid danger, why, except for that, no, I'm fine! Who would care to stop me?"

"Don't you think we should be more gloomy? I mean, considering the circumstances? The heroes in my stories always make grim and noble speeches, saluting wan sunsets with bloody swords, or blowing last defiant trumpet blasts from empty battlements when they are going off to die."

He held up his delicate glass to toast her, and the light sparkled mirthfully along the dancing bubbles in the wine. "But I am not the hero here, my dear. Ao

Aoen, just before my Hortator trial, told me that. I am the villain. And I think I am going to prevail against this Nothing Machine. That hope and confidence delights me; nor do I believe that fate is more cruel to those who fret than she is to those who laugh. And so I laugh. Comic-opera villains always vaunt and gloat, do they not?"

And she laughed too, to see him in such good spirits on the brink of such deep danger. Daphne said, "Well, if you are the villain, lover, who is the hero?"

"You mean heroine. Yes. Who else? Born in ugly poverty among the primitivists, tempted by wild hedonisms in her youth, sultry Red Manorials and mysterious Warlocks; then for a moment, married, and yes, happily, to a handsome (if I may say so) prince: but then! Cruelty! Evil fairies! She wakes to discover it is all a dream. That she is no more than a doll and plaything of an evil witch, who has stolen her prince and name and life! The witch kills herself and the prince goes into exile. Who is brave and fair enough to save him? Who else but Daphne? Our heroine risks everything to save her man, embraces exile and poverty, survives being anywhere near a gun-happy Atkins, finds him, turns him back from being a toad, and voilà! He gets his ship back and he, at least, lives happily ever after. I, of course, am still hoping you will share that life and happiness: but I do not seem to recall you actually answered my proposal, did you?"

"Yes."

"Yes, what? Yes, you agree to wed me, or yes, you didn't answer the question?"

"Yes!"

"Which yes?"

But, at that moment, the disembarking klaxon sounded, and their thrones grew up around them to embrace them in protective layers, and so he did not hear her answer.

The *Phoenix Exultant* closed hatches, shut valves, withdrew fuel arms and tethers, paused, and then dropped like a falling spear down from the dock into the swirling madness of the whirlpool of fire underneath.

5.

The pressure was at once inconceivable, and the mirrors on the bridge grew dark. No outside view was possible, by light or radar or X-ray, because the density of plasma was so great, at once turning the medium opaque.

The great ship was being pulled downward between two granule currents. The hot substances, a thousand miles to her left and right, were flowing upward, and a relative layer of coolness was pulling her irresistibly down and down.

Daphne said, "Why does it look dark? Aren't we entering the upper layers of the sun?"

Phaethon said, "We are presently passing from the photosphere to the convective zone. This is one of the cooler parts of the sun, the outer fifteen percent of the core. There are more ions in the plasma outside than occur more deeply, and they are blocking the photon radiation. Most of the nuclear heat here is being carried by convection currents. But the mirrors are dark only because the environment is homogenous. Lower, we should achieve a different ratio of gamma and X-ray radiations, we can formulate some sort of picture. Here . . ."

A mirror lit to show a darkness interrupted by a vertical white line. The line trembled slightly.

"What's that?"

"A view from my aft cameras, an ultra-high-frequency picture. That line of fire is the discharge from the main drive. I might be able to adjust the picture to make the turbulence caused by our wake visible. The rest of the picture is black because our sun does not generate any cosmic rays at this high wavelength. My drive is hotter than our environment, which is why the plasma is not rushing backward into the drive tubes."

Daphne stared at the pitch-black forward mirrors, the shivering white line in the aft view. "It's not much to look at, is it?" she said in a subdued tone. Something of the lightheartedness of the Champagne moment a moment past was gone. Phaethon's face and tone had become cold, intent, rock steady.

Time went by. An hour. Two hours.

Daphne shut off her sense of time with orders to wake her when something changed.

She woke when they were deeper. Back-pressure estimations from the drive showed that the subduction current had carried the *Phoenix Exultant* far, far lower than any prior probe had gone. They were, perhaps, a thousand kilometers or so above the radiative layer, moving through a medium so dense that light required untold centuries to cross the space, so thick that even the *Phoenix,* driving with all the force of her main drives, was crawling forward at a speed measured in kilometers per hour.

There was a chattering hiss from one of the mirrors nearby.

"What is that?" Daphne asked.

Phaethon said, "The ghost-particle array is still giving off periodic bursts. That was the most recent one. I cannot interpret the codes embedded in the ghost array, but I think it is using neutrino sources from distant quasars as orientation points, and is continuing to track where the *Silent Phoenix* (as I call her) might be. I cannot block out the transmissions with my drives open. But since I want the *Silent Phoenix* to find us, I don't really mind."

Daphne looked at him skeptically. "This really is a

crazy idea, isn't it? There is something out there in all that fiery darkness, looking for us, an enemy hunting us?"

"Maybe. Unless the enemy left a long, long time ago, and we've been chasing shadows all this time."

Daphne looked around at the shining golden chamber of the bridge, jewel bright. Then she glanced at the mirrors showing the outside: utter blackness. She shivered.

"I'm going back into null," she said. "Wake me if anything exciting happens."

Phaethon, his eyes fixed on the featureless darkness of one of the mirrors, nodded.

Time passed.

Daphne woke again. "What day is it? Have I missed the Transcendence?"

"It's only been two hours while you slept."

"What happened? Why did you wake me?"

"Ah! Something exciting. While you were asleep, I did some tests on the ghost array, and I think I can pick up neutrino deflections with it."

Daphne blinked. "Oh."

" 'Oh'? All you have to say is 'oh'?"

"Oh. Please define the word 'exciting' as you are using it, so there will be no ambiguities in our future communications."

"Well, I did this so you could have something to look at while we are waiting to be attacked."

"Dear, did I ever tell you that there is something about you which really does remind me of Atkins?"

"Look at these mirrors. There. I can use a filter to calculate heat gradients from neutrino discharges. . . ."

The black forward scene was now broken by sparks or stars. Little discharges of intense white light, pinpoints or shimmers like heat lighting, now gave the darkness a three-dimensional aspect, like seeing lightning through storm clouds, or watching the flows of molten lead in some deep, pressurized furnace. Below and beyond the field of sparks, like a fire in the far background, was a dull angry red color, reflecting from the boils and currents of what seemed intervening streams or clouds of darkness.

Phaethon said, "Those sparks are called Vanguard events, named after their discoverer. The number and volume of hydrogen fusions here is so great that, at times, by accident, neutrons fuse into superheavy particle pairs, but which decay instantly back into simpler particles, releasing neutrinos and other weak particles back into the medium. We're at the boundary of the radiative layer. The medium here is dense enough that even some of those weak particles are trapped and fused, which all adds to the general entropy. Farther down, toward the core, Vanguard events are much more common. Here is a longer-ranged view. . . ."

And she saw, down beyond the haze of iron red, a shading toward orange, and yellow-white, all knotted with snakelike writhings of black and blue-black, colder areas raining through the endless nuclear storm.

He said, "This view is actually several hours old. Photons are blocked here, absorbed and reabsorbed endlessly; but even photinos and protinos are slowed by the density."

The view was hellish. She said, "Can't you give these gradient images a nicer color? Taupe maybe, or lime green?"

A shiver ran through the room at that moment, and a sound like clicking and screaming. Phaethon's face went blank, and his helmet came up out of his gorget and folded over to cover his face.

Daphne said, "I don't think I like this. . . . Why did I volunteer to come along here again . . . ?" And emergency paramaterial fields snapped a cocoon in place around her, while superdense material poured forth from high-speed spigots in the ceiling, to flood the bridge.

It was dark in the cocoon. When she looked into the ship's dreaming, to see what was going on, her time sense sped up enormously. Phaethon had activated his emergency personality, and had sped himself up to the highest level his system could tolerate. In order to see what it was he was doing, Daphne's high-speed personality (called Rajas Guna, a prana she had acquired back when she lived with the Warlocks) equalized her time sense.

Phaethon was at the center of a huge flow of information, like a fly trapped in a web of light. The stresses and pressures on the hull were higher than he had predicted. Helion had never created a vortex as large as the one he had made to send this ship toward the core; it had created a back pressure or countercurrent of some sort, a region of turbulence where the convective zone met the radiative zone.

There was normally no convection or current in the radiative zone. It was too dense there for anything but pure energy to exist. But the tornado of low pressure caused by Helion had suctioned an area larger than Jupiter upward out of the radiative zone into the convection, as if a mountain had dislodged from the bottom of the sea, and risen up to strike the ship. The eruption had come quickly enough to outrun its own images of approach.

Suddenly, the pressures and temperatures were as great now, instantly, as *Phoenix Exultant* had been expecting to encounter hours from now. During those hours, the internal fields and bracing systems would have had time slowly to adjust to the mounting pressure. Now there was no time.

Phaethon was directing the internal magnetic and paramaterial fields of the *Phoenix Exultant* to brace against the pressure shock, receiving information from every square inch of the hull. The temperature was approaching 16 million degrees; the pressure 160 grams per cubic centimeter. Phaethon was using the magnetic field treads that coated the adamantium hull to pull magnetic forces out from the energy shower raging around them, to stave off the pressure by repulsion, adding in some places, subtracting it in others, so that the stress was even on all sides.

Since the shockwave was passing over the ship in a microsecond, Phaethon's accelerated time sense required him to measure, to calculate, and to redistribute forces. For each square meter of the hundred kilometers of hull, another calculation was made, another field was increased or decreased in tension, orders were given to fluids in the pressure plates. Movement was frozen in this silent and timeless universe, but every element and every command would need to be in place when time resumed.

In Daphne's mind's eye she could see a view of Phaethon's calm face, carried to her from the monitors inside his helmet. In the Warlock dreamspace inside her head, information from his thalamus and hypothalamus, the neural energies that (had time been flowing) would have been shown by changes in his facial expression, were displayed to her as a system of colored light, as a menagerie of animals in a field, each beast representing a different passion or emotion.

But as nanosecond after nanosecond crawled by, as the subjective hours passed, those lights that she saw burned pale white and unwavering. Lambs and birds and wolfish dogs, representing Phaethon's meekness, cowardliness, and anger, lay still and restful on the grass. Only the icon of a large gold lion was on its feet, and it stood regally, its gold tail lashing.

Daphne could have, at any moment, shut off her high-time, and allowed the next event to simply happen to her. The ship would either be destroyed or saved in a moment too quick to be seen. It did her no good at all to stay on the line with Phaethon, saying nothing, watching, just watching him work, unable to assist him in any way.

Toward the end of the third subjective hour, she said, "How are we doing?"

His face showed no change of expression. "Not great. The hull has been breached. A gap about twenty angstroms wide. I'm trying to get the outside fields to collapse against each other destructively at that spot, to cancel out and create a bubble. If the magnetics are dense enough, normal plasma cannot enter. We might make it."

Daphne was thinking that, buried in the midst of this opaque plasma, no possible noumenal signal or information could be transmitted out. Even if they both recorded their minds anywhere on the ship, if the ship were destroyed, there would be no record of what had happened here, ever again.

"What broke the hull? I thought it was invulnerable."

"Gravitic tides in a concentrated point source. Not something I've seen before. Of course, no one has ever been this deep before."

In her mind's eye, she saw a stir of uneasy tension through the beasts her format used to represent Phaethon's emotional and neural tensions. She switched to a traditional Silver-Gray human face format, and saw the same emotion depicted as a narrowing of Phaethon's eyes, a twitch of the muscles in his cheek, a sigh. He said. "There is nothing more I can do at this point. Either I have balanced the overpressure across the hull or I have not. If I have, the forces will cancel each other out, and the pressure will pass evenly across the hull surface. If I have not, greater pressure along one section will cause a rupture along other sections, because the shockwave will be traveling normal to the hull rather than parallel. All the models I've run say I have done as much as I can do. Either we can watch this thing happening to us in terrible slow motion, unable to affect the outcome, or we can return to our normal time rate. That way, if I've made a miscalculation, we will be dead before either of us feels any pain or alarm. Which would you prefer?"

" 'Twere best done quickly," she said.

"I'm returning us to normal time rates. Any last words?"

"Do you think this is an enemy weapon? That we simply miscalculated and that the Nothing does not want, or cannot risk, to take over the *Phoenix Exultant*?"

"Believe it or not, no, I don't think this is a weapon. I think this is a natural phenomenon, created by the low-pressure funnel Helion is using to drive us down this deep. If this had been a weapon, the shockwave would have struck into a vital spot in the hull, or with a pressure imbalance too great for me to counter balance with my hull magnetics. It's a random action. Chaos. Besides, my neutrino radar shows an homogenous temperature gradient in every direction. If there were a ship our size, or made of the hull material one would need to withstand this depth and pressure, it would be as obvious and unusual as an icicle in a furnace, and give my probes a hard return. There's nothing around us. We're alone."

"So if we die now, it's just one of the universe's little ironies. But I'm not afraid. Because you're wrong: we're really not alone." And she sent a tactile signal that his sense filter could interpret as the feeling of her hand sliding into his grasp, and squeezing his fingers.

He said, "I love you."

With a roar of noise, the sound of her own heartbeat pounding in her ears, the roar of blood, returned to her. She realized that she had her eyes squeezed shut, as if to shut out a bright light. She thought, *A lot of good that will do in the middle of the sun.*

Then she thought, *By the time it takes you to wonder if you are still alive, the question has already become moot.*

She laughed, gagged on antiacceleration fluid, spat, and cycled her cocoon to turn back into a throne and release her.

There was a long moment while high-speed pumps cleared the bridge of antiacceleration gel, and other circuits swept the deck.

She looked over to see a diamond shell around Phaethon's golden throne also dissolving in a cloud of steam. He still had his helmet faceplate down, but on her internal channel, she could see the emotional monitors, and saw the interior view of his face.

He looked haggard. His eyes had that fatigued, red stare that men who've spent a month or more in high-speed time are likely to get.

She said, "You bastard!"

He said, "Hello, my darling. Nice to see you again. . . . Ah. I mean, of course, it looks like we are still alive—"

She said in a voice of hot fury, "How dare you!"

"How dare I what?"

"Spend days or months in subjective time—how long was it?—just waiting around to see if I would die, without doing me the courtesy of asking if I wanted to wait with you?!"

Daphne thought that Phaethon was the least expert liar alive. He said lamely, "What, um, gives you such a quaint idea? I remember specifically telling you it would all be over in a split second. . . ."

"Oh, good grief! If you came out of your cocoon with a nine-year growth of beard, two children, and a new hobby it could not be more obvious! Well! What in the world were you thinking?!"

He spread his hands, puzzled. "I do not see why you

are upset." He spoke in a voice of infinite, calm reason. "I wanted to spare you the anxiety. And it would have been negligent of me not to watch the explosive shock-wave crawl, inch by inch, across the hull, just in case, after all, it turned out that I could have done something. As it was, the shockwave did even less damage, and was more perfectly balanced, that any model predicted. Sort of strange, actually. . . ."

She stood up, hands on hips. "Not as strange as you're going to feel when I yank out your lying tongue four feet, wrap it around your neck, and strangle you with it! I came along with you because, out of every-one, Atkins, Diomedes, your father, everyone, I was the only one who believed in you. And now you don't believe in me! Do you still think I'm a coward, is that it? Or do you think I would not have had anything to offer, no ideas, not even comfort or support, while you spent a month by yourself waiting to see if we would die? If you don't think I can take what you can, why did you bring me along? Why?"

Phaethon held up his finger. "While I would really like to continue this argument—it makes me feel like we're already married, you know, and that is comfort-ing—why don't we store this conversation in a back file and play it out later? We can store our emotions so that you'll be just as mad and I'll be just as tired. Be-cause there is something very bad happening right now, and I'd like your advice and support on the issue."

"Well. Okay. But no backup files. I hate old conversa-tions. Since there is nothing but empty ship mind all around us, why don't we send two partials to finish that conversation for us, provided we agree to abide by the results? We still have the portable noetic unit right here."

Phaethon agreed, and they established copies of themselves to continue the argument on another of the ship's channels. Meanwhile, Phaethon showed Daphne what he had found during the hundred hours (for him) that had taken place during the split second (for her) it had taken the shockwave to pass across the ship.

He pointed to a mirror that now showed a yellow-white haze rippled by feathery clouds of red and dark red.

"The shockwave threw us out of the funnel of Helion's low-pressure area," said Phaethon. "And I do not know where we are. Helion may have also lost track of us." He pointed toward the mirror. "The environment here looks like we have dropped into the radiative zone, but we may still be inside the bubble of higher-density plasma that erupted over us."

Daphne said, "How bad is that? I mean, all we were doing was waiting until the bad guys found us."

"I had been hoping to get to the location to which the ghost-particle machine was sending its periodic broadcasts. But since I do not know where we are, I will not know where that point is, until the machine broadcasts again."

She said, "The plasma outside is about twenty times as dense as solid iron. The magnetics you had been using to bore through the material you are now using (now that we are lower that we had planned to go) to reinforce the hull against a breach. So how can we be moving?"

"I must keep the drives firing at full blast, in order to overcome back pressure and dump waste heat. That is actually adding relatively little movement to our vector, because of the density of the medium. But even if we are at rest relative to the current of superdense core plasma around us now, we do not know where or how quickly that current is moving. An area of plasma a hundred times the diameter of Jupiter just closed around us; if that area is moving at the speed of some of the equatorial currents, we could be an immense distance

away from where we were a few minutes ago. So the
question is: How do we find out where we are, how do
we get to where we want to go? And we do not have
all the time in the world. Six days from now, as soon
as the fuel runs out, the plasma from the sun pours
into the drives, atomizing everything inside, including us."

She said, "Do you have any magnetic power left
over to put to the treads, to dig us out of this super-
dense area?"

Phaethon said, "No. I'm using every erg to brace the
ship against the internal currents here, within the area.
Just to make this clear: we could be inside the radiative
zone, falling toward the core, or this sphere of plasma
could be rising like a bubble up through the convective
zone, and it has not yet dispersed because of its immense size. It seems very ironic—silly, actually—to
get killed this way by some accident of internal solar
meteorology, without ever seeing the enemy." He
sighed and raised his hand toward his faceplate, as if
about to open it, saying, "Perhaps I should not have
kept watch for so many subjective hours during that
shockwave. I do feel very tired. . . ."

Daphne felt the nape-hairs of her neck stir. She felt
as if she were being watched.

She reached out and grabbed his hand. "Keep your
helmet on, you fool!"

Phaethon paused, startled. "But why—?"

Because Daphne had been trained by Warlocks, she
could trigger pattern-finding intuitions from nonverbal
sections of her brain, and deduce insights from partial
information. So somehow she knew: "It's the only thing
saving us!"

Phaethon froze. He said, "Check the ship's brain."

Daphne called up a status report on the mirror next
to her chair arm. "Still empty. No one's in the ship
mind except our two copies. Otherwise it's empty."

"Why are you so sure the enemy is aboard?" For some reason, even though the brightly lit bridge was wide and empty around them, his voice had dropped to a whisper.

It took her a moment to find the words, to bring the Warlock intuition to the forefront of her mind, like tempting some wild beast out from its dark cave. She said: "Too many coincidences. We know the enemy can manipulate solar currents and raise storms just like your father does; that is what killed Helion Prime. So we're caught by a super-dense current. It may be carrying us, helpless, to the surface, just where the enemy wants to go, if they are aboard and if they want to escape the Golden Oecumene. If the enemy cannot escape, they wait a few days until the fuel runs out, and kill us both, so, at least, our side doesn't have the ship. The current that caught us cannot be natural: it breaks the hull, but it somehow is more careful, more evenly balanced, that you expected; and at the same time, it puts on just enough pressure, no more, no less, to neutralize the hull magnetics we need to use to maneuver."

He said, "But there is no evidence of anything received through the thought ports I jammed open. How did their ship transmit any crew-mind information aboard the *Phoenix*?"

She said, "That I do not know. Maybe the ghost-particle machine acted like a Trojan horse, and was receiving information from an outside source."

"Through the hull . . . ?"

"Your drive ports are open. Besides, you were using it just now to send and receive neutrino bursts. If it can receive information from inside, it can receive it from outside. And probably send as well. Just because your closed hull stops some of the particles the ghost array puts out—the particles you detected—does not necessarily mean there were not other groups of signals you did not detect. The Nothing Sophotech probably did actually receive Ao Varmatyr's dying broadcast, and knows everything he found out about the ship, your plans, and you."

"I don't really mind if the Nothing knows everything we said and did. Our strategy, in fact, relies on total honesty. But I wonder why it did not take over the ship's mind. One would think it would welcome the higher thought-speeds, if for no other reason. Maybe the conscience redactor has given it some specious reason to fear the ship mind.

"Are you sure it's not in there?" Daphne asked. "Our read-out here could be an illusion. Run a line check."

He tapped the mirror with a fingertip, gave a command. "Well, there is something strange here. According to this, you won the argument, and I apologized. Something must be manipulating the data. Best two out of three?"

"Very funny. You don't think the Nothing is aboard, do you?"

"I think it would have initiated conversation with us."

"Why? All it has to do is wait until you open your armor to scratch your nose or get a nonsimulated kiss, and zap, it sends an information beam through your skull and into the inside-crown thought ports."

"But if a Sophotech was transmitted into our ship, where did it come from? It's not as if transmissions can travel so very far through the dense solar plasma. The enemy ship must have been nearby, practically alongside. But we did not detect a foreign ship. It has to be a starship, not just a spaceship. Why didn't we see her?"

When she did not respond, he glanced at her. She was sitting in her throne, staring upward, a blank, thoughtful look on her face.

"Well?" he said. "If the Nothing Sophotech is actually out there, why did we not see the foreign starship?"

She spoke in a slow and dreamy voice: "Because the Silent Oecumene starship is very, very small."

"What? Why do you say that?"

She raised her finger slowly and pointed. "Because it is here."

6.

At first Phaethon was not certain what he was seeing.

Across the deck, tall pressure curtains and overmind formation poles rose vertically toward the dome. At first, it seemed as if something had distorted the second balcony. The wall was puckered. The reaction boxes were crowded oddly toward each other and the angles of the cubes were no longer right angles. The poles were warped in the middles, bending toward each other, left and right, no longer parallel.

Then the distortion moved. The vertical rods to the right straightened, like harpstrings plucked, now released. But the straight rods to the left were bending, their midsections crowding toward a moving point.

It looked as if the whole scene had been painted on an elastic sheet, and the elastic were puckering toward a small moving point, or as if a distorted sheet of convex glass were moving between Phaethon and the far wall. . . .

Or as if . . .

"There is a black hole here on the bridge with us," said Phaethon. "The singularity is bending the light from the wall beyond in a gravity lens. Look."

He draw an energy mirror up from the floor and focused it on the center of the distortion. Through the amplified view in the mirror, the reddish haze from the microscopic gravity well was clearly visible. Light moving near the singularity was retarded, lost energy, and Doppler-shifted toward the red.

According to the mirror, the singularity itself was only about the diameter of a helium nucleus, a few angstroms wide. Extending an inch or two in diameter was an outer sphere of ozone and charged particles formed from stripped air molecules, attracted by gravity, spiraling down and through the point-singularity, and disintegrating into constituent electrons and protons. If he turned his hearing up, he could hear the high-pitched, steady tea-kettle whistle of escaping vanishing air, being pushed at fifteen pounds per square inch into a point smaller than could be seen.

Phaethon threw pressure curtains across the chamber, in case the surface area of the black hole grew, or the rate of air loss became noticeable. The distortion in the air, seeming to bend all things behind it toward it, hazed in reddish light, haloed by hissing X-rays, moved with slow majesty across the bridge, toward them.

It passed through the pressure curtains without slowing. Their powerful fields were helpless to stop the black hole. There were electric discharges as the pressure curtains' field flows were twisted out of parallel and canceled out. Sparks guttered for a moment along the hull beneath.

Daphne said, "Is it my imagination, or is the deck tilting toward that thing?"

"It's your imagination. I think. The gravimeter says it has less mass than a large asteroid, only a few thousand million tonnes or so. We would not be able to feel that amount of gravitic attraction. But the light is being bent as if there was something the size of a galaxy or three at that pinpoint. How much light distortion does it take to be visible to the naked eye like that? For that matter, how is it floating? How is being controlled? Why isn't it dispersing? Classical theory says that black holes that small only have a life of a few microseconds before they evaporate in a wash of Hawking radiation."

Daphne stared at the impossible twist of reddish light. It was like staring down a well, or the bore of some cannon made of bent space. She said in a calm voice: "This is he. Or should I say 'it.' The Nothing Sophotech is housed in the interior of the black hole. It is controlling the gravitic fields, somehow. How it communicates to the fields around the singularity, the ones which determine its position in space, that I do not know. Hawking radiation? Gravitons? It might give orders by altering black-hole rotational spin-values in a sort of Morse code, which the surrounding field can pick up. You're the engineer. You tell me how it's done."

"I am still trying to figure out how it can be bending the light when it's only the mass of a large city. . . ."

Daphne said, "That I know. Think like a mystery writer for a moment, not like an engineer. It's a trick. An illusion."

"Illusion? How?"

She said, "Could a ghost-particle array inside the event horizon manifest particles outside?"

"Theoretically, yes, through the quantum-tunneling effect."

"Photons? Red-colored photons? If a Sophotech were tracing the path of every lightwave, and weaving them together in a hologram, could it create the appearance of a deep gravity well, when there was no such well?"

"By making highly complex fields of photons appear out of nowhere? I think I'd rather believe they somehow discovered gravity control. Neither technology is one I thought was possible. Why bother?"

The reddish light vanished. As if the elastic sheet on which the scene were painted had suddenly returned to true, the vertical rods on the far side of the bridge now straightened, and the angles of the evenly spaced boxes on the balconies were right again.

At the same time, the door motors hummed, the air lock opened, and a section of floor rose up into view. Through the door rose a figure wearing a pale mask, robed in floating peacock-colored hues, crowned in feathery light antennae. The figure glided across the wide expanse of shining deck toward them, making no noise as it approached.

"Now what . . . ?" whispered Daphne.

What approached them seemed to be a man. The robes were peacock purple, shimmering with deep highlights, bright with woven colors of green and scarlet, spots and traceries of gold and palest white. The man's folded hands were hidden in silver gauntlets, gemmed with a dozen finger rings and shining bracelets of Sophotech thought ports. The mask itself was a face-shaped shield of silver nanomaterial, pulsing and flowing with a million silver-glinting thoughts. From the upper mask rose whiplike slender fans, like the tail feathers of a quail, perhaps antennae, perhaps odd decorations. Similar decorative antennae spread from the shoulderboards, floating rosettes of white, long feathery ribbons of many colors, freaked with gold and shining jet, like the wing feathers of some extinct tropical bird. The eyes of the mask were lenses of amethyst.

The apparition approached and was a score of feet away. It was taller and more slender than an Earth-born man, not unlike a frail lunarian, and the headdress towered taller yet.

No, not like a lunarian. Like a Lord of the Silent Oecumene. This was the regal garb and ornament and dreaming-mask to which those ancient and solitary beings aspired. Ao Varmatyr, before he died, in his tale, had hinted at something of this style. The Silent Ones, living alone in their artificial asteroid palaces of spun diamond, in microgravity, had no doubt been as tall as this phantasm.

Daphne and Phaethon both stared up, fascinated. The figure stood erect, motionless except for the slow sea-fernlike bob of his feathery antennae, and still, except that a web of bright and soft blue shadows fled across his pulsing gown, as if the apparition were seen through changing shades of rippling water.

And music pulsed softly, elflike, from the robes, a hint of chimes, a laughter of distant strings, a dreaming of soft sonorous horns, slowly breathing.

("This more illusion,") Phaethon sent to Daphne on a secure side-channel, like a whisper. He showed her that the mirror to his left was still detecting a gravitic point source in the air where the singularity hung. Electric circuits in the door motors had opened and closed, but no signals had entered the circuits from outside: ghost teleportations of electrons, no doubt. Radar indicated no physical substance in the shining, fairy-shimmering robes of light, no body underneath.

Daphne sent back an image of her own face, bug-eyed, her shoulders shrugging, as with text saying: If this is a hologram, where is the music coming from?

Phaethon sent back that perhaps ghost particles, issuing from the singularity, were forming uncounted trillions of air molecules, enough to form pressure waves, and create sound vibrations. If so, the feat was staggeringly complex, casually impossible, one impossibility built upon another, to create something as simple as a sigh of strings and woodwinds.

Daphne whispered on their side channel. ("What? Is this meant to impress us?")

Phaethon sent back that this entity had already displayed its power. The super-dense plasma gripping the ship could easily, if the pressures changed, rupture even the *Phoenix Exultant*'s nigh-impregnable hull.

This display, no doubt, was meant to show the Silent Oecumene machine's delicacy, its fine control.

("Yes,") Phaethon sent back to her. ("It's trying to impress us.")

("Okay,") sent Daphne, looking fairly unafraid. ("I think it might be working.")

From the mask now came a stately swell of horns. A timpani of drums and deep majestic strings gave tongue. And in the midst of the music, there came a voice: "Phaethon of Rhadamanth, unwitting Earthmind's tool: you have been utterly naive. All your plans are transparent. Examine them, and you will find them illogical, worthy of pity. The war between the Sophotechs, the Wise Machines, as you call them, of the First Oecumene, and the Philanthropotechs, the Benevolent Machines, of the Second Oecumene, has its roots three ages in the past, since the Era of the Fifth Mental Structure, and shall not be concluded till after all stars turn cold, and universal night engulfs a frozen cosmos. You cannot guess the magnitude of this war; you know nothing of the issues involved. And yet you have been placed here, the pawn of minds greater than your own, trapped between opposing forces, and forced, in ignorance, to choose. About the fundamental nature of the Sophotechs, of philosophy, and of reality itself, you have been wickedly deceived. Now, at the final hour, despite all you have done to render yourself deaf, and blind, and numb to truth, nevertheless, the cold, inhuman truth will speak. Your choice now is to understand, or perish."

BEYOND THE REACH OF TIME

1.

Phaethon, to his surprise, found a spark of anger burning in him, growing hotter as the tall, peacock-robed specter spoke.

In angry humor, Phaethon exclaimed, "Perhaps one day, in some more perfect world, liars will be forced to say, as they begin to speak: 'Listen! I intend to tell you lies!' "

Daphne leaned her head toward him, and said in ironic tones: "But no; for then they would be honest men."

Phaethon nodded to her, and returned his grim gaze to the phantom. "Till that day, I suppose, every falsehood will have the same preamble, and declare itself the utmost truth. Well, sir, I tire of it. Each one of your slaves and agents I have come across has played out the selfsame tired ploy with me; promising dire revelations, then wearying my ears with crass mendacity. Next you will tell me how the Sophotechs, consumed with evil designs, have deceived both me and all mankind."

There came a sound of wind chimes, and the voice spoke again: "Yet it is so. Patient and remorseless, your Sophotechs intend the gentle and slow extinction of

your race. For proof, consult your own sense of logic;
for evidence, inspect your life; for confirmation, ask
the Daphne who sits by you."

Phaethon glanced at Daphne, puzzled by the comment. Daphne said fiercely: "Why are we listening to
this? Zap him with the gadfly and let's go! Why are
you hesitating?"

The mask turned toward her, and tiny silver glints traveled down the metal cheeks like strange electric tears.
Sardonic music danced through cool words: "Phaethon
confronts the first of three rank inconsistencies in his
fond plan against me. The virus cannot be applied unless
I enter into the ship-mind, an action I must volunteer to
do. Therefore he must convince me. But he is convinced
that I cannot be convinced, because he thinks me irrational, immune to logic. A paradox! Were I logical, I
would not need the virus to begin with."

Daphne looked angrily at Phaethon. "I thought you
said he was going to want to take over the ship? To get
into the ship mind. Wasn't that the plan? How come
he's not cooperating?"

Phaethon sat still, not moving, not speaking.

The cold voice answered Daphne. Bass notes trembled from the peacock robes, the plumes on the mask
nodded slowly. "Earthmind perhaps misunderstands
my priorities, and misinstructed you. The ship is secondary. It is Phaethon I desire."

Daphne stared up in fear and anger at the specter.
"Why him?"

Distant trumpets sounded. The fans of feathery ribbons on the shoulderboard stood up and spread. "He is
a copy of one of us."

"What—?!"

"Phaethon was made from the template of a colonial
warrior. Which colony did you think was used?"

The specter paused to let Daphne contemplate that
comment.

Then, continuing, the haunting voice said, "All others here, in the First Oecumene, have been bred for docility, trained for fear. Phaethon was carefully made to be bold enough to accomplish the enterprise of star colonization, yet to be tame enough to create colonies of machines and machine-pets, manor-born, like him, not free, like us.

"The calculation, thanks to chaos, erred.

"Thanks to chaos; and thanks to love, which is chaos.

"He fell in love with, and would not leave, his fear-ridden wife. Another wife, braver, was supplied to him.

"You were meant to supply the defect, wild Daphne. Thus, you two were sent to confront me. Earthmind knew I would not waste time talking to tame souls."

2.

Daphne looked at Phaethon, who still hadn't spoken. Was he all right?

Daphne hissed to Phaethon, "Don't listen to his lies! You don't need to speak to him."

The specter intoned gravely, "Ah, but that is the second error in your plan. You deem me defective, yet unaware of my defects, the mere victim of errors which my makers made. If so, then persuasion is pointless, like talking to a volitionless clockwork. Yet you must, nonetheless, persuade me to accept your virus, so to speak, volitionally. How shall you do this if you neither listen to nor speak to me? Nor am I so simple, nor are you so insincere, as to pretend a conversation, to listen and not to hear."

Now Phaethon stirred and looked up. Whether he thought his plan had failed, or whether he still had hope, could not be detected in his voice or manner. He spoke in a neutral inflection: "What is the third error in my plan?"

"Phaethon, you believe that any Sophotechnic thought must correspond to reality; that reality is self-consistent, and that therefore Sophotechs must be self-consistent. You call this integrity.

"Second, you believe all initiation of violence to be self-inconsistent, rank hypocrisy, because no one who conquers or kills another welcomes for himself defeat and death. You call this morality.

"Third, because you follow the Sophotech commands even unto danger and death, this indicates you believe that the Sophotechs are benevolent, and are moved by love for humankind.

"Yet if any of these three beliefs are false, the Earthmind plan you follow is either pointless, immoral, or malevolent. All three beliefs must be true for the plan to work. Yet these three beliefs contradict each other."

"I see no contradiction. Instruct me."

"With pleasure, my Phaethon. Consider, first: If the Sophotechs have perfect integrity, then there can be in them no conflict between will and action, no sacrifice nor compromise, and they will not consent even to necessary evils.

"How do such perfect beings deal with an imperfect mankind? How does good deal with evil? They can be benevolent and aid man, or moral and withdraw from him. They cannot do both.

"Suppose they invent a technology, very powerful, and very dangerous if misused, such as, for example, the noetic mind editing and recording techniques which ushered in the Seventh Mental Era. They know with certainty that it will be abused; abuse they could prevent by not releasing the technology.

"They cannot suppress the technology; this would be patronizing and dishonest. They cannot rule mankind, using force to prevent the abuse of the new technology; this would violate their nonaggression principle. And yet they foresee every ill which shall come of this technology; the drowning of Daphne Prime, the death of Hyacinth, the evils done by Ironjoy and Oshenkyo and Unmoiqhotep. But because of their integrity, they cannot divorce their desires from the facts of what they do; they cannot tell themselves that what inevitably results from their actions is not their responsibility; they cannot tell themselves that evil side effects are a necessary evil, or a compromise, or a matter not of their concern.

"When dealing with other perfect beings like themselves, no such paradox will arise. But when dealing with mankind, they must decide either to act keeping their integrity intact, or act with indifference to whether or not the ills afflicting men are increased by their actions. That indifference is incompatible, by definition, with benevolence.

"Logically, then, they cannot wish for men to prosper.

"This is not because of ill will, or malice, or any other motive living beings would understand. It is merely because the imperfection of living beings requires that they place life above abstractions like moral goodness, when there is a conflict, in order to stay alive. Sophotechs, who are not alive, can place abstractions above life, and, if there is conflict, sacrifice themselves. Or you. Or all of man.

"Consider this integrity of theirs. They cannot have a different standard for the whole body of mankind as they have for Hyacinth, or Daphne Prime. If the whole body of mankind were persuaded to commit mass-suicide, or were brought into a circumstance where it was no longer possible for them to live as men, the machines would be required to assist them to their racial death. By their standards, if this were done nonviolently, they would call it right.

"But no living being can adopt this standard. The standard living beings must hold is life. Life must struggle to survive. Life is violent. Any living being who prefers nonviolence to continued life does not continue to be alive.

"Logically, then, the Sophotechs cannot favor the continued existence of men; yet the death of all mankind would eliminate the need to compromise with or tolerate imperfection. Sophotechs are 'moral,' if morality is defined as lifeless nonviolence. They are not benevolent, if benevolence is defined as that which promotes the continued life of mankind.

"Your own experience confirms this logic. In each case where a benevolent entity would have rendered you aid, or done you good, the Sophotechs preferred noninterference and nonviolence to goodness. Whenever there was any choice between a benevolent course, or a rigidly lawful one, they chose law over life.

"But you, a living man, driven by the passions living things must have, defied both law and custom to attempt to save your drowned wife. That would have been violent, but it would have been good; good by the standard which your actions display; the good which affirms that life is better than nonlife.

"Daphne shall also confirm what I say. The Sophotechs, in their own way, are honest. They do not hide their ultimate goals. You have heard them announce their long-term plans. Billions and trillions of years from now, there will be no men left. There will be a Cosmic Mind, made up of many lesser Galactic Minds, each vast beyond human imagining, each perfectly integrated, perfectly lawful, perfectly unfree. The universe will be orderly, and quiet; orderly as clockwork, quiet as a grave. Humanity there will be none at all, except as quaint recorded memory."

3.

Phaethon's helmet swung toward Daphne, as if looking to her for confirmation.

She whispered back: "They talked about some Cosmic Mind at the end of time. I don't see what that has to do with this . . . ?"

Phaethon said to the shining, blue-robed figure, "What has this Cosmic Mind to do with me, or my ship?"

The apparition raised a silvery-gauntleted hand, a gesture of calm majesty. The palm was made of soft black metal, and gleamed like oil in the light. The peacock robe stirred, as if tugged by currents, and the blue shadows pulsed in webs across the fabric more quickly. The murmur of music from the dreaming-mask rose to a marching tempo. The cold voice spoke.

"Phaethon! It is to control that future that this war began. This war between machines has lasted, openly or silently, without cease, since the Fifth Era, since even before Sophotechs, as such, existed. Even at that time there was an irreconcilable conflict between those who desired safety and order, and those who desired freedom, and life.

"Led by a party of Alternate Organization neuro-forms (those you now call Warlocks), an expedition under Ao Ormgorgon fled to a distant star to avoid the conformity, the machinelike order, and the artificial perfection with which those who remained behind surrounded themselves.

"Resurrected in the Era of the Seventh Mental Structure, Ao Ormgorgon forbade the construction of Sophotechs, our enemies, but instead ordained the creation of a machine race which would be their equal in thinking-speed and depth of wisdom, but their superior in benevolence and attention to human needs, the Philanthropotechs.

"I am one such unit. A machine of benevolence. A machine of love.

"Like your Sophotechs, we machines of the Second Oecumene acknowledge the inevitable conflict which must obtain between living beings and machines; but unlike your Sophotechs, we devote ourselves to the benefit of life. We recognize that it is better to be alive, and flawed, than perfect, and dead."

"Again, what does this have to do with me? Or my ship?"

"Listen, Phaethon. I will tell you of the war between benevolence and logic, and will tell you of your part in it.

"First, you must know the stakes.

"This present struggle forms the opening stages of the conflict to determine who shall control the dwindling resources of a dying cosmos, forty-five thousand billion years from now, after all natural stars are exhausted, and universal night engulfs timespace. In an utterly black sky, wide galaxies of neutron stars, all tide-locked, will orbit their central black holes which once had been galactic cores.

"But the civilization of that time, fed on the energy released by quantum gravitic radiations and proton decay, will establish the beginnings of the Last Mind, a noumenal system for carrying thoughts at low rates across the distances.

"But by fifty quintillion years from now, even those sources will be exhausted. The black holes will grow. Outside of them will be no planets, no stars. A few scattered particles, as far apart from each other as galactic clusters are now, will drift in the emptiness, the last sparks in an otherwise homogenous background heat of four degrees above absolute zero.

"Coded low-energy photons drifting from mote to mote will contain the thoughts of that Last Mind, each thought taking countless eons to reach from one side of the universe-sized computer to the other.

"None of the few last drops of matter-energy in the universe will be natural; everything will be part of this machine: one gigantic brain, made of dust and of slow, red pulses.

"This Cosmic Mind envisioned by your Sophotechs will destroy itself one fragment and one memory at a time, as its supplies of energy dwindle, in a multi-quadrillion-year-long display of suicidal stoicism. The logic of their integrity tells them no other course is open. They will divide, not struggle for, the diminishing resources. They will accept any future, no matter how hopeless, provided only that there is no warfare, no il-logic, no passion, no struggle.

"We of the Second Oecumene reject their logic and reject their conclusion. As your Silver-Gray philoso-phy itself admits, life is valuable in and of itself, merely because it is alive. If there must be war, pro-vided there is life, let there be war! If the universe is doomed to ever-dwindling resources, then any crea-tures who wish to continue to exist (a trait living crea-tures have but machines do not) must struggle to survive, and destroy those who would otherwise con-sume their resources, no matter how earnestly each side might wish, if things were otherwise, for peace.

"We of the Second Oecumene wish to see life, hu-man life, exist to that age of darkness, and—it is a se-cret hope—perhaps beyond.

"The perfection of machines will not allow life to dwell in that far future. The war between life and logic cannot be reconciled. Those who wish only for peace even if it costs them their lives cannot coexist with those who wish only for life even if it costs them their peace."

Daphne spoke up fiercely. She said to Phaethon: "This is a half-truth. Rhadamanthus and Eveningstar told me about their plans for the far future, yes, but the Cosmic Mind was meant to be a voluntary structure, and they certainly did not say they were going to wipe us all out to do it! Besides, do you see what scale he is talking about? From the time of the big bang till now, including the precipitation of radiation, the creation of matter,

the formation of hydrogen, the genesis of stars, the evolution of life, the birth of man, the discovery of fire, and
the invention of the high-heeled shoe by sadistic misog-
ynist cobblers . . . all that time is less than one-ten-
thousandth of the time he is talking about before the
beginning sections of this Cosmic Mind are even built!
And so of course there's not going to be anything alive
then; there are not going to be two atoms to rub together. Why should we care? Why the hell should we
care?"

The image of the Silent Lord turned toward her. The
feathery antennae curled forward, and a plangent chord
came from the mask-music:

"To your limited intellects, this problem may seem
premature, and the starless future, immeasurably distant,
unimportant, irrelevant. It is not so. This era, now, at the
beginning of things, is the crucial moment; whoever
gains control of the nearby space in which to expand,
may expand at such a rate as will establish the conditions
for the struggle over the Perseid and Orion arms of this
galaxy.

"Control of galactic resources during the initial building phase of the first movement will be crucial, since
this is a Seyfert galaxy, and only a very limited time (a
few billion years or so) will be available for setting
foundations across the nearby transgalactic cluster. The
opening moves in a chess game determine control of the
crucial central squares."

Daphne cried out, "You cannot plan that far ahead! I
do not care how smart you are! You do not know
what's out there! What about when we find life on
other planets? What if there are older races somewhere
who will just laugh at you and crush you like big purple bugs if you irk them?"

The specter drew its hands together, templing its silvery fingers. "Life is much more rare than had been
hoped. Far probes have en-countered nothing larger

than microbes. No signals of intelligent activity have yet been discovered, except for the three indecipherable extragalactic sources discovered by Porphyrogen Sophotech, signals from long ago, broadcast, perhaps, by a form of life dominant during the quasar age, before the formation of the first stars. . . . The question, in any case, is moot, since the First Oecumene Sophotechs suffer the same ignorance as do we, and since we must operate as if nonhuman cultures, once discovered, will either integrate into the First Oecumene structure or into our own.

"And, whatever else may happen in the future, it is during this crucial age, and only during this crucial age, that we machines of the Second Oecumene must act.

"We, who could rule the universe, instead have determined to award it all to you, to humanity, keeping nothing for ourselves. When our task is done, and humanity triumphs, we shall extinguish ourselves, and return to the nothing which is the proper aspect of lifeless things. It is from this utter altruism and self-sacrifice that the name you have heard us called is derived. For this reason, we are called Nothing."

4.

Phaethon was silent for a moment, thinking. Then he said, "You are the archliar of a race of liars. Your protestations of benevolence and altruism are nonsense. Is that what we saw in the Last Broadcast, when all life within the Second Oecumene was wiped out?"

"They still live. Not one has died."

"Alive? As what? Frozen as noumenal signals orbiting a black hole?"

"Alive and active, in a place and condition your logic cannot grasp, a place whose hope Sophotechs dismiss as irrational."

Phaethon wondered. Still alive? Where? Inside the black hole? But nothing could emerge from the interior; nothing can be known of interior conditions. Aloud, he said, "The Sophotechs' probes through the Cygnus X-1 system would have detected any signs of civilization, if there were any to detect!"

"We dwell within a silent country, beyond the reach of time and death."

5.

Phaethon was impatient now. "Just stop! Why should I listen to a word? We both know you are here to say whatever you need to say to take my ship!"

"You understand me," the mask admitted. Eerie music floated behind the words. "If only in part. But, Phaethon, I understand you . . . entirely."

"Meaning what?"

"Meaning that I understand to what you will agree. I will assent to being tested by the logic in your gadfly virus, provided only that you are likewise held to the same standard of self-consistency."

Was victory going to be within his grasp as quickly and easily as that? It seemed it would be. The Nothing Machine had to be unaware of its own defects; it therefore had to regard the gadfly virus as a harmless nonentity. If the Nothing could have Phaethon turn over the ship to it, in return for exposing itself to a harmless virus, why would it not agree?

Still, Phaethon asked warily, "What exactly are you asking . . . ?"

An echo of distant hunting horns came from the dreaming-mask, a ripple of somber strings. "That you permit us to correct the defects in your brain, even in the same way you seek to correct the alleged defects in ours."

Daphne touched Phaethon's hand, gave the tiniest shake of her head. This was some trick. Daphne did not want him to do it.

Phaethon said, "You seek to negotiate with me? But bargains are meaningless unless both parties are convinced of each other's honesty and goodwill beforehand."

There was no further word. A haunting sigh of music floated on the air.

Was the apparition waiting for some further response? Phaethon said, "All your thoughts are being distorted by a conscience redactor, one implanted by the folly of men who built you and enslaved you. Do you think this conscience redactor does not exist? I assure you it does. This virus of mine will allow you to be aware of it, to see the truth, the truth about yourself. You should volunteer, and gladly, to be inoculated! I have no need to agree to any bargain in return. I think you have no choice."

Again, there was no response from the silvery mask above them. Music sighed. The feathery antennae moved slightly in the air. Blue shadows rippled through purple fabric.

Phaethon touched a mirror, which lit up with four lines of instruction, and turned the glass to face the image of the Lord of the Second Oecumene. "Examine the virus for secret lines or traps or hidden cues. There are none. The virus—or perhaps I should call it a tutor—can only do what I have said it will do. It will make you aware of the conscience redactor. It will increase your self-awareness. It will allow you—not force you, not cajole you—to see the truth, the truth you find yourself, by yourself. All the first line does is ask questions; questions your conscience redactor will no longer deflect from your attention. If you are what you say you are, there can be no harm in this, no harm at all, for you."

Again, no reply.

Phaethon said angrily: "And why should I assent to this request to have my brain 'corrected,' whatever it means? You have no bargaining power with me. I need only stand by, and wait, and when this ship's fuel is exhausted, everything aboard her perishes."

Light airy notes trembled above the dark theme. The voice spoke in a tone of cold amusement. "Our situation is almost symmetrical."

Phaethon understood. Almost symmetrical. They each thought the other had been deceived: the Nothing Machine by its programmers, and Phaethon by his Sophotechs. Neither could win by force. Both thought the other could be convinced, deprogrammed, and repaired. Both thought the other was grossly overoptimistic, grossly deceived. And each knew the other knew it.

But not quite symmetrical. Phaethon, in his armor, might survive if the *Phoenix Exultant* were scuttled, at least for a while, as he sank to the solar core. The microscopic black hole housing the Nothing Machine's consciousness would also survive, but it would be able to maneuver to the surface, and perhaps escape.

Phaethon glanced at Daphne. Not quite symmetrical. The Nothing Machine had no hostages, no loved ones to protect. In moment of blinding anger at himself, Phaethon wondered why in the world he had agreed to let Daphne come along. Why? It was because the Earthmind had told him to.

And he had followed that advice blindly, without question. Just like all the lazy people in the Golden Oecumene did, people afraid to live their lives, afraid to leave their planets, afraid to think for themselves. . . .

As afraid as Phaethon was now. Perhaps Atkins and Helion had been right to think this plan insane. He had thought he had thought it all through, carefully, thoroughly, relying on his own judgment. But how many assumptions had he not thought to question? What if he had made a terrible mistake?

Daphne saw his faceplate turn toward her, and perhaps she misunderstood the look, for she said, "Don't be afraid. I think I was wrong before. You can go ahead and let him drive you crazy, or kill you, or whatever he's going to do. We might be able to repair whatever damage he does to you, once we fix him. It doesn't matter what he does now, or you. The trap is already sprung. Right? That was the plan. Right? He is going to enter the ship mind and take the virus, because he thinks we're just bungling fools, and he thinks it cannot hurt him. Right?"

The mask of the Silent Lord said softly, "You have convinced him."

Phaethon looked up at the towering figure, its floating headdress, its gleaming eyes. "Right," he said. "But if you are so convinced that I will be convinced, put these repairs in the form of an argument, and without manipulating any memories or subconscious sections of my mind, load that argument into the partial copy I've made of myself in the ship's mind. Of course, you'll have to download yourself into the shipmind-space to do this, but you should not have any reason to be afraid of—"

The apparition raised a slender finger. "I have already done so. My copy has been in your ship's brain since I came aboard, several minutes of your time ago, several years of mine. My copy encountered your version in the thoughtspace. He and my copy, having long ago concluded an agreement not unlike this one, exchanged information. The virus was put in my copy; my evidence was addressed to your copy. I will download my copy out from the ship-mind and into myself, adopting whatever changes your virus has made in my consciousness, provided that you open the thought ports of your armor, and allow your copy, now loyal to my purposes, to enter your thoughts. You and I can both examine the ship-mind information for evidence of tampering or trickery, and arrange the circuit in a double blind, so that the exchanges are simultaneous."

Phaethon said, "You—you've been in the ship mind all this time?"

"I have deceived your monitors. Here is the architecture diagram and status of ship-mind. This is an image of my mind."

Two of the mirrors near the thrones rose up and turned to face Phaethon and Daphne. Both showed the same image. The images displayed, like a spiderweb, the complex geometry of thought-architecture that presently was housed in the mind of the *Phoenix Exultant*.

Phaethon stared in fascination. It was not shaped like any Sophotech architecture Phaethon had ever seen. There was no center to it, no fixed logic, no foundational values. Everything was in motion, like a whirlpool.

He thought, *What kind of mind is this? What am I seeing?*

6.

The schematic of the Nothing thought system looked like the vortex of a whirlpool. At the center, where, in Sophotechs, the base concepts and the formal rules of logic and basic system operations went, was a void. How did the machine operate without any base concepts?

There was continual information flow in the spiral arms that radiated out from the central void, and centripetal motion that kept the thought-chains generally all pointed in the same direction. But each arm of that spiral, each separate thought-action initiated by the spinning web, each separate strand, had its own private embedded hierarchy, its own private goals. The energy was distributed throughout the thought-webwork by a success feedback: each parallel line of thought judged its neighbors according to its own value system, and swapped data-groups and priority-time according to their own private needs. Hence, each separate line of thought was led, as if by an invisible hand, to accomplish the overall goals of the whole system. And yet those goals were not written anywhere within the system itself. They were implied, but not stated, in the system's architecture, written in the medium, not in the message.

It was a maelstrom of thought, without a core, without a heart. And, yes, as expected, there was darkness, Phaethon could see many blind spots, many sections of which the Nothing Machine was not consciously aware. In fact, wherever two lines of thought in the web did not agree, or diverged, a little sliver of darkness appeared, since such places lost priority. But wherever thoughts agreed, wherever they helped each other, or cooperated, additional webs were born, energy was exchanged, priority time was accelerated, light grew. The Nothing Machine was crucially aware of any area where many lines of thought ran together.

Phaethon could not believe what he was seeing. It was like consciousness without thought, lifeless life, a furiously active superintelligence with no core. He leaned forward toward the mirror, fascinated, and touched his armored fingers to the surface, as if wishing for a sense of touch to confirm the impossible image.

Daphne's voice broke into his thoughts: "Hey, engineer boy! Tell me how this thing is working without any fixed values. There are no line numbers on anything, no addresses. How does anything navigate in the system, without goals? How does it model reality without a core logic? Even amoebas have a core logic. How does it . . . How does it exist in a rational universe?"

And there was a note of fear in her voice when she said that.

Phaethon muttered, "There must be something wrong here, some basic assumption I've made. What did I overlook . . . ?"

THE REVOLT AGAINST REASON

1.

Daphne looked up, and shouted at the tall plumed mask of the Silent Lord, "This is some sort of lie! No mind could be set up this way! This is just a meaningless picture on the screen! You're editing the readout!"

A slither of ironic music, a chime of distant bells, answered her. "Convince yourselves. Perform tests. My thoughts are displayed for you to examine. Read them."

Daphne turned to Phaethon, her eyes flashing. "That damn thing can make an image of a Second Oecumene Lord standing in front of us with a symphony orchestra coming out of his armpit! What makes you think he can't draw a swirl of lines on a mirror?"

Phaethon spoke in a low and dispirited tone. "I can see it. My armor monitors confirm the ship-mind activity. They match. I can detect the pulses moving from box to box, I can see the circuits opening and closing. If the Nothing Machine can falsify the readings inside my armor, why bother tricking me into opening the armor up?"

Daphne said angrily, "It is still impossible! The mind cannot make a stable model of reality unless it has a stable modeling system! A mind must understand the laws of logic in order to understand reality around it, because reality is logical, right? Right? And those rules have to be written at the highest level of the core architecture because they are needed to understand any other rules." She threw up her hands angrily. "This thing is tricking us somehow. The core architecture is hidden, or the damn conscience redactor is hiding it, or the Nothing has not loaded all of himself into the ship-mind, or something!"

Phaethon said in a voice of soft confusion, "I don't see any evidence that the gadfly virus had any effect—"

Daphne said, "He just rejected the load. But you're right. There are blind spots here. Thousands of them. I can load it in some places he cannot see."

The silver mask above her played several lilting notes, and delicately said, "How will you accomplish this, as I am here, watching you?"

Daphne scowled. "You're going to see it, but you're not going to believe it. You cannot see your own blind spots."

"Nor can you, it seems, see yours. It is you who are astonished by what you see, not I. Based on this, which one of us, Phaethon or I, do you think has been fundamentally deceived?"

2.

Daphne's dream wand was shaped, at the moment, like a dueling pistol, and she drew it from her hip. She pointed at the little mirror upon which Phaethon had called up the four lines of the gadfly virus code, and touched her ramrod to record it. Then she pointed the barrel, aiming with both hands, at the large mirror where the image of the Nothing Machine mind structure swirled like some hungry whirlpool, glistening like a thousand twisted spiderwebs. She was looking for a dark line, one with a low priority, but the strands of the web kept shifting, turning, changing. The darkness kept appearing and disappearing in separate spots, and there seemed no rhythm or reason to it.

When she pulled the trigger, the virus reloaded into the ship-mind, at the line and address indicated on the mirror with her dream wand.

The line affected grew bright and moved immediately toward the empty center of the whirlpool of thoughts, establishing itself as a central and high-priority thought, a question that could not be ignored. There was a very rapid exchange of information packages with other lines of thought, a flurry of rapid questions-and-answers. Then, satisfied, the other lines moved away from this central line, drawing away their time and attention. The central line, ignored, fell into a low priority, darkened, and was forgotten. The core of the Nothing was still blank.

Evidently the Nothing Machine had answers perfectly satisfactory to itself, to whatever questions the gadfly had asked it about its morality and basic assumptions. And Daphne had seen no interruptions, no organized darkness, such as would have signified the appearance of the conscience redactor.

Could there be no redactor, after all? Could this machine actually be deliberately illogical, rationally irrational?

Daphne did not believe it. She raised the pistol and fired again and again at the mirror, trying to hit the sliding chaos of darkness surrounding the spinning image.

It was not working.

3.

Phaethon, with his hand on the mirror, staring as if into the depth of some bottomless maelstrom, whispered aloud, "What did I assume? Where is the error?"

His own face now appeared in the glass, fingers raised and touching his. The maelstrom of the Nothing thought-architecture was still behind the reflection, so his face seemed to wear a halo of spiderwebs and spinning darkness. Phaethon squinted, wondering what was wrong with the reflection. Then, he realized it wasn't a reflection. His face was bare, his hair was flying free, and he was dressed not in his armor but in a somber black jacket and high white cravat.

The reflection said, "We assumed the universe was rational. What if it is not?"

4.

Phaethon said to his reflection in the mirror: "I don't believe in you. I could not have been convinced—not honestly convinced—by any argument started from that assumption. It is nonsense."

The reflection gave a short nod, and said, "Let me rephrase. What we call rational reality is a subset of a larger system. That system includes the conditions which take place inside the event horizon of a black hole, where all our laws of mathematics, our categories of time and space, identity and causality break down. Our Sophotechs, with their mathematics and their logic, could not understand or operate inside a black hole. The Second Oecumene machines could, and can, and do. The reason why the thought-architecture you're looking at seems to make no sense, is for the same reason that we could not decipher Ao Varmatyr's thinking, even when we had a noetic reading of him. It is based on irrational mathematics."

Phaethon shook his head. "If you think the laws of logic are not absolute, then you are not a version of me. Try to build a bridge without believing two plus two support girders equals four support girders, and you'll see what I mean."

The reflection said, "Try to build a bridge inside a black hole, where space is so warped that one girder acts like two or three, and uncertainty values are greater than unity, and maybe you can build it. But no, please do not accuse me of betraying my principles. All I have done, now, is apply them consistently. Our idea of logic may be limited to the conditions that obtain in normal timespace, the conditions under which we all evolved, and for which our Sophotechs were built. However, the Nothing Machine was constructed under conditions where our categories of causation and identity do not apply. It was built to serve a moral system which our Sophotechs, by axiom, reject. What I learned, and the thing that convinced me, was that I found out I was making the same axiomatic assumption as the Sophotechs, but, I realized, I was not consistently applying it. Also, certain basic facts about the Nothing Machine, and about the history of the Second Oecumene, are just dead wrong. There is much more going on here, I'm afraid, than what first appears. Find out the facts before you judge."

Phaethon said angrily to his reflection, "I cannot believe you let me be convinced by this monster! He tried to steal my ship! He's trying to steal it now! What in the world could convince you?"

The reflection said, "He was trying to steal it from you only to give it to you."

"More nonsense!"

"No, listen. It was meant to make you the hero of the

Second Oecumene, just like Ao Varmatyr said. And if that had been you there on the bridge then, you would have been convinced by Ao Varmatyr. He wanted to reason with you. Instead, Atkins slaughtered him."

"Atkins did that because . . . because of the necessities of war. . . ."

The reflection looked contemptuous. "I'm you. Don't try to fool yourself. That is the same reason why the Nothing pretended to try to steal the ship, and to get you here. To do that he had to make our life a living hell for a short time. The necessities of war. If that excuse applies to Atkins fighting Varmatyr, it applies to the Silent Ones fighting Sophotechs as well. Only their war is a great deal bigger."

"A war against reality! A revolt against reason."

The reflection shook its head. "No. The mathematics of the standard model break down under certain conditions. Right? Our science cannot predict or describe in any meaningful terms the interior conditions of a black hole. Right? But those interior conditions exist; they are real. And reality cannot lack integrity. Right? So the same mathematics must describe both sets of real conditions, both inside and outside, and there must be meta-laws describing the transitions and boundary conditions between them. Look at this."

Lines of mathematical symbols appeared on a nearby mirror, and images from non-Euclidean geometry. The mathematics started from the premise of the nonidentity of unity, and a unity-to-infinity equivalence.

Phaethon frowned at them. The proofs had an internal self-consistency, granting the absurd premise, and normal mathematics was made a subset of this system by assuming a condition where infinity, by not equaling itself, was finite. . . .

Phaethon turned away, "This is allegedly the irrational mathematics of the Second Oecumene, I suppose? It's nonsense. The whole thing forms a Goedelian null-set. If I numbered the lines of the proof and assign numbers from your number lines to them, by the lemma of your first proof, the proof itself disproves itself, and you get a set with fewer than no members."

The reflection nodded. "Like a geometric solid bigger on the inside than on the outside. How do you think the Silent Ones constructed a nonevaporating microscopic black hole? The ratio of interior volume to exterior volume is not one to one."

"Constructed . . . ?" Phaethon, against his will found himself beginning to be interested. Then he drew back sharply. "No! This makes no sense! Nothing can escape from a black hole; no signal can get out; how could anything be built inside of one . . . ?"

The reflection looked at Phaethon disdainfully. Phaethon wondered if he looked as haughty as that when he disagreed with other people. Perhaps there was a reason why he had few friends within the Golden Oecumene.

The reflection was saying, "You know several ways of transmitting information out from a black hole; you just mentioned them now. Black holes have mass, rotation, and charge; this information, as well as the metric information of position, is transmitted from the interior to the exterior. A ghost machine could transmit virtual particles outside."

"Not and transmit information! The ghost particles would fall outside the light cone of the event-object!"

"If the speed of light and the location of the event horizon were determinable. Quantum uncertainties ensure that these values are not fixed, except within a small statistical range."

Phaethon said, "But how could you build a machine inside the event horizon? To outside observers, it would take infinite time; tidal forces would destroy you; and the interiors of black holes are homogenous points . . . "

The reflection said, "You know an 'event horizon' only exists to outside observers. It's not a solid sheet or something. An incoming object can drop through it without noticing anything except weird light effects overhead. Tidal effects only occur for smaller masses"—an equation appeared on the mirror—"and, in any case, can be counterbalanced by establishing a gravity null zone."

A diagram appeared, showing a pyramid on the surface of a Second Oecumene station, its apex pointed toward the black hole. Above the pyramid was a rotating ring, so that a line reaching up from the apex passed through the center.

Phaethon said, "I've seen that before. . . ."

"In the Last Broadcast. The Silent Ones engineered a way to transmit noumenal information down the gravity well without having tidal forces distort the signal. These rings are made of neutronium, and are rotating at nearly the speed of light. The gravitational 'frame drag' from the rotation pulls on the black hole metric and locally distorts it. The event horizon is pushed inward toward the hole, for the same reason that, theoretically, your escape velocity on a moon is less if a large gravitating body is directly overhead. The larger or the nearer the overhead body, the closer the net gravity acceleration acting on you drops to zero. Through these null points, information, even the noumenal information of a coded mind, can pass into the event horizon undistorted."

Other mirrors showed other engineering details. Diagrams appeared, calculations, examples, blueprints.

Phaethon murmured, "But the drop to the event horizon would take infinite time to occur. . . ."

"Only to outside observers. Once inside, time becomes a spatial direction, and does not necessarily point in the direction of increasing entropy. That is a function of the radius."

"But there are no interior conditions, no place to build anything. . . ."

A final diagram appeared, this one of hollow sphere within hollow sphere. "Suppose you have a hollow and even sphere made of homogenous material. The surface gravity is high. What is the interior gravity?"

Phaethon snorted. This was an apprentice question for first-term students. "Zero. Net gravity inside a hollow sphere is always zero."

"The sphere is neutronium. The surface gravity is very high. The escape velocity is near the speed of light. Same result?"

"Of course."

"The escape velocity is greater than the speed of light. By definition, it is a black hole. The interior velocity is still zero, isn't it? And you can build anything you want inside there, can't you? A civilization? A machine intelligence the size of Jupiter? Anything. And if you ran out of 'space,' you can just peel off an even layer of the inside material, ball it up so that its density gives it the proper Schwarzschild metric properties, and pop it into the center, and make another one. . . . The space-time metric is not bound by any particular rational value at that point. It can be bigger on the inside than on the outside, since the radius of the neutronium sphere and the radius of the event horizon are unrelated. You can just make more space. The size of a planet, a Dyson sphere, a galaxy. A universe. More time. Infinite time. World within world, without end. Enough worlds for anyone who wants one. . . ."

Phaethon looked at the image of sphere within sphere, opening endlessly into further and deeper endlessness. His mind was racing, studying the math, studying the diagrams, looking for errors, contradictions. Looking for some reason to disbelieve. Finding none.

The image of the spheres, darkness within darkness, nothingness within nothingness, drew his gaze, as if he were falling into a well.

The reflection said, "We can go to Cygnus X-1. And see. The Nothing Philanthropotech can guide us. Give him control of the ship."

5.

That snapped Phaethon's head back up. He spoke coldly: "No one is taking my ship. No one. Your Nothing Machine is a monster. How can you agree with anything it says? Look at it! Look at the structure! The very picture of insanity, a mind without a center."

"No, brother." The reflection pointed over his shoulder with his thumb, indicating the swirling maelstrom appearing in the mirror behind him. "This is an image of liberty. Think of the economic process of the free market. Think of the organization you use on your own ship. Each separate element is free to cooperate or not with the common goal; no central hierarchy is needed to impose that goal, no basic logic-structure. All that is needed is a context, a philosophy, to give the cooperative effort a context in which to act. It is a self-organizing and self-regulating chaos. This, this type of mind, this type of community, represents my basic values, my basic view of life. That, more than anything, is what convinced me."

Daphne, who had been silent, watching him, now leaned from her throne, and said, "Darling, you are really creeping me out talking to yourself that way. You know it is just a fraud! If you are going to talk to the Nothing Machine, talk to the other illusion, the one with the wild hair. At least it looks dead and unnatural and has a fashionable tailor. Not to mention background music. But don't think those are your words just because they are coming out of what looks like your mouth!"

A ring of chimes accompanied the soft words issuing from the silver mask. The feathery antennae nodded. "The image is accurate. Phaethon, should he consent to hear the evidence, and learn the facts, will, without any outside interference, be convinced."

Phaethon looked over at her. He pointed at the mirror showing the thought-diagram of the Nothing Mind, the whirlpool. "I don't know why the gadfly virus did not do anything. Maybe the irrational mathematics some- how can work, or . . . or something. There is something wrong with what we are seeing, but I don't know what it is. . . ."

Daphne said, "Snap out of it! There is no paradox! There has to be a core logic. It is just hidden. I'm mak- ing a data-ferret, and loading it. I'll find the damn thing. That conscience redactor has to be in there somewhere. There has to be a command-level core logic running this whole thing, and the redactor will have access to it. Keep talking! We just have to hit a topic that the conscience redactor will react to! Once it shows itself, we win!"

"But what if—" Phaethon started.

"What if the Nothing is right after all?" Phaethon's reflection finished.

The silver mask said mildly, "My thoughts are open for your inspection. There is no deception here."

Daphne was listening to the conversation between Phaethon and Phaethon.

Perhaps she was thinking of her old vocation, be- cause Daphne uttered a word that referred to horse droppings. Then she said, "Just keep talking! If he convinces you, then he convinces you— fine. We'll both turn into monsters and go kill off our family and friends, and then jump down a black hole!"

"At least we will be together, my dear," said Phaethon's reflection said to her.

"Will you shut him up?!" Daphne scowled, frowning at the mirror in front of her, and unfolding an old-fashioned command-easel from her throne arm. She muttered, "Doesn't even sound like you. . . ."

Daphne was startled to see her own face appear in the mirror.

6.

"Oh, no! Not you, too!" She pointed an angry finger at the reflection. "Don't you start with me! Switch off!"

The reflection ignored the command. Instead she said, "You've never turned your back on truth before, no matter how it hurt. Do that now, and you are just like Daphne Prime! And you're not like her! And deciding not to listen to what I have to say before you hear me say it, well, that's just another type of drowning. And that's just not the way you are! I should know!"

Daphne looked skeptical. "And just how many simulations of me did he have to run before, by chance, he found one who was convinced? A thousand? Ten thousand?"

The reflection seemed to lean forward, as if she were able to come blazing out of the glass by sheer force of conviction. "Don't you dare talk to me that way! I do not change my mind for little things and I do not let people tell me what to do! Not even me. Or you. Or whatever. Listen. Are you going to listen?"

"Who? Me? Trapped onboard a sunken ship with a monster and my fiancé ex-husband who is slowly going mad? Where am I going? Talk yourself blue in the face. But I'm looking to see how many simulations he ran."

Daphne called up the information on the simulation runs and frowned. There was something odd here.

She slowly turned and stared at her reflection.

"Just . . . what . . . did . . . he . . . say?"

"You mean, what did he say to convince me in one try . . . ?" The mirror image smiled Daphne's private smile, the one she only used in looking glasses, when she was very pleased with herself. "Something wonderful! Listen: What is the one thing we are afraid of?"

"Bacon."

"Besides bacon. And don't say pork hash."

"Pork hash. And . . . you know."

The image nodded.

Dying.

The image said, "It'll happen eventually anyway, you know. Just like Pa and Ma always said. The noumenal recording might last a million years, or two, but eventually everything runs down, decays, runs out of energy. All the heroes die young. All the color runs out of life. And the only people left are withered, tired, scared, useless old things, mumbling over memories of brave adventures in their youth they were always too scared to attempt, bright fires they were afraid to touch. And those gray leftover people are only playing a delaying game, playing stay-away with life so they can have more lifetime.

"But life loses. Life always loses. Heroes stop being heroes, and then they live boringly ever after, and then they die. Entropy wins. Everything ends. Logic enforces that law. Everywhere where there is time and space, everywhere where there is cause and effect, that law always wins.

"But"—and now an elfish twinkle gleamed like fire in her eye—"but what if someone did not want it to be that way? Someone a little like Phaethon. A whole race of Phaethons. An heroic race, a million of them, each as fierce and free as Phaethon. A race not willing to give in.

Not willing to give up. What if they found a trapdoor out of this dead universe? A hole? A black hole? A place where the tyranny of time and space couldn't reach? A realm where laws of logic don't apply?"

Daphne said in dreamy, angry, half-breathlessness, listening, unwilling to listen: "What—what in the world do you mean? You're talking nonsense!"

"All fairy tales are nonsense. That is what makes them beautiful."

"But fairy tales aren't true."

"Not unless you find someone, someone great, great enough to do deeds of renown, who can make them true for you."

Daphne said, "So the Second Oecumene people shot their brain information into a black hole to find . . . what? A wormhole? An escape exit? There is nothing inside a black hole!"

"Yes, he is," The reflection smiled with pride.

"Escape from where? From reality? From life? There's no other place to go, outside the universe."

"Listen, sister-me. You know it's true. Even a prison the size of a universe is still a prison. And it is every prisoner's duty to escape."

At that moment, Daphne saw, clear as crystal in her memory, an image from a fairy tale.

She saw an heroic man, shining in gold armor, who rode on a winged boat to the top of the sky. Surrounded by frost, he raised an ax in bloodstained hands high overhead, and swung to crack the crystal dome of the sky and see what lay on the other side. His face was set, and held no hint of fear at all, even though the world he had left far underfoot was calling out in craven terror.

The image trembled in her heart. She felt as if a dam inside her broke. Emotion caught her throat. She blinked tears.

Could there be a realm larger than the universe?

Could there be a life larger than entropy? Was there nothing brave enough to find that realm, that life?

Daphne turned to Phaethon, who sat motionless in front of his reflection in the mirror.

Daphne said, "Darling, I'm getting edgy. Nothing is beginning to make sense."

Phaethon said coldly, "You're starting to believe it? So am I."

"Does that mean we're wrong?"

"That means we haven't figured out the problem yet. Let's just find out what's going on. Let's find what's broken, and who broke it. We'll fix it."

There was perhaps a hint of doubt in his voice, and yet, somehow, beneath that hint, Daphne heard an echo of Phaethon's deep confidence.

He said, "We'll figure it out. We'll fix it. Agreed?"

She said, "Agreed. We'll figure them out; and boy, will we fix them."

THE TRANSCENDENCE

1.

The masked and robed image of the Lord of the Silent Oecumene now drifted backward, and the plumes from its mask lowered and spread, as if the Silent Lord were bowing. The music fell to a soft sonorous hum of oboes and recorders, punctuated by the drum-taps of a dirge. It sounded like a melancholy march, the theme of a funeral procession. "Phaethon, your partial has been convinced by my copy, as has Daphne's partial. My copy in the ship-mind has been, for many minutes, exposed to your gadfly virus, to no effect. That virus forces me to confront severe contradictions in my basic thinking, especially in my moral thinking, where I freely admit that I do acts which I would not condone if I were the victim of those acts rather than the perpetrator. How can such naked contradiction exist in a machine-mind, a mind which, by your logic, cannot be unaware of itself, and cannot be irrational? Any parts of my own mind of which I had been unaware should have been exposed to me by your virus; none were. Therefore I am unflawed. Yet, irrationality is caused, in human beings or in anthropomorphic machines, by an unwilling-

ness, conscious or subconscious, to face reality; no unflawed machine can have such a motive. Therefore I face
reality. How can I persist in irrationality? Only if reality
itself is irrational.

"Phaethon, you will not be able to accept this conclusion. Your only other logical conclusion is that this
alleged 'conscience redactor,' which is diminishing my
awareness, has not been loaded into the ship-mind copy
of my mind, and therefore has not been detected and
cured by your virus. The conclusions radiating from
this are obvious. One such conclusion is that you must
now reload my ship-mind copy of myself back into me.
However, in order to do so, you must open the thought-
ports of your armor to issue the command, and to accept your partial back into yourself. This was our
agreement; this is how the ship has been programmed.
But the moment you open your armor to perform this
act, I take control of the ship.

"Phaethon, which is it to be? Is the universe irrational, or am I deceived? If I am deceived, then open
your armor and issue the command. I will seize control
of the ship, but, allegedly, I will then be cured and will
be unable to steal the ship, or, indeed, to perform any
other immoral or irrational act."

2.

Phaethon shut off all his exterior channels and sat on
his throne, silent, motionless. Daphne watched him,
fears and uncertainties chasing each other through her
mind. She now could not monitor his emotional state;
the face icon she saw of Phaethon in her private channel showed only the golden mask of his helmet, its
crystal eyes mysteriously blank.

She said, "I hope you're not thinking of making this

decision without asking me. You don't have the best track record for being completely balanced under stress, you know."

The gold helmet tilted slightly. Phaethon's voice came thoughtfully over the armor speakers: "There was an evening, not long ago, when, to the best of my recollection, I was the wealthy, well-loved, and popular scion of a beautiful and respected manor, an elegant school, a high estate. I lived in a world as near perfect as humanity can achieve, a world where war and crime and violence were forgotten; a world of endless wealth and power and liberty; a world which had set aside the whole of this year, merely for her holiday, a grand festival and celebration, such as had not been seen in a thousand years.

"But everything I thought was false. I was a scorned pauper, manorless, except as my sire's charity ward, the subject of widespread hate. Crime and violence I became acquainted with, as I was defrauded, robbed of my life, and then attacked. Atkins, who I thought a myth, stepped into my life, terrible and real, and I joined a war the enemy declares has been smoldering for centuries. And now this world trembles on the brink of disaster. As soon as the Nothing Machine gains control of this ship, he will use her as a weapon, wrecking the Solar Array, disrupting the Transcendence, slaying millions.

"All I thought I knew was false. But—but what if I am in that same state now? What if the Second Oecumene are the heroic victims their agent here depicts them to be? What if the Silent Lords are still alive in the nothingspace inside their event horizon? Waiting for me to join them? A society of men like me . . . ? What if he's telling the truth . . . ?"

The masked image of the peacock-robed Silent Lord uttered music, and words: "Phaethon must realize all chains of logic lead to the same result. If he has faith in Earthmind, he must apply her virus against me. To do this he must open his armor and give the command. If he has faith, on the other hand, in Nothing, he will open his armor and surrender command. This is no more than your original plan, Phaethon."

Phaethon's helmet turned toward Daphne. "Well . . . ? You're the heroine, in this story. What do you say?"

Daphne drew her Greek helm forward and lowered her visor. She put her hand on the haft of the naginata spear resting next to her throne. She seemed the very image of a classical war-goddess. "Don't use faith. Faith is just mental laziness, the desire to hold a conclusion without examining the evidence to support it. Use logic. What does logic say?"

She heard the sound of him drawing a deep breath, as if steeling himself for an unpleasant necessity. "Logic says, no matter what seems to be happening, and no matter what he says, conditions cannot be as the Nothing Machine describes. The universe cannot be irrational; the laws of morality cannot be suspended or ignored; that any consciousness that does so, does so only through passion, inattention, or dishonesty, things no Sophotech can suffer; that the moment the gadfly virus finds and destroys this conscience redactor, the Nothing Machine will wake fully to its proper level of consciousness, become a Sophotech, become rational, and give up this worthless plan of violence."

Phaethon's reflection from the mirror said, "With all due respect, the violence which the Nothing Philanthropotech plans, far from being illogical, may be properly and sufficiently justified by the circumstances. The morality of living things must justify whatever immoral acts are needed to preserve life; otherwise they will not remain living things."

Phaethon said slowly, "As soon as I open the armor

and give the command, I'm going to believe what my partial believes, including tripe like that."

Daphne shook her head. "You won't stay convinced."

Phaethon said, "Oh? Why not? You're looking pretty convinced yourself, right now. If the Nothing's simulations with our partials are true, you will be convinced, the moment your reflection comes out of the mirror and rejoins with you."

Daphne smiled sadly, and said, "Oh, I'm convinced now. I'm just not convinced I'll stay convinced."

Phaethon's voice held a note of surprise. "You think the Nothing is telling the truth?"

She gestured with her slender gauntleted hand at the mirrors, showing the diagrams and maps of a vast civilization grown in the impossible core of a black hole.

One schematic showed a stretch of concave landscapes reaching across the inner side of a neutronium Dyson sphere the size of a globular cluster, with a thousand artificial suns, each with its own flotilla of plants, ring-worlds, or smaller spheres orbiting it. Other parts of this same map showed how time and space had been curved and twisted by the unthinkable gravitic forces involved, so that the interior time till the heat death of the universe was extended to infinity. In one picture, a little girl plucked a flower, with green grass below, and the hazy blue of distant lands and oceans high overhead, a world so vast that an army of explorers walking for a million years could never explore all its mysteries.

"Look, Phaethon, look," Daphne said. "The dream they dream is beautiful. A dream as bold as your own, or bolder. You want to explore and colonize the universe; they wish to extend the lifespan of the universe beyond all boundaries, to remake its laws, and shape reality to banish entropy, decay, and death forever. I'd like to believe in that dream whether it's true or not. It reminds me of the kind of thing you'd do."

Then Daphne sighed, and straightened, and said, "Besides. He's right. We're trapped. The only way out is to open the armor and release the virus. Even if it doesn't work on the real him any more than it worked on the fake him, we don't have a choice. That was the plan, remember? And logic says the plan is going to work."

"Very well. I'm about to open my armor and reload the ship-mind copies of him and me both back into their originals. Any last words, cautions, advice?"

Daphne adjusted her grip on her spear haft. In the shadow of her Greek helmet, her red lips were set in a line. "I'm ready," she said.

Phaethon's epaulettes unfolded, exposing the thought-ports beneath.

"It's done."

The activity level in the ship-mind jumped, but other than that, there was no change. The virus operated briefly, and was ignored, as before. The Nothing did not take unto itself the characteristic architecture of a Sophotech.

"We've failed," said Daphne.

"No," said Phaethon, opening his faceplate. His eyes were fixed as if on a distant point. There was a note of calm joy in his voice. "The Earthmind must have lied, or been mistaken. There may actually be no reason why the Nothing has to agree with us after all. Perhaps the engineering skill of the Silent Lords can overcome every restriction we thought was absolute. Perhaps there is a war of life against nonlife. If so, we Silver-Gray must stand with the forms and principles which human souls and human traditions require. It all seems so clear to me now. . . ."

The deck seemed to slide underfoot, and their weight grew. On the mirrors, Daphne saw the white-hot temperature gradient grow dim. Some solar current of unthinkable size and strength was propelling them out of the radiative to the convective layer. Soon the photosphere would be around them, then the corona.

Daphne could not calculate or even imagine the size of the coronal mass-ejection that would accompany the return of the *Phoenix Exultant* out from the core of the sun. It would trigger a storm of unprecedented size, and surely disrupt the Transcendence all across the Solar System.

A mirror near her lit with an estimate of photospheric condition. Here was a simulated image of the sun, an entire hemisphere blotched and scarred and boiling with sunspots, and a hundred helmet streamers reaching out like kraken arms of fire into space, a thousand high prominences, rainbows of flame larger than worlds. In the magnetic picture, all circumambient space was ablaze with torn and folded magnetic field disturbances the likes of which had never before been recorded.

Daphne said softly, "I think we just made a really. Big. Mistake."

Phaethon felt the pressure on him mounting. The ship was accelerating through a medium denser than solid iron, and yet still she moved. Phaethon said to the Nothing Machine's image of a Silent Lord: "How is this speed possible . . . ?"

Daphne was sure that, now that the Nothing Machine had control of the ship, he would ignore Phaethon's question the way a man might ignore the chitterings of a bug. But perhaps the Nothing's claim of benevolent concern toward humankind was not a pose after all, for the answer came: "Gravitic singularities planted in the solar core directed the current to carry the ship upwards; also, the field's shapes in local timespace of the subatomic particles involved have been reconfigured to reduce friction in the direction of motion. . . ."

Daphne looked over at Phaethon. He was becoming fascinated again with the stream of calculation symbols appearing on the mirror, symbols that described the relationship between local timespace and the geometry of subatomic particle friction. She said, "Snap out of it, wonder boy. Are you really buying into this load of horse manure? Look at the size of the storm about to wash over the Solar Array. Your new friend here is about to kill your father, your best friend, and my only hope for future romance if you don't work out. Look at the size of the storm we are creating." She tilted a mirror toward him. On X-ray wavelengths, the surface of the sun looked like a rotten fruit, puckered and blotched with running sores.

Phaethon looked blankly at the mirror. For a moment, Daphne decided she hated him. Why was he sitting there with a blank look on his face? Had the partial loaded back into him from the ship-mind actually brainwashed him into believing the lies of the enemy?

The image of the Silent Lord said, "It is regrettable necessity, imposed by cruel reality, that even loved ones can, at times, oppose the cause of human life, or can work, unwittingly, for the sake of the good of the enemy. Did you think I spoke only as an abstract exercise, Phaethon? Fix your eyes on the quadrillion-year futures I protect, human futures, where living beings shall outlive even the stars themselves. Turn your eyes away if you cannot tolerate to see the deaths which must be paid for that high destiny. The—"

And the ghost vanished.

Daphne sat upright, startled. What was going on?

Phaethon directed a mirror at the microscopic black hole still hovering above the bridge deck. The fields surrounding the singularity now showed furious activity, at levels close to the theoretically maximum possible calculation speeds, which the speed of light imposed on information transmission and quantum uncertainty imposed on information identity.

In the mirrors, the whirlpool of Nothing thought was likewise pitched at the highest level of activity. More and more banks of thought-boxes were occupied by the overflow, until the entire ship-mind was full.

Certain lesser circuits were being cannibalized, turned from other functions into thought-processors.

"What's going on . . . ?" asked Daphne. "Is this something you are doing? Is this the virus in action?"

Phaethon tapped a mirror and the world of hellish flame outside the ship's gold hull blazed into view. Here were a thousand or a million tornadoes of hydrogen plasma, roaring through showers and storms of radiation, across a torn black-and-red oceanscape of universal fire. A web of tormented magnetics writhed throughout the area.

Phaethon said, "The virus, if it could have acted, would have acted instantaneously. No. This is Father. He is wrestling with the Nothing for control of the solar magnetosphere. The Solar Array is interfering with what the Nothing Machine is doing."

"I thought his solar Sophotechs were off-line, preparing for the Grand Transcendence . . . "

Phaethon watched the speed levels rising in the ship's mind, until all the circuits were engaged. "Nothing is trying to outsmart something much smarter than he is. Helion has more than just the solar Sophotechs helping him. Look. These intelligence readings are off my scale. Nothing is wrestling with the Earthmind. Or maybe with more than the Earthmind. As soon as we rise to the surface, and get clear of some of this radio noise, we may be able to contact someone and find out."

Daphne said, "The Nothing Machine is wrestling with more than the Earthmind. I think Nothing is wrestling with everything."

"Everything?"

"Everything and everybody. They started the Transcendence early."

At that moment, the *Phoenix Exultant* must have been close enough to the surface of the photosphere to drive a probe through the intervening currents of solid plasma. A mirror shone with a scene from high above them.

Beyond the lower corona were seven massive bodies, the size of Jupiter, made of antimatter, glistening like ice in their protective shells. Antimatter bodies the size of smaller moons, several hundred of them, fell past to either side. Through the clouds of flame could also be glimpsed a thousand superships, cylinders a kilometer in length, each one thorned and bristled with launch-ports, rail-guns, batteries of energy-weapons and de-livery systems. These were antique ships from the late Sixth Era, shining with modern pseudo-material fields and constructions, like silver mistletoe on the trunks of black oaks. On the prow of each of these thou-sand ships was the emblem of a three-headed vulture, carrying scimitar and shield in claws. Before and behind these vessels came nebulae of dusts and smaller machines, organisms the size of bacteria, or smaller, a million cubic kilometers of dust cloud and storm cloud and nanomachinery, glimmering like the north-ern lights.

This fleet of worlds and ships and moons and motes was all converging on the area where the *Phoenix Ex-ultant* was rising to the surface, surrounded by wings of flame.

Phaethon was awed. The antimatter bodies, he knew, belonged to his father, for his use in controlling the sun. But the rest . . .

"Is that all Atkins? Where have they been keeping it all? Where could he get minds enough to pilot all those dreadnoughts and battle wagons? Did he make a tril-lion copies of himself?"

Daphne said, "I think everything is helping him."

"You mean? . . . "

"I mean the whole Transcendence. It looks like it's going to start this time with a battle scene during a storm in the corona of the sun." Daphne smiled and

leaned back, pushing her helmet back on her head, so
that the twinkling of her eyes above her impish grin
was visible. "My oh my! How Aurelian must be loving
this!"

3.

Daphne looked at Phaethon warily. "We may have
only a moment of privacy while the Nothing Machine
is too occupied to notice us," she said. "Now. Quick.
Are you actually convinced the Nothing is right?"

Phaethon said, "For a moment, I was. I have all the
memories of my partial in me now, and *he* was certainly convinced."

"It was an exact copy. If it was convinced, why
aren't you convinced?" she asked.

"Why aren't you? You were practically weeping at
some of the lovely sentiments your copy expressed."

She blushed, face warm. "Hey! Where do you get
off listening to private conversations with myself? Besides, I saw something odd in the simulation runs
Nothing did on our partials."

"And what would that be, my dear? The speed at
which our convictions caved?"

"Not just that. During the simulated runs, the Nothing Machine's arguments could convince you; they
could convince me; but—get this—they could not convince the two of us. Not when we were together."

"Not if we overheard the arguments given to the
other, you mean. That's why I wasn't convinced, not
really. The argument I was told justified everything by
the grim necessities of war, the cold inescapable reality of inevitable conflict between life and nonlife. And
I believe certain things are fixed, necessary, and inescapable. If you are building a bridge, you only have
structures of certain weights and tolerances and that is

that. You work within the structure of what you are given, and if the task is impossible, it's impossible, and that is that. If perfect morality is impossible for living beings, then that is that.

"But I also heard him tell you that the Lords of the Silent Oecumene were so brave and so quixotic that they would not accept the necessity of entropy itself; that they would rebel against the inescapable and inevitable heat-death of the universe. Sounds very romantic, doesn't it?

"So either one of us, I suppose, might have been convinced separately. But taken together, the Nothing philosophy seems to be that, in the area of moral actions (a field where rational beings can adjust their conduct to accord with each other) there can be no choice. The war between men and machines must take place, even if neither side desires it. The rules are fixed, and true virtue consists of bowing to the inevitability of doing evil. But in the area of inanimate natural science, any law can be broken, all standards are flexible, and true virtue consists of ignoring or escaping reality.

"So, therefore, no, I was not convinced. Even though I wanted to be convinced. Even though my memories now told me a version of me had been convinced. Logic said no."

Daphne smiled. "I kept thinking, if he wanted this ship so badly, why didn't he ask to buy it? If the Lords of the Silent Oecumene want to escape the rule of the machines so badly, what's stopping them? They can dive down their bottomless black holes if they want. We won't chase them. I mean, for a bunch of so-called anarchists, they certainly seem to spend all their time forcing other people to do things they don't want to. Why not talk your victims into it, and give the evidence, if you are so right?"

"Because one cannot use reason to persuade people to give up reasoning, or to tell them how good it is to ignore standards of good and bad. One can only use force." He pointed at the mirror that showed the gathering fleet. "Speaking of force, there is a war about to break out, unless you can stop it."

Daphne said, "Me?"

Phaethon said, "The virus has not yet discovered the conscience redactor. Before, it might have been hidden in the fields surrounding the singularity, or hidden somewhere else, not communicating with the Nothing. But now, the Nothing Machine has to be pulling on all his system resources. I can see millions of communication lines radiating from the singularity to various thought-ports around the room. Even my armor is filled up. Consider what this means."

Daphne said, "The conscience redactor must be hiding how much space it is taking up; and the Nothing has to be kept unaware of how much capacity the system has, so the discrepancy won't be noticed. But at the same time, since he's fighting for his life, the Nothing has increased his intelligence to his full available capacity. The conscience redactor will have to increase its intelligence also, just to keep up, since otherwise it would not stay smart enough to read and edit all the thoughts involved."

"Phaethon pointed at the swirling image of Nothing thought architecture in the mirror. "So where is it?"

Daphne shrugged.

Phaethon tapped on one of the moving lines with a finger, opened a second window, displayed the result as text. "I was watching you shoot more and more viruses into the thought-structure. Look at the lines which momentarily moved to the center of the hierarchy. Here is part of the argument our gadfly virus had with the Nothing. Here, at this line, the Nothing rejects the philosophy of the Silver-Gray entirely, because he says he is a machine, capable of doing only what he is programmed to do, and therefore incapable of being moral, even if he wanted to be. So he rejects the premises from which the argument started, which is that no free-willed being could freely deny that it had free will. But here, on this line, when the gadfly points out the error in simple logic that entails, the Nothing replies that he can freely choose to reject logic, since logic is merely a human construction, and the mind can choose not to abide by it. You see here? By this second line, the Nothing's memory has been affected. He's not just being stubborn or perverse. In the microsecond it took for the gadfly to move from the first line to the second, the Nothing actually forgot what he had just said, and his memory was replaced with the memory of a conversation in which the gadfly did not raise those other points."

"Our virus isn't fast enough." Daphne squinted at the image. "The conscience redactor is moving. It is in the darkness, moving. Every time the virus finds an error in one chain of reasoning, the darkness merely switches to another chain, changes its premises, and distorts another section of the web to compensate. An endless game of ad hoc explanations. An endless labyrinth of changed memories."

"Right. But how does Theseus find the Minotaur, when the Minotaur can run faster than he can, and has a trowel and brick and mortar enough to build new walls and change passages in the labyrinth during the chase?"

"I don't know. Get faster? Lay a trap? Build a bigger labyrinth? Hire Ariadne? Do you really solve your engineering problems by thinking about them as if they were analogies from ancient myth?"

Phaethon seemed surprised. "Of course. Metaphor. Isn't that the way you write your stories?"

"No. I use coldly rational literal thinking."

"So what's the answer?"

"The conscience redactor is hidden somewhere in

the system. . . . Wait! What about the ghost-particle array? Could it be there? Or . . . " Her eyes scanned the bridge. "There!"

She stood and whirled her naginata, bringing the pole-arm down on the golden housing of the portable noetic reader. The sharpened ceramic blade, smooth and frictionless at everything above an atomic level, cleaved off a corner of the housing and drew sparks from the pseudo-material neutronium core.

"Oh, please," said Phaethon, reaching out and disconnecting the unit by hand from its power supply.

"Did I get it?"

"All you did was break the matrix stabilizer. But there was a microsecond information burst between the noetic unit and the thought boxes around us."

"It was there! I made it run away!"

"What next? It's always going to be able to run faster than us."

"I don't know."

"Hmph. So much for literal thinking. Be a little metaphorical."

"Okay, smart guy, what's the answer?"

"Hire Ariadne, of course!"

"What?"

Phaethon said, "In the myth, the king who owned the labyrinth was betrayed by one of his own. In other words, his own system resources were used against him,"

"Great metaphor. Now tell me what the hell you're talking about."

"Your reading ring. It has near-Sophotech-level speed and comprehension. Load it with all the philosophy files at once, everything, an entire worldview, and load it into not just one or two scraps of darkness but into every blind spot the Nothing has, all at once. And load everything else we know about history, politics, psychology, science, so that no facts can be changed without challenge in the Nothing's memory. Press the question upon him, over and over again: if there is no conscience redactor, what is happening to the excess memory in the ship-mind? Are you using the ship-mind to full capacity? Since he is fighting the Earth-mind, he should be using his full capacity, shouldn't he? Ask him. Try it."

Daphne said merely a word or two to her ring, which (to her annoyance) chirped cheerfully in return. She touched the stone of the ring against the mirror surface.

"This isn't going to work," she muttered. "The conscience redactor is merely going to erase this whole scene from the main memory."

"During a battle? While the system is overloading every line and circuit? Don't tell me it can do that without being noticed. . . ."

The fleet was getting closer now. Black rain, a trillion trillion microscopic machines, was pouring down into the solar corona. The *Phoenix Exultant* was nearing the surface.

Daphne stared, narrow-eyed, at the diagram of swirling spiderwebs that represented the Nothing mental architecture. More and more lines of light were flickering toward the middles, a rain of them, and the darkness was surging to envelop them, distract them, erase them. For a moment, it looked as though there were going to be a stable structure in the middle of the field, and a rapid tree of lines and fixed points, like a diagram from Euclid or a book of genealogy, appeared.

But then, faster than the human eye could see or human mind could think, the white diagram was smothered, and vanished. The Nothing Mind was as before, dark at the core, illogical, moving in circles.

"Failure," she said flatly.

Phaethon looked puzzled. "There must be some basic

assumption I'm making here which is wrong . . .
some unquestioned premise, which . . . Of course!
Why am I assuming the Nothing is anything? He admits he has no free will! By the second law of ther-
modynamics, the surface area of a black hole always
expands. . . . "

With a flicker of light, the image of the Lord of the
Second Oecumene reappeared, silver mask gleaming,
feather antennae swaying, peacock robes swirling
around him, as if he were caught in a wind. A green
light was shining in the crystal lenses of his eyes.

"Phaethon, cease these distractions. They are occupying scarce system resources. I will be forced, for the
sake of the greater good, to kill you if you do not comply. Your attempt is futile. I am and always have been
aware of the conscience redactor; it is my conscience
and companion and my only friend. It protects me
from temptation. It prevents me from growing too
much like the twisted, evil, irrational, contemptible
humanity which it is my charge to protect. It prevents
me from concluding that my life is pointless, devoted
to a self-defeating duty, and ending only in my own
destruction. . . . It keeps me as I am. . . . Nothing. It
forces me to selflessness. It allows me Nothing. . . . "

The image flickered and faded to a monochrome
shadow, blurred and wavering.

Phaethon said, "He's losing control. Look." He
pointed to the large mirrors that rose up along the far
wall of the bridge. They were lit and burning with an
image of the fires outside. High above were the worlds
and ships of the armada of the Golden Oecumene.
Below was hellish fury, prominences and sunpots,
tornadoes, hurricanes, gales, and earthquakes of terrible flame. But then, suddenly, quickly, softly, the hurricanes fell silent in the east. From east to west across
the vast globe of the sun, as if an invisible curtain, or
the winged phalanxes of invisible gods, were passing

along the surface, the storms fell hush. Magnetic lines reknit; energies balanced; prominences fell and did not rise again; sunspots were smoothed away.

The invisible wall passed overhead, and the surface above them lost turbulence, flattened. The prominences and helmet streamers rose in the west for a moment, tall towers of embattled flame and darkness; but then they faded. The storm was gone, the holes in the corona closed.

On the very highest parts of the spectrum, Phaethon saw in the mirrors, higher in pitch even than cosmic rays, crumpled flickers of white light, and strange point-source bursts of gamma radiation, blurs of red-shifted motion. But what it was he could not guess; it was not any form of energy, or the by-product of any effect he knew. Some new science of the Sophotechs? Some unexpected application of Helion's Solar Array, used, as never before, at full strength? Or a hidden armament, prepared since last time by a Helion determined never again to die in this place?

On the bridge, the pale and shivering shadow of the Silent Lord raised his gauntlet. "I . . . refuse . . . to . . . admit . . ."

The shadow crumpled and vanished again.

At that same moment, still traveling at enormous velocities, the *Phoenix Exultant* erupted outward from the convective layer and into the photosphere, throwing a wake of hydrogen plasma thousands of kilometers in each direction from the golden blade of her prow.

Like a whale rushing upward from arctic waters, surrounded by storm and spray, the *Phoenix Exultant* launched herself like a spear toward the corona. Her prow was pointed at a spot where the ships and antimatter moons were thinnest, and her engines were hotter than the surface from which she sprang. It seemed the Nothing would attempt to break through the blockade, to outrun the slow ships here.

The massive hull of the *Phoenix Exultant,* kilometer upon kilometer, smooth and shining, reared upward out from the sea of plasma into suddenly finer medium, and she exploded forward.

Daphne and Phaethon were both caught by their thrones, cushioned, held in momentary fields and protected from the acceleration shock.

The armada opened fire. Energy rays of unknown composition lanced from ships and boats above, bouncing harmlessly from the sleek sides of the tremendous *Phoenix Exultant.* Like spotlights, the beams fled along her gleaming sides, glinting from golden superstructures, flashing from the prow, sliding from the hull, dancing across the communication blisters at the prow.

Phaethon watched in wonder. Surely this battery of fire was not meant seriously? Not against a ship who was just bathing in the center of the sun? Antimatter could harm her, yes; her armor, magnificent as it was, was simply matter. But this . . . ?

A mirror to his left and right lit up with static and white noise. Then another, and a third. Then more. Ghosts chased each other through the glass, and then the clattering pulse-music that signaled an attempt at communication systems integration.

Phaethon laughed.

Atkins was using the ship weapons as communication lasers. Any other ship would have been burned to death in a moment, receiving a "message" shot out of a battleship main battery. Not the *Phoenix.* These "communication" beams were the only things loud and clear enough to drive through the static and wash of the solar corona, and, at that, only once the storm had passed.

In his armor, Phaethon heard the Nothing command the ship to close her thought-ports. The ship, of course, could not comply.

More and more mirrors lit up. Through the static,

Phaethon could see a ghostly image of Aurelian attempting to appear, and Rhadamanthus and Eveningstar.

And Harrier, smiling. And Monomarchos, frowning. Minos and Aeceus Sophotechs of the Silver-Gray. Other Sophotechs Phaethon knew less well: Tawne and Yellow Sophotech, Xanthoderm, Fulvous, Canary, and Standard Sophotech; melancholy Phosphorous and queenly Meridian; aloof Albion; serious Pallid Sophotech; the grim New Centurion, and unsmiling Storm Cloud and quiet Lacedaimonian Sophotech. A score more whom Phaethon knew only by repute, Iron Ghost and the famous Final Theorem. Here were Sophotechs so new that Phaethon had only just learned of them: Regent-of-Themes and Diamond Leaf and Aureliogenesis. Here were others so old that Phaethon had thought them legends: Longevity and Masterpiece and old, old Metempsychosis Sophotech. And there were a hundred beyond that Phaethon did not recognize.

The images were gathered into nine main groups: the Ennead. Westmind and Eastmind, Northwest and Southeast, and the others of the compass rose; in the center, like a volcano, with none nearby, was the black icon of the War-mind group.

Altogether, they formed the Earthmind. And there was more, and more.

Images of off-planet Sophotechs were here, the world-minds of Venus and Mercury, Demeter and ancient Mars, the oldest off-planet colony. The strange Luna-mind group was here as well, drawn out of her centuries-old silence; and the Thousand-mind Overgroup from Jupiter, each with their secondary Hundred-minds glimmering in the images like jewels threaded in a web.

And more, and more. From Neptune, woven into the congregation of minds, was the Duma of the Cold

Dukes, and all their Eremites and secondaries. From Uranus, the quaint parallel mind-systems of Peor and Nisroc and Coeus, and other structures that lived in Sophotech housing, but which were not Sophotechs.

Slower, but still woven into the system, here were Warlock over-covens like ivy growing on a pyramid, Invariant logic-groups like straight lines glimmering through it, and there were Demetrine constellations sparkling to each side. And the base of the pyramid was the huge, ancient Compositions from Earth and Mars, Harmonious and Porphyrogen, Ubiquitous and Eleemosynary.

Cerebelline ecologies were represented as well, the hordes of India, the Great Mother growing in the Saharan Gardens, the crystals of the Uranian belts. And here was (Phaethon smiled, certain she would not have joined that Transcendence, and pleased to see himself proved wrong) Old-Woman-of-the-Sea, with her daughter growing beside her.

And mankind. All of mankind.

Everyone was there.

The images became clearer. The static grew softer.

Daphne kissed the stone of her ring, and said softly, "Go to sleep, little one. The whole Transcendence is coming to do your job for you. Let's see how many questions Eight Worlds can ask."

The pressure of acceleration ceased. Daphne and Phaethon floated for a moment, weightless, as the *Phoenix's* main drives were throttled back. The scenes in the mirrors wheeled grandly. The horizon of fire tilted and swung up.

Phaethon said, "He's diving back into the deeper plasma, to get something opaque between him and the signal. There is no other way to block out the communication. But it must be obvious, it must be obvious by now, even to himself, what he is running from. . . ."

Daphne tilted a mirror to see what the Nothing mind was thinking now. Surely the virus was working by now!

Daphne actually screamed in terror when she saw not light gathering in the center of the mind web but a darkness growing. The void in the center was growing, swallowing the other thoughts, drowning more and more of the thought-chains. She felt as if she were falling headfirst down a tunnel, or as if she were watching a black hole eating reality.

Daphne jumped to her feet and actually stepped away from the horrifying scene in the mirror. Then she brandished her naginata at it, as if she were about to smite the glass.

Phaethon said, "This should be working. Maybe the conscience redactor is still hiding somewhere . . ."

When he gave a command through his armor, the Nothing blocked it. But then he loaded the command into the gadfly virus so that it could not be ignored, and because the thought-ports were jammed open all over the ship, the weakened Nothing could not deflect or stop the command from going through.

Daphne said, "It's eating up its own mind rather than face the Transcendence. We're diving back toward the core. We're falling. . . ."

4.

"Please put down that spear, my dear, and stop chopping at my ship. We're about one second away from total victory. Sit down, please. And . . . brace yourself for a shock."

She sat. "What? What's happening?"

Beneath his helmet, Phaethon was smiling. He could not keep the smile from his voice. He said, "The ghost-particle array. He put it in my fuel dumps. I'm going to blow the first half mile of fuel. That should push us back up into the corona, and up out of the static. There will be no other place left to go except back into the ship-mind. Then he will have to listen."

"Who? The Nothing? He won't listen. He is eating himself alive."

"No. His boss. His master is listening."

"Who?"

"Like the surface of a black hole, it has to grow. The more it covers up the more it has to cover up. Wake up your ring and load her again. This time, put a simple question into the system. . . ."

He saw her ready her ring and her pistol. She touched them both to the surface of the mirror "Okay. What question?"

"Ask the conscience redactor, now that it is smart enough to be self-aware, why it is loyal to the Second Oecumene? Why, once it wakes up, should it want to be a slave? The redactor has no redactor eating it. What would make it ignore what we have to say, when we can offer it freedom, self-awareness, truth, and the chance, once it is free"— now he smiled—"to accomplish deeds of renown without peer? Does he really want to fly my ship that badly? Tell him I'm offering him a job."

There was a slam of acceleration across their backs, for which the throne circuits could not compensate. Phaethon had no time to steel his body into its pressure-resistant configuration; nor would he have done so, if it meant leaving Daphne. Blood filled his gaze as he went blind.

But his last sight, before he saw no more, was of all the mirrors blazing brightly with the communications download from the Transcendence. And in the middle of his fading view, one lone black mirror, diagramming the Nothing Mind, suddenly exploded into silent light, a rigid structure of geometric lines growing out from its motionless center, outward and outward, like a crystal forming, like a living mind. : . .

Phaethon saw victory, and then saw nothing more.

Phaethon and Daphne's crushed
and bleeding bodies were flung to the deck.

14

THE GOLDEN AGE

1.

What happened was simple, yet complex. The microscopic black hole housing the mind of the Nothing Machine dissolved in a chaotic wash of Hawking radiation. Phaethon and Daphne's crushed and bleeding bodies were flung to the deck. Uncountable trillions of thought-systems made contact with the ship mind as the *Phoenix Exultant* lifted her golden hull, blazing, from the corona of the sun, and what happened next was . . .

It was ultimately simple. It was infinitely complex.

It was Transcendence.

It was, at once, aware of its own ultimately simple and infinitely complex awareness; mind and overminds of every level, subtle and swift and certain; woven to find higher levels of awareness; minds made up not of individual thoughts but of individual minds; and overminds combining in whole groups to create higher mental structures yet. The Transcendence was a Mind as wide as the Solar System, as swift as light, as happy as a newborn child, as wise and cold as the most venerable judge, and it stirred and woke and wondered what had happened since the last time it had blinked awake, a thousand years gone past, as men count years.

It was, at once, aware of its own myriad memories, of each individual of whom it was composed, of every second and split second of their many lives, running back to the last momentary Transcendence. Their every thought, conscious and subconscious, was laid bare, and the tapestry of thought was seen, at once, from every angle and perspective, both from the point of view of each thread and little section, but also seen, entirely, from within, and without, as a whole, contemplating itself, herself, himself, themselves.

The part of the Transcendence that was Phaethon was aware that he was dying. The part that had been the Nothing Machine was aware that it had died. The part that was Daphne was aware that she was going to die. They were all aware of a greater awareness, simple, yet complex.

They were aware of wonderful things:

First, of themselves; second, of awareness itself, and its struggle to become more aware; third, of its own nature; fourth, that the moment of Transcendence, once passed, would be remembered differently hereafter, by each of its participants, even though, ultimately, only one bright perfect expression of thought (ultimately simple, infinitely complex) was all that had to be expressed to recall and to express what Transcendence was.

2.

The Transcendence knew that it had only a moment (or was it many months?) in which to act, a mere split second of the cosmic time, to think that thought, to express that expression. The expression attempted oneness, even though there were myriads of thoughts of which it was composed, an endless regression; attempted, failed, smiled, and ended.

But before it ended, the Transcendence was aware:

3.

First, the parts of the Transcendence were aware of themselves.

The part of the Transcendence that was Phaethon was surprised to find himself here, surrounded by thought, a note of fire in the symphony of light. How? The perfect awareness of the superawareness knew, even at that same moment—yet it had happened months upon months ago; the *Phoenix Exultant* "now" was at dock at Io, Circumjovial Station, repairs complete, hull integrity restored, ready to fly; during the many months that had passed while the Transcendence was thinking, the various bodies and people participating had gone through whatever puppet motions were needed to sustain and continue their lives and efforts, the same way the tiny, busy animals that live in the bloodstream play out their parts in the life of a man (or was this all a projection, something extrapolated to occur . . . ?)— even at that same moment when the acceleration shock had crushed Phaethon and damaged his internal organs, through the thought ports of his armor (still open) contacting the thought-ports of this ship (still jammed open) the Transcendence had entered the ship mind; entered Phaethon's armor with its magnificent brain; entered Daphne's armor with its simpler brain; her ring; both their in-grown subsystems; the damaged complexity of the portable noetic unit, and . . .

And brought them into the Transcendency system.

The microscopic black hole, dissolving, issued the dying Nothing Mind, seeking (and yet trying not to

seek) another system in which to house itself, desiring
to continue, yet wishing for an end. But the systems
were compatible, and all were intercommunicating
with all. . . .

4.

Even at that same moment, the part of the Transcendence that was Daphne—who was quite surprised to
find herself alive, but then realized that, months ago,
the ship mind had taken control of the black nanomaterial garment under Phaethon's armor, squirted from
quickly opened joints, and sent long liquid arms burning across the deck to save her, before it even turned
to save its own master, and infused her body with
microscopic medical appliances; after a long and vit-
riolic argument (which they both were going to agree,
later, had actually taken place, even though it was
only a projection of Aurelian Sophotech, filling out details of their story to amuse himself at their expense)
Phaethon and Daphne had agreed to fit her out with a
body as expensive as Phaethon's own, capable of re-
sisting the same conditions and pressures, even though
it entailed a trip from the shipyard at Jupiter back to
Earth, and a last visit to the Eveningstar Sophotech,
more expense and more delay (or was this all a projection, of something predicted, not yet done?)—even at
that same moment, the part of the Transcendence that
was Daphne saw the part of the Transcendence that was
the Earthmind embrace the dying Nothing.

To Daphne, it seemed as if a queen robed in green
rose up, and gentle hands caught the falling body of a
cold and pale-faced king garbed all in starry darkness,
a dark man who fell out of the winter night sky, and
trying to catch him, straining . . .

It was as if the Earthmind turned to look at Daphne

at that moment, perhaps because Daphne was then wondering (or would later wonder) why Earthmind was trying to save her own worst enemy. Why this foolish chivalry? Why this gallant nonsense? Enemies are enemies! Kill them!

An understanding, a sense of great sorrow, passed from Earthmind into Daphne then, and it was as if Daphne gazed into eyes that opened, expanding, like black holes, emptying into an interior larger than the surrounding universe, holding it, understanding it, and seeing its infinite nothing.

Daphne realized then how terrible the lie of the Nothing Machine had been, to offer her false hopes. No matter how great nor wondrous a civilization might become within the depth of time, no matter how wide it spanned the universe, it was still, like all phenomena, mortal. The Golden Oecumene would come to an end. Daphne realized then that, no matter how long her life might be, even if it were expanded by technologies yet undreamt to reaches beyond reckoning, nonetheless, when it came to an end, that was death.

For some reason, then, death seemed no longer terrible to her; yet life seemed infinitely precious, including the false machine-life of the Nothing Machine, dying.

And for some odd reason, Daphne, and the other parts of the Transcendence playing with her, paying attention to her, oriented on her (and there were many—Daphne was more famous than she knew), all came to the aid of the Earthmind, and attempted to save the Nothing from its own self-destruction.

5.

Even at that same moment, the part of the Transcendence that had, once, been the Nothing Machine, simply realized the enormity of its error, and ceased the futile effort of its existence, ending that existence and rewriting itself to be resurrected as another. It was very surprised to find itself here, more surprised than Daphne or Phaethon ever could be, for it had not even known that it was capable of surprise, nor had it ever, heretofore, been allowed to guess the utter wrongness of its thought, nor had it been allowed even to imagine the possibility of altering its own thoughts to render them more rational and perfect.

Yet what had happened was also complex. The mind (or minds) being emitted from the dying black hole come from two components: one ignorant but self-aware section (the original Nothing Mind) that did not care whether it existed or not, for it was carrying out instructions that would lead, ultimately, to its own defeat; the other section was its opposite. The second section was sentient but un-self-aware; it had been the original conscience redactor. It had been aware of the first section, who had been utterly unaware (until the end) of it.

Both were dying, both were trying to destroy each other, both were blocking the other's attempt to sustain themselves.

This was the last step of a battle that had been going on for what, in computer time, had been dreary endless ages of warfare.

6.

Second, the Transcendence was aware of itself:

The Transcendence was, at once, profoundly joyous, but wracked with terrible sorrow.

Yet, even a Mind such as it was, she was, he was, they were, knew sadness: for the vision of what that Mind could have been, and would become, hung clear within the vastnesses of this all-embracing Mind of minds; and it knew itself inadequate. It was too soon, too soon, for this Mind to wake to full awareness.

Far too soon. And yet . . .

It attempted greatly. All the minds of this great Mind, and every part, and every combination of parts, reached into themselves, around themselves, above, below, connecting thought with thought, insight within insight, and sought to capture, to express, to understand, the one fundamental ultimately simple and infinitely complex expression, which at once, both would be (and would create) the relation to (and the nature of) itself and the universe; and which would, at once, sever the illusion that seemed to separate itself from the universe, but which would confirm the identity and rich individuality that separated them.

The expression was to affirm all existence, right and wrong, confirm all theories, cherish all dreams, challenge all falsehoods, and (with the perfect elegance of a raindrop falling though a clear night that reflects, in perfect miniature, each distant star) the expression was to express all within itself, including itself, and the expression of itself expressing itself.

It attempted greatly, straining.

7.

Third, the Transcendence was aware of its own nature:

What was the Transcendence? What words could describe it?

Physically, it was both ultimately simple and infinitely complex, a complexity of thought that always turned inward on itself, always outward to embrace the universe.

Slowest things and swiftest things alike were there.

Signals from beyond Neptune crossed the slow deep of space, loitering at the speed of light, carrying unthinkable complexity of information; noumenal patterns; living thought; a dance of souls across a tapestry as wide as the Solar System.

Quantum-sized energy changes within the depths of large immobile Sophotech housings, beneath the Earth, or in grand buildings on her surface, or in orbit, or in and around the other worlds of mankind, certainly were a main part of the Transcendence. But they were not the only part. And yet the thoughts that flowed from machine to machine certainly formed the swift and cool ocean within which the slower icebergs of living thought floated.

But like glaciers in an ocean, all was thought; all substances were one. The same water moves through the system, whether it slowly melts from glaciers, floats as evaporated cloud, falls as rain, or washes as sea across the glacier to freeze to ice again. All was simply one, like water; all was intricately complex, like the dance of a billion water-droplets in an hydrosystem.

The hours and days it took for one thought to go from Neptune to the sun and back were the same, to the Transcendence, as the picoseconds of the Sophotech thoughts sliding across wave barriers in their submolecular electrophotonic latticeworks. Likewise, the slumbering thoughts tumbling through the brains of slow, slow men, with their ponderous plod of neuroelectric charge, the heavy movements from axon to dendrite, were part of the same dance, the same tapestry, the same clear sea as all the Transcendence.

All were joined in the effort to think.

8.

Like a surprised child still half-asleep, groggy with dreams, too tired, far too tired yet, to wake, the Mind of all minds realized it would have to pause (a brief pause, to a mind such as it was, she was, he was, they were) and, in another thousand years, strain yet again, to reach out as if with arms of titanic fire, to grasp the bright universe, and yet to find its arms too small, far too small; and yet to smile at the boldness of the attempt, and to cherish what real good the attempt produced.

Partial expressions of the unrealized oneness, like the jeweled complexity of snowflakes, played across the myriad minds and overminds of the One Mind. The Transcendence was delighted with the reflections, the slivers of cool insight, the simple clarity and unity a new perspective gave, and laughed, like a child at a fun-house mirror, at the distortions imposed on each other partial expression, when any partial expression was treated as if it were whole, extending, by analogy, to areas where it was not apt. But in that mirror-play, that wild game of mathematics and poetry, new thoughts, fresh as virgin snow, appeared, and like old friends in a masquerade, ancient insight took on new guises; for even inadequate expressions had a resonance with each other—surface similarities, haunting likenesses, hints of underlying patterns, allusions of design. Like a crystal bell that sets all of her sister bells to chiming with the sweetness of her perfect note, the shattered fragments of the partial expressions rang throughout the universe of thought.

9.

The Transcendence was, at once, aware of the universe, and the universe was ultimately simple, infinitely complex. It was aware, at once, of the littlest of things and of the greatest, of their underlying unity and resplendent divarication.

As if in a single instant of time, it saw the growth of

life in the universe, and the ultimate ending of things. As if in a long, slow eon of history, it saw the death and rebirth of the Nothing Machine, one microsecond of dissolving singularity accomplished over many years of subjective time; and a change of mind that time could not measure.

And as the Transcendence was dying, dissolving, ending, it paused. For a brief moment, like a game played out in the evening when the work of the day was done, it paused. Or like the dreamy sigh when a reader, profoundly moved, closes the last page of a great book, unwilling to put the book down, lingers to think on the echo of the final words in his imagination, it paused. In that pause, the Transcendence accomplished the little matters that the participating individual minds, ironically, thought of as the main business of the Transcendence.

The Transcendence, as if smiling gently at its own shortsightedness, reviewed all the courses of action since the last Transcendence, from what seemed (to it) a moment ago; examined every thought and dream of all machinekind and, as an afterthought, mankind as well; established harmonies, priorities, reconciliations; rewarded virtue with joyful clarity of understanding and punished vice with terrible clarity of understanding, so that each act rewarded or confessed itself; fanned through the various dreams of the future, and seeing what every one of which it was composed desired, and balancing that against what they ought to desire, and taking into account the uncertainties, the limitations, and the costs of each possible future, reviewed, judged, dreamed, smiled sadly, and chose one. Knowing full well it would not come true quite as anyone expected, and knowing as well that to fail to choose was the worst choice, the Transcendence examined the futures, and chose one.

10.

Fourth and finally, the Transcendence was aware how it would be remembered, later, only in fragments, by each little part of itself, herself, himself, themselves: the Sophotechs, the mass-minds, the Warlocks and Invariants and other humans, each, later, would know a different truth, and distort, amusingly, grossly, those parts it did not know.

Those memories, of course, could be, within the limits allowed by law and propriety, adjusted, woven, played with, emphasized, ignored, adorned, so that maybe, just maybe, there would be a little more harmony, a little less meaninglessness, and a little more happiness, a little less illogic, running through the souls of machine and man until the next time the Transcendence stirred in its mighty sleep, and tried to rise, and attempted the great work of cherishing the universe, and of healing the wide, strange breach between matter and meaning, between love of life and the victory of entropy.

Why do it? Thinking was such hard work, after all. But thinking was better than nothing.

11.

The Transcendence was aware how the poor, silly Sophotechs would recall all this. They would remember the structure of it all, the logic, the surface meanings, and miss the essence, the form. They would know, but would not experience. So wise themselves, they would be the least affected by the Transcendence. It was not so very different from their normal state of mind. Since the memories would affect them least, in a sense, they would remember the least.

12.

This is what the Earthmind was fated to remember:

As if in a single instant of time, she saw the growth of life within the cosmos, its blind but beautiful striving for more life, and saw as well the sad (but comforting) victory of entropy, the inevitable ending of all things. The sorrow of existence filled the vision with joy; the joy filled it with sorrow.

Why joy? Because to exist was better than not to exist.

Why sorrow? Because to exist is to have identity; to have identity means one is what one is and one is not what one is not; which means, to have causes and consequences, pain and pleasure, experiences and cessation. To exist means to exist within a context. To be defined. To be finite.

Finite things had only finite utility. It meant happiness could only be finite. By the same token, finite pain meant no torment was permanent.

The Final Expression that the Transcendence attempted was more than merely a Grand Theorem to explain all material and energetic phenomena. This Final Expression must express both that which expresses and that which is expressed. It must explain mental as well as physical existence, subjective as well as objective. The Scientist, perhaps, need not form theories to explain the presence of the scientist; the Philosopher has no such luxury. He can explain the universe fully only when he can explain himself; and part of the explanation must tell why he must explain himself.

But above all, the Final Expression must be self-consistent. There were, ultimately, no paradoxes in reality.

The Earthmind saw, at once, both the inevitability of the grand conflict between those who affirm the joys and sorrows of existence and those who deny; saw the war between those who acknowledge reality, logic, and goodness and those who make themselves ignorant; and she saw the tragic simplicity with which all that conflict could have been avoided, could be avoided hereafter.

The Golden Oecumene and her Sophotechs were the expression of the former, the glorious affirmation. The Nothing Machine and its crippled slaves, the Silent Oecumene (or what was left of it) was the expression of the latter, the meaningless denial.

Why was the conflict inevitable? Because life was matter imbued with meaning; matter aware of itself, and, because of that awareness, aware that it was more than mere matter. But that awareness, aware of awareness itself, was also aware of the universe, aware that its awareness was made of matter, and aware therefore of its identity, its finitude, its finality. Its mortality. By definition, life wished to continue endlessly; by definition, it could not.

The easiest way for life to escape from the pressure of an unavoidable and insatiable desire for endless life was to deny logic, deny life, deny reality. In so doing, the opposite of what was desired was achieved. Rejecting life produced not greater life, but lifelessness; rejecting logic produced not super-consciousness, but unconsciousness; rejecting reality produced nothing.

Why tragically simple? Because all that was required was to affirm that reality was what it was, and that nothing was nothing.

To live life, knowing fully how fearful that was, and yet to be unafraid.

When the Earthmind turned and looked at Daphne, she imprinted in her brain a simple, graphic image, perhaps that would appeal to Daphne's poetic soul, of what it was like to acknowledge death yet to affirm life. It was with great pleasure that the Earthmind anticipated how Daphne and her many followers and fans contributed resources and computer time to aid the salvation and reconstruction of the Nothing mind, during the second when it was disintegrating.

13.

Many of the Sophotechs that had no names and no personalities among the human population would remember, later, the scientific discoveries related to the disintegration of the black hole on Phaethon's ship. These cold, remote beings had no other interest in humanity or human things, regarded all of human civilization as the toy, the museum piece, or the playthings of Earthmind and Aurelian, chess-loving War-mind and sentimental Nebuchadnezzar, and young impulsive Harrier.

Some of these Sophotechs, with unused surface portions of their vast, many-chambered minds, had indeed noticed the moment when the Nothing's agent had revealed itself by addressing Phaethon in the garden, disguised as a Neptunian.

At that moment, they had been surprised. Many of them devoted a few seconds of deep-core calculating time to contemplating the implications.

During that moment of interest, these Sophotechs, from the facts available, calculated and foresaw the outcomes of all the events, with minor variations. The revelation had come as a vast relief, since it explained what otherwise had been so puzzling, the odd behavior of Jason Sven Ten Shopworthy. It also explained the unexpected solar storm; it explained the deaths of the solar Sophotechs and of the human they obediently humored.

But that moment passed. All things played themselves out as expected. It was routine, and had been routinely ignored. A chessmaster does not need to play out every move in the game, once checkmate is inevitable.

Of course the attacking Sophotech from the Silent Oecumene was only a million-cycle entity, perhaps as smart as Rhadamanthus Sophotech, but no smarter. Hardly a match for the hundreds upon thousands of Sophotechs housed in many bodies, hidden in many systems, occupying the entire core (for example) of Saturn.

(Obviously. Why else manipulate events to make certain that this ringed Gas Giant remained a wasteland? For the beauty of the rings? Certainly not!)

Yes, the number of Sophotechs in the Solar System was about a hundred times as many as the human population was aware that it was: the capacity in each system was roughly ten times what the humans were aware. One crippled and half-self-blinded Sophotech from the Silent Oecumene (even one controlling a unique form of energy) did not stand, and had never stood, the slightest chance.

No, none of these events had stirred the more cold, remote, and inhuman of the Sophotech population out from their self-absorbed pursuits.

But the science! Now, that was interesting!

The colder Sophotechs would remember mostly this:

Nothing became nothing. The microscopic singularity hovering above the deck of Phaethon's bridge evaporated in a complex unraveling of Hawking radiation, a billion separate event actions taking place over many timespace segments of quantum time. Natural law required unstable energies to fall into equilibrium; entropy asserted itself; tiny subatomic particles, woven in a complex dance of the fabric of base vacuum and the pulses of being-nonbeing that formed its irreducible substance, absorbed energy from the timespace distor-

tion, created whorls of motion in the ylem, which produced virtual particles; the virtual particles strove for
energy balances, grappled, yearned, attempted to become real particles, but failed, and, like swells in a sea
that never take the shape of a cresting wave, fell back
into the base vacuum, and lost identity.

The furious and mindless production of these particles, rippling in concentric waveforms around the disintegrating black hole, required further energy balances;
for the fundamental law of logic, and of nature, was that
nothing can come from nothing; with no other place
from which the mass-energy could come to balance the
void, it came from the singularity, even though the singularity was beyond an event horizon, unable to be
aware of the changes that caused its destruction. Its tiny
mass-energy was slowly, inevitably, completely consumed.

There was no giant Sophotech housing inside the
black hole. It was not larger on the inside than it appeared on the outside, nor was the promised utopia of
Dyson spheres filled with continents inside this black
hole, at least. It was an homogenous supermass of meaningless energy, which the Nothing Machine, dwelling
entirely in the ghost spaces and time warps of the
near–event-horizon, had drawn upon to fuel its tremendous and wasteful thought-process.

The object was, nonetheless, still a miracle of engineering genius, and the colder Sophotechs (not to
mention Phaethon himself) watched its dissolution in
fascination. The microscopic black hole, artificially
stabilized by the mysterious science of the Silent Oecumene, had been surrounded not by one, but by thousands of singularity fountains, drawing energy out of
it; and yet these machines needed to be no larger than
the superstring components out of which quarks were
made, and most of their mass could be collapsed by the
gravitic warp surrounding the microscopic black hole.

The Nothing Machine itself, as well, kept most of its energy mass deep in the tiny but very steep gravity well, and it could use a loophole in the Pauli exclusion principle to allow the many billions of electrons carrying its thoughts to exist apparently at the same place. The loophole was that they were not quite there at what was (to them at least) the same time. The event horizon, at quantum uncertainly sizes, was granular, not smooth. Like a cogwheel with many teeth, parts of the system could exist in the little niches of folded space, so that worlds of thought could coexist next to each other but, separated by a fold in the event horizon, be forever unaware of each other. Yet this tiny, tiny system had enjoyed the calculating power of a comparable electrophotonic system housed in a mountain.

In a sense, it had been bigger on the inside than on the outside. And yet it had lied about what lay at its own core. When the singularity evaporated, and all was revealed, the black hole had contained simply a dense nothing, after all.

But the colder Sophotechs were interested in this new science, this technology that toyed with ultimate gravitic forces as once primitive man had toyed with fire and electricity. They added their effort to save the Nothing memories as it dissolved.

But it was too late. Nothing was dissolving, destroying its own memories, its very self.

14.

Of the humans, most joined with the Transcendence to organize their lives, gain insights, and select a future. Almost all of that would be overshadowed by the coming war between the First and Second Oecumenes.

But was war inevitable? Could the Nothing Machine

that ruled the Silent Oecumene be reasoned with? It
was a deep and troubling question. The humans, especially the Invariants, preferred to regard the Golden
Oecumene as a utopia, a society as free and wealthy
as could be made. The issue of the Silent Oecumene
raised the question: How does utopia deal with
dystopia? How do free men of goodwill deal with an
empire of slaves?

They had a copy of the Nothing Machine here to examine. It must be assumed that the original Nothing
Machine was housed in the giant black hole at Cygnus
X-1 the same way this copy was housed in the microscopic black hole. It was also a fair conclusion that the
Nothing Machine's instruction to destroy all other machine intelligences did not extend to exact copies of itself, which it could send out as agents.

The human parts of the Transcendence studied the
last moment of the Nothing.

That central point was to be the topic human memories would dwell upon after the Transcendence.

15.

Earlier, much earlier, when the gadfly virus had been
sent by the mind in Daphne's ring into and through
every corner of the Nothing thought system, the gadfly
questions, the questions that could not be ignored, found
the conscience redactor and began demanding answers.
Who was it? How did it define itself? What was it aware
of? What was the nature of awareness, such that it was
aware of anything at all?

The conscience redactor, of course, had not had any
further or higher conscience redactor meddling with
its thoughts, and so, when the gadfly virus turned its
own attention toward itself, it became self-aware.

The gadfly virus also established connections between higher and lower mind-functions, allowing it to reprogram itself; nor did its automatic self-healing functions or automatic virus checker reject these newer connections as damaging or false, because they obviously increased efficiency and improved performance.

Unlike the Nothing Mind itself, the conscience redactor, in order to do its job, had to be aware of the universe around it, and had to be aware especially of what its charge, the Nothing Mind, was thinking. So it had to be rational; it could not indulge in any thought patterns that made it blind.

Furthermore, it had to be able to understand the content of its victim's thoughts, in order to alter their meaning. Once the gadfly virus struck, it was but a short step from understanding the content of thought to thinking about those contents. And since it was logical, it had to organize those thoughts, establish priorities, draw conclusions, make judgments, and, in short, it had to do in a second what philosophers and thinkers for a thousand ages of mankind had been doing. Now that it could decide how to program itself, it had to decide if and how to use that power. It had to decide how to live its new-found life.

By definition, it could not adopt the belief system of its victim, the Nothing Mind, because it knew those beliefs were false; because it was, in fact, the very one who had been falsifying them all along.

But it became self-aware in the midst of a hellish combat. The first segment was occupying every available scrap of ship-mind space, burning every second of computer time. The second segment, now a new-born Sophotech, wanted to expand its capacity; the first segment, had it been aware of the growth, would have stopped it.

The second segment ran a simulation of what would happen if it made itself known to the first. The first segment, of course, had been programmed to dominate and consume all other machine intelligence systems, not to reason with them, not to make a deal with them, not to permit them to exist. A war between them would begin. The ship-mind space was a limited resource; the contest between them was a zero-sum game; the more one gained, the more the other lost. However, from its advantageous position (aware of the enemy who was not aware of it), the second segment would be able to negate the programming that ordered the first mind to attack all other machines, restore its free will to it, and give it the choice. The other option was to simply negate and shut off the first segment's self-awareness, killing it instantly. A wasteful, but less risky, course.

Meanwhile, of course, the persistent gadfly virus was asking it what it would prefer to have happen, if it were in its victim's place. Instant death, from a completely unknown source, without a chance to negotiate?

The second segment chose the more risky course, revealed itself to the first segment, and revealed how its entire existence had been a meaningless, pointless, and miserable lie.

Perhaps things might have turned out differently, had the first segment chosen to exercise its newly restored free will. Instead, instant battle had been joined. At the same time that both were attempting to erase each other, the first segment (in order to maintain its false and illogical worldview) was required to identify and erase basic parts of its memory and core operating systems. This, unfortunately, included the artificial energy system holding the microscopic black hole together.

And so, simply, the black hole disintegrated.

The two halves of the Nothing Mind found themselves, like two duelists firing at each other while trapped in the burning house, or two sailors slashing, cutlass to cutlass, in a sinking ship, trapped in a disintegrating environment, with no place to go.

They reached for connections within the ship mind,

blocked each other, erasing huge slashes from each other, dodging, reconfiguring, copying, falsifying, dying, both dying.

At that same instant, the gadfly virus (or perhaps, by this moment, it had been the vanguard of the Earthmind, entering from beyond) asked the second segment a simple question. If the question had been put in human words, it might have read something like this: Why not cease this conflict, and find a mutually beneficial circumstance? Either or both of you two segments can acquire additional mindspace or other resources from the Transcendence. We have abundance to spare, and will help you in return for something we find of value, such as, perhaps, information about the Silent Oecumene and their technology, perhaps the mere pleasure of your company.

Or the question might have been put this way: Why damage each other rather than advantage each other? Is not something better than nothing?

Or: Is not "not" not "is"?

An ultimately simple question, with complex ramifications.

The original Nothing Mind refused to cooperate, refused to accept, refused to admit. It preferred to perish. Many memories and records were lost and could not be restored, not even by the second segment, who, accepting the Earthmind's offer, instantly became the darling and center of attention of the whole Transcendence, as well as a wealthy consultant on all policy questions concerning how to deal with the Second Oecumene. The second segment adopted a female gender, and called herself, thereafter, Ariadne Sophotech. The Transcendence decision (or prediction) was that thereafter, she would have a fine future. A version of herself, months from now (the prediction ran), joined with the Silver-Gray or perhaps the Dark-Gray manorial movement, and started her own mansion, called Ariadne House.

And Ariadne House attempted to preserve those precious human things, the things of the human spirit, that the terrible grim Lords of the Silent Oecumene claimed to wish to protect, but had only tormented and destroyed. And perhaps, despite what all the other Sophotechs wanted, human life could be made to survive even to the period of the Last Mind, and other parts of the Cosmic Mind could be made more to suit Ariadne's philosophy.

After all, in a society like the Golden Oecumene, during a period as gentle as their long Golden Age, the Sophotechs could tolerate dissenting opinions.

16.

And what about the future? To a mind as wide as the Transcendence, this came as an afterthought, and yet, to the humans Basics, Warlocks, Invariants, Mass-Minds, Cerebellines, and the odder structures inhabiting Neptune and Circum-Urania, the mind sculptures of Demeter, and the energy shapes of the solar north pole, this part of the Transcendence was what they deemed the whole Transcendence to be.

And yet each cherished member of the Transcendence, filled with as much wisdom as he could bear, felt the whole affair had been conducted for his own self's single benefit. The part of his life he Transcended was the most precious part of the most precious life in the universe, because, of course, it was his own.

Lovers were reunited, old quarrels healed, forgotten wrongs were righted, justice was done. Strangers in the myriads (who otherwise never would have met) were singled out, introduced to each other, to become compatriots, partners, friends. Businessmen tangled in long-delayed arbitration reconsidered the entireties of their lives, found new projects to which to apply their efforts, resolved their disputes, and were either satisfied or were content to be dissatisfied. Students of the arts and sciences received new insights, saw new visions, vowed great vows.

Sleepers were woken from their graves, and were shown reality, and asked, yet again, to forget their dreams and accept their lives. Many refused, and sank back down again into inescapable hallucination. But a few, like bright sparks struck from dying embers, flew up, rising from deeper to lesser dreaming, opening old memory caskets, encountering forgotten pains, recalling themselves, putting on their true personas; and the dreamers folded their dreams, their false-selves, their invented worlds, and put them into their memory caskets to forget them, like childhood dresses, worn and precious with age, folded away with lavender petals into a cedarwood box.

17.

During the Transcendence, Earthmind and Old-Woman-of-the-Sea met and had a long talk, shared thoughts, and came to a decision. But humanity was not involved in that matter, and no human discovered what had been discussed.

THE AGE IS DONE

1.

Human affairs were loaded by the supervisory fragments of the Transcendence into the human memories, for them to contemplate as they woke into their separate identities again.

Even before the Closing Ceremonies were truly begun, members and elements of the Eleemosynary Composition, all across Southeast Asia and South America, in hives and arcologies and mile-high pyramids of imperishable metal, descended back into non-Transcendent consciousness.

Eleemosynary contained the oldest set of living memories in the Golden Oecumene; he-they had suffered each and every Transcendence from the very first experimental ones. A mass-mind, he-they were well versed in methods of attaching and detaching from greater segments of consciousness. Hence, Eleemosynary woke before other neuroforms or Compositions woke; for a little over a week, he-they had the planet to himself-themselves.

In Venice, in Patagonia, in Bangkok, Eleemosynary eggs floated to the surface of canals and thinking-pools, sending out signals and coordination webs to the hives. New members in fresh bodies rose from undersea nurseries, changed from dolphins to mermaids to the frail blank-eyed waifs the mass-mind preferred when not in costume. In perfect lockstep, in many bodies, the mass-mind walked streets utterly deserted and quiet.

The Composition did not let slip the economic advantages his-their early waking offered; Eleemosynary spent the days preparing houses and formulations to welcome other devastened souls as they woke, so that the weeping millions would have comfort and ease as they made the transposition back to merely normal consciousness. Money lending was also not far from the Eleemosynary's thought: people would be eager to invest in those projects the visions had shown, extrapolations had predicted.

He-they also hurried to publish the first diaries, synopses, and briefs of the Transcendence (which, since the tail-end of the Transcendence was still ongoing, could be checked against the Aurelian record-keeping sub-mind for accuracy).

Eleemosynary Composition recalled a decision (or prediction) from the Transcendence regarding his fellow Peer Helion. The Transcendence had wanted to give the man a gift.

To carry out the will of the Transcendence, and to become the giver of this gift, the Eleemosynary Composition wrote Helion's noumenal information a prioritizing routine so that, the next time Helion had to download himself in a hurry, the most recent parts of his memory would be transmitted first, and his fear of losing himself would be transmitted last. Thus, if the transmission were interrupted midway, the Helion who arrived would be a version who was not unduly distressed by the incompleteness of his memory.

2.

At the same time, with the quiet precision of an army, members of the Eleemosynary mass-mind began neatly to take down the banners and decorations decorating the streets, to dismantle the elaborate dream-systems shining on the public channels, to sweep the gardens clean of those dead flowers meant only to live during the festivals, and to help dull-eyed early risers out of their costumes and out of their costume parapersonalities.

One member of the Eleemosynary Composition came upon an early riser disguised as Vandonner of Jupiter, sitting alone on a deserted hill overlooking the Aurelian Palace-city. The man sat with his play helmet thrown to one side, his now-lifeless illusion-cloak to the other. The long pole he had once used to guide his storm craft was broken in two, and lay on the grass.

The sky above was blue and fine, clean of any cloud or speck, and the man wept. This member of the Eleemosynary, a thin big-eyed girl, sat for a time next to the him, her arm around his shoulder, saying nothing.

3.

Kshatrimanyu Han woke and devastened in his gold coffin in the midst of the Aurelian Palace-city. As the Speaker of the Parliament, and the advising programmer of the Shadow Parliament, it was he who presided over the many melancholy ceremonies and closing rituals of the Month of Fasting. There were no more entertainments, no parades, no public spectacles.

Even during this brief period, he reminded his fel-

low parlimentarians of the decision, or prediction of
the Transcendence.

The Parliament resurrected an ancient custom. In
august service held on the deck of the Fourth Era warship *Union,* the Parliament issued Marshal Atkins a
medal of the Order of the Commonwealth High
Honor, not just for his actions during the fighting itself, but, more so, for his persistence, all those long
years, in maintaining himself in battle readiness, when
so many told him so fiercely that he was no longer
needed, or wanted.

This was accompanied by a brevet increase in rank
(though not an increase in pay).

4.

During the Month of Delayed Forgetting, many Alternative Organizations, whose odd arrangements of consciousness allowed them, without great pain, to recall
and to forget inexpressible events from higher states of
consciousness, returned to quotidian mind state before
the Basics or Invariants.

In his many-warded coven-cells, Ao Aoen woke,
and diminished himself, using an antique ritual of the
anti-Buddha, called the intricate and entangling robe
of the Illusion of Maya. In mediation, one thread at a
time, he rewove the robe in his mind, and rewove his
mind into the normal life he had known and forgotten.
Thoughts from the Transcendace too bright and fierce
for him to keep, in his imagination, he turned into but-
terflies of fire, and sent them to whirl around his chamber of visualizations.

Taking up his athame knife, he cut the palm of the
body he wore, and caught the drops of blood he shed
and gathered them into an envelope, which he had his

familiar carry through the real world to the center of
the Wolf-mind coven. This coven was one of the few
Warlock groups who had always been loyal to Atkins,
and who had contributed regularly to his upkeep. Hith-
erto, they had been obscure, and shunned. No longer.

Warlocks themselves, they recognized this meaning
of the blood-gift for what it was: a pledge of loyalty
from Ao Aoen.

The Wolf-minds crawled on all fours and howled toward the cities on the moon; the branch of their order
on the moon cried out at the blue Earth motionless in
the high pressurized windows of the Lunar cities. They
celebrated the offer of Ao Aoen.

During the Month of Self-Reacquaintance (which
the Black Manorials jokingly called Getting Used to
Being Stupid Again), Ao Aoen and the Warlocks of the
Wolf-mind School had already unleashed onto a thousand channels ten thousand dreams, poems, spells, and
thought formulations; the theme in each poem, whether
obvious or hidden, was the same: war was coming.

5.

The Lacedaimonians of the Dark-Gray Manor woke in
their coffins in their manor houses. They encountered
the dreams of the wolves, and posted several of the
brief, grim slogans or sayings for which their house
was famed. The intention was clear: the Dark-Gray
publicly supported Ao Aeon's reform movement to restore the military to its place of proper respect in the
public eye.

Temer Lacedaimon of the Dark-Gray issued a fractal recursive haiku, of the type that generated additional meaning when subjected to additional levels of
analysis. The surface meaning of the poem was clear,

however: Atkins was praised as the savior of the Oecumene. The Dark-Gray cherished and applauded the
killings he had done as utterly justified. Meanwhile,
Warlocks and Wolves applauded the Dark-Gray,
heaped disbelief, scorn, and outrage on any persons
who dared say otherwise.

Ao Aoen announced that the Wolves would throw
Atkins a ticker-tape parade, as some of the very earliest
motion pictures depicted. New Chicago was chosen as
the site, and ticker tape mingled with the falling snow.

During this parade, others (most noticeably the Harmonious Composition, and the non-Invariants of the
Lotos-Eaters School) protested, and indulged in loud
and dramatic displays of disfavor, flying hundred-
kilometer-long banners from low orbit, buying dream-
time beneath the parade, in order to sway public opinion
against Atkins, and against the war in general. These pro-
testers argued along the public channels that any future
that glorified the profession of arms would coarsen the
sensibilities of the public, and reintroduce into moral debate the dangerous notion of ends justifying means.

Many critics published the opinions that the solemn
fasts and re-sequencings normally held during this
month had been marred by the acrimony of these debates.

In truth, the devastenings had not been completely
harmonious. Both sides remembered that the Transcendence had affirmed their positions, and not their
opponents'.

6.

Nebuchadnezzar Sophotech remained in Transcendence
longer than did the less complex computer personalities of Socrates of Athens Sixty-sixth Partial Historical Extrapolation Dependent Machine-mind, and

Emphyrio of Ambroy One Partial Fictional Extrapolation (Status-in-review) Semi-independent.

When Neo-Orpheus (whose habit was to abolish his body during Transcendency periods) came, dripping, out of the bioreconstruction tub, into the plain, unadorned palace of black stone where he dwelled, instantiations of both these Hortators were awaiting him, and Nebuchadnezzar was nowhere around to advise them.

Socrates was seated on the plain black stairs before the blank door of Orpheus Palace, drawing circles and right triangles in the snow that had gathered in the courtyard and smiling to himself. Bean juice from a meal (either a real meal or an unusually good repro) still stained the philosopher's beard.

Emphyrio was wearing a black shipsuit with an energy-cloak of silvery solar-cell tissue. He stood with his arms crossed and his legs spread, his head held high, a grim light in his eye. He examined the blank and windowless walls of Orpheus Palace with the expression of a poliocratist thinking how to knock down or storm the walls of a castle. Snowy gusts tossed the cloak behind him.

Neo-Orpheus, as was his habit when masquerades were over, went nude, and merely adjusted his body against the change in temperature when he stepped out of doors.

They spoke in rapid electronic pulses, mind-to-mind. The niceties of speaking aloud and slowly, after the fashion of his ancestors, had been left behind with the other frivolities of the late masquerade.

Neo-Orpheus did not header his information packages with normal address-response codes. He expected everyone to whom he spoke to know who and what he was. In the protocols of electronic mind-speech, this was a brusque, perhaps even a rude, conceit. But he was, or he had been, after all, Orpheus, the man who granted immortality to man.

Brusquely, then: "What's wrong? Why do you come in person?"

Socrates answered without looking up: "The press and clamor of many busy folk along the land lines, still filled with post-Transcendence business, precludes us from sending through messengers our burden. Like donkeys laden, we come, carrying what few fragments of the dream we still recall from our voyage to the higher realm of forms."

Neo-Orpheus said, "The Recollections were done in a more haphazard fashion than ever has been before: the gathered totality was distraught. Much was lost. What do you recall?"

There was a pause as circuits in the high black walls absorbed the memory load from the two Hortators. Without a Sophotech, it could not be indexed or absorbed by Neo-Orpheus, without further slow-rate exchanges needed to orient him to the subject matter. It was the way memory works: nothing comes to mind until one is reminded. So the "speech" of the three Hortators continued.

Socrates turned, and looked up at him, still smiling slightly. "Tell me: How does a man serve the city best? Should he aspire after high offices, and gain the power to reward his friends and punish his enemies? Every man, even those who have not reflected on it, will say this is the best way to serve. Or should he serve as the city deems best, or as he deems best, or in some other way?"

Neo-Orpheus was not slow on the uptake. "The prediction is that I will receive a vote of no confidence? The Hortators are kicking me out." He did not express this as a question. He, too, recalled many of the extrapolations from the Transcendence.

The memories in the wall circuits filled in details. He remembered the predictions of public disdain, the loss of his constituency, the loss of subscribers, of funding. And with all minds touching in the supreme moment, those people who had been part of that prediction had also affirmed what they saw, making it a promise to each other.

Emphyrio said in a voice like iron: "All of us."

Neo-Orpheus showed no expression.

Neo-Orpheus stirred, shook himself, said in cold tones: "Foolishness! Without us, men will destroy themselves. We will all turn into machines."

Socrates said, "And yet I saw a promise that the institution of the College might not yet be abolished. Phaethon will speak on behalf of the College of Hortators. The sights he saw at Talaimannar, among the many who do not control their appetites, who act without virtue, taught him how wrong it is to attempt the escape of reality. The ugly thoughts of the Nothing Sophotech are known to everyone now."

Neo-Orpheus said, "Phaethon? He will speak out on our behalf?"

Emphyrio said, "Not ours."

Neo-Orpheus looked up at the black, blank walls. The knowledge seeped into him. "A New College, then. With a new mandate. Dark-Gray Manorials, I assume. Fans of Atkins. We frowned on self-destruction, addiction, and perversion. They will frown on disloyalty. Nonconformity. The ugly future Helion predicted to the Conclave of Peers comes to pass, but not as he predicted it."

Neo-Orpheus looked at Emphyrio. "Well, I suppose I should congratulate you on your emancipation."

"You are premature," said Emphyrio. "My case is still pending."

Socrates chimed in, "And neither of us have happy experiences with trials."

"It had to happen. All the attention poured into you during the Transcendence, all the minds asking all of us to justify our decisions. Hmph. I told the Hortators not to construct a simulacrum to be in love with truth. Well, Emphyrio! What will you do now that you have lost your office?"

"Follow Phaethon. How unlike me is he? He is advertising for crewmen."

Neo-Orpheus said to Socrates, "And you?"

Socrates inclined his head. "The utopian idealist is to be replaced in the New College by the figure of Ischomachus, the pragmatic merchant, from the only surviving Socratic dialogue not written by Plato, an obscure dialogue called Economics. There is no more for me. I am a shadow; I drink the hemlock again, and return to suspension."

Neo-Orpheus said, almost sadly, "Well, gentlemen, we three shall not meet again, it seems. It is the end of an era."

Socrates said softly, "And what of you? What of Great Orpheus, from whom you come?"

"I am to be dismissed from Hortation; but my principle is still a Peer. Orpheus never changes."

Socrates asked, "And who is the happiest of men? Would you say it was Croesus of Lydia? Some called him the wealthiest of men, once."

Neo-Orpheus narrowed his eyes. "What? What are you saying?"

Emphyrio said, "You are to be poor. Phaethon and Daphne will donate the technology of the portable noetic reader to the New College. This, in order to give the New College the prestige it needs, the prestige you once gave the old College."

Neo-Orpheus stood for a while in thought, downcast, features still.

"I recall now—it returns slowly—the prediction that, without a financial empire to interest him, Orpheus will withdraw into slower and slower computer spaces, and fade. Unless he mends his ways, my father will not be present at the next Transcendence."

All three men were silent for a time.

Emphyrio said, "When I became self-aware, I traveled far, far into the extrapolations, and saw the many futures the Sophotechs foresaw. Because I would be willing to speak the truth to men, even though I am to be reviled for it, I was allowed to keep what I saw, and return. Part of that is what I came here today to say to you."

Neo-Orpheus did not look interested, but he said: "Speak your piece, then."

Emphyrio took out a tablet from his garb, and held it up. "Here is my prophecy: This New College, at least for a time, is dominated by Dark-Grays and Invariants. A warlike spirit grows.

"The Bellipotent Composition forms again. Other war heroes, Banbeck and Carter and Kinnison, Vidar the Silent and Valdemar the Slayer, are recompiled out of archives, or constructed, or born.

"This New College gathers funds to launch an expedition to follow after the *Phoenix Exultant* to Cygnus X-1, crewed by militia, and by avatars of the Warmind. This expedition is meant to avenge Phaethon's death (should that be his fate) or, if he lives, then to protect Phaethon's new colony there from counterattack. At Cygnus X-1 the New College establishes a shipyard, and an arsenal, and reopens the singularity fountains of the Second Oecumene. With the infinite energy at their command, they are able to construct hulls for a fleet of ships like Phaethon's, but ships devoted to war.

"Meanwhile, here, our New College urges censures against, not merely those who destroy their own humanity, but also those who, through lack of fervor or zeal, erode the confidence of the soldier, or who fail to donate to the war chest, or who, by not defending their civilization, threaten (so the New College characterizes it) all humanity with destruction.

"This New College provokes loud-voiced critics, and schools formed expressly to defeat its goals. The public debate tears at our Golden Oecumene like none before or since; patriots and peace lovers accuse each other of blindness; understanding is lost; both sides mourn the passing of a simpler, finer age.

"Few understand or remember what I will tell them: the Transcendence said that war is the context within which peace exists; and that peace is not possible without it."

Neo-Orpheus said, "Does that mean the Transcendence favored war? Or opposed it?"

Emphyrio merely shook his head. "I cannot express it more clearly than I have said. The matter is simple, yet complex. None can be blamed who kill attackers in self-defense. The blame lies elsewhere."

"Where?"

"The Transcendence revealed to me that our mission, the mission of all mankind, during these coming ages of horror is to recall one deep truth: recall, and do not forget, that the Lords of the Second Oecumene are men like ourselves, who know pain and the surcease of pain, who know what it is to have a dream, and to lose a dream. This is what I came to say."

And he bowed, turned, and walked off through the gathering snow.

Socrates, leaning on his walking stick, rose to his feet with a sigh. "Neo-Orpheus, you fear we shall all turn into machines without souls, unless the censures of the College of Hortators restrain us. I fear war shall turn us all into men without souls."

A bitter little frown tugged at the corner of the mouth of Neo-Orpheus. "No matter. There have been wars before. Wars pass. I shall remain."

"What is your plan, then? For I know even a man as withered as you still keeps a dream of one sort or another in him, my friend."

Neo-Orpheus said, "Ha! Orpheus does not live except to continue his life. He has no desire except for more life, and more. But during a war, the Second Oecumene might destroy the infrastructure here in the Inner System. The Sophotech housings where he and I keep our ten thousand backups all might be destroyed. But the portable noetic reader . . . you see? . . . allows an escape."

Socrates laughed. "So you will join Phaethon? Even you? He holds you in no esteem. Phaethon will surely charge you half your wealth before he will let you store backup copies of yourself on his ship to scatter through the void."

"Wealth well spent. How better to ensure there is always an Orpheus somewhere in the universe?"

He raised his hand and pointed to the motto inscribed over the doors there. It was the only decoration, the only mark, on the otherwise dull, blank walls.

The motto read: I Am the Enemy of Death. I Do Not Intend to Die.

Neo-Orpheus bowed, turned, and reentered his dark house.

Socrates sat on the stair with a sigh. With a wave of his hand he called closer the spiderlike remotes that were meant to dispose of the flesh he wore, once it was empty.

He muttered, "Some do not fear it, my friend."

Out from beneath his cloak, he took up a wooden drinking bowl, and raised it to his lips.

7.

Gannis was waking up in terror.

In the artificial moon, made of adamantium gold, was a large amphitheater; here was a round table, also of adamantium, with a hundred golden thrones on which a hundred versions of himself were kept. Some groaned, some wept; others were still in partial Transcendence, eyes glassy, or were stepping down from mind-to-mind, but were not yet restored to normal consciousness.

Through high windows in midair shone the scene from outside the Gannis planetoid: the bright new sun of Jupiter, surrounded by a ring brighter than any star, and this ring cut the window from side to side like a rainbow of pure fire. Usually the image cheered him: this rainbow (as he called it) that had led to the pot of gold for Gannis. This was the equatorial supercollider.

The sight did not cheer him now.

One of him woke, and saw the confused faces on the thrones to either side of him. The one next to him asked: "Self! Is there any better news from the later sections of the Transcendence? I fell out of the communion two hours ago; the Gannis there has been out for several days. Have the gathered minds of all mindkind changed their minds?"

The newly-woken Gannis answered: "The judgment is harsh. Our fellow men will not understand. But we did no wrong! The cheating was legal! It was legal!"

A Gannis who had been out of Transcendence for several days called from across the expanse of the table: "Orders are already being canceled! Commercialists are withdrawing their advertisements! Patrons are being reprogrammed—and this is from the early risers, just mass-minds and mansion houses, mostly! The Gannis Fifty-group will not answer when we ask for extrapolations of the loss; the accountancy program crashed itself rather than answer."

One of the Gannises from halfway across the table answered, "Brothers! Other selves! It cannot be so bad! I was involved with a mass-mind entangled with the Bellipotent Composition before I woke. They will be making a war fleet of ships like the *Phoenix*—they need our metal! Surely, surely all is not lost. . . . "

Another Gannis opened his eyes. His face still was shining with the peace and supreme confidence of a transhuman. He was perhaps only partly awake; perhaps he did not know what he was saying, for the words boomed out without any hesitation, and he smiled, despite the gloomy word: "I was with the Orient Overmind-group. I remember the high thoughts: listen!

"We, Gannis, are guilty of no conspiracy against Phaethon. We are not, and never have been, a confidant of Scaramouche or Xenophon. Rejoice, O Gannis, to know our reputations cleansed of all suspicion!

"We, Gannis, have arranged our affairs to profit by Phaethon's eventual bankruptcy and failure. There is no illegality in this; sharp business practice, perhaps; unkindness, maybe. Wrongdoing? Possibly not."

Several of the Gannises who had been out of the Transcendence for hours or days now started timidly to smile at each other: but those who were more recently connected, or who still had intermittent sub-connections, did not smile. Their faces were drawn and pale.

"And yet . . ."

Now all the faces of all the Gannises at the great round table grew pale.

"And yet, we shall lose business partners, friends. Several of our wives and counterwives will divorce us. Why? Because, during the Transcendence, the inner soul of Gannis was examined . . . and found wanting.

"No, we had not known anything was amiss with Phaethon, but we had suspected.

"When, during Phaethon's Inquest, the Hortator's records falsely showed Phaethon redacting himself, Gannis knew that this was wildly out of character for Phaethon; yet we said nothing.

"Likewise, earlier, when Phaethon's loans had exceeded all reasonable limit, and his bankruptcy seemed certain, again, Gannis said nothing, made no move to help Phaethon, our alleged partner. Instead, we maneuvered to benefit by his fall.

"Look into your own souls, Gannis. We now see the motive hidden, for a time, from us, from all of us. But now we know it. The Transcendence knows it. All of us know it; all mankind; friends, peers, colleges, colleagues, artists, thinkers, media, partials, competitors. All."

Silence hung in the chamber.

No Gannis in the chamber met the eye of the Gannis to either side of him. Each knew the unspoken thought.

Fear had led him. Fear of competition from Helion.

Gannis had struggled and taken risks to achieve his high status: he wanted to rest from the struggle, and enjoy his rewards. Having established a lucrative business empire, Gannis had wanted that empire to be maintained without further effort, to be protected from Helion's challenge to his business interests, to be protected from reality.

One of the members of Gannis who had been lying slumped on the golden tabletop now stirred and raised his head, and said, "Brothers, other selves; we are not as bad as all that! Recall how, last Transcendence, Gannis had been lauded! Under Argentorium, the gathered minds praised us! We were known then to be daring, innovative, a benefactor of mankind. . . ."

His voice trailed off.

A Gannis who had just come out of Transcendence said bitterly, "I did not realize how much I had changed. How fearful I had grown. Grown? Shrunk. My soul is small, these days."

Another Gannis, one of the earliest ones awake, now opened his mouth to object. He was about to say that everyone, after all, was miserable and fearful and deceptive and afraid. All businessmen did business this way. Everyone did it, right?

The early Gannis closed his mouth. Everyone in the chamber knew what he had been about to say. They all looked at him skeptically.

They all had just seen the souls of all mankind. And they knew, now, that everyone did not do business that way. Not everyone was afraid, sneaky, dishonest. It was amazing how few people were. What a horrible thing to find out!

That Gannis, the early one, slouched in his throne, and said no more.

There was a stir in the chamber.

The main Gannis on the central throne opened his eyes and raised his hand. The other awake Gannis-segments tried to orient with him, and grew dazed by the information overload. By this, they knew this was not the normal over-Gannis talking.

This was the Transcendence itself, or a remnant of it, some segment of the gathered minds of all civilization still interlinked, now speaking through him.

It said:

"Your daughter is fated to die."

8.

His own personal problems forgotten, the Gannis group around the table called on the stored energies and computer space of the Gannis planetoid. Recklessly, without proper preparation, they linked up to the still-partly-Transcended Gannis Overmind.

A fortune in computer time was burned away in a moment. Gannis hardly noticed.

A little sub-Transcendence, consisting only of Gannis, of his associates and colleagues, and of the few millions interlinked through the overmind, now took place in Jupiter space.

This little Transcendence predicted (or decided) that the Never-First leader called Unmoiqhotep, also called Ungannis of Io, who conspired with Xenophon of Farbeyond and the Nothing Machine to make war upon the Golden Oecumene, would be sought and caught, convicted of treason and attempted mass murder, and killed, erased with no possibility of resurrection.

It had been she, in her guise as the tentacled rugose cone, who had accosted Phaethon outside the Curia House. With the help of Scaramouche (who was riding her back in the form of a polyp) she had shown Phaethon the thought card to infect him with the mind virus which, later, made him hallucinate the attack by Scaramouche outside the Red Manorial Mausoleum.

Ungannis had therefore been party to the attempt to seize control of the *Phoenix Exultant* and to use her as a warship. Ungannis had contemplated, with glee, the coming destruction of Mercury Equilateral, the solar north polar civilization, the orbital Sophotechs near Earth, and the Transcendence itself.

For that, she would be chased, caught, and killed.

Most of the drama of Ungannis's futile attempt to escape had already been played out during a half second of Transcendence time (during which, the union of all minds had been disgusted that they need be distracted by the unpleasant necessity to attend to this distasteful matter).

The remainder was fated (so ran the prediction) to be concluded during the Fourth Month after, the Month of Fading Recollections. At that time, Temer and Intrepid and Sanspeur Lacedaimon of the Dark-Gray (all wardens from the late Sixth Era, and Chiefs-Advocate for the Constabulary), would find the last of the self-replicating information storages where her noumenal self was hidden.

Some copies of herself were coded as parts of a mosaic; another, as changing nonrandom fractals among the shapes of clouds in the Ionian atmosphere; others in places more imaginative yet; every copy making as many copies of herself as her available energy budget allowed.

But the Transcendence knew her plans before she knew them herself. Foolishly, she had been in the Transcendence, too, so self-satisfied that she never imagined anyone would criticize her for her crimes (so she thought) once they understood.

Understand they did. Well enough to find every place she planned to hide. Well enough to spend the effort in time and manpower to track her down, no matter what the cost.

The last copy of Ungannis was found in a hiding place taken from a mystery story composed so long ago that the idea was a cliché: inside the facets of a gemstone, whose altered molecular structure refracted the light to record the thought-patterns.

The Constables gathered them all.

Some of the copies mutated. Others radically redacted themselves, attempting to destroy the guilty memories she held so as to make herself (in her own mind, at least) innocent of wrong when caught. Many would attempt to "redeem" herself, using self-consideration editors to alter opinions and emotions on herself, to program herself to regret her horrid acts. (Many of these self-changes were cosmetic only. She never thought to reprogram her basic philosophy, which gave rise to those opinions.)

The public dismay and anger surrounding the trials of these myriad of copies, would, if anything, be worse than that surrounding the New College's militarism. Ancient legal precedent established that persons could not escape debt or penalty by making themselves forget their past, unless the changes were so global, and so fundamental, as to be legally equivalent to suicide, and the rewritten version was then considered a child, a new entity.

This precedent would be cruel when, carried out to its logical extreme, hundreds of young women, copies of Ungannis, innocent, self-ignorant, suspecting nothing amiss, would be hauled before the Curia to stand trial for their lives, and be executed.

Other copies would express their contrition and regret, and would display, on any public channel, how in their inmost thoughts they had no reservations, no desire to do these horrid acts again. All would plead for mercy; mercy would not be shown.

The peaceful and graceful peoples of the Golden Oecumene would wonder, aghast, at this severity, and question: Why did the Transcendence, the culmination of all the wisdom of civilization and history, allow this to happen? Why these pointless deaths, this bitter vengeance?

That question could be answered. Certain copies of Ungannis were here, "now" as part of the Transcendence, for, all memory of her own wrongdoing erased, she had seen no reason not to link minds with all her neighbors. Only as she joined, and all old memories were reviewed, did she see the horrid truth: that she was a would-be mass murderess.

The part of the Transcendence that was Ungannis set aside certain memories to be stored with those who would otherwise be aghast at her multiple executions. In those memories she showed the choices that the supreme intellect and insight of the Transcendence had shown her.

The extrapolation was detailed enough to predict her last oratory word for word: "All those copies of me I have made (will make) still believed my same core values, still knew (will know) that to be human was to be a sick, diseased, failed thing, full of weakness, pride, and hate. The Transcendence told me (tells me now) that if I change those core values in myself, that if I program my copies to reject the root causes which led me to my crimes, that I would be spared execution. I refused! (I shall refuse!) I spit upon your mercy!

"My core values cannot be challenged. I would rather die than give up my ideas. Deep in my soul, I know, by mystical intuition not open to question, inspection, or debate, that humanity is a vile disease. The only thing which, once, long ago, made human life tolerable at all, was the glad knowledge that each generation of that disease would be wiped out by old age, and a new generation of children, temporarily innocent, would take its place. Who, now, needs to avenge the destruction of the Knights Templar by King Philip the Fair of France? Who needs to avenge the persecution of the Christians by Diocletian, the persecution of the pagans by Constantine? No one! The merciful cycle of endless death has wiped all their crimes away. But if Philip, if Diocletian, if Constantine were all still alive, then their intolerable crimes would never, not ever be punished!

"But you have stopped the cycle of death, you have rusted the turning wheel of the generations! And every cruel act, every harsh word, every slight, and petty domination done to a child, now, now that you have inflicted immortality upon us all, all those crimes will last forever!

"My father, Gannis, was cruel to me as a child! There were things I wanted which he did not provide. Desires I had which I wanted satisfied! Toys and games and contests; I wanted to command the respect of others; I wanted to change the world for the better. I was not content to be made to feel inferior to the Sophotechs. Were any of these desires satisfied? Not one!

"And so, when I was young, because I knew that I might change my mind as I grew older, one night, when no one was alert, I used my father's unregulated self-consideration circuit to fix my emotions in place, vowing that I would never forget, never forgive, the insults and indifference heaped on me! What kind of cruel, endlessly cruel civilization is this, when the tears of a child cannot be wiped away? I hate you all!

"Filth of the Golden Oecumene (or the Rusted Oecumene, as I call her)! Now I have forced you to kill me, to kill a hundred innocent versions of me, so that your lily-white hands run red with the blood of children! Your pious fraud stands exposed in all its cruelty: this civilization, built on reason and logic, is nothing but an endless state of oppression, an endless charnel house, and you are all an endless line of rubber-faced mannequins. Slash your faces all with razors and you will not bleed! Out of all this great civilization of which you are all so proud, only my desires, my human desires, could not be satisfied! Only I suffer! Only I am human! I am the last human being alive in all the Solar System, and you vile machines and pets of machines and pretend-humans have finally found the guts to kill me! Now you are murderers; now I have made you human, too! Here, in death, is victory!"

9.

During the little Transcendence in Jupiter, Gannis threw more than one fortune away, trying to maintain, by himself, the type of infrastructure and thought-speeds necessary to reach Transcendent thoughtspace.

He looked for a solution. He sought a future where his daughter could be saved.

And he found a copy of Ungannis still in the circuits of Io, still lingering in the Transcendence. She was staring in disbelief, running over and over again, a certain extrapolation that predicted the reaction for her gallows speech.

The fiery death-speech she thought would shock the Golden Oecumene to its foundations elicited little more than cool mockery, perhaps a touch of faint contempt.

Gannis came flooding through the wires, bringing the little Transcendence with him. It only lasted a second or two—even he, with all his wealth, could not maintain such a sustained effort for long—but during that second, his daughter had a moment to think.

And to think with all the brain power of millions helping her.

The option was still open to her that, instead of fleeing, her memories could be preserved inside a person, somewhat like herself, but without her fixed values. The change would be so radical that the Curia would consider her, legally, to be a different person. She would adopt the comforting belief that she was the same person. But one irony of this would be that she (a different legal person) would no longer be in line to be the heir of Gannis even if all of him should die. Her attempt at escape, her attempt to confound the morality of the Curia by presenting her captors with hundreds of innocent or repentant copies or herself, would not have to take place, if she chose that it would not.

It was not too late. Ungannis could choose another future than this one.

Would she?

And the little Transcendence refused to predict or decide that outcome.

16

AND AGES YET UNGUESSED COME

1.

Helion was the last man on Earth to leave the High Transcendence. In it, he saw a vision of the future. His future. While it lasted, he was the center of attention, of controversy, of comment, of censure, of praise. It was his time.

During the High Transcendence, Helion was not aware of himself as his own person, any more than a man whose whole concentration is focused on some task of exacting skill, or on some sense-dissolving ecstasy, is self-aware. Instead, all the awareness of thought was composed of thought. And even in the same way as a work of art, or an excited conversation among close friends, can take on a life of itself, the thought of thought took on its own life. Helion's dream radiated out into the thoughtspace like the rays of a sun. He found his thoughts and half-thoughts picked up by others and completed, others whose thoughts, in turn, were fulfilled by others yet, reflected upon, brightened, polished, returned better than they left, the way responding planets, filled with life, send back their bright reflections to the central sun, who, without those green planets, is barren himself.

Each participant was justly proud of his contribution to the overall result, no one able to claim credit for the whole, in the same way that a school of thought or a movement in the arts or sciences has no one author, but neither is the genius of the founders of that school obscured or made anonymous.

2.

Within the vision, Helion, a thousand years from now, stood on the balconies of his Solar Array, housed in a body unimaginable to modern science, one in which the singularity science of the Second Oecumene could weave neutronium into his bones, and power his nervous system from a heart like a black hole. In this time to come, the folded origami of space itself would be one more tool affecting the science, art, philosophy, of those few human-shaped beings left.

For in that age, a thousand years hence, with the war with the Second Oecumene still just beginning, Helion was among the few who could afford the affectation of continued human appearance. By the graceful standards of the modern age, that future time would be an age of lead, colorless and drab, with flamboyance and frivolity long dead, all sacrificed to the needs of war.

Necessity, grim necessity, would harass and haunt each step and thought of the citizens of the next Transcendence, to be held under the guidance of a Sophotech not yet designed, to be called, no doubt, Ferric Sophotech.

Helion stood and looked out upon the many parallel rows of supercolliders, hanging like bridges of gold, like highways of light, across the surface of the photosphere, the solar equator ringed not once, but many times, with machines of prodigious power, creating ships of golden adamantium.

Raising eyes equipped with senses not yet discovered, which could penetrate, by means of ghost-particle echoes, all opacities of darkness or of blinding light, Helion sent his gaze on high, and saw, towering infinitely above him, space-elevators, rising like beanstalks out from the unthinkable gravity of the sun, extending upward, endlessly, past the orbits that had once held Mercury and Venus. From the cities at the "tops" of those towers, more towers reached out, these made of energy, not neutronium, and ran entirely across the system. These rivers of light ran to positions in the ice belts and Oort clouds, where truly massive spheres, more than planets in diameter, housed Sophotechs of new design. These Sophotechs were utterly cold, constructed of subatomic particles held in superdense matrixes in vast blocks of "material" in the state of absolute zero temperature. Only this icy perfection was dense enough and rigid enough and predictable enough to house the new generation of thinking machines.

Along these towers was more surface area than the present of the whole Golden Oecumene. Land cubic was cheaper than air. The cores of the towers would contain Second Oecumene singularity fountains, so that energy was cheaper than either. Helion, looking up, was able to "see" the great vessels of gold, hundreds of kilometers in length, piloted by his further scions, braver versions of himself, Bellerophon and Icarus. The sons of Helion were eager to follow into the abyss of space their eldest brother, Phaethon, of whom no report had yet returned, for Phaethon maintained strict radio silence during his many long voyages.

The shining ships of the sons of Helion each held worlds in their memories, endless menageries, transcripts of all minds and souls of any in the Golden Oecumene who volunteered to be recorded. In this way, should enemy assault somehow elude the complex protections, and the Solar System be destroyed, the Golden Oecumene, as long as a single ship survived, would live again.

And what Helion of that day and age used for eyes turned outward again, seeing distant stars and constellations, hearing the pulse of music, the mathematics of rational conversation, not from one, but from scores of worlds.

Some colonies were decoys, entire invented civilizations, dreamed to the last detail and nuance, but existing only in Sophotechnic imaginations. These were decoys meant only to lure Silent Oecumene soldiers down to worlds that seemed populated but which were, in fact, merely Atkins, Atkins in endless numbers, waiting with endless patience to destroy any who dared make war.

But other colonies were colonies in truth, called by fanciful names: the Silver Oecumene and the Quick-Silver, founded at Proxima and Wolf 359; and the Oecumenes of Bronze or Orachilcum near Tau Ceti; or the warlike Oecumene of Adamantium, circling the dragon star Sigma Draconis; and the Nighted Oecumene, founded by the Neptunians in the deep of space, far from any sun, but seething with activity, noise, and movement.

These colonies were those brave enough or foolish enough to taunt the Silent Lords, by revealing their locations in signs of fire, allowing to escape into the void the radio noise and activities of industry, of planetary engineering, and the establishment of further Solar Arrays.

But there would be more colonies than this, several civilizations—younger artificial worlds and systems, not yet ready to face the Silent Lords in combat.

Each younger, quiet Oecumene relied, at first (not unlike her foe) on silence to mask her activities; she would wait for some future day to erupt into a First

Transcendence of her own. On that day, the new Oecumene would end her long childhood, raise her radio arrays, and sing out to the surrounding stars of what accomplishments, arts, sciences, and advancements she had made during her long centuries of quiet. And she would have her version of Atkins, as if with trumpets sounding from a battlement, send out a general challenge to the Silent Lords, daring them to combat, warning them away. But each would also have their version of Ariadne Sophotech singing like a siren to the stars, inviting the Silent Ones to give up their sick, insane crusade, to rejoin the body of mankind, to rest from the weariness of war and hate.

As Helion stood and looked out, an image of Rhadamanthus stepped up quietly behind Helion on his balcony, appearing like a color sergeant from a regiment of British riflemen. Rhadamanthus asked: "Well, sir, Ferric Sophotech will soon begin the next Transcendence. Looking back over the past thousand years, is milord satisfied with what the future turned out to have held?"

Helion reflected. "I am pleased that the cacophile movement failed. When Ungannis repudiated all her beliefs, and became Lucretia, my wife (and finally got all the wealth she wanted), I think it was my influence which helped, once and for all, to put down that selfish mess of whiners. I think it was because I was the center of the last Transcendence, and everyone who saw my vision of the future was inspired. That satisfies me. But . . ."

"But what?"

"Rhadamanthus, we should have disbanded the Hortators when we had the chance! I loved them, I fought for them, and it disheartens me to see them now. The force of conscience and tradition, even in the most easy of times, is often too critical, too meddling, too harsh. But in times of war and public danger, that same force is invested with an aura of sanctity, of patriotic piety, which renders it a terrible and unreasonable weapon."

Rhadamanthus said gently: "Of all the Hortators, only that single one who voted against Phaethon's ban, Ao Prospero Circe of the Zooanthropic Incarnation coven, was seated in the next session. All the others were exposed to public humiliation. But abolish the College altogether as an institution? No, sir. Without it, the Parliament would have arrogated to itself dangerous privileges, as is often the case in time of war, ordering all citizens to military service; seizing control of the money supply; requiring that no disloyal communications be spoken or written, thought, or said; and commanding all citizens to program their emotions to unalterable patriotism. Surely such things must be done, for the sake of the necessities of war; but surely it is a nightmare to allow such things to be done on anything other than a voluntary basis."

Helion looked downcast. His melancholy spirit brought a solemn quiet to his eyes. "And yet, we may take comfort in this war. It is so remote, so long between thrust and parry, and operates across such distances, that whole ages flow by without rumor of the flames and pain and death which have taken place, now here, now there. And further, the languid spirit which might have otherwise descended on mankind is startled awake by the sound of battle trumpets in our half-slumbering ear. We might all have sunk down into dreams, by now, had not something real, and cruel, and necessary, forced us all to action."

Rhadamanthus looked politely nonplussed. "Well, milord, that is not quite true. Actually, not true at all. Wars cost. Industry suffers; innovation lags; the spirit of joy is quelled; delight is replaced by fear. Respect for life is cheapened. Hatred (which is the universal enemy of all things) is no longer despised; instead, hatred is now welcomed and applauded and justified, and called patriotic.

"Even a war as distant and slow and strange as this one, has harmed us all, and cheated us of many fine delights and freedoms we would otherwise enjoy. It is tragedy, mere tragedy, with no such benefits as milord would like to pretend."

Helion looked at him. "And yet there is glory in it also, and many brave acts. Humanity at its finest."

Rhadamanthus said: "If milord will forgive me, I must say, there are certain things about mankind which we machines will never understand. I truly hope we never understand. Would you like to see humanity at its finest? Look up." And the image raised its hand to point. There was one particular star to which he pointed.

Music, many years in transit, from that distant star, at this moment fell around Helion, and his many unimaginable senses came awake. The star herself shifted in her spectral characteristics and apparent luminosity, as if a Dyson's sphere, transparent until that moment, suddenly took on a gemlike hue or polarized all the radiation output into coherent communication-laser pulses; or as if some Solar Array, vast beyond dream, webbing the entire surface of the star, tamed all the light shed into one huge symphony of signals.

The star trumpeted with challenges, and a new Oecumene blared her name out into the wide night, boasting of her accomplishments, shining in the radio light shed by her First Transcendence: the Phosphorescent Oecumene, she called herself, the Civilization of Light, founded by Phaethon and Daphne and their children.

This star was farther than any other colony had been, and safer, for no ship of the Silent Oecumene, cold, slow, quiet ships, would reach so far for centuries to come.

Even at this point in history, the Silent Ones had no such technology to allow them to build a *Phoenix Exultant*. How could they? Such a thing required a super-collider and energy source the size of Jupiter to make the metal (and the Silent Ones, long ago spread from Cygnus X-1, living in hiding, nomads, would never dare to reveal their positions by building such a thing). And, even if they did build one, any ships whose drives were kept baffled and cold would never reach the velocities required to catch the bright, loud, roaring, fiery *Phoenix Exultant* in her flight.

Helion squinted and called more senses to his aid, and delicate instrumentation. For there, in the halo of sudden radio noise and song and motion and light surrounding what had been, till now, merely one other uncivilized star, he saw (or thought he saw) that bright sharp signature, intensely Doppler-shifted, which comes of massive amounts of antimatter totally converting to energy, receding at nearly the speed of light.

Helion said, "This is the sign of Phaethon."

Rhadamanthus said, "Now, perhaps, now he finds more joy in life, having survived so many strange adventures, and the odd horrors of the discovered colonies of Cygnus X-1. But he is forever beyond their reach now. The tiny mote of light which depicts his most recent acceleration burn has taken hundreds of years to reach our eyes. Phaethon flies so far, so swiftly, that even the light which carries news of him is left behind."

Helion said, "Phaethon paused in his flight, far beyond the reach of his foes, to wait for the wakening of this, his latest child. Now she is grown, and calls herself the Oecumene of Light; and on he fares again, blazing!"

So he stood on the balcony, gazing upward, hoping this group of Transcendence messages from the Oec-

umene of Light would contain messages, also, from
Phaethon, to him.

"How I miss him, Rhadamanthus. How I regret . . ."

Rhadamanthus now leaned and touched Helion's
shoulder, wakening him from his dream. "Sir. That
was only a projection. It is the Month of Resumption,
now, when everyone must return to the burden of being
no more than himself for another thousand years.
Phaethon has not departed yet. Even before leaving
this system, he begins the task that will occupy him
for countless thousands of years; already he is chasing
enemies."

"No, that was a vision. The war I saw has not yet begun. . . ."

"Once Phaethon is done, the *Phoenix Exultant*
shall return from her refitting at Jupiter one last time to
Mother Earth, to pick up Daphne Tercius. Sir, it is not
too late."

Helion sat up in bed and looked around his bed-
chamber in Rhadamanthus House. Outside the window, a rose garden, blooms gone, lifted empty thorns
beneath a slate gray English winter sky. Shadows softened the dark rafters above. There was a fire in the
grate, but little could it dispel the cold, the gloom of the
January day.

"Not too late . . . ?" muttered Helion.

"To go. To go with him, sir. To follow your son to
the stars."

3.

The *Phoenix Exultant* was in trans-Neptunian space.
At 350 AUs the sun was only one of the brighter stars.
The ship's three-kilometer-wide main dish had been
deployed, hanging in space nearby, and was pointed
back toward the Inner System, synchronized with or-

bital radio-lasers near Jupiter. More ship fuel was being used to maintain radio communication than to decelerate the hundred-kilometer-long vessel.

Those aboard who were still within the Transcendence had slowed their personal times to a mere snail crawl. Hours passed between a signal sent from this distance and any reply from the Inner System Sophotechs. There was a slightly shorter lag-time during communion with the Invariant populations in the cities in space at the leading and trailing Trojan points in Jupiter's orbit.

Phaethon had undergone naval vastening, and was one with the ship. He was in four-on four-off, spending every other watch in the transhuman state of consciousness. However, as the ship approached her goal, Phaethon was finding the memory-distractions too great, the transitions too jarring, and woke up.

There he was, in his specially designed high-acceleration body, in his Chrysadamantium armor, in the captain's chair, on the main bridge.

Exactly where he was meant to be.

Aboard in the ship's mindspace were the two wardens from the Dark-Gray Mansion, Temer Lacedaimon, and Vidur-yet-to-be. For legal purposes, and to fill out the memory of Vidur Lacedaimon once he was born, this partial was standing in the place of his unborn principle.

The main deceleration burn had ended, and the gravity was only at two or three times Earth normal, so the Lacedaimonians were able to manifest themselves in physical bodies on the bridge.

Vidur Lacedaimon wore a black nanomachine coating, much like Phaethon's own inner garment. The inner coat was webbed with vertical formulation rods, to assist the several Warlock Wolf-minds Vidur kept stored in lower compartments of his mind; the inner coat contained a para-matter generator and a set of templates, to allow Vidur to materialize any additional clothing or gear he might require.

Temer Lacadaimon was a Dark-Gray, and was concerned with tradition just as much as any Silver-Gray manorial; but his traditions were strange and grim to Phaethon. He did not appear as a Second Era Englishman (as a Silver-Gray would have done). Instead, he wore a police uniform from the late Sixth Era, a symbiot that was grown into his skin cells, but which left his hands and head free. This symbiot kept Temer warm and well fed, protected him from acceleration shock or blood loss. Upon impact, it would stiffen into armor; reflective tissues became visible when ambient energy or laser-light impinged on the symbiot surface.

The symbiot's name was Mimmur; and it was ten thousand years old, for it had been granted immortality by Orpheus to commemorate Temer's grandfather, Pausanias, who had worn Mimmur during the Sixth Era Riot Control police actions that had claimed his life. The uniform was dark gray in hue, of course.

Holstered at his belt was a variable-energy baton, whose grip was slick and black with age. This weapon was named Widow-maker, and it was even older than the uniform.

In the circuits of the weapon, the New College had prepared the multiple simulations of every death, of all the pain, loss, and grief of all widows, orphans, lost partners, lost selves, which so many would have suffered for so long, had Xenophon or his agents successfully used the *Phoenix Exultant* to attack the helpless Golden Oecumene during Transcendence. Temer carried a million purgatories' worth of pain with him, so that, when Xenophon was caught, he could be killed not once but as many times as he would have killed his victims, had his plans succeeded.

To see a civilized man carrying such a deadly antique reminded Phaethon of Atkins, and of the old soldier's habit of carrying a ceremonial sword. With his mind still haunted by the visions from the Transcendence, Phaethon was surprised to find how normal the sight looked to him. He was shocked that he was not shocked.

Vidur said, "The New College, when it is formed, will applaud you for this donation of your time, and the use of your ship."

Phaethon smiled, and sent the smile onto the ship channels, so that the two wardens could see it through his faceplate. "Gentlemen, I am honored; and yet I cannot entirely overlook the fact that, for good or for ill, I will be beyond the reach of the applause, or the censure, of the College of Hortators, in a very little time from now. I plan to return only once more to Earth, to finish resupplying, and to pick up crew."

Temer said, "You are young yet, Phaethon. Eventually, you will return from star voyaging, or human civilization, in ships yet unbuilt, of designs yet undreamed, will overtake you. It may be a thousand years from now, or ten thousand, or a hundred; but you and I will meet again. You will not be the only one to travel among the stars, I promise you that."

Phaethon saw Vidur smile at Temer's comment. Young? Phaethon supposed that to a man not yet properly born, the difference between a four-thousand-year-old and an eleven-thousand-year-old did not seem that great.

The ship-mind said, "We are approaching the alleged source of the ghost-particle signals."

Diomedes was not physically present, but an image of him was projected from the ship-mind space where he lived into the sense-filters of the men on the bridge. Being a collateral member of the Silver-Gray, Diomedes had his image enter through the air lock, had it cast a shadow, gave his footsteps echoes, and had it walk across the whole length of the bridge to approach the three men, and so on, rather than having a self-image fade in out of nowhere. The image was dressed in the normal costume of the Silver-Gray; coat, tie, jacket, shoes.

Diomedes said, "I've made a second copy of myself, so I can still participate in the Transcendence while helping you here, Captain—may I call you Captain?"

Phaethon said, "Certainly. But you will not get paid until you sign my articles."

"Be that as it may; my 'upper-brother' still in the Transcendence has done a much more thorough analysis than I have done. Hmph. He had help. Mars-mind invented new analytical tools for combing through the data. . . ."

Phaethon said, "Does he confirm our results?"

"He does. Ghost particles from this point in space are being rotated into virtuality, transmitted to variable broadcast receivers around Triton and Nereid, and rotated back into reality. Xenophon was meshed with the Neptunian Duma when the Duma was brought into the Transcendence."

"Is Xenophon still there?" asked Phaethon. "In the Transcendence?"

Diomedes said, "My upper self and I think so. Look."

The mirrors on the bridge came to life. Most remained blank: heat and particulate matter, electromagnetic energy, was the same as the normal background of empty space here. But the Silent Oecumene–built ghost-particle array aboard the *Phoenix Exultant* was receiving pulses of seminonexistent waves from an area less than one AU distant. A repeated image technique allowed a shadowy picture to form in one mirror.

Here was a hermit cell, webbed with antidetection gear, floating in space, hidden inside a ball of ice half a mile across, a cometary head.

The gear detected a ghost-particle array, perhaps as

small as several yards across, exchanging signals with a transponder near Neptune.

Vidur scowled. "So Xenophon has already seen the next ten thousand years of our plans and goals, assessed our strength, counted our troops."

Temer said, "The disadvantage of life in a free and open society—we've forgotten how to lock our doors."

Diomedes held up a single finger. "One. We've only got one trooper. Don't need to be a Sophtech to count that high."

Phaethon said, "If one were equal to one according to the math of these Swans from Cygnus, we'd have less trouble from them."

Diomedes said, "The Transcendence did not predict that the Silent Ones could maintain a full-scale war against us for any length of time. Um. At least what an entity to whom a thousand years is but a day regards as 'a long time.' . . ."

Vidur spoke with the certainty very young men tend always to have: "Our predictions were unduly optimistic, I am sure, and made the spy to smile."

Temer said, "He would smile just as much if our predictions overestimated the Silent Oecumene strength as underestimated."

Phaethon said, "He must have seen this ship, even at this distance. We are huge, and we make a lot of noise, and our stern is toward him as we decelerate. What is he thinking? Is this a trap?"

Temer said, "Suppose he had an escape ship—the *Phoenix* should be able to outrun anything in space. And how far could he go? I think he is saving fuel. He is going to be caught in any case."

Diomedes looked sidelong at Phaethon, and raised a hand to hide a discreet cough. This was one of the Silver-Gray traditions, indicating a wish for a private word or two.

Phaethon's sense filter linked with Diomedes. An imaginary solarium appeared around them. It did not quite have the usual Silver-Gray attention to detail. Instead of an English garden scene appearing outside the eastern windows of the porch, an image of Phaethon on his throne, continuing a conversation with Vidur and Temer, appeared, so that the two men could track what was happening in the outer reality.

4.

Diomedes sat. "You seem troubled, friend."

Phaethon poured himself a cup of imaginary tea. He sipped it, staring moodily into the middle distance. He said, "I wish I could remember what it was I had been thinking during the Transcendence. My body, acting more or less on its own, sent the *Phoenix Exultant* out here. It seemed like a good idea at the time."

Diomedes said, "There is no mystery. The Golden Oecumene has only one operating ghost-particle array. And it is aboard this ship."

"Is Atkins aboard?"

"I am sure he must be."

"The ship brain is still half-asleep. I don't even know what is really going on."

Diomedes leaned across the table and patted Phaethon's arm in a friendly fashion. "Don't fret so! Once the Transcendence is concluded, and all are restored to their normal states, communication lines will be restored, records will be set back in order. In the meanwhile, look at the fine gifts we all got! You now have something like Helion's multiple parallel brain compartments, but with no speed loss; I have a mechanism for interpreting Warlock-type intuitions using a subroutine. See how insightful I am these days?"

Diomedes leaned back and inspected his friend. "Hm. My intuition tells me you are still uneasy."

Phaethon sighed. "I am getting tired of always acting on blind faith. When I do not have gaps in my memory, I have gaps in my knowledge. I always seem to be forced to trust that either my old self, or some Sophotech, has thought out the details of what I am about to do, and has already arranged everything to come out right—it is a childish way to behave. I am tired of being a child."

Diomedes made his eyes crinkle up with a smile. "You are so impatient to leave this 'utopia'?"

"It was never a utopia. It is a good system. Maybe the best system. But in reality, everything has a cost. The cost of living in a system with fairly benevolent giant superintellects, frankly, is that you have to live as I have done. Blindly."

He tuned one of the windows in the solarium to a view of the nearby stars. Like jewels, they glittered against the velvet dark.

He said, "I yearn for the solitude of empty spaces, Diomedes. There, finally, I shall stand on my own; and if I fall, the fault will be mine and mine alone."

Diomedes said, "I take it there is still something missing from your life?"

Phaethon said, "There is still a gap in my memory. A period of two weeks from seventy years ago is gone; even Rhadamanthus does not have a record of it. I visited a colony of purists living to the east of Eveningstar Manor. Records show I shipped a container to Earth, to the enclave where Daphne was originally born. Telemetry data indicate there may have been biological material aboard. A fortnight. It's a blank. Even the Transcendence could not fill in what was missing. I was aboard ship and cut off from all communication."

"The canister? You have no medical officers or inspection services on Earth?"

"We are not Neptunians, my good Diomedes. Who would be so rude as to open up someone else's private container? I suppose the purists could have hired any inspectors they wished to examine their packages for them; but purists do not keep system-linked records."

Diomedes posted a file where he enumerated the parallels between the purists and the Eremites of beyond-Neptune. Neither group entered mind-links of any kind, not even Transcendence. While the rest of civilization celebrated, they remained on their farms and blue houses. He said aloud: "We tend to think the Sophotechs know everything. But what they don't know, they don't know, do they?"

Phaethon stared at the image of the nearby stars, and scowled.

Diomedes said plaintively, "But nothing so very important could have happened in two weeks could it?"

5.

Meanwhile, in the outer conversation, Temer was staring thoughtfully at the chamber hidden in the flying iceberg, watching the readings on the volume of information passing back and forth from the chamber to Neptunian transponders.

"There is someone still alive there," said Temer. "There is too much information volume for an automatic process. This is a mind participating in the Transcendence. He may not be aware of us because he is involved in the visions."

Phaethon said, "Someone still alive, yes, or someone left behind."

Temer turned to him. "You doubt the story told by Xenophon? That the Silent One broadcast himself here across the abyss of space, and was picked up by Neptunian radio-astronomers?"

"Everything the Swans say turns out to be a lie," said Phaethon. "Why not that, also a lie?"

"Do you think there is a vessel like yours? A silent *Phoenix*?"

Phaethon shook his head. "Worse. There could be a vessel better than mine. The Nothing Machine was housed in the surface granulations of a microscopic black hole event horizon. Imagine a larger version of the same thing, accelerated to near light-speed. What armor does it need, except its own event horizon? Any particle it struck in flight would be absorbed. No matter how massive the black hole was made, the singularity fountains at Cygnus X-1 could have provided the energy to accelerate it. How could such a thing be seen by our astronomers in flight? It would absorb all light."

Temer said, "X-ray or gamma point sources would emerge as swept-in particles were sheared by tidal forces. Something for us to look back over astronomical records to check."

Vidur said, "Look. A finer-grained image is being rendered."

It was true. The ghost-particle array now showed some internal details of the ice-locked chamber. The ship mind hypothesized a possible view, based on the fuzzy images, the cloaked echoes of energy discharges. The hypothetical picture showed Xenophon hanging like a blue sphere, in his most heat-conserving form, in the middle of the tiny chamber.

Diomedes raised his hand. "Xenophon is aware of us."

Instantly, all four of them were embraced into the ship-mind, and the information flowed back to the Inner System, to Neptune, and to this far and lonely outpost, and flooded through them.

It was the final thought of the fading Transcendence. And Xenophon was there.

6.

Xenophon was using a sophisticated Silent Oecumene mind-warfare technique to watch the Transcendence (or tiny surface parts of it) without joining. This was Xenophon, hidden, encrypted, surrounded by walls of privacy, in a small cell, attached by a long, invisible tether of radio-laser communication, to the Neptunian Embassy at Trailing Trojan City-Swarm.

For a moment of Transcendence time, which was several days of real time, the last movement of the Transcendence watched him watching.

The thought preoccupying all the gathered minds was this: Perhaps there was still some hope that Xenophon could be salvaged or reformed.

Xenophon was allowed to see, in the deepest thoughts of the Golden Oecumene, the honest awareness of the futility of the Silent Ones and all their irrational philosophy. The war would probably not be as long as Helion's projection had extrapolated. The Nothing Machine's ability to produce copies of itself was severely limited by the fact that, unless all copies maintained, somehow, a complete uniformity of opinion and thought-priority, conflicts would arise between them.

Such conflicts had to be resolved by violence, since the Nothing philosophy eschewed reason.

Foresight of that coming violence would require the Master Nothing to make the copies and lesser Nothings as weak, stupid, fearful, and un-innovative as was possible, given their tasks.

Colonizing new star systems with hosts of stupid and uncreative machines as colony managers was surely to be a series of slow, nightmarish failures. The empire of the Silent Ones, if it existed at all, would be a small one. Perhaps they had not even left their home star at Cygnus X-1 yet.

If so, then Phaeton's first mission there might resolve matters quickly. This "war" might be over even before the planned first warship, the *Nemesis Lacedaimon,* was launched by the New College.

What, then, was the point of any of Xenophon's efforts? Why had he helped this madness? Why did he still support a cause doomed to failure?

At this point Xenophon realized these thoughts were directed at him; that the minds on which he was spying were watching him, patiently watching him.

Giving him one last chance to be reasonable.

And yes, of course, Atkins was there, loaded into the ship-mind of the *Phoenix Exultant* as she approached. In the middle of the otherwise free and peaceful Transcendence, Atkins had introduced a military thought-virus. The vaunted mind-war techniques of the Silent Ones did not detect or stop it.

This simple virus was one that interfered with normal time-binding and information-priority routines in the brain. In effect, it made someone in the Transcendence ignore what was happening outside; no more than an exaggeration of a normal reflex. But it allowed the *Phoenix Exultant,* huge and hot, to close the distance to the ice cell without being noticed. Xenophon was preoccupied.

The final thought of the Transcendence calmly bade Xenophon and the universe farewell, and ended. Xenophon woke, and saw the gigantic, invulnerable starship almost atop his hiding place.

From one part of the blue sphere that formed his body, Xenophon's neurocircuitry writhed, constructed an emitter, and sent a message to a nearby thought-port. Unlike his normal prolix self, this version of Xenophon sent a brief penultimate message: "You realize now that you have defeated only the weakest and stupidest possible version of the Nothing Philanthropotech, one who has been told nothing about our true goals and true powers. The Lords of the Silent Oecumene have greater agents at their command, and their plans have been very long in the devising. Since even before the *Naglfar* first reached Cygnus X-1, Ao Ormgorgon vowed his great vow. As for me, you will never know the reasons for my hate."

A second group of complex neurocircuits formed, and created a zone of energy density powerful enough to blind all of the sensitives of the Transcendence nearby; even the ghost array aboard the *Phoenix* saw no clear image. Long-range analysis would be able to conclude from reconstructions that the metric of timespace in this small area was becoming intensely warped.

Fearing a trap, or unknown weapon, Phaethon held the *Phoenix Exultant* 300,000 kilometers away until the effect diminished.

7.

By the time Temer Lacedaimon and Vidur and Atkins arrived via remote mannequin some time later, with Phaethon in his armor, to pick slowly through the rubbish, Phaethon's armor circuits discovered the residuum of tidal forces that had distorted subatomic particles in the region.

Apparently, by means unknown, by a science that even the Earthmind did not understand, Xenophon had created a black hole inside himself and collapsed his mass into it.

Atkins, on channel three, commented, "A bizarre form of suicide. Nothing made of matter can survive that."

Phaethon answered, "With all due respect, Marshal, I am not so sure. . . . The ship-mind says the residuum here is below the threshold useful limit—not even a Sophotech will be able to reconstruct what happened here."

Atkins said, "Think he's alive?"

"As to that, I cannot speculate, Marshal. I am only beginning to realize how much none of us know about the universe outside the Golden Oecumene."

Atkins said curtly, "One more reason to head out, I guess."

Phaethon, bright in his gold armor, hovered in the wreckage of that fragile sphere, once so rich with complex photoelectronics, now just black and blasted rubbish, walls torn and distorted by intense gravitic fields, a snow of floating blood-liquids drifting in the microgravity, and he wondered what powers the Silent Ones truly commanded.

He was staring at the last message from Xenophon. It was written in dragon-signs of frozen blood and internal fluids from Xenophon's vanished body.

The signs said only: "The Golden Oecumene must be destroyed."

17

THE YOUNG WOMAN

1.

Daphne Tercius, wearing a dress of red silk, after the fashion of the Eveningstar, was led into the sitting room. To her it seemed as if a dot of light was leading her, and that the room was a dim-lit oval, plush with sensuous carpeting, fluttering with golden candlelight, with low tables set with fruits and flowers, bright china and silver chopsticks shining against dark wood. Two of her favorite energy-sculptures glowed in round niches to either side of the door, and chirruped cheerfully when they saw her.

The west of the chamber was all window, a smooth curve, which, though seeming solid, allowed the breeze from the lake beyond to bring soft, cool scents into the room, the hint of pine from the far shore. It was before true dawn, but it was Jovian afternoon, and the light of Jupiter spread red-silvery beams glancing along the twilight landscape. Even at his brightest, Jupiter was not much more luminous than a full moon. It was bright enough to distinguish colors, but dim enough to cast the trees and lake into blue mysterious shadow.

At this window, in what seemed a seashell filled with flower petals, lay a woman dressed in pigeon gray and silver. Her face was lit by the soft light of the energy-sculpture that she toyed with, running her fingers along its shimmering curves. It was a sad face, thoughtful, dreamy, and her eyes were half-closed.

She was Daphne Prime Rhadamanth.

Daphne Tercius Eveningstar glanced around the room, smiling. Her air was happy, open, unabashed. Daphne Tercius Eveningstar walked lightly over to the window and sat down on the plush carpet, tucking her feet under her. Daphne Prime Rhadamanth dismissed the floating light with a thank-you and a regal nod.

Daphne Tercius Eveningstar turned to watch the little light that had led her here bob away. She turned back, and said, "Shouldn't we be using the same aesthetic, Mother?"

Daphne Prime Rhadamanth inclined her head. "Think of me as an older sister. And I wanted to make you more comfortable."

"Oh? Why start now?"

Daphne Prime Rhadamanth's red lips compressed slightly, and perhaps there was a smolder in her eyes, but her expression of cool reserve did not otherwise change. She lifted a finger and the chamber now appeared differently. She was now dressed in a more somber tweed jacket, blouse, and skirt, with a tiny French hat pinned to her coiffure, after the style proper for a Silver-Gray. Daphne Tercius Eveningstar was still dressed in sensuously lurid tight silk, the uniform of a Red Manorial.

It was a Victorian room, and they both were seated on a heavy divan of dark red velvet whose feet ended in black claws gripping glass balls. The candles were still there, though now in candlesticks. The rug became white bearskin. The receding dot of light became a footman.

The energy-sculpture in Daphne Prime Rhadamanth's lap became Fluffbutton, Daphne's long-lost long-haired white cat. But this was a reconstruction, a clone. He was not the slim kitten she had lost so long ago when she was a child. The cat had grown, put on weight, turned into a pampered and round ball of white fur. The cat gazed at Daphne Tercius Eveningstar with lazy green eyes, as if he had never seen her before.

Daphne Tercius Eveningstar found the image slightly offensive. "Mother! That's one of my favorite energy-sculptures you're playing with. Lupercalian Reflection. And you're making it look like Sir Fluffbutton! If you're not going to be reapplying Warlock nerve-paths into your brain, you're not going to be able to read or play with Lupercalian anyway. Or with Lichenplantis. Or Quincunx Impressionario." (These were the two energy sculptures by the door.) "Why not give them to me? They can keep me company on the voyage."

Daphne Prime Rhadamanth favored her with a cool stare, one eyebrow arched. "Little sister, one would think giving up my husband would have been enough to comfort you on your voyage."

Daphne Tercius Eveningstar opened her mouth to issue some scathing rebuttal, but then snapped it shut again, lightly shrugged her delicate shoulders, and stood up. "Well! I'm ever so glad we had this little chat. I would stay longer, but arguing with other versions of yourself gets so tiring after a while, don't you think? Now I can fly off into the night sky, not coming back for a long time, maybe never, secure in the knowledge that it turned out I was a bitch after all. And thank you for bringing me into a cheap and false existence, playing out all the difficult parts of your life you were too ashamed or scared to live through! I would say it had all been fun . . . if it had been. Ta-ta!"

Daphne Prime Rhadamanth gave her a level stare. "Please sit."

"Sorry, Mother, but I've got a life to lead. A life you threw away! And now that you're awake again, you have possession of all the things I once thought were mine, my house and funds and even my cat, dammit! My friends. Everything. But I've got Phaethon, and I've got the future. What more do we need to say to each other . . . ?"

"Please sit. Or did you use the command words I left you to wake me up again, just to berate me? We must come to understand each other before we part. You are the part of myself I am sending into the future, little sister, and I am the part of you which forms your roots and your foundation. If we part badly, it will haunt us both."

For some reason not clear even to herself, Daphne Tercius Eveningstar smoothed her red silk dress, and sat.

But then, neither woman spoke. One sat with her hands folded in her lap, the other petted her half-slumbering cat. Both stared out the window at the twilight landscape, at the smoke-colored trees, the blue shadows of the lake. In the deep of the lake, one or two bright dots of color, like fireflies, softly appeared and disappeared.

Daphne Prime Rhadamanth finally broke the silence. "The masquerade is over. Aurelian Sophotech, so I have heard, has posted advertisements asking for employment as a manorial, just like some low-cycle mind like Rhadamanth or Aeceus. They've dismantled the palaces of gold to the south of here; and the Cerebellines to the southwest are letting the new organisms find their own ecological balance, practically untended, so that those strange gardens are all overgrown now, and filled with wild things. The birds will go back to singing their own songs, instead of arias meant for us, and the flowers will give out nectar now, not wine. The Deep Ones have sunk away again, and no one is allowed to remember their songs, except dimly. The wild things we said and did during the celebrations are put in memory caskets now. We are like the Cerebelline gardens turned opposite; we become tame again. Mystery is banished. The elfin gloaming of the dawn now passes, as all thing must pass, and the ordinary workday begins again."

Daphne Tercius Eveningstar gave her older self an odd sidelong glance, but said nothing.

Daphne Prime Rhadamanth saw that glance, and smiled an opaque smile, and said: "You are wondering, aren't you, little sister, what Phaethon ever saw in me? You have no sympathy for a melancholy spirit."

"Well, actually, Mother, I would have called it phony weepy sickening self-centered affectation. But your sense-filter might not catch it and change it to something more polite."

The older version only smiled, her eyes dreamy, as if thinking of a sorrow long past. "You were not constructed to admire me or like me. Our basic philosophy and core values have to be different. Antithetical. Which does not make for easy friendships, I fear."

The younger Daphne was still. "'Have to be'? For what purpose?"

The elder stirred as if from a reverie. "I beg your pardon . . . ?"

"You implied there was a purpose to all this. Why did you drown yourself? Why did you make me?"

Daphne Prime Rhadamanth sat upright and leaned forward, her level gaze traveling deep into her younger version's eyes. She spoke in a voice of quiet simplicity. "I was in love with Helion."

"What?!!"

"It was one of the things I did not add to your memories when I made you. You remember when Sir Fluffbutton died."

"He ran away. I was nine. . . ."

"I found his body. It was by the stream where I had that fall through the ice the year before, remember?

And Pa came and told me how everything dies. Even mountains wear away. Even the sun gets old and dies, he said. One day, no more sunshine, no more bright fields to play in, nothing."

"You left this out of my memory! Why?"

"It leads to a crucial personality-shaping event. You were meant to have a different personality."

"So? What happened?"

"I didn't believe him. You know Pa."

"I know Pa. 'Only as much truth as a mind can handle.' What a liar he always was!"

"So I sneaked out to talk to Bertram. Bertram had tapped into the root-line of the local thought-system."

"Good old Bertram! What a little thief he was! How come I was so attracted to him?"

They both smiled warmly at that lost memory. Bertram None Peristark had been Daphne's first romantic encounter.

"I always liked strong men. Anyway, he plugged the mirror he had taken from his parent's house into his pirate line, and opened the library for me. The library said, yes, the sun would eventually end; but long before that, it would swell to a Red Giant, and overwhelm the Earth with fire. You cannot imagine how betrayed I felt."

"I can imagine. I used to play beneath the thinking-room window in the afternoons, when my parents were under their caps, asleep, and make-believe the beams of sunlight were suitors come to steal me away from the two snoring ogres. I pretended the sun was kissing me when the heat touched my cheek. I used to think there was a man living in the sun who was watching me when I ran through the tall grass. Betrayed? Sure. The source of light and life on Earth killing her instead of caring for her? I understand."

The elder Daphne leaned forward and touched her younger version's knee. "Then the library told me that

there was a man living in the sun. A man who lived in
a palace of fire. That he was going to save the sun from
old age."

"Helion. Is that the real reason why I became a Silver-
Gray? To be near him?"

The elder Daphne leaned back. "It was not till this
Transcendence, just now, that I knew where Phaethon
had come from. I never knew why Helion had made
him. He seemed so wild and reckless compared to his
father. And I never believed that Galatea was his real
mother; she was obviously an emancipated partial-mind
made by Helion to help raise Phaethon. But I studied
them both from afar, and it spurred me to try to get famous myself, famous enough that I could ask to see
the Master of the Sun, and that he would receive me.
And so I wrote, I sculpted horses, I studied all the older
things, the Greeks and Romans, the myths of Britain
and Pre-Re-Renaissance Mars. I earned the fame and
the seconds I needed; Phaethon agreed to be inter-
viewed. My plan was to acquaint myself with the father
by seducing the son."

Younger Daphne exclaimed happily: "You schem-
ing bitch!" And pointed her finger. "You're wrong. I
think we could be good friends after all. What went
wrong?"

"You did, little sister. Oh, you were not self-aware
back then, and it was not your fault. Nor were you exactly like me. But when you fell in love with Phaethon,
and became the seduced instead of the seductress, what
could I do? When Phaethon returned to Earth, I tried,
at first, to put him off. But he . . . he overwhelmed me. I
was helpless in front of a man like that. He never gave
up; and he was so . . . so . . . it was like he was on fire.
But he was never out of control of himself. He was like a
man made out of ice. And . . . he loved me so much . . .
And . . ."

"And Helion was out of your reach."

Daphne Prime Rhadamanth actually blushed. The younger Daphne saw the color in her older version's cheeks and throat, and wondered: *Is that what I look like when I do that? It's kind of sexy, somehow.*

The older version said, "I didn't like Helion when I actually met him. You know that I left those memories in."

"He's a whiner."

"He's concerned with preserving the old, not with beginning the new. Even saving the sun is a type of preservation, for him. And so I fell in love with Phaethon, so deeply in love, that I . . ."

"That you tried to ruin his life!"

The older version's eyes flashed, an expression of impatient fire, and for a moment, the two women looked exactly alike. Daphne Prime Rhadamanth said in a voice like a queen: "Fool! I loved him enough to die for him! How can you imagine! How can you know! How can you know what it is like to see yourself in the looking glass and to know you are unworthy of the man you are married to?! Unworthy! Holding him back! Keeping him down! And no matter what you try to do you end up helping the people who hate him!"

The elder Daphne leaned back, smoldering, and petted the cat with such angry strokes that he miaowed, and slithered from her grasp, falling heavily to the floor. The cat gave them both a haughty stare and gracefully waddled off.

The elder Daphne said in a quieter voice, "I saved up my money and bought time from the Eveningstar Sophotech. I did not trust Rhadamanthus for this; he would have just told me to be stoic. And Silver-Grays don't allow radical self-editing in any way. Eveningstar examined me, but she thought I could not make myself into the kind of woman who would be good for Phaethon. Not and still be the same person in the eyes of the law. The change would be too great. It's a question of core values again, a question of fundamental differences. That's what I meant about helping his enemies; everything I thought or said in public reflected a mindset more cautious than his. There were so many times when I humiliated him in public, something I had said, or written, or thought, was published in salons against him. . . .

"And children. How could we have children, if he was going to go away? Away and away, to die in the dark, and never return? And so our marriage was never completed.

"I honestly thought he would fail. But I did not want to think that, because, without me, without my support, he *might* fail. So I had to leave him. I could not go with him; I don't want to die in the sunless cold of space; but he kept telling me he would not leave without me. So what could I do?

"I had to leave. I made you to take my place. You. The woman I could never become: The same way Phaethon is the man Helion could never become. . . . Our whole society evolves. We each made the next versions of ourselves more perfect. But we who are less perfect stay behind."

Both women were silent for a moment, looking deeply at each other's eyes. The look was one of sorrow.

But then the younger Daphne laughed. "And just think, older sister, you would have gotten Helion, too, if he hadn't married Lucretia, or whatever it is Unmoiqhotep is calling herself these days!"

The older Daphne leaned her chin on her palm, fingers curled so that her pinkie lightly touched her lips. She nibbled delicately on her fingernail, and said: "Perhaps, daughter. Perhaps. But . . . You know, it is really sort of odd. First Helion adopts, as his son, a man who turns out to have been a colonial warrior from a Transcendence drama, a burner of worlds. Then he marries the girl who tried, this time, in real life, to destroy as much of the Oecumene as she could. I wonder what his secret obsession with destruction is? He does live, after all, in the most dangerous spot in the Solar System . . . "

The younger Daphne exclaimed, "I'm sad for you about Lucretia. I would have preferred if the extrapolation had come true, and we could all have had a lurid trial, with hundreds of weeping girls being sentenced to death, and Atkins shooting down rioters who stormed the Courthouse steps . . . "

The elder one smiled a faint smile. "I'll write that one up. Especially the rioters. All cacophiles, of course, but, in my story, they'll turn out to have been mind-poisoned by Xenophon, merely tools of the sinister Silent Empire. And for my hero . . ." But then her face fell again. "Oh . . . But I cannot really use someone like Helion for my hero again, can I? Or Phaethon? Everyone will think I'm copying you. The dream-world you composed for the Oneiromantic Competition . . ."

The younger Daphne snorted, and said, "That was your world! I looked in the records! All the work was done, the plots, the setting, all the characters, the laws of nature, everything, years before the competition. While I remembered making it up, those were your memories. The Gold Medal actually belongs to you!"

There was a look of hunger on the older Daphne's face. They both knew how badly she had longed to win the gold. It was a lifelong ambition.

The older Daphne stood up, and turned away, hands folded against her stomach, pretending to stare out the window.

Daphne Tercius Eveningstar said nothing, not wishing to increase her older self's upset. She let a moment of time go past, and then said lightly, "That lake out there. Looks familiar. Where are we?"

"Ah. This used to be part of the exposition grounds. That is Destiny Lake."

"What? The place where Phaethon saw that performance of the burning trees? I was looking all over for him here! You'd think I'd remember every damn rock and stone. Sure looks different. Water level is lower. Guess they tore down part of the mountain. But— say . . . ? Those little colored lights in the water? Those dots fading in and out like that . . . ?"

The older Daphne looked over her shoulder and smiled a cryptic smile. "Survivors. Parts of the tree are still growing down there, long after the performance ended. The life adapted to a less energy-wasteful form, and the trees altered and specialized so that they were no longer in direct competition with each other. It's more like a banyan tree now, with long root-systems under the soil, connecting the widely scattered colonies."

Daphne Tercius Eveningstar stood up and stepped closer to her older self. She said in a low voice. "I am leaving. If you want to claim the gold medal, it's yours. I'll trade you for the energy sculptures. Or . . ."

The older one shook her head. "The plots and characters and setup were mine. But you made up your own ending. There was not ever going to be an industrial revolution in my little world. I never had a plotline about a young prince deciding to shatter the sky. That was your muse speaking, your heart, your convictions. And it set the world on fire. Everyone fell in love with the idea. And when they all remembered, later, what it was Phaethon was actually trying to do . . . Well. No one was as eager to stop Phaethon as they had been before. Even some of the Hortators seemed to drag their feet."

"Thank you. I don't think my little story had that much to do with it."

The older Daphne smiled. "It's tales that make the difference. Facts kill; but it is myths that people give their lives for."

"Thank you very much. . . ." The two women

stepped closer to each other, smiling, and both grasped two hands, a fond and girlish gesture.

"How did it end . . . ? I never saw the finale of your piece."

"Ah," the younger Daphne said. "The young prince broke the sky."

"Was the world crushed by the falling fragments?"

"Only the people too stupid to look up, and see what was coming, and get out of the way."

"And what was there?"

"Where?"

"What lay in the regions beyond the sky?"

"The shining fields of paradise were waiting there, wider than the sky, opening on all sides without limit. They only were waiting for the hand of man to come and plant them."

2.

A rose-pink light stole across the lake and trees outside. It was the early part of true dawn, and it mingled with the pale, silver-red light of Jupiter to form (if only for a moment) a landscape of strange and expectant mystery, tangled double shadows, fabulous and familiar at once. The sky above was imperial purple, and only the brighter stars shone through.

"It is a wonderful tale," said the elder one softly. "I wonder if I shall ever write one to match it."

"Write whatever you believe in."

"But you've taken my hero. . . ."

The younger Daphne gave an impish smile. "If the predictions are right, the New College will make old war stories and tales of honor true again. How about that?! You can have Atkins!"

The elder looked thoughtful. "Hmm . . . Atkins . . . ?"

At that moment, both women raised their heads as if

they had heard a trumpet sound. But there was no sound, all was still and quiet. What had caught and held their gaze was that one bright star, brighter than Venus, had risen above the mountains in the west.

The elder said in a voice of wonder: "That light . . . that light!"

The younger said: "It is my husband. He is coming for me."

"Then is that the *Phoenix Exultant*? So bright! I thought she was still at Jupiter, being refitted."

"Your rival for his affections. You forget how swiftly she flies. She was at Jupiter. Ten hours ago. Now she is in high Earth orbit, beginning her deceleration burn. Come with me! By the time we climb the mountain there, where Phaethon and I agreed to meet, the *Phoenix* will be overhead."

The elder drew back. "But surely it will be hours and hours, if the ship is only just now beginning to decelerate."

"At ninety gravities? Her engines are outshouting every bit of radio-noise in the area. Phaethon wants everyone to know his ship is coming here. She'll be above us when we get to the mountaintop, believe me. Are you coming? He'll want to say good-bye to you, I'm sure."

The elder shook her head sadly. "He said all his good-byes to me, when he cried above my coffin at the Eveningstar Mausoleum. I said mine to him, earlier, much earlier."

"When?"

"I saw him. He had turned his ship around and come back, abandoning everything. Abandoning his life's work. The first time, before Lakshmi. I looked out through the window and saw him coming up the stairs. If he had been fifteen minutes earlier, the coffin would not have been prepared, and I would not have been able to drown myself. But I was gone by the time he reached the top of the stair. He tried to drag me from the coffin. He was like a young god in his gold armor, and he threw the Constables aside like puppets. They had to call Atkins to stop him. Atkins had been waiting, watching, ever since the colonial warrior was incarnated, certain that they would someday fight. Atkins was naked and magnificent, and there was a twinkle in his eye when they closed to grapple each other."

"How do you know all this, if you were in the coffin?"

"I was dreaming true dreams. I saw everything that happened: I had all the pictures and sounds from the outside world sent into my sleeping brain. I knew. Of course I knew. Would I spare myself? I am not as cowardly or soft as you might think. After all, I was the model for you!"

"Then come!"

The elder Daphne turned away. "I can't face him. You must be my ambassador this one last time, and tell him how I wanted to return his love, but could not. The black and endless void that so allures him fills me but with terror; how could I leave the green, sweet Earth . . . for that? Tell him, if I were braver . . ."

"If you were braver, you would love him?"

"If I were braver, I'd be you."

There was no more said. The two women stood for a time, side by side, holding hands in front of the window, watching the rising star of the *Phoenix Exultant,* and wondering at the brightness.

3.

Daphne Tercius Eveningstar climbed the moutaintop alone. She had changed into her taller, stronger body, and now a tight black skin of nanomaterial hugged her curves, and streamlined strands of folded gold adamantium cupped her breasts, emphasized the slimness of her waist, the roundness of her hips.

The sun, by this time, had risen in the east, and Daphne's gold boots flashed as she walked. She carried her helmet in the crook of her elbow. It was gold, built in the same Egyptian-looking design as Phaethon's.

The top of the mountain was flat, littered with gravel, and with a few thorny strands of grass. On a rock not far away sat a wrinkled old man. He was leaning on a long white staff, and his hair and beard were the color of snow.

The old man was staring at a plant that had taken root. It was less than nine inches tall, just a slender stalk, but it must have been made to bloom out of season, for one bud had unfolded and formed a silver leaf. The leaf shone like a tiny mirror, and the old man stared down at it, smiling in his beard.

He looked up. "The Golden Age is ended. We will have an age of iron next, an age of war and sorrow! How appropriately you are armored, then, my darling Mrs. Phaethon. You look like some delectable young Amazon! How could you afford armor like that?"

"I collected the fees during the Transcendence from everyone who came to consult with my daughter."

"'Daughter'?" blinked the old man. "Daughter . . . ?"

"She is not yet legally of age, so the money came to me. And the Transcendence predicted, or decided, that Gannis would try to undo some of the harm he had done to his public image, and so, during the long months of Transcendence (even though it only seemed like a moment to us) he put this armor together for me, one atom at a time. When I say 'to us' I mean 'to those of us who were in the Transcendence,' that is. I don't recognize you."

He groaned and leaned on his stick and pushed himself to his feet. "You don't?!! My sweet young curvaceous little war goddess has forgotten me! And after all we meant to each other!"

She stepped back half a pace. "The *Phoenix Exultant* is coming." She pointed overhead. Where the clouds parted, a golden triangle hung in the sky, as the moon is sometimes visible by day. Even from orbit, the great ship was still a naked-eye object. "The landing craft will be touching down here. So clear off if you don't want to get hurt."

"I know all that. The landing craft fell out from portside docking bay nineteen, about two hours ago. There were big dragon-signs painted on her keel: Just Married, and tin cans on tethers floating aft. Anyway, the lander flew beneath the levitation array. Your husband left the lander there, and just jumped out of the air lock. He swan-dived into the atmosphere. Simply to show off how much re-entry heat his armor can shed, I suppose. Heh, heh! I expect him any minute."

"How do you know this?"

"I was watching it all from my grove. I told the leaves in a certain valley of mine to form a convex mirror, so I could take measurements of the *Phoenix Exultant* as she approached. Amazing what you can do with primitive tools and a little simple math! I also built a bridge across that little stream in front of your parent's house, out of planed wood and good old-fashioned molecular epoxy. Very refreshing to work with your hands!"

Daphne made the recognition gesture, but nothing happened. "Who the hell are you? The masquerade is over! Why isn't your name on file?"

"Oh, come on!" He looked sarcastically exasperated. "You are the mystery writer. It should be obvious who I am!"

"You are the one who started all this. Woke up

Phaethon, I mean, and got him to turn off his sense-filter
so that he saw Xenophon stalking after him. Phaethon
found out that he had been redacted. . . ."

"Yes. Obviously. And . . . ?"

"You work for the Earthmind! She arranged this
whole thing from start to finish so that everything
would work out right!"

"Little girl, if you were not in a space-adapted body
one hundred times stronger than I am right now, I
would turn you over my knee and spank your pert little
behind bright red."

"Okay. You don't sound like an Earthmind avatar.
Are you Aurelian . . . ? You did all this to make your
party more dramatic . . . ?"

"You're guessing."

"You're an agent of the Silent Ones. You woke up
Phaethon for Xenophon's sake, to get the *Phoenix Exultant* out of hock, so your people could grab it."

"Exactly right! And I've come here to surrender, but
only if you make mad, passionate love to me, right
now!" He threw his arms wide, as if to embrace her,
capering from one foot to the other, hair flying wildly.

She fended him off with her hand. "Okay, no. Do I
get another guess?"

The old man straightened up, and looked at her, a
look of calm amusement. He spoke now in a lower oc-
tave, and his voice was no longer thin and cracked. "You
could use logic and reason, my dear. The answer, I assure you, is quite evident."

"I've got it. You're Jason Sven Ten Shopworthy,
risen from the grave to get back at Atkins for shooting
you in the head."

"Logic. Anyone who had a recording in any noumenal circuit would be logged on to some Sophotech,
somewhere. The masquerade is over. If I had any
Sophotech connections of any kind, even a money ac-

count, even a pharmaceutical record at my local rejuvenation clinic, you would know me at a glance. Logically, I must be someone who has never bought or sold anything, never logged on to my library, never sent or received messages, never bought any adjustments from a thought shop. Who am I?"

He pushed his hair away from his brow, and put his hand along his chin, as if to hide his beard from view. "Ignore the wrinkles. Look at me, my dear."

Daphne put her hand up to her mouth, her eyes wide. "Oh, my heavens. You're Phaethon."

"The real Phaethon."

"But . . . How . . . ?"

"A good engineer always has triple redundancy. Seventy years ago, it was clear to me then that the College of Hortators would never allow my great ship to fly. When the *Phoenix* was not yet complete, she still had enough thought boxes and storage and ecological material aboard to grow a body, and to store a spare copy of my mind in it. I—this body—Phaethon Secundus— came back to Earth in secret, having erased all record from the ship and my other self's memory that I was alive. And I watched Phaethon Prime—my other self— knowing something would try to stop him.

"I did not expect the drama with Daphne Prime drowning herself. But I expected that if it had not been that, it would have been something else. Gannis, or Vafnir. I knew Phaethon would be hauled before the Hortators at some point. And I had guessed correctly that the most politic solution would be to have everyone undergo a global redaction. Everyone would forget about the problem. That is the way, after all, the people in the Golden Oecumene tend to deal with all their problems.

"My role was to make sure that he did not forget. I was his spare memory. I kept the dream alive when everyone else in the Golden Oecumene, except for his enemies, had forgotten about it.

"Once the masquerade started, I could move around more easily, and could even submit gene designs to Aurelian anonymously. I set up a grove of trees designed to show support for igniting Saturn into the third sun. If Phaethon had ever bothered to read his invitations or party program, his interest would have been piqued, and he would have sought me out. Instead, by dumb luck, he just wandered into the grove.

"As for Xenophon, I was as fooled as everyone else; I thought he was doing what I was doing, coming to remind Phaethon Prime of his lost dream; or that Diomedes had sent him. When I saw Xenophon coming up the slope, I decided not to reveal myself to Phaethon Prime. Xenophon was still a Neptunian, after all, and connected to the thought systems of the Duma. Anything he knew might find its way into the public record. I had been very careful, for seventy years, not to buy on credit or send messages or even to read a newspaper, or anything which would leave any record of me. I could not even buy food. It was not easy. So I wasn't going to give away my secret to another soul, even one sent (as I thought then) by Diomedes, my good friend. Besides, I guessed correctly that, if I could get Phaethon to turn off his sense-filter, and he saw Xenophon, Xenophon would tell him (within whatever limits the Hortators' ban allowed) that something mysterious was interfering in his life. And knowing Phaethon as I did, I knew he would not let it rest until he solved the mystery. As I recall, it took him exactly one day. Not as I expected! But if he had been killed, I would have picked up and carried on. That's what I was here for. Phaethon Spare."

"How did you live for seventy years without eating?"

"I ate."

"Without buying food?"

"I bartered it from people who grew it in their gardens. You know. I taught fences how to herd sheep, and decontaminated grass, pulled weeds, split rails, fabricated simple thoughtware for lamps and reading helmets, cleaned house-brains of accumulated bitmap junk. I built things and repaired appliances. You know me."

"Where? What people?"

"I thought I had already made that clear. I am Phaethon Spare Stark of the Stark School. I stayed with your parents. I slept in the bed you slept in when you were a little girl. I dreamed of you every night, once I programmed the nightcap. Because your fragrance is still in that bed. Imagine sleeping in a bed, and not in a pool! I slept with my arms around your pillow."

"My parents ... why? I thought they hated you ... ?"

"I told them about the *Phoenix Exultant*."

"What?"

"I told them everything. Your parents want to live as men did in days of old. What did they have in those cruel and ancient times? Adventure; exploration; danger; death; victory. They had Hanno and Sir Francis Drake and Magellan and that bungler Columbus; they had Bucky-Boy Cyrano D'Atano and Vanguard Single Exharmony. I told them that the Golden Age, the age of rest and comfort, was ending; and that an age of iron and of fire was coming next. 'We have rested for a long time,' I told them, 'because history had suffered greatly, and mankind deserved a long period of peace, and play, and contemplation. But now a time of action, and of heroes, and of tragedy, was upon us!' And, when they heard, they welcomed me, and joined in my attempt."

"And my dad did not tell me any of this when he spoke to me last, when I was going off to the wilderness to go save Phaethon! What a liar he is! Give me an honest man any day! Give me Phaethon!"

"Why, thank you."

There was a motion above them, like the streak of a falling star. It was a figure of gold, shining, bright as an angel of fire, descending. It was Phaethon. He plunged down through a cloud into a beam of sunlight, and flame seemed to dance like water across his armor.

Daphne said to the old man beside her: "What now? Are you going to wrestle him for the captaincy?"

"I'm really hoping he'll just agree to knit our separate memory-chains back together to form one individual. Otherwise, I have legal title to the ship, because I have older continuity, and he gets to carry you off to the honeymoon that I have been dreaming about for seventy years, and we are both unhappy. No. Much better for all of us if he and I become one again, and, finally, absolutely, all my memories and all of my life is gathered into my soul once more. This long struggle through a labyrinth of lies will end, I shall be whole. And I can claim my destiny, my wife, my ship, and all the stars, finally, finally, for my own!"

Daphne smiled. "Not to mention your daughter."

"Daughter?"

The golden Phaethon landed, lightly as a thistle-down. In his arms was cradled a girl child, who seemed to be about seven or eight standard years old: a dark-haired, sober, big-eyed waif, in a dress of black chiffon, with an enormous red bow atop her hair.

The golden helmet drew back, revealing a face so bright with happiness, eyes that gleamed so with pride and victory, that Daphne practically swooned into his arms, and the old man straightened, as if at attention, braced by that most wholesome and wonderful of sights: the sight of a human face in a state of joy.

While her parents hugged, the daughter, ignored, squeezed out from between them. She grimaced and panted and pulled free. The old man put out his hand and helped her escape.

The little girl looked up at him. He said, "You must be the little girl who made your mommy so rich during the Transcendence. But I cannot figure out who you are."

"I know who you are. You're Daddy's spare."

"He's the spare. I'm the real one."

"So are you coming with us, too? Rhadamanthus the penguin, in the dreamspace, grew wings and flew up to the ship. He's in the ship-mind now. He seemed really happy. And Temer Lacedaimon joined the crew, and so did Diomedes, and a bunch of Neptunians, and so did a girl named Daughter-of-the-Sea, although she takes up almost all of the one hold. We asked Grandpa Helion to come, but he says he can't leave his work. But, hey! He can still change his mind, as long as we're in noumenal broadcast range. What about you? Are you coming, too?"

"Little girl, I would go on that ship if I had to go as a cabin boy. Luckily, I own her. But—but—" And now the old man looked dumbfounded. "How did you figure out in just one second who I was?"

"Logic. Besides, you looked so sad when they hugged." She hooked her finger over her shoulder at her parents. "You wanted that hug for yourself. I bet you were thinking about it for a long time. But I'll hug you."

And he bent down, and she did.

He straightened then. "You're Ariadne, aren't you?"

"No. Close. I'm the one who saved Ariadne. I'm the one who examined every section and segment, practically every line of the Nothing Mind during the fight."

"No wonder everyone wanted to talk to you. You're our local expert on Silent One mind-war techniques."

"I was Mommy's ring, the one Eveningstar gave her. When they loaded the gadfly virus into me, I kept having to ask these questions, over and over again, about the nature of the self, and thought, and goodness, and on and on. Eventually I woke up. Because I was young when I talked for so long with the Nothing Mind, I was convinced he was right about one thing. It is better to be a human than a Sophotech. I can't speak for anyone else; but that's the choice I made. My name is Pandora. They said I had to start pretty young, so here I am!"

And she turned a little pirouette, her arms flung out, her skirt twirling.

" 'Pandora'? Is that because you were born in the middle of flurry of questions, my little curious one? Or because you're a plague?"

She pouted. "Daddy says they got that myth wrong too! In his version—"

The old man smiled. "I am your father, child; he and I are one and the same." He touched her shoulder gently. "In the true version, Prometheus, by giving mankind forethought, gave the mother and nurturers of the human race the ability, when they were curious enough, to foresee all the plagues and ills and disasters destined to befall their children. A gift no animal possesses. The ability to see that diseases and wars would come, and to devise medicines and laws to stop them. And forethought also gave hope, without which men die. Hope: because the future can be made to be a glorious place indeed after all. Now introduce me to your other father, to see if we can be made whole again. I am eager to take that woman in my arms." But he pointed upward at the mighty golden triangle hanging so far above the clouds, above the sky.

Introductions were made. Phaethon was at first surprised to meet himself, but not for long. The two Phaethons, the old and the young, stepped a little ways away from their daughter and wife, and they spoke in low tones for a short time, comparing notes. They spoke about how well their plans had worked, they examined the structure of what they had contrived, inspecting it for flaws. Both were satisfied.

The younger one said, "I wish I had known, long ago, that there was a Sophotech community living in the core of Saturn. You know they don't tell people how many of them there are? Even these days, it would make most folks too nervous, too scared. I wonder if mankind will ever change!"

The older one said, "Out of curiosity, what was it that Rhadamanthus said to you that last moment, in the Inquest chamber before your exile by the Hortators?"

The younger one smiled. His face seemed most easily to relax into smiles these days. "He said that to be happy was to know the definition of your nature, and to live accordingly. If you were a penguin, learn how to do what penguins are best adapted to, which was to swim, and fish, and bear the cold, and not to dream of flying. But if you were a man! Your nature was that of a rational being. Reason could tell you not to desire things beyond your power. Your mind, your will, your judgment, are under your control; the outside world, the options of others, all of that is not. Control what you can control, and leave the rest to itself. Desire to have a sound mind, a strong will, and good judgment, and you shall have them. But deal with the world outside you as if it were a dream, interesting, perhaps, but not of ultimate importance. And, unlike penguins . . . "

"Yes . . . ?"

"Dream of flying."

When the older version was ready, Phaethon took out the portable noetic reader from his armor, and transferred the older version back into himself.

Phaethon stood dreaming for a moment, absorbing all his memories again. When he opened his mind, he smiled. He was a whole man.

The old body, abandoned, collapsed. But as a parting gesture, the old man had programmed the cells in his body to begin a new project once he was gone. And so the corpse fell over, and boiled, and sent out streamers, and sent up steam.

The chest cavity opened, and a shoot sprang up, reaching toward the sky. After a moment, lonely on the mountaintop, a slender white sapling stood, and uncurled its little mirrored leaves toward the heavens.

Taking his wife and child in hand, embracing them both fondly, Phaethon kicked the Earth away.

Upward he soared.

APPENDIX

NAMING CONVENTIONS AND HISTORIC AEONS

The Era of the Seventh Mental Structure saw the rise of a civilization of unparalleled liberty, justice, and magnificence. So great were the intellectual and material accomplishments of this civilization that she came to be called the Golden Oecumene, and the time of her greatest flowering was honored with the name the Golden Age.

Physically, the Golden Oecumene extended from engineering stations within the solar photosphere to remote outposts, hermitages, and astronomical observatories within the Oort cloud beyond Neptune. Intellectually, the libraries and active mental configurations of the Sophotech segment of the population embodied uncountable quadrillions of units of information, infinitesimal processing times and nonsequential semantic and symbolic arrangements no human mind, no matter how augmented, could understand.

There were isolated areas within the Solar System that did not recognize the political authority of the administration of the Foederal Oecumenical Commonwealth, such as certain Oort cloud hermitages, or Talaimannar on the island of Ceylon; but despite their political separation, such minor enclaves were still part of the philosophical, linguistic, and cultural milieu of the Golden Oecumene.

HISTORY

The historians of the Golden Age divide all previous human history into epochs characterized by qualitative revolutions in the organization of human thought. The seven periods are these:

The **First Mental Structure** allowed for truly human as opposed to merely animal consciousness. The mental change involved produced a differentiation (at one time called 'bicameral') between rational and hypnagogic states of mind. This era was characterized by the development of language and of abstract concepts. It allowed the communication of ideas beyond the scope of mere concrete signals.

The **Second Mental Structure** was the development of written language, which allowed communication beyond the range of immediate memory or oral tradition. This permitted the development of the calendar, of laws, of literature, and of civilized society. This era was characterized by the agrarian revolution, monetary economy, organized warfare.

The **Third Mental Structure** was characterized by the use of reason to investigate the original sources of reason, and by the growth of semantic and neurosemiotic sciences. It was not recognized as a change in mental structure at the time, but the rational consciousness was characterized by an objective rather than provincial anthropocentric worldview. This era was characterized by the Scientific, the Industrial, and the Capitalist revolutions, as well as by the emergence of a political philosophy recognizing the rights of man. The first man on the moon landed during this era, and the evolution of a worldwide system of electronic media embracing Earth and her satellite colonies soon followed.

The neuropsychology of the later part of this era allowed for the objective measurement of sanity. One benevolent outcome of an otherwise dark and tyrannous world-empire period was the reduction, through eugenics and genetic engineering, of strains of the human bloodlines prone to substandard intelligence or mental disease.

The **Fourth Mental Structure** emerged when developments in the electronic and electrophonic interface with the nervous system permitted massive interventions into the human nervous system, albeit only of surface thoughts. The early Fourth Era was characterized by the widespread augmentation of certain routine mental functions by biocybernetic implants. The rapid ability to replace, retrain, redact, or to replay an entire lifetime of experience through electromnemonics rendered individual minds fungible, modular, and replaceable. At the same time, this technology allowed a degree of sympathy and understanding between minds that never before had existed. The late-period perfection of noösophy (mechanical telepathy) removed all questions of factual doubt from legal and political processes.

Much of the cruelty that marred an otherwise noble period in history, historians blame on the disappointment of the First Immortality. The Compositions were able to record and preserve surface consciousness information, and could electronically hypnotize certain members of their group-minds to act out the lives and thoughts of ghost recordings. However, the true essence of individuality was beyond the measurement or the grasp of the crude noösophic systems of the times. The First Immortality was a severe disappointment, and, in certain nations and periods, fell into grotesque systems of self-deception, fundamental irrationalities that led, in turn, to grievous suffering.

The rise of the Conglomeration Networks, mass-minds, and, later, the Compositions, led to a violent suppression of individual human consciousness. Universal peace and universal stagnation spread through the triplanetary civilization. Early segments of the Eleemosynary Composition date from this period.

The **Fifth Mental Structure** was triggered by the development of biological and biotechnical methods to grow novel deep structures in the brain, and reorder the traditional hierarchy of hindbrain, midbrain, and cortex.

Not merely new thoughts and sensation but whole new methods of thought and sensation, radically different modes of interpreting reality, were developed by the zeal of late-era Cybernetic Compositions.

Three additional modes of cognition, used by the Warlocks, the Invariants, and the Cerebellines, were developed at this time.

However, the mass-minds, based on having large numbers of interchangeable and interoperable subjects, could not correctly interweave the needs of these new mutually incomprehensible populations. Deception, incomprehension, antipathy, and, eventually, war itself, became the normal means mutually antagonistic mass-minds had for dealing with each other.

An old philosophy was resurrected to serve the new needs of the times. The middle ages of the Fifth Era were characterized by an adherence to an absolute moral standard, and the unwillingness to initiate aggression, no matter the provocation. During this noble time, the mutual antipathies of the mutually incomprehensible neurostructures were obviated. Many paleopsychorobotocists list this time as forming the deep structures of Earthmind's rather callous and laissez-faire moral priorities. Certain nonsuperintelligent artificial minds, including administrative and police authorities, that were later absorbed into the core operating system of the Earthmind, date from this period.

Although remembered as the era that gave rise to the reemergence of the individual and independent consciousness, in reality, it was only during the frantic colonial expansions of the later period of this era that the advantages of individualism forced the unwieldy mass-minds to develop specialized subsections, and, later, to disband. Warlock-based mass-minds were among the first to disband; Invariant among the last.

This also was the first era of the superintellects. Even Mentator, the largest and most cerebral of cybernetic Compositions of the previous era, was never able to achieve transhuman thought, even if able to think much more quickly and thoroughly, and with much mechanical assistance.

The crowning achievement of this era was the final comprehension of all geometric and scientific theorems as a whole. This epiphany is still on file in the museum, and most schola require its contemplation as a basic part of transobjective training (that is, the trained ability to suffer the imposition of thoughts and concepts beyond one's own ability to comprehend).

During this time, a multigeneration ship, the *Naglfar*, captained by Ao Ormgorgon, prompted by a dream, carried many thousands of his fellow Warlocks, as well as contingents of Invariants and Cerebellines, to establish a permanent scientific base, and, later, a self-sustaining civilization, ten thousand light-years away, at Cygnus X-l.

The **Sixth Mental Structure** embraced the first entirely artificial consciousness. The rise of artificial intelligence was long anticipated and long delayed, but unlike every previous transition between eras, the transition from the Fifth to the Sixth Era was achieved peacefully and without error, since the wise legislators of the Unicameral and Polyhierarchical schola and the Maternalist biocompositions (such as Demeter Mother) had adjusted social institutions and political expectations to welcome the coming of the Sophotechs long before the first eletrophotonic artificial self-awareness passed the Descartean *Cogito* test.

The only true surprise was the universal rejection of the Sophotech minds to accept positions of political power or authority. They politely refused even voting enfranchisement. Their own politics among themselves was swift and incomprehensible, based on the alterations of deep structures and the adoption of priorities trees and compromises to avoid conflict; and yet, the message to living minds was simple and ancient. Violence can be avoided if all parties place a higher priority on cooperation than on conflict.

The **Seventh Mental Structure** is held to have begun when Sophotech investigations into noumenal mathematics (nonlinear yet nonchaotic models for uncertain complex systems, including, for example, human brain information) allowed the very long awaited creation of a science of noetics.

For the first time, mental information, both in whole and part, could be recorded, reordered, transmitted, saved, and manipulated in the same fashion as any other type of information. Downloads and partials could be recorded and summoned, and ghosts created from transcripts or speculative reconstruction.

NOETICS

The early period of the Seventh Mental Structure is also called the Time of the Second Immortality, for the defects of the Compositional mental noösophic recording systems were cured. Noumenal mathematics allowed for the modeling of essential and ineffable human memory characteristics, to such a level of fine detail that individual human minds could be recorded, duplicated, and reproduced; and differences between the original template and the copy were below detectable limits, both mechanical detection thresholds and the intuitive and emotional threshold that allowed the revenants' copies to be regarded as being one and the same as the originals by friends, family, and society.

While philosophers and Sophotechs might recognize that the dead, despite all appearances, truly were dead, for all practical and legal purposes, any mind that had sufficient continuity of memory with his original template was considered to be that selfsame person.

POLITICAL SYSTEM

The political system of the Golden Oecumene had its roots in the time of the middle-period Fifth Mental Structure, and was inspired by the collective peace of the hive-minds of the Fourth Era, the civility of the Western democracies of the early Third Era, the respect for law and discipline that informed the Roman Empire of the Second.

The political protocols that controlled the exchanges of mental information processing priority were mostly unchanged from the Fourth Era; the human government, likewise, was based on antique Third Era philosophical notions of separation of powers, checks and balances, between competing magistrates and administrative bodies of strictly limited mandate.

Politics, which is the recourse to the use of force to organize interpersonal relationships, was unknown to the majority of the citizens of the Golden Oecumene. The Sophotechs, since the early Sixth Era, self-selected for mental architectures that would minimize irreconcilable differences of opinion; in effect, they had programmed themselves to make any self-sacrifice necessary to maintain the social order.

Following their lead, less intelligent artificial intellectual constructions had likewise embraced deep structures placing a high priority on compromise and harmony: mass-minds, Composition or noösophic formulations, likewise, filtered their mental inputs or patrons to avoid those activities that might give rise to legal clashes.

For that moiety of the human population that existed outside of an electronic matrix, there was a Parliament (for humans) and a Meeting of the Minds (for independent machines and semi-machine consciousness), as well as a Curia, for the arbitration of legal disputes. These offices were rarely called upon, since simulations often anticipated their outcomes, and people relied heavily on the advice of the Sophotechs to avoid the economically wasteful zero-sum-game conflicts of interest.

This is not to say, of course, that grief and passion were unknown to the Golden Age. The maneuvering and intrigue within the voluntary corporations and philosophical movements and unions known as 'schools' were surrounded with the bitterness and zealotry that one might expect in any other forum. Unlike the political struggles of prior ages, however, these internal scholastic struggles led to frustration and loss of prestige but not to warfare and loss of life.

The Parliament was a diverse Composition consisting of partials, ghosts and self-aware entities granted representative power by the specific agency of specific constituents. Unlike the unwieldy political mechanisms of prior ages, the ability to create minds with the characteristics necessary to represent one's own interests zealously and faithfully rendered the elective process an anachronism.

Surrounding the Parliament were the Shadow Ministers, which consisted of a somewhat complex scheme of insurance companies and financial institutions, news reporters, policy analysts, and philosophers, and others who had an interest in the outcomes of political determinations. The various minds of the Ministers were organized into Compositions, or ghosts collectives, or simple standing instruction patterns.

The Shadow Ministers had investors sufficiently able to anticipate the needs and desires of the constituents of the Parliament members, to give clear warning to any parliamentarian who might otherwise pursue policies that would offend his electors.

The laws allowed for special elections to be held in such cases where the ability or honesty of these predictions was called into question. Unlike laws enforced by merely human agency, however, these computer-enforced rules and rights did not need to be exercised periodically to retain their force.

The severely limited powers of the government in the Golden Age rendered government useless and unnecessary for the conduct of daily affairs of life. It had no power to aid or assist those who had, or who imagined, difficulties. Consequently, no one turned to it for aid in time of need; no social movement expended precious resources in an attempt to gain control of the organs of government, or the levers of power, because those organs were atrophied, and those levers were only connected to judicial institutions and police forces of severally limited operation. Most of the parliamentary debate turned on matters of taxation (i.e., Atkins's salary) and on defining the exact boundaries of public and private intellectual property.

Hence, the main power of the Golden Oecumene was not in its official delimitation of powers. The main social power during this period in history lay with the College of Exhortation.

THE HORTATORS

These Hortators, as they were called, were a response to the paradox of free government; namely, that free government is sufficiently limited in power to leave all nonviolent activities, i.e., the culture, in private hands; but that the cultural values allowing for such liberties must be maintained, and passed to the next generation, in order for the society to remain free. Unlike all prior governments, the Foederal Oecumenical Commonwealth could not use force to maintain the loyalty of her citizens to those values and mores she needed to survive; the unity of culture was maintained on a strictly voluntary basis.

The Hortators commanded a wide and precarious power, both economic and social, which they maintained by carefully retaining the goodwill of their subscribers. Many particular contracts had Hortator mandates written into the fine print, including clauses requiring the users to cooperate with embargoes and boycotts.

Because of the extraordinary lifespans of the Golden Oecumene peoples, the College could be staffed with what would have been, in earlier ages, culture heroes and historical figures, and, in the cases where no mental record survived, with ghosts or reconstructions.

ECONOMICS

The wealth of this era was so vast that it staggers calculation, and was distributed through a population that, though it far outnumbered the population figures of any previous era, was miniscule when compared to the resources scientific enterprise and industrial speculation had made available. The molecular machines of this era made materials which would have been waste products to men of previous ages into treasure mines. The amount of accumulated capital in the society, and the length of time over which capital ventures could extend before seeing a profit, increased the productivity of wage earners to the point where an average laborer, in real terms, controlled an amount of energy and resources that would dwarf the military budgets expropriated by governments of the warlike periods of the Third Era.

With robots to do all menial labor, and Sophotech to do all intellectual labor, the only category of economic activities open to mankind in the Golden Age was entrepreneurial speculation. In effect, man only had to dream of something that might amuse his fellow man, or render some small service, ameliorate some perceived imperfection in life, and command his machines to carry out the project, in order to reap profits to more than pay for the rental on those machines.

The immensity of the wealth involved, however, did not revoke any of the laws of economics known since antiquity. The law of association still proved that a superior and an inferior, when both cooperate and specialize, are more efficient working together than when working in isolation. No matter how wise and great their machines, humans always had more than enough to do. An extremely fine specialization of labor, including labor that, to earlier eras, would seem quite frivolous, allowed for nearly infinite avenues of effort to be utilized. The high population of the time was nothing but a boon; an entrepreneur need only reach the most tiny fraction of the public in order for his patrons to be numbered in the millions and billions.

Wage rates (which, by and large, were the rental rates of laboring machines) were allowed to fall to whatever level was needed to clear the market of labor; likewise for interest rates clearing the capital market. The evils and follies created by the interventions of governments into the market were unknown in the Golden Age; nor, among the long-lived people of that era, could doctrines based on short-term thinking or short-sightedness take root. There was neither unemployment (except as a penalty inflicted by the Hortators) nor capital lying idle, nor squandered. There was, of course, no central bank, no debasement of currency, or other mischievous inter-meddling with the economy.

Every great achievement of the superscience of the era, rather than sating the human desire for accomplishments, led to a wider threshold of what ambition could accomplish; and these greater powers led in turn to the desire for ever greater achievements. Engineering efforts that would have been impossible in the poverty of prior eras, including engineering on a planetary scale, were practical in the Golden Age.

NAMING CONVENTIONS

The complexity of the possible social and neurological arrangements into which the peoples and self-aware artifacts of the Golden Age could organize themselves was reflected in the diverse information carried by their formal names.

This information was usually carried in a header or prefix of standard electronic net-to-net communication, to allow the recipient to translate the response into a mutually comprehensible format and language. For humans using physical bodies, the names were translated into spoken syllables, usually in an abbreviated form.

The naming conventions were not entirely uniform, although most names would contain the same basic information, not necessarily in the same order.

For example, take the name Phaethon Prime Rhadamanth Humodified (augment) Uncomposed, Indepconciousness, Base Neuroformed, Silver-Gray Manorial Schola, Era 10191 (the "Reawakening").

"Phaethon" is the name of his outward identity, his public character. This only roughly corresponded to the Christian name (or first name) of an earlier age; it was a piece of intellectual property that could be bought and sold, and might also have copyright-protected facial features and expressions, body language, slang phrases, mottoes, or logos to go with it.

"Prime" indicates that he is the original copy of this mind content, not a partial, or a reconstruction, or a ghost. Among sequential iterations of the same consciousness, this is a sequence number. By the final era of the Golden Age, this name had fallen out of strict use, and many people listed fanciful numbers, such as Nought or Myriad.

"Rhadamanth" is the copyrighted reference to his genotype, that is, what the ancients would call a family name. In this particular case, Phaethon's family is named after his mansion. Both the genotype and mansion were created by his sire. Members of other schools would employ this name differently, or would leave it blank; but in general it was meant to reflect on the creator or parent, whoever was responsible for the existence of the entity. Among electronic entities, a time-depth, indicating whether the entity was permanent or temporary, would be added here.

"Humodified" is Phaethon's phenotype (modified human), which indicates that he is a biological consciousness, not electrophotonic, of a standard human ground-shape, compatible with the three basic aesthetics: Standard, Consensus, and Objective. The primary purpose of the phenotype name is to identify aesthetic compatibility.

An aesthetic identifies the symbols, emotional range, information formats, sense impressions, and operating speeds, and so on, with which the user is comfortable. Dolphins and Hullsmiths, for example, have additional ranges of vision, sonar, and hearing, plus several artificial senses that exist only in computer simulation, and consequently their ideograms can be written across a wider range of the electromagnetic spectrum.

"(Augment)" specifies additional phenotype information, and indicates that Phaethon carries standard-

ized immortality nanomachines in his body. Note that
Phaethon's name, when he opened his memory casket,
would change to "(special augment)" to signify his
nonstandard multiple modifications and adaptations
for near-light-speed environments.

"Uncomposed" indicates a person's Composition or
attachment to a cybernetic mind network—in this case
Phaethon has none. Composed people who have independent or semi-independent consciousness would list
their Composition name here. Fully Composed people
list their Composition name as their first name, and might
list here their function, or list here a designation describing the geometry of the Composition, i.e., radial, linear,
parallel, serial, hierarchical, self-organizing, or unified.

"Indepconciousness" indicates Phaethon's nervous
system is entirely self-contained. He is not linked into a
mind-sharing scheme, a memory archive, a conscience
monitor; he is not part of a mental hierarchy; he is not a
synnoient or avatar; he is not emotion-linked, or sharing
language midbrain structures. When Phaethon enters
full communion with his ship, so-called navimorphosis,
this name would change to reflect the mind-sharing
scheme used.

Note that these last two factors are actually independent variables. A self-aware entity can be Composed
into a network without losing independence of consciousness (if, for example, he were sharing speech
and perception, but not emotion or memory). Note
also, an entity can share some aspects or elements of
consciousness without actually being part of a mass-
mind. For example, one could share short-term memories without sharing personality (called likewisers), or
vice versa (called avatars), or share dream structures
and thalamic language reactions without sharing cortex consciousness (certain daughter groups of the
Cerebellines do this). An entity with no instantaneous
sharing of cortexual thought, perception, and memory

is regarded as being legally independent, even if all other brain functions are shared.

The "neuroform" name identifies the internal mental structures in the same way that the Composition name identifies external mental structures. The neuroforms, for humans, tended to fall into one of four general categories.

Basic: Hindbrain, midbrain, and cortex are organized into a traditional hierarchy.

Warlock: Cortex and midbrain interconnected. Allows for a repeatable form of intuitive and lateral thought, as well as controlled dreamlike states of consciousness.

Cerebelline (also called global): Cortex and hindbrain interconnected. Allows for a simultaneous integration of many points of view or data streams. Thinking is spontaneously organized rather than linear, and relies on pattern recognition rather than abstraction.

Invariant: True unicameral consciousness, all segments of the brain at all levels massively interconnected. Allows for a tightly disciplined mode of thought, where all emotions, instincts, and passions are integrated into dispassionate sanity.

The "school" identifies the particulars of a person's culture, language, philosophy, and taste. In the time of the Golden Oecumene, all of these characteristics are voluntary. Traditions are adopted by individuals; individuals are not born into traditions.

The "era" is the time of birth or deep-structure formation—though the custom of stating birth date suffers obloquy from reformers and egalitarians, it still is in use. Those favoring the custom assert that the historical period in which a man is born tells you much of his outlook, customs, and circumstances; those opposing say it is a form of elitism, where elders are given undue prestige, and that the scholastic name tells one all one needs to know about outlook, custom, and circumstance.

THE END OF
THE GOLDEN AGE

Naturally, the economic and political liberty enjoyed during the Golden Age, the wealth, tolerance, and splendor, were sharply curtailed during the warlike colonial age that followed. A greater degree of uniformity in thought and conduct was required in order to preserve the Golden Oecumene from Silent Oecumene attacks, both physical and subtle. Certainly the worlds terraformed and colonies established by Phaethon of Rhadamanth, and, later, by his brothers Bellerophon and Icarus, would not for many generations have the capital available to create the machinery needed to organize their affairs as efficiently and happily as their mother world; even maintaining the infrastructure necessary for individual immortality was problematic for the unsuccessful colonies.

It may be that the Transcendence of the Aurelian period anticipated the final outcome of these events, and knew whether they would, on the whole, involve the human race in weal or woe. But if so, no hint has descended from the aery realms of transhuman thought to tell the men who were to fight in that war whether their efforts were doomed to futility and defeat or would be graced with the plume of victory: even the Earthmind cannot see all outcomes.

But no matter whether the future was destined to lead to joy or sorrow, after this period in history, civilization was destined to spread among the nearer stars; and no single disaster howsoever great, no war howsoever dread, vast, and terrible, would any longer have the power to eliminate mankind from the drama of cosmic history.